VICTOIRE

VICTOIRE

by
Clare Darcy

WALKER AND COMPANY
NEW YORK

1

Eastcott Park, as any guidebook is happy to inform one, is the principal seat of the Earls of Eastcott and one of the finest examples of Restoration architecture extant in Sussex. The orange-pink colour of its brick is much admired; its park, laid out by Capability Brown, is justly famous; and one of its reception rooms is embellished with rose-pink Gobelin tapestries depicting the return of Baldwin the First from the Crusades.

None of these facts, however, on a bright afternoon near the end of May, was of the least comfort to the Third Earl of Eastcott as he sat in his library awaiting the arrival of a pair of visitors whom he did not at all wish to see. He looked very cross and very uncomfortable, and, if the choice had been his at that moment, he would doubtless have given up all his precious Gobelins for the assurance that he need not face the interview before him—a bargain for which he would later have been exceedingly sorry.

Even the presence of the wife of his bosom and her elderly cousin, the Honourable Miss Amelia Standfield, who had been

C. 2

a Lady-in-Waiting to Queen Charlotte until her health had obliged her to resign her post, did not sustain him, for he did not consider the matter that was to be the subject of the forthcoming interview a suitable one for female ears. Lady Eastcott, however, who never paid the least heed to her husband's wishes, had stated categorically that, since the Marquis of Tarn was *her* brother's son and not Lord Eastcott's, she certainly had every right to see the latest of his *chères-amies,* especially if this one had been clever enough to induce him to offer her marriage.

"Which he never seems to have done for any of the others," she remarked, surveying with approval the tip of one celestial blue kid sandal peeping from beneath the broad flounce embellishing the narrow skirt of her high-waisted morning dress, "at least as far as *we* know, Nigel. Of course what he did during those years he was abroad one can never be sure of—though it *does* appear, from what I have heard, that he was far too busy with expensive Cyprians and Portuguese countesses who already had perfectly good husbands of their own to have had time to think of marrying."

Lord Eastcott said, in the despairing and outraged tone of a man who has already made the same remark several times before without the least effect, that he did not believe Tarn had ever had any intention of marrying.

"It's a plot," he said. "Mark my words, Eleanor, it is all a plot of this fellow Duvenay's. He thinks if he brings the girl here our sympathies will be engaged."

"Yes, but no matter how much they are engaged, he must realise that *we* cannot make Lewis marry the girl," Lady Eastcott said reasonably. "As a matter of fact, you know very well that you would not if you could. The man *may* be a gentleman, and his sister a lady, but the whole thing has a very odd sound to me."

Miss Standfield, who was engaged in knotting a fringe,

sitting very erect in a winged armchair with the air of un-wearied graciousness that appeared to have rubbed off on her from her long association with Royalty, here gave it as her opinion that Lady Eastcott was quite right.

"You will be obliged, no doubt, Eastcott," she said, with kindly condescension, "to decide whether or not it is worth your while to buy him off. I recollect very well a similar situation many years ago, when His Majesty found it necessary to expend a considerable sum in purchasing a number of indis-creet letters written by the young Prince of Wales to a female who apparently possessed a most accurate awareness of their market value."

This interesting information appeared to do nothing, how-ever, to lessen the sense of injury under which Lord Eastcott was labouring.

"Yes, but deuce take it, Amelia," he said, "*I'm* not responsi-ble for what Tarn does. He is four-and-twenty, you know —and even if he were not, *I* could never do anything with the boy!"

"Oh, no! No one could, except Lionel," Lady Eastcott agreed, referring to her brother, the late Marquis, whose resemblance to his son in both person and character had been such as to make it scarcely a matter of surprise that they had dealt together very well. "I have always thought," she went on, "that it is the greatest pity he died when Lewis was only eighteen, for it would certainly have saved the family a world of trouble if he had not. Though I *do* think," she added fair-mindedly, "that if he had not been gooseish enough to allow Olivia to persuade him to name *her* as Lewis's guardian, in-stead of you or my brother Edward, things might not be in quite so bad a case as they are today. For what can one expect a wild, unmanageable boy to do, when his own mother is so freakish as to remove from his home and make him his own master when he is no more than eighteen, but to run into all sorts of foolish excesses?"

3

Lord Eastcott was silent, gloomily aware that he was held responsible by a great many people for permitting his sister-in-law, the Dowager Marchioness of Tarn—who had never in her life deigned to follow any piece of advice given her by anyone—to leave Tarn House upon her husband's death, on the ground of refusing to allow what she termed "the deplorable tendencies" even then apparent in her son's nature to contaminate his two young sisters. It was six years now since that unhappy occasion, but it still seemed to Lord Eastcott that, whenever Tarn was involved in some new scandal, accusing eyes were turned upon him. Whereas, if justice were to be done, he thought bitterly, it was Tarn's mother who would be obliged to bear the blame—or, to come down to fundamentals, the late Marquis himself, whose own morals and manners, while he was yet alive, had given his wife such a baleful idea of what she might expect of their son.

This was ancient history now, however, and could have nothing to say to his present difficulty, which involved a letter from a gentleman named Fitzhugh Duvenay, of Duvenay Manor, County Kerry, Ireland, announcing his intention of waiting upon him, in company with his sister, Miss Anne Duvenay, that day at Eastcott Park. Why *he* should have been selected as the recipient of this visit, rather than the young Marquis of Tarn himself, Lord Eastcott was only too unhappily aware, since the latest duel in which Tarn had been involved—a highly irregular affair emanating from a disagreement at the Cock-Pit Royal in London—had resulted in his nephew's being obliged to flee the country a few weeks before.

This was a necessity which Tarn's noble family had been able to bear with equanimity, for they had had quite enough to endure in the way of unpleasant notoriety in the six months that had passed since he had returned to England from a prolonged sojourn abroad; but Lord Eastcott, faced now with the possibility of himself being pitchforked into a very untidy scandal, owing to his nephew's inopportune absence from the

4

country, was at the moment somewhat unjustly inclined to consider that Tarn had contrived the whole affair of the duel simply in order to be able to leave his eggs of indiscretion, like the cuckoo, in someone else's nest.

He was unable to enlarge upon this subject, however, for at that moment Philbrook, the butler, entered to announce Mr. Fitzhugh Duvenay and Miss Duvenay. Lady Eastcott, who had been looking bored, at once brightened, and fixed an interested gaze upon the door.

She was rewarded almost immediately by the appearance of a very large gentleman of an age approaching forty, attired in proper but somewhat shabby travelling dress, who solicitously shepherded into the room a much younger lady—so young, indeed, that she appeared, to Lady Eastcott's astonished gaze, to be scarcely out of the schoolroom. The fact that her burnished chestnut curls were crowned by an exceedingly dashing bonnet, with a huge, upstanding poke-front lined with French green silk, served merely to emphasise her youthful appearance and gave her rather the look, to Lady Eastcott's experienced eyes, of a young damsel who had taken advantage of an older sister's absence to try the effect of one of her bonnets.

She looked about her with frank interest as she entered the room, but evidently with some embarrassment as well—an emotion not shared, it seemed, by her brother. That gentleman, advancing upon the little group seated together near the windows, bestowed a courtly bow upon Lady Eastcott and Miss Standfield; he then seized the nerveless hand of Lord Eastcott, who had risen on the young lady's entrance, and shook it with an air of dignified formality.

"You, I apprehend, are Lord Eastcott?" he said. "May I present myself, sir? Fitzhugh Duvenay, Esquire, of Duvenay Manor—and this is my little sister Nancy, the unhappy cause of our meeting today. Nancy, my dear," he went on, drawing the obviously reluctant Miss Duvenay forward, "make your curtsey to Lord Eastcott, and to—Lady Eastcott?" he concluded, looking enquiringly at her and the Honourable Miss Stand-field, both of whom were subjecting Miss Duvenay to such a frank scrutiny that the colour rose vividly in that young lady's face.

To say the truth, Lady Eastcott, who had seen the dashing barques of frailty on whom her nephew had bestowed his attention during the six months he had spent in England prior to his recent hurried return abroad, had been startled quite beyond civility by Miss Duvenay's appearance. The girl was certainly attractive, she thought, in a rather strikingly unusual way: she had the beautifully fair skin that often accompanies titian hair, a short straight nose, wide-set hazel eyes, and a firm little chin, and her figure, in a walking dress of French green silk (also bearing the air of borrowed finery), though still childishly slender, was graceful and elegantly formed.

But Tarn, of all men, Lady Eastcott thought, to have conceived a *tendre* for this child! *And*, she added mentally, in indignant disapproval, to have deceived her as well! She had never before this been inclined to take as severe a view of her nephew's character as had the other members of his family, for, having raised quite a few eyebrows herself in her own younger days, she had a certain tolerance for her young relation's scandal-ridden career. But this, she thought, was the outside of enough. The girl was obviously both innocent and a lady, and she decided on the instant that this time there was nothing so scathing that the rest of his family might say about Tarn with which she herself would not wholeheartedly agree.

She accordingly rewarded Miss Duvenay's curtsey with a sympathetic smile and presented her to Miss Standfield, who shook her head and, evidently imbued with similar sentiments, said tersely that it was a great pity.

This statement was immediately taken up by Mr. Duvenay.

"Alas, ma'am, what you say is all too true!" he said earnestly. "A *great* pity—and if it appears so to you, who have but just clapped eyes for the first time upon this unfortunate child, what do you conceive it must be for me, who have stood, so to speak, *in loco parentis* toward her since the death of our parents a dozen years ago? To see her cast off, slighted, humiliated—"

Lady Eastcott, perceiving that he was about to be overcome by his own eloquence, requested the visitors to sit down. She then glanced meaningly at her husband, who, resigning himself to the necessity of taking the situation in hand, said rather testily to Mr. Duvenay that he quite appreciated his feelings, but did not see what he himself was to do in the matter.

"You must know, sir, that I have no control over my nephew's actions," he said. "Not likely, either, that anything *I* say will have the least effect upon him. The thing is, you've wasted your time in coming here. The only advice *I* am able to give you is that you apply to Lord Tarn personally."

Mr. Duvenay, casting a reproachful glance at him from a pair of mournful brown eyes, remarkably like those of an intelligent spaniel that has just been unforgivably disappointed in its master, cleared his throat and ventured to suggest that this scheme might involve certain difficulties.

"I understand," he said, "that his lordship has left England and gone abroad, owing to—how can I best express it?—certain unfortunate circumstances, and has no settled residence there. To pursue him across the Continent is, I fear, quite beyond my present straitened means and, as it appears that the date of his return is indefinite—"

He broke off, looking appealingly at Lady Eastcott, as if he trusted to her feminine sympathy to suggest some course of action to him. Lady Eastcott, however, whose sympathy did not extend to Miss Duvenay's brother, merely shrugged, and it remained for Miss Standfield, still placidly knotting her fringe, to bring them all to the crux of the matter.

"And exactly what, Mr. Duvenay," she enquired, "would you hope to gain if you *were* to succeed in approaching Lord Tarn? Do you wish us to understand that he has offered marriage to your sister? Or that you merely apprehend that he is bound in honour to do so, because of certain indiscretions engaged in by the two young people?"

Miss Duvenay, at this piece of frank speaking, blushed, though looking, as both Lady Eastcott and Miss Standfield noted, fierce rather than embarrassed; and Mr. Fitzhugh Duvenay appeared wounded to the quick.

"My dear ma'am!" he said reprovingly. "Pray remember that you speak of, and before, an innocent child! My sister has been bred up in the strictest principles—"

"Yes, yes, I daresay," said Miss Standfield agreeably. "So, unfortunately, have a great many other young females who find themselves under the necessity of securing a husband as rapidly as possible. But I can assure you, my dear sir, that if you are thinking of making this child the Marchioness of Tarn on the basis of any such necessity, you are wasting your time. Furthermore, I believe you know that quite as well as I do."

Mr. Duvenay, registering affront, begged leave to inform Miss Standfield that no such vulgar necessity existed.

"There are, however," he said, tapping his breast-pocket with the air of one disclosing the presence of a trump card in his hand, "letters, I may inform you—letters so compromising to Lord Tarn's honour that I cannot believe that either he or his family would care to have them read as evidence in a court of law. Which," he continued nobly, "repugnant as it is to my feelings, I am fully prepared to see done, ma'am, should this be the only means open to me to secure redress for the injury done to my sister's young heart."

Upon hearing this, Miss Standfield, laying her fringe aside, said, "I thought so," still in a quite unperturbed voice, and, turning to Lord Eastcott, enquired what he meant to do.

"It is plain that Mr. Duvenay intends to ask you for a sum of money, Eastcott," she said, "and I believe it will save a great deal of time if you inform him whether or not you are prepared to meet his demand. For my own part, I do not advise it.

8

Distressing as it must be to have Tarn's indiscretions publicly aired in a court of law, one must remember that he is not, after all, Royalty, so that the necessity under which His Majesty laboured in regard to the Prince of Wales in the case I have just cited does not precisely apply."

She then informed Mr. Duvenay in a quite kindly voice, considering the statement she had just made concerning him, that he had the appearance of suffering from bilious disorders and recommended the use of James's Powders, after which, declaring that she had no further time to spare, she rose and left the room.

Mr. Duvenay, not unreasonably a trifle bewildered by this abrupt change of subject, turned a bemused gaze upon Lord Eastcott, but that gentleman also appeared to have lost the thread of the conversation momentarily, so that it was Lady Eastcott who was obliged to step into the breach. Her method of doing so was to cross the room to the sofa on which Miss Duvenay had seated herself and, sitting down beside her, to take one of her gloved hands in her own.

"Now, my dear," she said, "this is a horrid business, to be sure, and I daresay Tarn deserves to be flogged for his part in it, but if your brother is speaking the truth and there is really no need for you to be married at once, I think I should tell you that you would be well advised to return to Ireland and forget that you ever clapped eyes on him. He is a scandalously wild young man, you know, and would make you the very worst sort of husband if he *could* be induced to marry you—which I am frank to tell you that he will not be. And as for bringing an action against him for breach of promise—I am persuaded that you cannot know in the least what such a matter would involve, or you would never so much as consider it! To be obliged to describe the tender passages that must have occurred between you and my nephew publicly in a common court—"

She broke off, suddenly becoming aware that there was something odd in Miss Duvenay's response to her words.

9

There was neither obstinacy nor embarrassment—either of which she could have understood—in that young lady's face, but rather a desperate sort of indignation, for which nothing in the conversation appeared logically to account. Lady Eastcott saw that her gaze was fixed upon her brother, and instantly jumped to the conclusion that the emotions expressed upon her young guest's face represented her revulsion at having the secrets of her first youthful passion callously exploited by that gentleman for gain.

"Oh, you poor child!" said Lady Eastcott, impelled by a new wave of sympathy. "I daresay you were—*are*—very much in love with that wicked young nephew of mine?"

Miss Duvenay, finding the eyes of the entire company fixed upon her, was obliged to make some response. A furious blush rose swiftly in her face and she said, in a scarcely audible voice, "Please—I do not wish to speak of it."

"Naturally she cannot bring herself to discuss the matter!" said Mr. Duvenay, himself speaking so rapidly upon the heels of his sister's words that he hardly allowed her the time to complete them. "I should not, my lady, be guilty of such monstrous cruelty as to propose that this child be called upon to convince you by her own account of what has transpired between her and your nephew. But *here,* if you please"—he took Miss Duvenay's left hand and gently removed the glove from it—"*here* is proof positive of the business. An engagement ring, you will perceive!"

Lord Eastcott, raising his quizzing-glass to survey more closely a very fine diamond glittering upon Miss Duvenay's slender hand, said in a decidedly cross tone that he didn't take that point at all.

"No proof that Tarn gave it to her," he said. "Anyone might have done so. Well, you, for example. Simplest matter in the world to walk into a jeweller's shop and order a ring. Done it myself, more than once."

Mr. Duvenay did not deign to respond to this insinuation.

10

Instead, he drew from his pocket a small packet of what appeared to be letters, tied together with a bit of pink ribbon. Undoing the ribbon, he proceeded to look with care through the documents it had contained, selected one, and handed it to Lord Eastcott.

"If you will read that, my lord—" he said simply.

The quizzing-glass was raised again and his lordship surveyed a single sheet of paper, on which the following was written in a bold masculine hand:

> *Lovely Nancy,*
> *Never fear. I shan't fail you. You shall have the ring*
> *as soon as ever I come next or nigh a jeweller's shop.*
> *Till tonight. Tarn.*

That was all, but to his lordship's unhappy gaze it was quite enough. Whatever else the small packet of documents still in Mr. Duvenay's hand might contain, these few words —unmistakably in his nephew's hand—were enough to give that gentleman the best possible grounds for hope that he might bring an action against Lord Tarn to a highly successful conclusion.

2

It remained for Lady Eastcott to keep her head sufficiently to see to it that her husband's ingrained dislike of anything that threatened an upset in the placid routine of his existence did not lead him to sit down immediately and write a draft upon Hoare's Bank to satisfy the expectant Mr. Duvenay. Having been informed only that morning by her spouse that it was quite out of the question for her to expend the sum of three hundred pounds upon a grande-toilette of lace over white satin in which she wished to shine during the forthcoming visit of the Allied Sovereigns to London in celebration of the recent defeat of Bonaparte, she was scarcely in the mood to see an amount perhaps many times that large go into Mr. Duvenay's pocket from her lord's purse. Letters or no letters, she informed that hopeful gentleman, nothing would be settled that day, as her husband, she said mendaciously, would be obliged to consult with other members of his family on what could be done in the matter.

Having then ascertained that Mr. Duvenay and his sister were stopping at the local inn, the George, she promised that Lord Eastcott would let him know his decision as soon as possible and thereupon dismissed him.

This stratagem she was soon to look upon as a manifestation of the purest genius upon her part, for shortly after luncheon the arrival of another visitor at the house with a piece of news from town put an entirely new complexion upon the affair.

The newly arrived guest was another of her nephews, Mr. Bruce Fearon, who had come to spend a few days at Eastcott Park—an event which frequently occurred when he found that the dissipations of town life, with their concomitant drain upon his purse, made it advisable for him to go into the country on a repairing lease. As he was a bachelor not yet in his thirtieth year, of a handsome person and pleasing address, he was always welcome in the homes of his more affluent relations, where he invariably repaid his hostess by making himself agreeable to any fellow guests whose entertainment was found by her to be the most difficult or boring at the moment. Middle-aged ladies in general pronounced him to be the most delightful of companions, and more than one matchmaking mama had deplored the perverse fate that had bestowed a title and a fortune upon Tarn, while leaving his more deserving cousin with only the crumbs, so to speak, from the family table.

The one consolation that remained to them was the hopeful expectation that a young man as wild as the Marquis, with a strong predilection for duelling and the more dangerous forms of sport, must sooner or later be overtaken by some disaster that would put a period to his existence and place Mr. Bruce Fearon, who stood to inherit in the absence of any male off-spring of his cousin's, in possession of his title and estates.

On the present afternoon he was all amiability as he walked into the tapestry room, where Lady Eastcott and Miss Standfield were discussing the events of the morning, and bowed in turn over the ladies' hands. Lady Eastcott, who invariably

14

disclosed any matter that was occupying her mind to anyone who would listen to her, at once began upon the topic that was uppermost in her thoughts. She found Mr. Fearon an attentive auditor, but he made no comment until she had concluded her narration of the morning's events, when he remarked, replying to her last vexed statement that she had no doubt Eastcott would allow himself to be bled handsomely only to be rid of the man, that he believed his uncle need no longer concern himself in the matter.

"Tarn, my dear Aunt, has returned to London," he said. "In point of fact, I saw him there myself just before I set out, and informed him of your being in expectation of a visit from this fellow Duvenay. You will be relieved to learn that he assured me he would come into Sussex himself immediately and take the matter out of my uncle's hands."

He got no further, for Lady Eastcott, staring at him incredulously, interrupted at this point to exclaim, "Tarn in London! But surely he cannot be! They say that horrid creature he fought that disgraceful duel with has been lingering at death's door these past weeks, and Eastcott assures me that Tarn has only to set foot in England for the Bow Street Runners to be after him! He cannot be so utterly imprudent as to have risked *that!*"

Her nephew took a very handsome Sèvres snuffbox from his pocket, unfobbed it with an expert flick of a finger, and refreshed himself with a pinch of its contents.

"Oh, he ran no risk, ma'am," he observed, when he had accomplished this. "The fellow—Fryde, *Captain* Fryde, I believe he calls himself, though a Captain Sharp is as much as I'd say he could properly lay claim to—is quite out of danger now, so that there is no longer a question of Lewis's being obliged to stand his trial for murder. And it appears as well that another member of the family—my cousin Marmaduke, in this instance—has succeeded in inducing Captain Fryde to make a statement that obviates any need for Lewis to remain abroad."

15

Lady Eastcott, who found herself somewhat more in charity with Lord Tarn, now that there was no longer any necessity for her husband to become involved in his lordship's tangled affairs, said warmly that she was very glad to hear it.

"And I will say this for Duke," she added, referring to the Honourable Marmaduke Standfield, who enjoyed the relationship of cousin to both Mr. Fearon and Tarn, as well as that of nephew to Miss Standfield, "that, though he may be a very frippery young man and have the least supply of brains of anyone in the family, he is always willing to exert himself when one has need of him. But of course I daresay Tarn will repay him any sum he was obliged to put out in the matter—which I *must* say I am persuaded he would have done for Eastcott as well, if he had been put to the expense of buying off Mr. Duvenay. Only heaven knows how long it might have been before Tarn heard of it, if he were still wandering about the Continent."

Mr. Fearon, who had employed the period occupied by this speech in dusting his fingertips with his handkerchief and replacing his snuffbox in his pocket, observed at this point that perhaps, in the long run, his uncle would have found the necessity of putting a sizeable sum of money into Mr. Duvenay's pocket a small price to pay for the tranquility that would have been his had Tarn remained abroad.

"At least while he was on the Continent one was merely obliged to hear rumours of his excesses," he remarked. "It is infinitely more tiresome—as you must have learned yourself during these past months, dear Aunt—not to be able so much as to enter a drawing room or walk down Bond Street without having his latest escapade flung into one's face."

Miss Standfield, who had been observing the rather bitter expression upon Mr. Fearon's face as he spoke of his cousin, now said, with her customary air of regal finality, that she believed he was refining too much upon the matter, since it was very possible that marriage, when the young Marquis

16

decided to take a wife, might work a salutary change in his way of life.

"I have often observed this to be so," she said, "even in the case of young men whose families had quite despaired of them. Indeed, I am persuaded that if Mrs. Fitzherbert had been of sufficiently exalted birth to have been received into the Royal Family as the Prince's wife, the Regent might be a quite different man than we see him today."

She would have gone on, but Mr. Fearon interrupted, looking up quickly, "Good God, ma'am, you do not mean to tell me that you consider Lewis might marry this little Irish nobody? Is the jade clever enough to have brought him so far into her net?"

"No, no, you must not call her so!" Lady Eastcott protested, before Miss Standfield could reply. "I vow, she is the merest child, Bruce, and has not the least notion of feathering her nest. It has had me in a puzzle ever since I laid eyes on her to account for Tarn's being taken with her at all. But I daresay the truth of the matter is that he was merely amusing himself with her because there was no other presentable female at hand, for you know that when he was in Ireland he was staying in quite an out-of-the-way place."

"Yes, I know all about that," Mr. Fearon said impatiently. "He went over with Neddy O'Bannon to have a look at a pair of prime hunters O'Bannon wished to sell him. And I must say I should never believe that Lewis would be the man to lose his head over a pretty face."

"Oh, he has not! I am persuaded of that!" Lady Eastcott assured him. "Even the girl's brother has obviously not the least idea that Lewis will marry her, and the child herself seems quite sunk in despair; she had scarcely a word to say for herself all the while they were here."

Miss Standfield here gave it as her opinion that such a marriage would be highly unsuitable, Miss Duvenay's position in life in no way fitting her to take her place as a member of the

17

higher nobility, but added enigmatically that Tarn might do worse.

"Not unless he marries a barmaid," Mr. Fearon said brutally, "which I must say I live in daily apprehension of hearing that he has done."

The striking of the hour then put them all in mind that it was time to dress for dinner, and they separated to go to their various rooms.

The next morning, while they were still at breakfast, they were surprised to receive an early call from Tarn. Lewis Lionel Wystan Fearon, the Most Noble the Marquis of Tarn, was a very tall young man, the most noticeable features of whose appearance, beyond his height, were a certain air of tautly controlled muscular strength in the way he moved and a pair of arrogant dark eyes, violently alive in a young, harsh-featured face. He was dressed in a dark green coat, buckskins, and boots quite lacking in the extravagantly long white tops affected for country wear by such patterns of fashion as Mr. Bruce Fearon; a handkerchief was knotted about his throat in place of a cravat; and his black locks were carelessly arranged in a manner bearing no resemblance to the cunning disorder of the *coup de vent* style into which his cousin's fairer curls had been brushed.

His arrival occasioned an outcry of questions from everyone at the table except Miss Standfield, who merely remarked in her usual unruffled manner to Lady Eastcott that she had best order Philbrook to lay another place and fetch ale and more bread and butter and ham, for young gentlemen, in her experience, were notoriously sharp-set in the morning.

"Oh yes, by all means!" agreed Lady Eastcott, nodding to Philbrook. "And a few slices of that nice red sirloin, I should think—for if you have breakfasted at Tarn House," she went on, addressing her nephew, "I daresay they gave you nothing but coffee and cold toast. It is the commonest gossip, you know, that Mrs. Timbs is growing *quite* peculiar, and that it is as much as poor Timbs can do to bring her to part with a groat,

18

even for the most necessary expenditures. But I expect you will have seen for yourself the state of the house, which is a very good thing, for it must be *years* since you have visited it, and certainly it is high time that something was done—"

Lord Eastcott here interrupted testily to enquire if his wife meant to go prosing on forever.

"Give the boy a chance to say a word for himself!" he said. "Must say, you had us all in the deuce of a fidget yesterday, Tarn! Time you came down and took hold of things here. I suppose everything is settled now with that fellow Fryde?"

The Marquis, who had taken the chair held for him by a disapproving Philbrook and accepted the tankard of ale hastily fetched by one of his underlings, regarded the assembled company with his customary and, as Lady Eastcott later described it, *maddening* imperturbability.

"Why, yes, sir," he said. "I believe it is. Thank you, yes, ham, if you please, and I *will* have some of that sirloin."

"Lewis, if you are going to talk of nothing but food, I shall scream!" threatened Lady Eastcott. "Here you walk in looking as if the only thing you cared about was your breakfast, when you have been causing everyone in the family the most dreadful anxiety!"

"Not Bruce," said his lordship, glancing briefly across the table at his cousin. "*He* looks in prime twig."

"Thank you, I am," said Mr. Fearon, with his white-toothed smile. "I must confess, though, coz, that I should rejoice in even greater health and spirits if I were not obliged to suffer the constant shock of your highly unconventional actions. First this affair with the somewhat less than respectable Captain, and now, it appears, an impoverished Irish squireen threatens to publish to the world that you offered marriage to his sister and then abandoned her."

"Oh—that," said Tarn, discussing bread and ham with an appetite that appeared quite unimpaired by this news. "Well, I fancy I can put a stop to that fast enough." He looked at his uncle. "Fellow turned up here yet?" he asked. "Bruce told me you were expecting him."

Lord Eastcott nodded. "Yesterday," he said, frowning. "Of course you know, Tarn, this sort of thing is very disagreeable for the family—very! Bad enough to keep the town on the tattle about your affairs with the muslin company, but when you take to deceiving respectable young females—"

Tarn shrugged, his mouth curling. "Is that how he described her?" he said, in a tone that caused Lady Eastcott instantly to cry out upon him.

"There was no need for him to describe her!" she said. "He brought her to see us, and—oh, Lewis, I own I was sadly shocked, for you must know that she is the merest child! Indeed, it is too bad of you, and I am excessively sorry for her!"

"Well, you needn't be," Tarn said callously. "If that is how she appeared to you, she is a more accomplished actress than I gave her credit for being." He glanced again at his uncle. "I hope you weren't cozened into laying out any of your blunt to buy her off," he said. "If you were, I shall repay you, of course."

"No, no!" Lord Eastcott said. "I am not so easily bamboozled, my boy! Though I must say," he added doubtfully, "that it appeared to me that Eleanor is right about the young lady, Tarn. Dash it, hardly more than a schoolgirl!"

"A schoolgirl! Nancy Duvenay!" Tarn said, in derision.

"Lewis, that is quite unfair, and you know it!" Lady Eastcott said severely. "The fact is, I expect, that it has been so long since you have spent any time in the company of respectable females that you are not able to recognise one when you see one. You have behaved quite scandalously towards that poor girl, and excusing yourself by trying to make it appear that she is no better than one of your lightskirts does you no credit, I will tell you. Indeed, for all your faults, I believe no one has ever been able before this to accuse you of seducing school-room misses."

"Thank you!" Tarn bowed ironically to her across the table.

"Nor are they able to now, ma'am, though I daresay it suits Miss Duvenay to lead you to believe otherwise." He got up from the table. "Well, if you will tell me where this innocent is to be found," he said, "I shall settle my account with her—*and* with her brother—and you need hear no more of them in future."

Lord Eastcott said disapprovingly, but with a certain air of relief, that the Duvenays were putting up at the George, and the Marquis was about to leave the room when Miss Standfield requested him to stay a moment. He paused, looking at her interrogatively.

"Yes, ma'am?"

Miss Standfield regarded him thoughtfully. After a moment she said deliberately, "I have never regarded you as being deficient in understanding, Tarn, and I can scarcely believe that even the highly improper mode of life you have been indulging in has altered you in that respect. I therefore apprehend that you have a surprise in store for you, and I must beg that you do not allow it to arouse your temper—which I fear is a somewhat ungovernable one—to an extent that you will later regret."

She concluded this entirely cryptic speech by announcing her intention of going to her room to follow the regimen of complete immobility after meals prescribed by the eminent Dr. Newlyn, and made a stately exit.

Tarn, his eyebrows raised, looked at Lady Eastcott. "And what, I wonder, am I to understand by that?" he asked.

"I have not the least notion!" she confessed. "Really, Amelia is growing so odd of late! But I must admit that she is excessively clever at knowing the sort of things no one else so much as suspects, like telling Lady Corbishley that that perfectly charming French dancing master she had for Lucilla meant to run off with her." She wrinkled her brow. "Still, I cannot think she meant anything of the sort in this case—that you might run off with Miss Duvenay, I mean."

"I should sincerely hope not," said Mr. Fearon languidly. "I warn you, Lewis, that I find myself unable to sustain any more shocks just at present, and if I should discover that, by some miracle, you *do* have honourable intentions towards this totally ineligible young female, I fear that it would be quite too much for me to endure."

"You may make yourself easy," Tarn retorted. "I have no such intentions."

And, with a bow to his aunt, he was gone from the room.

"Well, I *do* think," said Lady Eastcott, looking after him discontentedly, "that he is the most unaccountable young man! To walk in here and eat breakfast with us as if he were used to doing it every day in the year, tell us absolutely *nothing* of where he has been or what he has been doing—"

"No, no," interrupted her husband earnestly, "far better he didn't do *that*, my dear. *I* don't want to know what he's been doing—or what he's about to do now, as a matter of fact. As long as he gets rid of that fellow Duvenay, he may go about it any way he chooses. Much more comfortable to know nothing about it! Don't you agree with me, Bruce, my boy?"

The Marquis, whose mode of attacking any problem that presented itself to him was nothing if not direct, drove his curricle immediately to the George upon leaving Eastcott Park and, tossing the reins to his groom, strode inside the ancient, thatch-roofed hostelry and demanded Mr. Fitzhugh Duvenay of the landlord. That worthy, who had not laid eyes upon his lordship for a matter of almost five years, nevertheless recognised him at once, and greeted him with many expressions of surprise and gratification.

"Yes—very well!" Tarn cut him short, unmoved by this effusive welcome. "But Duvenay?"

"Why, I'm sorry to say, my lord, that he's not here," the landlord confessed. "Gone off to visit a relation of his, he said, down Bexhill way—so it's not likely, either, that he'll be back soon." He added, as he saw the impatient look upon Tarn's face, "But miss—that is to say, the gentleman's sister—didn't go with him, if you was wishful to see her as well, my lord. She stepped out for a bit of a walk just now, but I don't doubt you might overtake her if you liked, for she set off down the lane not ten minutes ago. She was going in the direction of Tarn House," he concluded helpfully, "and wearing a regular dasher of a green bonnet, so I shouldn't think it was at all likely you could miss her on the road."

The Marquis, having rewarded him for this information with a coin dropped into his hand, strode out of the inn and set up a shout for his groom, who, in the expectation that his master would make a more prolonged stay in the house, was indulging in a heavy-wet in the bar. He came reluctantly, with a barely repressed mutter of surly words, for, like all his lordship's servants, he had early discovered that Tarn was not one to stand on his dignity, merely laughed at impudence as long as his horses were well looked after, and was only dangerous when one of his retainers baulked at accompanying him on one of his more foolhardy adventures. The groom who had served the Marquis just previous to the present occupant of the position had gloomily predicted to his successor that, after *he* had been overturned half a dozen times by his lordship's driving hell-for-leather over roads where even a prime whip—which he wasn't saying his lordship was not—needed to use a bit of caution, he would think even the handsome wage the Marquis paid him insufficient to compensate him for the risks he ran.

At the present moment, however, the groom found that his master's intention was no more alarming than to drive at a very moderate pace along a country road—and even this pleasant mode of travel was brought to a conclusion at the end of no more than five minutes when his lordship, rounding a turn, came upon a slim figure in an extremely fashionable French green gown and bonnet walking before him in the road. Before the groom could imagine what he was about, he had halted the horses, tossed him the reins, and sprung down from the curricle; the next moment he was striding along the road towards the green-clad figure before him.

She had turned her head at the sound of the approaching

carriage and then, stepping to the grassy verge along the side of the road, continued on her way. The sudden cessation of the rattle of wheels, however, together with the sound of rapid footsteps behind her, caused her to pause and turn again just as Tarn, coming up beside her, grasped her somewhat ungently by one arm.

"Now, my girl—" he began, swinging her about to face him, and then paused, his hard eyes expressing the blankest astonishment. "The devil!" he ejaculated. "You aren't Miss Duvenay!"

The young lady, whose own face expressed quite as much surprise as Tarn's, looked at him enquiringly and not entirely cordially.

"Yes, I am Miss Duvenay!" she said. "And who are you? I wish you will let me go at once! Why do you stop me?"

"*You* are Miss Duvenay?" His lordship's hand dropped from her arm, but it must have occurred to her that those cold black eyes, mercilessly searching her face, held even more menace in them than had that rude grasp. He added slowly, "Miss *Nancy* Duvenay?"

"I do not at all see what affair that is of yours! Will you let me pass, please?"

"No, I will not let you pass!" said Tarn. "Just what kind of rig is it that you are trying to run, my girl? You are not Nancy Duvenay—though I'll lay odds I've seen that bonnet before, and on Nancy Duvenay's head!"

He recalled at the same time Miss Standfield's odd prediction that he had a surprise in store for him, made an instant connexion between the "schoolroom miss" who had been described to him and his present companion's innocent, questioning, rather stormily indignant face, and heard, with some satisfaction, the startled gasp that now broke from her.

"Oh!" she said. "You are not—you cannot be—Lord Tarn!"

"Yes, I'm Tarn," he said grimly. "And who are you, you rogue?"

Her chin lifted. "I did not lie to you, my lord," she said. "I am Victoire Duvenay."

"The devil you are!"

"But I *am*! I am—*your* Nancy's cousin. And I do not at all blame you,"she continued frankly, with a sudden air of fair-minded acknowledgement of the niceties of the situation, "if you would like entirely to kill me, which I can quite see that you do! *C'est infame*, to play such a game with you, no matter how badly *you* have behaved!"

His lordship, finding the wind somewhat taken out of his sails by this candid statement, was able to retain a grasp upon his temper, but it was in no very cordial tone that he retorted, "Generous of you to say so! And what, precisely, *is* your game, Miss Duvenay? No—you needn't trouble to tell me; I believe I can guess. Extortion—blackmail—by what name do *you* call it?—with my uncle playing the pigeon, since I was safely out of the country and he had never clapped eyes on either you *or* Nancy. The only thing I *don't* understand is why this mas-querade was necessary. Or did Nancy decide that she couldn't spare the time from her Irish admirers to make the journey?"

Miss Duvenay, who had been regarding him with what seemed a mixture of the liveliest curiosity and the deepest mortification, said at this, in a hushed voice, "Oh no, my lord! You see—she is dead!"

"Dead!" Tarn stared at her incredulously. "Nancy? Gam-mon!"

"No, no, indeed she is dead!" Miss Duvenay insisted seri-ously. "It was the fever, you understand. I was not there when she died, but I was told that it carried her off very quickly —which often happens, you know, with the fever, for I have seen it myself with soldiers—"

She was interrupted by the approach of a gig along the road. She and the Marquis were obliged to step aside to allow it to pass, undergoing as they did so a severe scrutiny from the elderly gentleman in rusty black who was driving it.

"The devil!" said the Marquis impatiently, bestowing a highly unfriendly regard in return upon the elderly gentleman. "We can't stand here talking in the road! Come along; I'll take you up with me."

"But I do not wish to go with you!" objected Miss Duvenay, showing some slight alarm at this proposal. "Indeed, there is no need! I shall explain to my cousin that you have returned to England and have seen me, so that it is not possible that you will pay him any money now for all the things my cousin Nancy suffered because of you—"

"Thank you!" Tarn interrupted unaccommodatingly. "But there are a few things I should like you to explain to me as well, my girl, and you are not going to do it while we stand here in the road!"

He took her arm as he spoke and compelled her to cross the road to where his groom had drawn the curricle up. With the latter's curious eyes upon her, she evidently felt it beneath her dignity to resist, but she said in an urgent, imploring undertone, "Please—I do not wish to go with you! I have told you the truth, my lord! Please let me go!"

"We'll see that," Tarn said, in an unmoved voice, ruthlessly handing her up into the curricle.

She stole a glance at him as he mounted beside her; only his profile was presented to her, but the set of the lips was enough to tell her that her explanations had not succeeded in mollifying his anger to any noticeable degree. She sighed suddenly, as if resigning herself.

"Very well," she said. "I shall go with you. After all, I daresay I am quite as much to blame as my cousin Fitz—Fitzhugh —Ah, bah! I cannot say it properly!"

Tarn glanced down at her briefly as he gave his horses the office to start.

"French?" he asked. "That is something else that you may explain to me, Miss Victoire Duvenay—at the proper time."

She cast a glance, following his, at the groom, who had

resumed his place perched up behind them, and relapsed into what appeared to his lordship to be a rather forlorn, considering silence. There was, in truth, something in the determinedly gallant erectness of the little figure beside him that made it difficult for the Marquis to continue to regard her in the light of the scheming jade she had appeared to him in the first hot moments of his wrath; but he was still exceedingly angry and had not the slightest intention of letting her escape from him before he had wrung the whole story of this outrageous masquerade from her.

With his groom present, however, even Tarn's faulty sense of the proprieties forbade him to enter into the matter of Miss Duvenay's duplicity, and it was not until the curricle had bowled up the imposing but highly overgrown drive leading to Tarn House some quarter of an hour later and swept to a halt before the front door that he turned to his young passenger again.

"Get down," he instructed her briefly and, tossing the reins to his groom, jumped down himself and came round to the other side of the carriage to assist or compel her to comply with his order.

Victoire looked down at him dubiously, and then at the noble façade of the huge Tudor house before her, which bore an appearance of such obvious neglect that it seemed to be quite uninhabited.

"Here?" she enquired.

"Yes—here!" said Tarn, in a voice that brooked no opposition.

Victoire, faced with the prospect of being haled ignominiously from her seat if she refused, capitulated and allowed herself to be assisted to alight. His lordship's hand beneath her elbow propelled her irresistibly forward to the front steps, which were alarmingly weed-grown to her eyes. She baulked at the foot of them and said rather breathlessly, "Is this *your* house, my lord? Surely no one lives here now!"

Tarn gave a short laugh. "What—losing your courage, sweetheart?" he jeered. "If you wish to fill Nancy's shoes, you must play Nancy's game. *She* would not have drawn back at the notion of an empty house in my company!"

Victoire made no reply. Tarn's hard fingers, gripping her arm, again impelled her forward. She took a step, halted—and then, before he could be aware of her intention, suddenly wrenched herself free and, doubling like a frightened hare, went speeding off down the avenue in the direction of the huge iron gates.

It was an unequal chase. In a brace of moments Tarn had caught her up; a long arm grasped her shoulder and, as she struggled wildly to free herself, she tripped over an encroaching tree root and tumbled to the ground. Tarn, instantly down on one knee beside her, held her pinioned there ruthlessly.

"Oh, no!" he said. "It's not to be so easy as that!" He added deliberately, "You little vixen!"—awaiting tears, cajoleries, even gutter threats, if it developed the girl was not so much a lady as she would like to appear.

What he got was a wide, soundless, unwinking stare from fierce hazel eyes that might have belonged to some forest bird doubled there, helpless, beneath his grasp. He could see the pulse beating wildly in her throat, but the eyes never wavered. She lay there, waiting; he felt muscles quivering and bunching for the struggle that his next movement must inevitably trigger.

His grip loosened slowly; he rose.

"Get up!" he said harshly. He bent and put a hand under her elbow to assist her, but she scrambled to her feet, disdaining his aid, and stood facing him. "And don't try to run away again!" he warned her.

She said, on an oddly childish, resentful sob, instantly suppressed, "No! You can run too fast. It would be—of no use." And, with even darker resentment, "I wish very much that my father was here!"

He gave a grim little laugh. "Well, where is he? Is he a part of this charming little plot of yours, too?"

"No! He is—dead."

"Like Nancy? Your road appears to be strewn with corpses, my girl!"

She drew in her breath at his flippant tone. "He was killed—at Wagram," she said, in a low, furious voice. "And you will not *dare* to speak disrespectfully of him!"

Tarn's eyes narrowed suddenly. "A soldier?" he asked.

"Yes! He was Colonel John Duvenay. I daresay you must have heard of him!"

The Marquis knit his brows. He had not spent almost five years on the Continent without having been regaled there with tales of the famous Irish soldier of fortune whose exploits in several armies had reached their apogee in the gallant but disastrous Austrian stand against Napoleon's army at Wagram. He had *not* heard, however, of the Colonel's having left behind him a chestnut-haired young daughter, and he was cynical enough to reflect that Miss Duvenay would not be the first to take advantage of the coincidence of a name to claim a relationship quite above her touch.

He accordingly said, "Yes, I have heard of him," in a non-committal voice, which apparently conveyed his thought to Victoire, however, for she flushed hotly and began to say something defensive. But she then appeared to recollect that the matter between herself and the Marquis scarcely had to do with her parentage, for she shut her lips suddenly, and when she spoke again it was only to say, in a gruff little voice, "*Enfin*—what do you mean to do?"

Tarn, regarding the very flushed, apprehensive young lady facing him with such a valiant attempt at composure, had to blame the violent temper of which Miss Standfield had warned him for not allowing her to depart at once. That temper was still up, and stubbornly insisted upon getting to the bottom of the affair, with a view towards visiting condign chastisement upon its perpetrators, and he therefore announced bluntly to Miss Duvenay that he intended to do exactly what he had been about to do when she had run away from him—namely, escort her into the house.

"You needn't look so mulish," he added impatiently, as Victoire, stiffening, cast a harassed glance about her as if in search of succour. "The house isn't empty. In point of fact, my old butler and housekeeper are both there, and either of them would like nothing better than to screech the house down if they thought I intended any mischief to you. Come along!"

His hand grasped her arm. She allowed herself reluctantly to be led back up the drive towards the house, up the weed-grown steps, and in at the deeply recessed Tudor doorway.

The loud creak of the huge front door on its hinges brought—to Victoire's obvious relief—a white-haired butler into the hall. He stared disapprovingly at the pair before him and muttered something, with a strong Sussex accent, to the effect that Master Lewis had ought to known there was no likelihood Mrs. Timbs would take kindly to the thought of scurrying round for refreshments for any young ladies. He did not add, "who have no business to be here in the first place," but it was plain, from the censuring look he cast at Victoire, that the thought was in his mind.

Victoire, whose notions of the Marquis's temper had been formed from her own present unhappy collision with it, was a good deal surprised to find that this outrageously insubordinate behaviour on the part of his butler drew only a grin and a mocking word from his lordship. But indeed, she thought, her gaze travelling wonderingly about a great hall where dusty figures in armour and stained marble busts austerely surveyed neglected hangings and furniture swathed in holland covers, his lordship must be a peculiarly indulgent master on other points as well, if he was content to see his house in such a shocking state of disarray.

She followed him into one of the stately reception rooms

31

opening from the hall, her trepidation somewhat allayed by the comforting knowledge that a respectable-appearing and testy old servant, who called the formidable Marquis "Master Lewis" and was not at all averse to giving him a sharp set-down, was on the premises.

Inside the room, Tarn swept the covers from a pair of chairs and indicated with a gesture that Victoire was to seat herself upon one of them. He himself did not sit down, but, going across to the window, pulled back the dusty red damask draperies to let the May morning sunlight into the dim apartment. Turning back to his unwilling guest, he then said, "Well?" in an impatient voice.

Victoire, who had been regarding in some awe the portrait of a fierce-looking gentleman in a Tudor ruff and peasecod-bellied doublet glaring balefully down at her from over the carved stone mantelpiece, jumped.

"W—what?" she stammered.

Tarn said, with no marked air of politeness, that he was awaiting her explanation.

"My—my explanation? Oh! You mean, why did I pretend to be Nancy?" Victoire wrinkled her brow. "But—where should I begin?" she asked.

"At the beginning, I should think. And I may as well warn you that I've no mind to spend the morning over this business. Give me a plain story, girl, or, by God, I'll shake it out of you!"

Victoire drew herself up with an air of umbrage. "I would not *lie* to you," she said, deeply offended.

"No?" Tarn laughed shortly. "You seemed ready enough yesterday to lie to my uncle."

"Yes, but *that* was different."

"Was it? Why?"

Her defenses appeared to crumble suddenly; she made a hopeless gesture and said after a moment, in a small voice, "I daresay you will not understand. I know I should have gone away when I found out what Fitzhugh wished me to do."

"Well? Why didn't you?"

"I—I could not." Tarn saw her hands clench together tightly in her lap—a betrayal of nervous emotion that even his own rather brutally dangerous behaviour of a few minutes before had not elicited from her. "You see," she said, "there is only *Maman,* and she does not want me in the least. That was why she sent me to Ireland, to my cousin Fitzhugh, when—when the trouble came in France—"

The Marquis, who began to perceive that the explanation of Miss Duvenay's masquerade was going to be considerably more involved than he had bargained for, sat down.

"I *said* you'd best begin at the beginning," he said curtly. "Well—do so! And *don't* snivel," he added unsympathetically, seeing the tears welling up in Victoire's eyes.

"I am *not* snivelling!" Victoire sat up indignantly. "But how can I talk properly—or think properly, for that matter!—when you have done your best to frighten me half to death, and sit there now looking as if you would like very much to murder me?"

"Well, I am not going to murder you—or, at any rate, I shan't do so if you will stop arguing with me and tell me what I want to know," Tarn said, with what was apparently, to him, the utmost reasonableness.

His words at least had the effect of reassuring Victoire to the extent that she was able to marshal her thoughts to recount her story to him in a fairly coherent fashion. She was, she again insisted, indeed the daughter of Colonel John Duvenay, and when he had been killed at Wagram in '09 she and her mother, a Frenchwoman of good birth, had been left almost destitute—a fate which Madame Duvenay had promptly remedied by marrying for a second time.

Her new husband, Victoire said, with a wrinkling of her straight nose that was far more expressive of her opinion of him than were the few brief words in which she described him, was a man who had risen from obscurity during the Revolution to become one of the minor lights of the Napoleonic Court.

"*Bien entendu*," she said disparagingly, "he wished to forget that *Maman* had ever been married to Papa. He was always frightened of his own shadow, that one, you understand; *au vrai*, I do not think he would have married *Maman* at all if she had not been so excessively beautiful that he could not help falling in love with her. And it did not at all suit him, either, to have me about to remind people that he had married an enemy of Bonaparte's, so I was sent off to Normandy to live with his mother, Madame Rollon, in a little manor house he had bought for her in the country—very remote, *vous concevez*, because she was not at all *à la mode* and so he liked to keep her also quite hidden away, like me. Madame hated me very much, I think, because she quite worshipped Bonaparte, and I"—Victoire lifted her chin—"I would not permit her to speak ill of Papa, which she *would* do, because he had fought against the Emperor."

She looked enquiringly at Tarn, as if to see if he might be sympathetic to this point of view, and, observing no encouragement in his dark face, shrugged her shoulders and said,

35

"But I see you are not at all interested in that, so I will go on. When Bonaparte was obliged to abdicate and leave France, you will understand that it was a very bad time for Monsieur Rollon—I do not call him Papa; I will *never* call him Papa," she added firmly. "And Madame Rollon—his mother—had the misfortune to fall ill just then; if you must know the truth, she ran quite mad, and said that the Emperor was hiding in her garret, and a great many other very foolish things, and so they said I must not live with her any longer. Only *Maman* wrote that I could not come to her, either, because she and Monsieur Rollon were obliged to leave France and would probably emigrate to America, and meanwhile I was to go to my cousin Fitzhugh Duvenay in Ireland, whom she had never seen, but she had heard my father say he had a considerable estate in County Kerry, and she was sure he would look after me much better than she and Monsieur Rollon would be able to do for a very long time to come."

Tarn gave a short laugh. Victoire looked at him questioningly.

"A *considerable* estate," his lordship said derisively. "Yes, I've seen it. A huge old barracks that is fast tumbling to ruin, and lands reduced to a beggar's allowance."

"Oh!" said Victoire, enlightened. "But of course you have seen it. *That* is where you met my cousin Nancy—*n'est-ce pas*?" She added, with some interest, "She was very beautiful, I suppose—like *Maman*. Is that why you fell in love with her?"

The Marquis did not reply to her question; he was frowning over another part of this speech.

"Deuce take it," he said, after a moment, "do you mean to tell me you've never met her?"

"*Mais non!*" said Victoire. "How should I have met her? I have never been in Ireland except when I came to my cousin's house two weeks ago. And she was already dead then, which was why I was sorry for Fitzhugh and said I would come here in her place—because he was quite in despair, you see, over her

36

having died of a broken heart just when he was about to bring her to England."

"You said a few minutes ago that she died of the fever," Tarn interrupted, with the utmost skepticism.

"Well, yes," Victoire admitted conscientiously, "she had the fever, *too*. And I think myself that it is a great piece of foolishness to say that one dies of a broken heart, for I am sure, if it is true, I should have done so when Papa was killed and *Maman* married Monsieur Rollon. But Fitzhugh says that my cousin Nancy was a person of the utmost sensibility, not at all like me, and so it was natural that she pined away and died after you had treated her so cruelly. Which was why it seemed to me that it could not be such a very bad thing, after all, if I did what he wished and pretended to be Nancy, because if she had lived and he had brought her instead, you would have been obliged to make some recompense for your wicked behaviour."

"My dear girl," Tarn said irritably, his ire beginning to rise once more at these extremely frank animadversions upon his conduct, "my *wicked behaviour*, in the case of Miss Nancy Duvenay, consisted in buying her every trinket she expressed a wish for, at the price of a few kisses and a great many promises delivered by her. She was the most accomplished flirt in the county, as Neddy O'Bannon warned me—and he should know, for she'd had him and half a dozen others dangling at her shoestrings for a year or more, while she debated which of them could offer her the most."

Victoire looked doubtful. "That is not what Fitzhugh says," she remarked.

"No, I daresay it is not—for a bigger rasher-of-wind I never clapped eyes on, or a more accomplished liar!"

"Well—yes," she was obliged to agree. "He *does* lie a little, I think—but, you understand, it is not that *he* does not believe what he says. He likes very much to—cut a dash, do you say?—and then he is carried away sometimes."

"He'll be *carried away* to Newgate one of these days, if he tries running many more rigs like this one," Tarn said, rather grimly. "And you, too!" he added, looking at her with some severity. "You're old enough to know better than to lend yourself to a harebrained fetch like this! How old *are* you?" he broke off to enquire abruptly.

She drew herself up. "I am *quite* old. I am nearly eighteen."

"Well, you don't look it—or you would if you hadn't got yourself up like a piece of Haymarket-ware in those things of Nancy's," he said, with unfeeling frankness. He added critically, "I suppose you know that bonnet has got devilish squashed"—a remark that sent Victoire flying up out of her chair to examine it in the tarnished mirror above the pier table beside her.

She found his lordship's words to be only too horridly true. The plumes that had been arranged by a milliner's clever fingers to rise in a dashing cascade above the upstanding poke-front of the modish confection had been quite crushed in Victoire's fall, and hung dejectedly to one side. The Marquis, accustomed to female shock at any such sartorial disaster, was quite unprepared for Miss Duvenay's singular reaction to it: she merely gave vent to a ripple of laughter at the sorry picture she made, and then, looking guilty, said she was very sorry to have ruined the bonnet, since her cousin had so little money and she had no doubt it was a vastly expensive one.

"But I daresay it does not matter now," she said, instantly recovering her spirits, "since you have found out that I am not Nancy and will not give him the money, *de toute façon*. And if we are to live in a cottage, as he says we must when the mortgages are foreclosed, my own clothes will do very well, because they are not at all fashionable and will be quite *convenable* in a cottage."

She took off the offending bonnet as she spoke and tossed it on the table, thereby destroying the last vestiges of doubt in Tarn's mind that he might be dealing with a hussy capable of cleverly plotting to pluck him like a pigeon. Miss Duvenay's hazel eyes—wide, enquiring, and almost uncomfortably direct—looking out at him, unshadowed now by the monstrous bonnet, from beneath a mass of burnished chestnut curls, were a guarantee written in highly legible letters of a nature totally unskilled in devious dealing.

The enquiry in those wide eyes gave Tarn the notion now that their owner, sensing the relaxation of his anger against her, was waiting hopefully for him to dismiss her; but, though his wrath towards her had indeed considerably cooled, he was by no means in such a charitable mood as far as Mr. Fitzhugh Duvenay was concerned. He wanted a word with that gentleman, and it would not suit him to have Miss Duvenay return to the George and inform her cousin of the miscarriage of his plan before he—Tarn—had had an opportunity to have that word. And if he knew anything of Mr. Duvenay, his young cousin's account of her morning's adventures would be sufficient to send him posthaste back to his diminished ancestral acres in Ireland, and that would be the last that would be seen of him in Sussex.

Tarn frowned thoughtfully and unobligingly at the expectant figure before him and enquired, "When does your cousin return to the George?"

"When does he—? Oh, he said he would surely come back before dinner," Victoire replied, "because he wished to go again to Eastcott Park today—" The words broke off suddenly; she looked at him with dawning apprehension in her eyes. "Why do you wish to know this?" she demanded.

"My good girl, surely you don't think I shall let him play such a dog's trick as this on me without giving him good reason not to do it again!" Tarn retorted. "I am not quite so tame-livered as *that!*"

Apprehension deepened to positive alarm on Victoire's face. "*Mon Dieu*, are you going to shoot him?" she gasped.

"Shoot him? No! What could put such a bird-witted idea into your head?"

"It is *not* bird-witted! Fitzhugh says you have shot a great many people." She looked at him hopefully. "*Enfin*—perhaps *that* was a lie, too?" she enquired.

The Marquis had the grace to flush slightly, and said that "a great many people" was an exaggeration. Victoire's curiosity then got the better of her apprehension, and she enquired with interest how many persons he *had* shot.

"That is none of your affair," Tarn said dampingly.

Victoire regretfully agreed that it was not, but said that one couldn't help wondering.

"Of course," she said, "in a war one shoots a great many people, but then it is quite *comme il faut* and one does not regard it. But there is no war now, and I should not at all like you to shoot my cousin Fitzhugh, even though he is a very silly person—"

Tarn, interrupting, begged her with some impatience to disabuse her mind of the notion that he meant to do anything more lethal to Mr. Fitzhugh Duvenay than to put the fear of God in him to a sufficient extent that he would never again be tempted to come it over him.

"The point is, though," he said, still frowning over his problem, "what am I to do with you? If I let you go now, it's Carlton House to a Charley's shelter you'll tell him the whole story the moment you clap eyes on him, and he'll lope off before I can come up with him." He looked at her speculatively. "I expect I *could* lock you in one of the rooms here—"

"Oh, no—please!" Victoire implored him earnestly. "I promise you I shan't tell him, if you do not wish me to!"

The Marquis remarked skeptically that he did not believe he cared to rely upon a promise from such a quarter, and then made matters worse by saying that he had no taste, either, for playing nursemaid until the dinner hour to a schoolroom miss, or for loitering about the George till Mr. Duvenay returned, so that it appeared to him that lock-and-key was the only solution, after all.

Victoire tilted her chin. "Very well," she said. "You may lock me up if you wish, my lord, for I do not think I shall be able to stop you. But as soon as you are gone I shall scream and scream—oh, *mais affreusement!*—and then no doubt your butler will come and let me out."

"Not if he hasn't the key," Tarn said unanswerably.

But his face betrayed the uneasy knowledge that Miss Duvenay, unless actually bound and gagged, was capable of creating such a disturbance inside her locked room that he might return to find that Timbs had summoned half the county to her aid. The Marquis had flouted convention with what his noble relations considered an entirely callous indifference both in London and across the greater part of the continent of Europe, but to create a noisy scandal within the precincts of Tarn House, under the eyes of an ancient family retainer who had been long enough employed by his lordship's father to have dandled the present Marquis on his knee, was more than even he was willing to bargain for.

Victoire, seeing her advantage, handsomely enquired how the Marquis had had it in mind to occupy himself that day.

"If it was to take a gun out, or to go fishing, I am quite willing to go with you," she offered, "because I do not think you are savage with me any longer, and so no doubt it will be very safe."

Tarn, however, appeared unresponsive to this compliment, and merely said unencouragingly, "In those clothes?"

"But yes!" insisted Victoire. "It is very dull at that inn, where there is no one to talk to and nothing to do, and no doubt it would be even more dull if you were to lock me up in a room here. Joseph," she added, seeing that the Marquis still looked quite unconvinced, "who is Madame Rollon's grandson, often let me go fishing with him, and sometimes permitted me to shoot, as well—but I do not suppose that you would do *that*?"

"Let you get your hands on one of my guns? No, I would not!" said Tarn unhesitatingly.

"*Eh bien*, I did not really expect that you would," Victoire said regretfully. "Madame Rollon was used to scold Joseph very much when he let me shoot *his* gun, and she did not at all like it, either, when he took me fishing, because she wished me always to sit very straight in a chair, like herself, embroidering altar cloths or hemming handkerchiefs. Sometimes we would run away," she went on, her eyes kindling with enthusiasm as she recalled these incidents of gross insubordination, "not *sérieusement*, you understand, only for a day, to the woods —and then she would send Jean-Baptiste, who was the groom, and Guillaume, the coachman, after us; but they were both fat, and I could run just as fast as Joseph could, and so they could not catch us and we did not go back until we were *quite* ready to. Madame was always very angry then, *vous savez,* and lectured me for hours, because she said it was much worse for a *jeune fille* to act so than for a boy—but she is not here now," she concluded buoyantly, "and there are some pretty clouds today and a little breeze, very suitable, I think, for fishing, and so we might do *that* until my cousin returns, *n'est-ce pas?*"

The Marquis appeared to consider, regarding her fashionable French green frock and mutilated bonnet with some disfavour.

"I daresay we might," he said unpropitiously, "if you wouldn't look such a Bartholomew baby, going fishing in that rig!"

"*Moi*, I shall not regard that," said Victoire loftily. "And it will not frighten the fish, I think."

This was too much for the Marquis; he burst out laughing and said if the fish did not mind it, no more would he, and thereupon dragged Victoire off with him to find a rod and line suitable for his sport.

By the time he had succeeded in doing this, and had instructed a rigidly disapproving Timbs to have Mrs. Timbs put up a nuncheon for them to take along with them, he and his unwilling guest were on much friendlier terms. In fact, when

Timbs, returning with the nuncheon neatly packed into a small basket, suggested to Victoire, with a still disapproving but somewhat anxiously paternal air, which revealed that he had reached the same conclusion concerning her innocence as his master, that she ought not to go jauntering about the countryside alone with the Marquis, she looked quite surprised for a moment, and then said, "Oh! I see! You think he is not enough respectable, *n'est-ce pas?*"

Timbs, with a dour glance at his master that strongly suggested that he was refraining, out of a perhaps mistaken sense of loyalty, from saying everything he could on the subject, remarked that it did not seem respectable to him, in any case, for miss to be where she was without some other lady to bear her company.

"Now that's enough," Tarn said authoritatively, beginning to look thunderous again. "If you think I'm throwing out lures to a schoolroom chit, you're fair and far out, you Friday-faced old surly-boots."

Timbs, looking affronted, said he wouldn't so demean himself as to do anything of the sort, but added darkly, as he departed, that what my lady would think of such goings-on he didn't know. This appeared to be a shaft that he was diabolically sure would reach its mark—a certainty justified by his lordship's immediately damning him roundly, which sent the old man off in chuckling satisfaction.

"Who is 'my lady'?" Victoire enquired curiously.

"That too is none of your affair," Tarn said promptly, rising from the edge of the table on which he had been sitting. "Come along now."

Victoire took up the basket and obediently hurried out of the room beside him, endeavouring to keep up with his long strides.

"Why is your house in such a sad state?" she asked, undaunted by this snub. "And why have you no more servants? Are you poor? Fitzhugh says you are very rich."

"I am. And you ask entirely too many questions, brat! What are you stopping for now?" he demanded impatiently, as they passed the door of the reception room to which he had first brought her.

"My bonnet," said Miss Duvenay firmly, and set down her basket on a table in the great hall to dart inside.

When she emerged, the injured bonnet now upon her head, she found herself staring up at a portrait hanging above the table on which she had placed the basket—a portrait of an arrogant dark face so very like the Marquis's that she paused involuntarily to study it. The gentleman in the portrait wore the elaborate ball dress of thirty years before—satin knee-breeches and a claret-coloured coat of velvet embroidered in gold, with lace foaming at throat and wrists and great diamonds glinting upon his long white fingers.

"*Mon Dieu, qu'il est beau!*" breathed Victoire, in much admiration. She turned to survey the Marquis. "I think you would look so, too, if you did not crop your hair and wear such entirely uninteresting clothes," she said, critically surveying his lordship's casual country dress. She returned to the portrait. "Is it your father?"

"Yes," said Tarn briefly.

"Dead, like mine?"

"Yes. Now come along."

"No, no! One little moment—"

She was looking at what was obviously a companion portrait to the one that had first drawn her attention: it represented a coldly handsome lady in a gown of pale blue silk, enormously hooped *à la française,* one delicate hand resting upon the shoulder of the dark little boy of two or three standing beside her. The lady's rather close-set blue eyes were slightly raised, as if in severe contemplation of higher things, and the child, in spite of the artist's obvious intention to create a pleasing family piece, looked remote, uncomfortable, and rather sullen.

"And that is you, and your *maman*?" Victoire demanded.

44

"Tiens, she is very beautiful, too, but not so beautiful as my *maman*. Is she dead, too?"

"No!" said Tarn, grasping her hand and ruthlessly dragging her away from her contemplation of the portrait.

"But she does not live here?" Victoire went reluctantly out the door with him, still endeavouring to look round at the portrait. As she emerged with him into the pale, cloudy spring day, she gazed up wisely into his face. "You do not like her very much, I think," she said.

The Marquis laughed shortly. "You would better say—she does not like me, my dear."

"Because you make a great many scandals? Ah, bah! I do not believe that," Victoire said. "She is angry with you, perhaps, and scolds you sometimes—"

"My mother," said Tarn, in a curt, unpleasant voice, "never scolds—or perhaps it might be more accurate to say that she never *did*, for I have not set eyes on her these six years." Victoire looked shocked. "If I am not to lower myself still further in your opinion," his lordship continued, "I see that I had best hasten to tell you that that is entirely by her wish. She said when I was eighteen that I would go to the devil—which prediction I am happy to say I have not disappointed—and, as she had no wish to contaminate either herself or my sisters with acquaintance with that gentleman, she decreed then that we should live better apart."

There was a very bitter look in his lordship's eyes as he pronounced these words, but it did not remain there long; the next moment he shrugged and said indifferently, "It is just as well; we never dealt together. She is very content as she is, and sent me word only last month that if I could contrive not to involve myself in any further low, disgusting scandals for a time, she would be able to make a quite eligible match for the younger of my sisters."

Victoire found herself wishing very fiercely at that moment that she might give the Dowager Marchioness of Tarn a large piece of her mind—an emotion which somewhat surprised her, as there had certainly been nothing in what she had seen of the young Marquis up to this time to suggest that he stood in need of a champion against anyone or anything. But looking up into his face, with that suddenly bleak and withdrawn expression upon it, she could not help saying, not without a little difficulty, for it was not easy for her, either, to speak of her own deepest disappointments, "*Eh bien, ma mère*—you understand, she does not at all wish to have to do with me, either. Some women are like that, I think. But that does not mean that we—that you and I—are not—" She paused, searching for the right words with which to express her thoughts; finding none, she gave it up and, tilting her chin, said valiantly, "At any rate, I do not any longer regard it, *moi*. And you—you must not do so, either, for truly one can see from the portrait that she is not at all *une femme sympathique*, and that she did not cherish you even when you were an *enfant tout à fait charmant*, which is to me a thing incomprehensible."

This description of his juvenile self caused the Marquis quite unexpectedly—not only to Miss Duvenay but also to himself—to burst into laughter, which made him look much younger and banished the bleak expression from his face entirely; and then he and Victoire, quite in harmony with each other, walked together across the neglected lawn in the direction of the Home Wood.

5

During the ensuing hours Tarn discovered that it was not the most disagreeable fate in the world to be accompanied on a fishing excursion by a young lady who was able knowledgeably to admire his skill in the delicate art of handling a blow line rod, showed no squeamishness about touching his slippery catch, and was willing to fall accommodatingly silent whenever he commanded her to do so. Women of many types and nationalities he had been acquainted with, from rural Sussex beauties to Continental courtesans queening it in the demi-monde of several European capitals, but with none of them could he have felt so agreeably free of the necessity of making trifling conversation or, indeed, of taking into account at all the fact that he was in company with a female.

He looked at her with an appearance of some approval as they at length sat down together on a fallen log to enjoy their nuncheon of cold ham and cheese. The green bonnet dangled by its ribbons, quite disregarded, on her back, where it had been pushed by her upon its first encounter with a low-hanging tree branch, and the skirts of her fashionable green gown, sadly wetted by an imprudent excursion too near the water's edge, were spread out to dry with no more dismay at their condition being displayed by their wearer than his lordship was evincing over his own splashed and muddy leathers.

"I'll tell you what," he said to her magnanimously, feeling that such evidence of a proper spirit deserved its own reward, "I'll drive you back to the George when we've done here, and if your cousin hasn't returned yet I'll trust you to say nothing to him of your having seen me. If it's his intention to see my uncle again at Eastcott Park this evening, I'll come up with him there—though," he added frankly, "if he takes you along with him again, it beats me how he expects to hoax them into believing you're Nancy Duvenay. My uncle's not a clothhead, and you can't open your mouth without making it plain you weren't reared in Kerry or anywhere near it."

"But I speak English very well," said Victoire, somewhat affronted. "I always spoke English with Papa! Though perhaps I am a *little* out of practice now," she conceded, "which is no doubt why Fitzhugh told me that on no account was I to speak unless it was most strictly necessary, and then only in a very low voice." She paused, seeing that Tarn was looking at her with a rather curious expression upon his face. "But what is it?" she demanded. "Why do you look at me so? Have I said something wrong? *Je crois que non!* I tell you, I speak English *very* well!"

Tarn grinned. "And so you do," he said. "No, there was nothing wrong with your English, brat; it's that it just occurred to me to wonder—well, from what I've heard of your father, he was usually careering all over the Continent, looking for the hottest spot to be found there. Do you mean to tell me that he dragged *you* along with him?"

"But yes! *Bien entendu!*" Victoire looked surprised. "*Maman* and I always went with him—*naturellement*, not

48

when there was a battle, which made me very angry that I was not a boy, because I had turned thirteen before he died, you know, which is *quite* old enough to have gone to a battle if I had not had to be a horrid *jeune fille* and sit at home with *Maman* instead, learning Italian and sketching silly water colours!"

At the expression of total revulsion upon her face as she recollected this unfair trick of fate Tarn could not help laughing—a piece of callous indifference that caused her to round on him with an indignant frown.

"Yes, it is all very well for *you* to laugh," she said, "but I daresay that is not how you were obliged to spend *your* time when you were abroad!"

"I was older than you were," said his lordship incontrovertibly, drawing the curtain firmly upon this aspect of his past.

But this did not prevent his companion from subjecting him to an interested examination as to the countries he had visited during his sojourn abroad, her envy being aroused by the news that his travels had taken him as far as Constantinople, while her own had extended to no more exotic capital than St. Petersburg.

"Which I did not like at all," she confided, "because it was always cold, and Papa was bored because he was obliged to attend often at the Court, and I had a horrid German governess who rapped my knuckles with her knitting needles when I could not recite *all* the Holy Roman emperors. So I was very glad when we went to Vienna instead, where Papa *very* often took me to the *confiserie* for lovely chocolate creams, or we would go to the Woods together and he would put me up on his Campaigner, who was a beautiful *big* black horse and had been in *five* battles—"

Miss Duvenay's enthusiasm for the mode of life she had enjoyed in Vienna was so fervent that she knocked the nuncheon basket over in a sweeping gesture meant to convey an impression of Campaigner's great size, an action that caused his lordship to burst out laughing again, and they went back to their fishing with Miss Duvenay expostulating vehemently because he refused to take her reminiscences seriously.

Later that afternoon, however, as they walked back to Tarn House together, she with the empty basket and he with his highly satisfactory catch for the day, she became more pensive, and at last, looking up at him, said with a slight air of constraint, "I have been thinking about—about my cousin Fitzhugh. *En effet*, what will you do to him?" Tarn's face, which had looked perfectly good-humoured up to that moment, darkened slightly, and she went on, a trifle anxiously, "*Moi*, I think it will be better if *I* tell him that you have found him out and you do not see him at all, because perhaps you will be angry again if you see him, and you are very—very *formidable* when you are angry, my lord. Very," she added impressively, as Tarn halted to look down at her.

He grinned, the dark look disappearing. "Did I frighten you?" he asked. "I'm sorry—but you deserved it, you know. And your cousin deserves a good deal more for trying to serve me such a backhanded turn. Deuce take it, if I hadn't turned up here in the nick of time, he might have choused my uncle out of a handsome sum."

"Yes, he said so," Victoire said, with a slight sigh. "And of course I know it was very wicked of him—only it is quite uncomfortable, you understand, when there is an execution in the house and they carry off the furniture, and he says that soon, if he cannot come by a large sum of money, there will be no house, either, for they will take that away from him, too, and we shall be obliged to go and live in a cottage. As I told you before, *I* shall not regard that, but he does not at all wish to do it."

"No, I daresay he does not," Tarn said, but now a trifle absently; he was frowning over a new thought that had suddenly struck him. "See here," he said abruptly, "*must* you continue to live with that fellow? He may be your relation, but he's not at all a fit sort of person to have charge of you. There must be someone else you can go to, if it's true that you can't get in touch with your mother. I daresay Duvenay would be glad enough to be rid of you."

"Well, yes, I think he would," Victoire acknowledged, "now that he cannot make your uncle believe any longer that I am Nancy. But I do not know at all where *Maman* is now, or how long it will be before she is settled in America, and unless Madame Rollon has recovered her wits, I do not see that it will be possible for me to go back to France, even if I had the money to do that, and I have not any money at all, you see."

Tarn, looking down at Victoire's face as she pronounced these words in a determinedly matter-of-fact voice, was moved for perhaps the first time in his life to a disagreeable anxiety over the future—a future, moreover, that had nothing to do with his own interest or pleasure. Fitzhugh Duvenay, he knew very well, was a scoundrel—a gentleman-scoundrel, but a scoundrel nonetheless, and to hand back to his keeping the very young lady walking beside him seemed an entirely callous, not to say disastrous, thing to do. He had already embroiled the girl in a highly illegal scheme to extract money from Lord Eastcott, and if he was indeed in such dire straits financially as she had indicated, it was not at all improbable that he would not hesitate to make use of her again in any way that might appear profitable to him, without the slightest regard for her safety or reputation.

Still, Tarn asked himself irritably, what was *he* to do to remedy matters, and what concern was it of his? He had only just met the chit, and certainly had not the least right to interfere in her affairs. Endeavouring to salve that newly awakened anxiety for Victoire's future, he told himself that he was no doubt making a mountain out of a molehill, and that the girl's mother would remove her from her cousin's care before any irreparable harm had been done. But he promised himself, at any rate, that he would take advantage of his forthcoming interview with Mr. Fitzhugh Duvenay to deliver a few home-

51

truths to that gentleman as to the responsibility he bore towards his young relation.

He had not long to wait for that interview. When his curricle swept to a halt before the George a short time later, the first thing he clapped eyes on was the portly figure of Mr. Fitzhugh Duvenay, emerging from the front door in what appeared to be a state of considerable agitation.

"My lord!" he ejaculated, making a quick recover from what was obviously the distinctly disagreeable shock of finding his young cousin in the Marquis's company, and coming up to the curricle as Tarn tossed the reins to his groom and jumped down to assist Victoire to alight. "What am I to think of this? I return here to find that my cousin has disappeared—that you had enquired for her this morning—is it possible that you have been with her all the day?"

Tarn smiled slightly, showing his teeth. "So she has become your cousin now, has she?" he said, lifting Victoire down from the curricle and then turning at once from her to Mr. Duvenay. "I believe she was your sister yesterday when you introduced her to my uncle." He glanced with some displeasure at the landlord, who had come hurrying out of the inn at the sound of carriage wheels, and said in a curt undertone to Mr. Duvenay, "Let us go where we may be private. I have a word to say to you."

Mr. Duvenay drew himself up in some hauteur, for the words had decidedly been couched in terms of a command, but, seeing the expression upon Tarn's face, thought better of remonstrating with him and walked back into the inn with him instead, followed by Victoire. The landlord, once more profuse and obsequious in his greeting to the Marquis, ushered the trio, upon his lordship's demand, into a private parlour and suggested refreshments—a suggestion immediately dismissed by Tarn. He closed the door unceremoniously behind the landlord's departing figure and turned at once to Mr. Duvenay.

52

"Now what the devil do you mean by it, you fat flawn," he demanded, in a voice that made Victoire jump, "trying to mace my uncle of his blunt by a damned Banbury tale like this?"

Mr. Duvenay, with a glance at Victoire, merely raised one plump, remonstrating hand.

"My lord!" he said in tones of deep affront. "I must beg that you will moderate your language! Remember that you speak in the ears of Innocence!"

The Marquis, who quite evidently had entirely forgotten Victoire in his rekindled wrath at seeing her cousin, looked round at her and said peremptorily, "What the deuce are *you* doing here? Go to your chamber."

Victoire, who had been looking anxious, observed rather tentatively that she thought she had better stay.

"Well, you hadn't," said Tarn bluntly, and added impatiently, "Good God, girl, will you rid yourself of the notion that I intend to put a bullet through this ginger-hackled court-card! Now take yourself out of here before I put you out!"

Victoire, quite aware by this time that his lordship was perfectly capable of literally carrying out his threat if she did not obey him, reluctantly went to the door. With her hand on the latch, she paused and said, in a voice from which she could not quite banish all trace of regret, "I will bid you good-day then, my lord, and—and good-bye, if we should not chance to meet again."

The Marquis's acknowledgement of this civility was exceedingly brief, and Victoire found herself outside in the hall, with only one last glimpse of her cousin's alarmed eyes following her as she departed.

Upstairs in her own chamber, she had not long to wait to learn the outcome of the scene she had been obliged to leave below. What his lordship had had to say to Mr. Duvenay had evidently been brief, pungent, and exceedingly to the point, for within ten minutes she was able to hear him shouting for his groom below her window and the sound of wheels as his curricle departed. A few moments later her cousin joined her, his rather florid face now poppy-red, and with such a strong sense of injury animating his breast that for several minutes he could do no more than walk up and down the room, throwing out violent objurgations against toplofty young wastrels.

Victoire sat listening to him in some impatience, and at last asked, reasonably enough, whether it was not to be expected that Lord Tarn would be very much displeased when he learned of the deception that had been practised upon his uncle.

Mr. Duvenay halted in his pacing and glared round at her. "Displeased!" he choked. "What has *he* to be displeased about? *His* pockets are not the lighter by a penny over this affair, but as for me—*I* am ruined! And what," he went on, his recollection of the part *she* had played in the downfall of his plans brought to the fore by her interruption of his tirade, "did you mean by it, girl, to let it out to him who you were? If you had told him you were Miss Smith—Miss Jones—any name in the world but *Duvenay*, when he accosted you, we might yet have carried the business through! But no! To add to all my other misfortunes, I am saddled with a hen-witted female without brains enough to protect her own interests."

"Well, I do not care!" Victoire said unregenerately. "I think you have told me lies about Nancy, for Lord Tarn says that he did not ruin her, as you said, and I believe him, so that it is not at all proper that he should be obliged to pay you any money."

"You believe him!" Mr. Duvenay stared at her incredulously. "My poor deluded child, you would put your faith in the word of such a man as Tarn!"

"Yes, I would," said Victoire obstinately. "*Quant à ça*, he may be very wicked, but he does not lie, I am quite sure. And now," she concluded practically, "I find this talk entirely unprofitable, *mon cousin*. There will be no money from Lord Tarn—*enfin*, what must we do now? Go back to Ireland?"

"No!" said Mr. Duvenay explosively. "If he has the least

notion that he can insult me so grossly and go unchastised—"

"But, *mon cousin*," Victoire reminded him, a slight, mischievous smile in her eyes, "he is younger than you and, I think, much stronger; or if it is to fight him with pistols that you wish, have you not told me yourself that he has already shot many men? It would be very dangerous to call him out, *n'est-ce pas*?"

"Call him out? Who said anything about calling him out?" said Mr. Duvenay, repulsing the very idea of such madness with obvious alarm. "You must be all about in your head even to think of such a thing!" He continued peevishly, "Besides, how would that remedy the matter? I should not gain a groat by it, and it is money—money, girl, money!—that I must have. Has the idea not yet penetrated into your head that I have scarcely enough of the ready and rhino in my pockets now to take us back to Ireland?"

"Well, if it is money that you are thinking of, I am very sure that he will not give you any," said Victoire positively, "so it appears to me that it would be much better for us to go back to Ireland at once and forget all about him. And perhaps we shall be able then to think of a way to get money there."

"I tell you, no!" Mr. Duvenay said again, in obstinate resentment. "He has not done with me yet, though he may flatter himself that he has taken the trick this time! Damme, he is an impudent young jackanapes, and I'll not—" He broke off, and looked speculatively into his young cousin's candidly disapproving face. "And you, miss," he said, suddenly hopeful once more, "did he offer you any discourtesy today? You were all day in his company, were you not? By the Lord, if he has played fast-and-loose with *you*—"

"I wish you will not be so silly!" Victoire said severely. "He did not try to make love to me, if that is what you mean to say, and it is *tout à fait* foolish for you to think you will now ask him for money because of the damages he has made to *my* reputation."

Mr. Duvenay raised his plump shoulders regretfully. "Very well," he said. "I shall let it pass. But all the same," he added darkly, "he shall bleed." He resumed his pacing up and down the low-pitched little chamber, his hands joined together behind his back. "I must think!" he announced impressively. "A plan—I must devise a plan—"

"I think you are indeed very silly," Victoire repeated, shaking her head. "How can you make Lord Tarn give you money if he does not wish to? *C'est ridicule!* He will not do so, I tell you now."

"No?" said Mr. Duvenay. He paused in his walking; a slight gleam had suddenly appeared in his eyes. It grew slowly, until gradually it lit his entire countenance with a beatific glow. "No?" he repeated, but now in a quite changed, almost exultant voice. "We shall see, my dear girl; we—shall—see. At this very moment a plan has entered my mind which, if I can succeed in carrying it out—and I have not the least doubt that I shall be able to do so—will quite reverse the undeserved misfortune that has up to this time dogged my footsteps, a plan of such genius—But I must not waste time on idle words," he broke off, in mounting excitement. "Perhaps at this very moment that young scoundrel is planning on leaving the neighbourhood, on going to London, or to Brighton—"

"And why should he not go to London or to Brighton?" Victoire demanded suspiciously. "What is this plan of yours, *mon cousin*? What will you do?"

Mr. Duvenay waved an impatient hand. "Dear girl, do not interrupt me!" he adjured her. "I must—yes, I positively must see Martin at once, and then—"

"You must see Martin?" repeated Victoire, jumping up. "But that is your cousin—*n'est-ce pas?*—the one you went to visit today? Why must you see him so soon again?"

"Fortunately," said Mr. Duvenay, paying not the least heed to her, "the days are long at this season, so that I should be able to arrive before it is quite dark. But I must see the landlord at once about hiring his gig."

"*Voyons*, do you mean to go off and leave me here again in this inn?" Victoire demanded, placing herself firmly between him and the door as she saw his intention of departing from the room. "When will you return, then?"

Mr. Duvenay regarded her with marked asperity. "My dear child," he said, "I shall return as soon as I am able—no doubt by tomorrow noon, at the very latest. Meanwhile, you will remain here—and not, I trust, go jauntering alone about the neighbourhood as you were so foolish as to have done today. Now step aside, if you please, for my business is urgent."

"And Lord Tarn? What has all this to do with him?" Victoire insisted. "Why must you go away if you wish to see him?"

Two large, plump hands put her firmly aside, and Mr. Duvenay stepped past her into the hall.

"I am not so totty-headed as to tell you *that*," he retorted, "after you have made mice feet of this business today by your totally bird-witted actions! No, no, leave this in *my* hands, my dear, and you shall soon be queening it in Ireland in silks and purple."

He went on hastily down the passage, a portly, self-important figure, and Victoire retreated, frowning, into her chamber, closed the door, and sat down to consider.

"*Tiens*, I do not like this!" she said to herself. "Why must he go now to see his cousin, who is, he says, a person entirely respectable, but cast down in the world so that he must be employed as agent on the estate of Sir Antony—I cannot remember his name, but he also is entirely respectable and not at all, I think, connected with Lord Tarn. And why is it necessary that Lord Tarn should not go to London, or to Brighton? *Vraiment*, it seems to me that my cousin means mischief to him, for he is truly very angry with him, and also very disappointed that he will not pay him any money." Her brow wrinkled suddenly. "Perhaps I should go to warn him—but no!" She shook her head firmly, a slight flush rising in her cheeks. "He will think I do so only that I may see him again, and he does not wish to see *me*; of that I am very sure, for when he said good-bye to me he did not even look at me. *D'ailleurs,* he is very well able to look after himself, that one, and it is not at all likely that anyone so foolish as my cousin will be able to make him pay money if he does not wish to." She drew a long breath, her eyes suddenly alight. "Perhaps if he knows I am still here he will come to see me himself, and I can warn him then. Perhaps—"

The flush crept higher; with a fierce little gesture, Miss Duvenay jumped to her feet.

"*Imbécile! Bête!*" she said aloud. "He is a great lord, and you are a beggar, with a fat rogue for a cousin! You will not sit here daydreaming! You will not! Ah, bah!" She shook her head, her shoulders drooping forlornly. "It would be better for me, I think," she said, "if I were back again with Madame Rollon!"

58

6

"And what," asked Lady Eastcott, regarding in some displeasure Tarn's tall figure lounging before the fireplace in the library at Eastcott Park, his big shoulders propped against the green jasperware Wedgwood mantelpiece, "am I to tell Eastcott when he comes in?"

"Tell him I'm off for London in the morning," recommended Tarn. "*He* won't want to hear more than that."

It was the day following his interview with Mr. Duvenay, and he had come—with unwonted consideration, Lady Eastcott privately thought—to inform his uncle that he need no longer concern himself over the matter of Miss Nancy Duvenay. Lady Eastcott, as she regarded her nephew's more than six feet of hard male presence, now lazily at ease before her, was, as usual, inclined to cast a forgiving eye upon the disgraceful conduct he had been guilty of, and to wonder why some people found that dark, harsh-featured face, with its big, curling mouth and heavy-lidded eyes, unattractive. Poor little

Nancy Duvenay, at any rate, had not done so, she thought with a sigh, and, recollecting that young damsel's unenviable plight, she roused herself to say, with some severity, "Well, I *do* think it is too odiously provoking of you, Lewis, to tell us no more of the matter than this! Have you done anything at all for that poor child?"

"Nothing at all, ma'am," said Tarn, quite unmoved by the censure in her voice. "To tell you the truth, it appears to me that that is a matter that no longer concerns either my uncle or yourself."

"Well, *there* you are quite mistaken," Lady Eastcott said feelingly, "for I am excessively sorry for that poor girl. Indeed, it is infamous of you, Lewis, to pretend that she is only another of your lady-birds, and that she entered into this affair with eyes quite as wide open as yours were. Did you see her yesterday yourself? Surely even you must have been touched—"

Tarn made a gesture of irritation. "Oh yes, I saw her," he said. "But how can *I* remedy her situation, ma'am, short of marrying her, which I daresay even *you* would not have me do?"

Miss Standfield, entering the room at that moment and overhearing the last words of this speech, remarked placidly that she had no doubt that marriage would be very beneficial to his lordship—"though somewhat wearing, I expect," she concluded, "upon the young female you choose as your wife, for I cannot think that she will have at all a comfortable time of it—at least until you have accustomed yourself to a somewhat less *eventful* mode of life."

"I have no intention of marrying, ma'am, so you need not waste your sympathy upon this fictitious female," Tarn retorted. He pushed his shoulders away from the mantelpiece. "Well, I'm off," he said shortly. "Cousin Amelia, your servant—Aunt, your very obedient—"

60

"Do not," said Miss Standfield agreeably, "add sarcasm to bad manners, Lewis. I daresay Timbs and Mrs. Timbs, at any rate, will be happy to see you go, so that they may return to falling quietly to ruin along with your house. It will no doubt disappoint you to learn, however, that your mother has never come near enough to it to see its deplorable state, so that, really, I fear you have quite wasted your efforts in so determinedly condemning it to decay."

She looked up to give him a perfectly cordial nod of dismissal as she concluded this speech—an action which sent Tarn off in a mood halfway between violent exasperation and grudging admiration of a perspicacity quite lacking in his other relations.

His mood was not improved when he returned to Tarn House to find a missive awaiting him there, which Timbs informed him had been delivered in his absence by one of the servants from the George. He tore it open impatiently, expecting renewed demands or threats from Mr. Duvenay, but, to his considerable surprise, it was the name *Victoire Duvenay* that appeared at the foot of the page.

The message itself was very brief. *My lord,* it read, *I hesitate to appeal to you, but, having nowhere else to turn, I make bold to do so. If you will be so very kind as to come tonight to the lane behind the George at ten o'clock, I shall explain to you everything. Please do not fail. I am in despair.*

Tarn frowned, and said, "The devil!" under his breath. He had for a moment the cynical notion that little Miss Duvenay was not, after all, quite so innocent as she had led him to believe on the previous day, and was casting out her lures quite as expertly as her cousin Nancy had done; but remembrance of a pair of wide, hazel eyes almost immediately banished this notion from his head. It was far more probable, he thought, that her rogue of a cousin had made matters so unpleasant for her, because of the part she had played in his —Tarn's—discovery of the deception practised upon him, that

61

she had concocted some plan of running away from him, and had turned to Tarn for aid as a last resort.

And if he were to aid her? He could not, he thought grimly, do her a worse turn than to do so; the chit was mad even to suggest such a thing. Mad, or simply frightened and too innocent to see what must be the outcome of it if the Marquis of Tarn were to involve himself in any way in her affairs. He had a sudden impatient desire to box Miss Duvenay's ears and try if in that way he could bring some modicum of prudence into her head—a procedure that would most certainly not remedy her situation, but would at least give some outlet to the irritable sense of uneasiness that situation had succeeded in arousing in him.

At any rate, he thought, he must at least go to the George that night and hear what the chit had to say. It was not beyond the bounds of possibility that a self-centred rogue like Duvenay might have abandoned her entirely in that wretched inn —though, if that were so, why his own interview with her must be conducted in secrecy and after dark he could not imagine. No, it was more likely, he thought, that Duvenay had merely uttered threats, in his anger over the failure of his plan, that had frightened the girl—in which case a few well-directed threats of his lordship's own might succeed in inducing him to take a milder tone towards his young relation.

The evening came on overcast but mild, and at half past nine the Marquis, having dined in a rather Spartan manner on a dish of hasty mutton and haricot beans, which was all Mrs. Timbs' frugal notions had permitted her to prepare for her noble master, strolled out of his cheerless home for his rendezvous with Victoire. There was no moon, even had the clouds allowed it to be seen, but Tarn, having been brought up in this country, knew it like the palm of his hand, and made his way without the least hesitation to the rough lane behind the George that Victoire had appointed as their meeting-place.

This was thickly overhung with pines and hollies, from one of which prickly retreats an owl hooted sepulchrally as he entered the lane. The Marquis, however, whose thoughts were occupied elsewhere, failed to note this particularly; but a moment later an answering call behind him brought him suddenly to the alert. He swung round, at the same instant hearing running footsteps behind him, and, before he well knew what was happening, he had been struck a staggering blow on the head by a dark figure emerging abruptly from the trees beside the lane.

Fortunately—for the blow had obviously been delivered, not with a fist, but with a stout cudgel—the shallow-crowned beaver he was wearing absorbed the brunt of the impact, and he was able to remain on his feet and whirl to face his attacker. The Marquis, who was well-known for his sporting prowess, and who had been a constant patron of Gentleman Jackson's fashionable Boxing Saloon in Bond Street during his recent stay in London, was not an easy man to overpower, even half dazed as he was from the blow he had received, and, grappling immediately with the shadowy form before him, he sent it flying into a clump of bushes beside the road in a swinging fall.

But almost at the same moment he found himself again engaged from the rear. He turned swiftly upon a second dark figure, apparently even bulkier and broader of shoulder than the first he had dimly glimpsed. A purposeful right to the jaw sent it careening backwards, at the same time that his first attacker called urgently from the bushes from which he was engaged in extricating himself, "Jem! Jem! Leave them horses and lend a hand here!"

There followed a violent scuffle, the first attacker launching himself once more upon Tarn and succeeding, after some confused in-fighting, in obtaining such a dogged grasp upon him that he was held long enough to receive several punishing body hits from his second opponent. He wrenched himself free at last, staggering and gasping, and, delivering a blow that sent one attacker crashing into the bushes, turned to face the other, only to receive at that instant a stunning blow from behind from some heavy object that dropped him where he stood. As he struggled to regain his feet he heard a hoarse voice say breathlessly, "Hit him again, Jem! Dang it, hit him again!"

There was another shock, as if the entire world had heaved over and fallen upon him, and he slid into oblivion.

When he began to come to himself it appeared to him that the world was still moving unsteadily and painfully beneath him—motion which, in his dazed state of semiconsciousness, he at last succeeded in interpreting as the jolting of some sort of vehicle in which he was being conveyed over a rough road. He opened his eyes and found that there was nothing at all for him to see but inky, smothering darkness. An attempt to move then made him realise that he was lying on his side, his hands and feet both tightly bound; at the same moment he became aware that what was impeding his breathing was a gag thrust into his mouth and tied securely with some kind of cloth about his face.

The vehicle in which he was lying gave a lurch at that moment that jolted his violently aching head to such malign purpose that he slipped again into unconsciousness, but not before he had known a moment of such utter fury, directed impartially at Miss Duvenay for the part she had played in bringing about his present plight, and at himself for having been such an easy dupe to her lure, that he thought it must have choked him. Perhaps fortunately, the state of the road over which he was travelling was such as to prevent him from regaining consciousness sufficiently to be able to piece together again the connexion between his present discomfort and Miss Duvenay's imploring letter, and it was not until the vehicle in which he was lying had rumbled at last to a halt that he was able to command his dazed thoughts to the extent of attempting to take stock of his situation.

Three men, he recalled now—it must have been three, though he had grappled with only two, the third, no doubt, having been the unseen "Jem" who had come up behind to deal him the final *coup de grâce*—had seized him in the lane behind the George and had conveyed him away from it in the wagon or cart in which he lay. That they were Fitzhugh Duvenay's tools, there could be no doubt, or that Mr. Duvenay had made use upon a second occasion of his innocent-appearing young cousin to bring the Marquis again into his toils—this time, it must seem, for the purpose of holding him to ransom.

He was not long permitted to indulge in reflection uninterrupted, however, for almost immediately the rough sacking with which it seemed to him that he must be covered was dragged from his face and a hoarse voice, recognisable as the one he had heard in the lane, recommended the man called Jem to "look lively and take hold of his legs, now."

The next moment he found himself being lifted from his uncomfortable resting place and carried along by unseen bearers, one of whom complained of his being "tedious heavy," only to be unkindly advised by his companion to "dub his mummer and not give him any argy-bargy about it." Tarn, with the night air now fresh on his face, felt the confusion of semiconsciousness leaving him under its revivifying influence, and was aware of a rhythmic rush and murmur of water, a smell of salt, which informed him that he must be near the sea. For a brief time he feared that his captors meant to put him on board a boat and carry him abroad, in order better to foil any search that might be made for him, but a few moments sufficed to lay that idea to rest. For he was being carried now, he was sure, down a flight of steps; a door swung gratingly open; and in a moment he was dropped upon an exceedingly hard floor with a thud that made him violently aware of the excruciating pain in his head and the excessive soreness of his body.

A dubious voice spoke above him. "Adone-do! If he ain't dead he's done to a cow's thumb and that's the truth! Better take that handkercher out of his mouth, Jerry, and let him draw a free breath now."

Tarn opened his eyes, disregarding an alarming tendency of his surroundings to dissolve unsteadily before them, and found himself looking up, by lantern light, into the faces of a pair of stout fellows in frieze coats and gaiters. He was in a small cellar, it appeared, which, as he painfully turned his head to look around, seemed to be empty except for a few sticks of broken furniture, a sack or two piled in a corner, and some coils of rope.

The signs of life he had indicated appeared to afford the younger of his captors some satisfaction, for he remarked in a relieved voice, "Well, he ain't slipped his wind, and that's a good thing," and dropped to one knee to untie the gag that had been thrust into Tarn's mouth.

His companion regarded these proceedings sourly. A large purple bruise on his jaw gave evidence of the fact that he had been one of Tarn's attackers in the lane, as did also a hideously discoloured eye.

"Ay, but don't you go to untie him any further than that," he warned, "for I'll cap downright I never see a cove with a handier bunch of fives, and I don't want him a-coming at *me* again."

The other, meanwhile, had produced a flask from the pocket of his coat and, supporting Tarn's head so that he could drink from it, held it to his lips. Tarn drank, tasted good French cognac, and managed an unpleasant smile.

"So that's it!" he said. "Smugglers. How much does Duvenay pay you to bring you into *this* game?"

The man called Jem looked startled and a little alarmed at these words, but the other merely recommended Tarn to save his breath, as nobody cared to hear anything he might say, and all he needed to know, for his own part, was that the sooner his relations came down with the pitch-and-pay, the sooner he himself would be free.

"Ransom, you mean?" Tarn asked, his suspicions confirmed; but the larger man, with a jerk of his head, merely signed to his companion to precede him to the door and, following him with the lantern, went out behind him. Tarn heard a key turn in a lock—a quite useless precaution, he thought bitterly, in his present condition; and then he was alone in the damp blackness of his cellar-prison, with only the stealthy scurrying of a rat to break the silence that fell upon it.

7

He had no way of knowing how long he lay there before he heard a key turn again in the lock, for he was still in a half daze that made it difficult for him to do more than cling grimly to consciousness. In his state of extreme discomfort—his head throbbing fiendishly and his limbs growing cramped and numb—it had seemed an aeon, but he believed that actually it could not have been long. He heard the door open, and a chink of light fell along the floor; then Victoire's voice, rather breathless, came unmistakably to his ears.

"*Mon Dieu!* Did you hear, m'sieur? Surely there is someone in the yard!"

There was the growl of a masculine oath and the sound of heavy footsteps plunging up a flight of steps; the next instant the door had opened wider and Victoire herself, carrying a candle, slipped into the cellar.

Tarn rallied his forces to greet her suitably.

"An unexpected pleasure, my dear," he said, with biting

civility. "I confess I had not anticipated *your* paying me a visit here."

Victoire seemed not to hear him. She had come across to him quickly and dropped to her knees beside him, setting down the candle.

"*Nom de Dieu*, what have they done to you!" she ejaculated, in an anxious whisper.

Tarn, infuriated by this seeming solicitude, lost his air of detachment and attempted to sit up, but the effort only made his head swim and nausea rise in his throat; he turned, and was vilely sick upon the floor.

"*Voyons!*" said Victoire indignantly. "They are monsters to use you so!" She took out her handkerchief and proceeded with serious efficiency to wipe his lordship's sweating face. "If only I could untie these horrid ropes!"

"Well, why can't you?" said Tarn, feeling that there was no use in trying to keep up his dignity now, and therefore speaking with considerable asperity and in a far more natural tone than he had used on her entrance. "That would do something, at any rate, to make up for that damnable trickery of yours!"

Victoire cast a glance over her shoulder at the door. "No, no!" she said, in the same rapid whisper. "He will return in a moment. But I will come back later; truly I will! I promise you—"

Before he could speak again she had sprung to her feet and, with a nonchalant air, turned to face the man Jem as he entered the cellar.

"There warn't nobody there, missy," he said, regarding her suspiciously, and then looking searchingly towards Tarn. "Here, you ain't been meddling with them ropes, have ye?" he enquired.

"But not at all!" Victoire said disdainfully. "I think he is not pleased to see me, and—*enfin*, he has been very sick, which is quite as he deserves, for to me he has been abominable, and I am truly glad to see him so."

70

Jem grinned, looking at Tarn a trifle more sympathetically. "Shot the cat, eh, lad?" he said. "Well, it's no great wonder, for danged if I ever see a cove take such a pounding before he'd give in to own himself grassed."

"*Au vrai*, he quite deserved it," Victoire said severely, "and I hope that he will be very uncomfortable, and that you will leave him here for a long time—exactly so!" She turned to observe Tarn critically. "Perhaps he will even die, for certainly he looks very pale. Me, I have experience of such things, and I can tell you that it is not at all unlikely."

An uneasy look crossed Jem's face, which, in the light of the lantern he carried, appeared to Tarn to be rather more flushed than it had been when he had first assisted in carrying him into the cellar.

"Surelye to goodness, you're an unaccountable bloodthirsty wench!" he said reprovingly to Victoire. "First you must come down to see for yourself that we've got him here all right and tight, and now you're wishing to put him to bed with a shovel! A hem set-out it will be for us if he sticks his spoon in the wall! The Nubbing Cheat—that's what it'll mean for Jerry and Nate and me!"

He reached into his pocket as he spoke, and again produced the flask from which he had earlier regaled Tarn and offered it to his lips.

"That's right!" he encouraged him. "Have a good swig, lad, for there's plenty more where that came from."

From the reek of his breath as he bent over the Marquis, it was clear that he himself had been following this advice upstairs, which perhaps accounted for the improvement in his humour. Tarn, somewhat revived by the fiery liquor he had swallowed, said, endeavouring to take advantage of the situation, "It scarcely seems worth the risk, does it? You won't find my uncle such an easy pigeon for your plucking, you know. He'll have the Runners down on you before he pays. My watch and ring and purse would be safer loot."

"Lord bless you, lad, you don't think we've not had *them* off you long since!" Jem said indulgently. "But it's not little pickings we're after now. We'll set up as gentlemen on *this* business or you won't see daylight again; that's certain!"

Victoire nodded corroboration. "That is true," she affirmed. "He is very rich, my cousin says, and can afford to pay well for his freedom. But now I do not wish to remain here any longer, if you please, for truly it is very damp and altogether disagreeable in this place." She added loftily, "*I* do not wish it, but it appears to me that it would be a great deal better, if it is true that you do not wish him to come to harm, if you untied him, so that he is not obliged to lie on this damp floor."

Jem looked doubtfully at Tarn.

"*Allons*, he is sick and weak, and you have a pistol," Victoire said scornfully, turning her back on him and walking towards the door. "Even *I* should not be afraid of him if I had *that*."

Jem hesitated for a moment longer, but, after again scrutinising Tarn's undeniably pale face, bent and untied the cords that bound his legs.

"There!" he said. "You'll be a deal more comfortable now, and with them fives of yours still trussed up, I misdoubt you'll be making mischief for us."

And he thereupon picked up the lantern and followed Victoire from the cellar.

Tarn, left alone, occupied himself for several minutes in trying to restore the circulation to his numbed legs, and eventually succeeded in getting to his feet. He was obliged to sit down immediately, however, for he was still dizzy and sick. In the pitch blackness of the cellar there was little, at any rate, that he could accomplish in the way of attempting an escape. The door, as he ascertained presently, after a dogged and exasperating search for it that sent him blundering, it appeared to him, into every moveable object in the cellar, was a stout one, which it was quite beyond his present power to break down, and there seemed to be nothing in the collection of articles he had glimpsed in his prison that would be of the least use to him in attempting to free his hands. The rope with which these were bound had been knotted so tightly about his wrists that movement was impossible, and, as they had been tied behind his back, he could not make use of his teeth to undo the knots.

His only hope of escape seemed to lie in Victoire's whispered promise to return, and whether he could rely upon that he had not the least idea. Certainly she had seemed for a few moments, upon first seeing him lying there bound and battered, to have felt some compunction over the part she had played in the affair, but apparently any feeling of this nature had quickly vanished, and she had even exulted over his plight. No doubt, he thought bitterly, she was as changeable as any other woman, in spite of her deceivingly candid appearance, and to expect her to do anything to help to free him from the position into which she herself had lured him was the height of wishful thinking.

But in this opinion, he presently discovered, he was doing Miss Duvenay a great injustice. Again he had no notion for how long a period he had been left alone in his cellar, but to the best of his calculations no more than an hour could have passed before he again heard the grating of the key in the lock and the door swung open to admit Victoire. She was carrying a lantern, which she set down immediately upon the floor, and as she came towards him he saw the sudden flash of steel as she produced a knife from the folds of her gown. He had a sudden startled and quite unpleasant instant of suspicion that she had actually come down to murder him, and stumbled to his feet, facing her, but she said at once, in a breathless, impatient voice, "Turn around! How am I to cut the cords if you do not? Please, we must hurry! I do not know when they may discover that the key is gone!"

Relief made his voice almost lighthearted as he turned obediently and said, "So you have come to rescue me, sweetheart!

I have been heaping curses on you these past hours, but it seems I have wronged you, after all!"

She paid no heed to him, exerting her strength to cut through the cords as quickly as possible.

"Can you walk?" she asked anxiously, as the cords fell away and he drew his arms before him with a gasp of relief. "You are still very pale, and there is blood on your head."

"Oh, yes! I shall do famously now," he said, but his actions belied his words. He was still far from clear-headed, he found, and even the slight exertion of walking across the small cellar to the door sent him spinning dizzily into the wall. "Oh, the devil!" he ejaculated. "Where am I, and how far must I go to get out of the reach of these fellows?"

"But you cannot go like this—*cela se voit!*" Victoire exclaimed, coming over quickly to lend him the slender support of her arm. She looked up at him worriedly. "If you could ride, there is a horse in the shed—"

"Can I risk that? Won't they hear?"

"I do not think so. They have all drunk a great deal and now they are asleep; that is how I was able to steal the key."

"Well, I'll take that knife, at any rate, if you don't mind," Tarn said rather grimly, reaching out a numbed hand to take it from her and dropping it into the pocket of his coat. "If they *should* chance to wake, I've no wish to let them shut me up here again."

He mounted the steps with her help, and they passed through what was evidently the back door of the house into the open. Tarn found himself standing outside a low little house that seemed to be the only habitation in sight under a heavy dark sky. It stood at the end of a lane—little more than a track —leading upwards across the dunes away from the sea, the quiet expanse of which he could make out below him only as a more intense blackness beneath the sky. There was not a light to be seen anywhere.

"Where is your horse?" Tarn asked, finding to his great

annoyance that the cool night air, instead of clearing his head, only made it ache more blindingly, so that he could scarcely manage two consecutive thoughts. "I think I must risk taking it, after all."

"Yes, I think so, too," Victoire said decisively. "It is in the shed there." She pointed to a small ramshackle structure standing at the end of the yard. "We must have the lantern, I suppose."

She darted back into the cellar after it, taking the precaution of closing and locking the door behind her before she climbed the steps again to rejoin Tarn. She found him steadying himself against the outer wall of the shed, quite evidently scarcely able to keep on his feet.

"*Mon Dieu*, how can you go like this?" she exclaimed, a hint of panic in her voice. "The horse is old and safe, I think, but if you faint away you will fall and you may be killed."

He roused himself to speak reassuringly to her. "Gammon! I shall do very well," he said. "Put a bridle on the brute for me and I'll guarantee to stay on its back."

She did not reply, but looked at him searchingly for a moment in the light of the lantern and then slipped at once into the shed. He heard a low whinny and the sounds of a horse shifting uneasily in a stranger's presence. In a very short time Victoire appeared again, the lantern now extinguished, leading a large, rawboned animal that looked quite unwilling to have its honest slumbers disturbed at such an unseemly hour. She led it to a log that evidently did duty as a mounting block and, before Tarn knew what she was about, had sprung quickly up to seat herself upon the horse's broad bare back.

"I am going with you," she said, as he stared in astonishment. "Come, please!" she added imperatively. "Can you mount behind me? I could not take the time to saddle this horse; if they find us it will be very bad, you know!"

"Yes, but—"

She said impatiently, "You cannot ride alone, my lord; it is a *bêtise* to say that you will do so! *Ainsi donc*—I will take the reins and you will hold to me tightly and not fall off."

Tarn was well aware that, under normal circumstances, a dozen reasons would have presented themselves to his mind why he must not allow Miss Duvenay to do anything so foolhardy as to come with him; but in his present half-dazed state he could find words to marshal none of them, either for her consideration or for his own. It was quite apparent, at any rate, that she was right in believing that he could not make his escape alone; the battering he had received had obviously been too severe for him to be able to recover from it within a space of hours.

Another anxious, impatient command from Victoire decided him; he moved forward and, with an effort, managed to mount up behind her. The exertion made his head swim sickeningly, and he found himself slumping heavily against the small, firm figure seated before him.

"And you must *not* faint, my lord," a severe voice penetrated his consciousness. "I shall do all the rest, but that *you* must do."

He grinned a little, in spite of his racking head. "Little Trojan!" he said. "Very well. I won't fail you."

"*Bien!* Then we shall go."

He felt the horse move under him as she gave it the office to start, and the next moment they were proceeding slowly away from the house, towards the track leading up from the sea.

For several minutes he was too much occupied in a grim effort to keep his promise to Victoire to be able to take any account of their progress, but eventually his head cleared somewhat and he glanced around him.

"Where are we?" he demanded. "I don't recognise this place."

Victoire shook her head. "I do not know," she said, "except that it is on the sea. It was already dark when Fitzhugh brought me here and—as you see—it is a very lonely country. It is a

76

journey of three hours or more from the George, and to the southeast; that is all I can tell you."

"Three hours!" ejaculated Tarn. "The devil you say!" He looked around at the flat country to which the sandy dunes near the sea were giving way—a sullen, marshy land with nothing but a few thornbushes and willows, and the intersecting dykes traversing it, to interrupt its eerie loneliness. "The Marshes, of course!" he muttered, more to himself than to Victoire. "Good God, I daresay they must have taken me into Kent." He frowned, trying to concentrate his thoughts, and said at last, rather thickly, "We might do better to remain near the sea; we may be near Lydd, or New Romney. At any rate, you had best leave me at the first house we come to, for it seems I am not in case to travel far."

She glanced round at him in quick alarm. "No—please!" she said. "We must not stop so soon, and so near the sea. These men are smugglers, and have many friends along this coast, Fitzhugh says, and I think it is entirely likely that those friends may not wish to help you if they learn what has happened to you."

"Probably not," admitted Tarn. "It's true there are few people along these coasts who haven't to do with the Gentlemen in one way or another. But how came your cousin to be able to find such a set of rogues so ready at hand? Is he so well acquainted in these parts?"

"No, but he has a cousin who is the agent for a gentleman living somewhere near here, and many quite respectable persons, he says, know of the smugglers and have dealings with them because they wish to buy the brandy they bring in from France. Is this true?"

"Very true," Tarn assured her, a faint smile twitching his lips in spite of his aching head. "But do you mean to tell me that this cousin of his knew why he wished to be put in touch with these fellows?"

"*Mais non!* He is of a respectability most complete, Fitzhugh says. I am sure he knows nothing of this, but that Fitzhugh told him some entirely false story."

"And Duvenay himself—where is he now?" asked Tarn, wishing that the dark landscape would cease its disconcerting habit of swimming dizzily before his eyes. "Behind at the house with the others?"

"Yes. He too has drunk very much cognac, and now he is asleep. The man they call Nate has gone back to Eastcott Park, where he is to collect the money your uncle will pay him when he learns you are in the hands of these men." She added, practically, "Will you fall off if I make this horse go faster?"

"Won't you?"

"But no! Papa taught me to ride well."

"I should think so!" murmured Tarn, feeling the steady ease with which the little figure before him sat their sorry steed. "Well, go on! I promise to warn you if I find I am about to—as Jem put it—shoot the cat again."

She dug her heel into the plodding horse's side and it responded clumsily, with a jolting gait each step of which seemed to Tarn to drive a thousand needles into his burning head. They were on a rough, zigzag road now, which he hoped might lead them to a village or at least to some farmhouse, but it soon appeared that Mr. Duvenay, with the advice of his confederates, had chosen one of the most isolated sections of the coast for his exploit. Victoire, with no light to guide her, either from the sky or, at this hour, from any habitation that they might be passing, could only endeavour to keep the horse on the road and to put as many miles as possible between the Marquis and his captors. She pressed on persistently but a little desperately, knowing from the long silences that occurred that her companion was fully occupied with his own problem of preventing himself from giving way to a dangerous lapse into semiconsciousness, and feeling, therefore, entirely cast upon her own resources.

At length a lightening of the darkness, a greying of the heavy sky above her, made her realise that a new danger was threatening: the night was paling into dawn, and it must soon be light enough for pursuers to see them. She might hope that her cousin and the men he had hired to help him had drunk enough that their slumbers would be uninterrupted for some hours still, but if they had not, and discovered their prisoner gone, they might attempt pursuit; and on a lonely road a contest between a girl and a half-stunned man on the one hand, and a pair of armed ruffians on the other, could have only one outcome.

"Dieu me sauve!" she thought, in panic. "I must find a house," and, as if in answer to her unspoken prayer, the glimmer of a light shone off to the right from behind a thicket of furze bushes.

Reining in the horse, she found that a rutted lane led off at that point in the road in the direction of the light, and, having no doubt now that she had hit upon a farmhouse or shepherd's cot where the early-rising inhabitants were preparing for their long day's work, she turned the horse at once into the lane.

Tarn, rousing himself at this change in direction, enquired indistinctly what she was doing.

"I have seen a house," she said. "They will take us in, surely, and then you will be safe, *n'est-ce pas?*"

She pointed ahead to where the small light was now clearly visible across the marsh.

"If," Tarn said, still in that rather blurred voice, "they don't turn us away for a pair of vagabonds. I wonder if it has occurred to you that we must present a decidedly off appearance, and in these parts they are suspicious of strangers, you know!"

"Oh, no!" she said, in quick dismay. "They would not do such a thing!"

But such a thing, it soon appeared, was precisely what the farmwife who appeared at the door of the small house at the end of the lane, as the plodding horse with its two riders approached, had it in mind to do. Her first action was to slam

79

the door shut in the face of the pair of strangers emerging so suddenly out of the grey dawn; her second, evidently, was to summon her husband, for in a few moments a burly individual purposefully holding an ancient fowling-piece in his hands put his head from a window and requested them in no uncertain terms to take themselves off.

"But you cannot turn us away!" Victoire said indignantly. "This gentleman has been severely hurt!"

"Drunk as a wheelbarrow, both of them!" the incensed voice of the farmwife was heard proclaiming from behind her husband's broad back. "*And* I'll warrant that horse is stolen, for they've taken it off without a saddle to its back! If they try to come closer, Jeremiah, do you let that thing off at them!"

None of Victoire's earnest entreaties succeeded in shaking the irate dame's conviction that she was dealing with a pair of shameless roisterers, and from Tarn's silence Victoire gathered that the effort of joining in the argument himself was beyond him at that moment. In despair, she said at last, "Then will you tell me at least if there is an inn near here where I can take him? *Mon Dieu,* I must have help!"

"One o' them foreigners, that's what *she* is!" the farmwife said, working up to another round of bitter disparagement. "Shameless hussy! Jauntering about the countryside with her fancy-man at this time of day! Her kind ought to be whipped at the cart's tail!"

But her husband, less convinced, it seemed, of the nefarious character of their unusual visitors, said more mildly that Fairford was just up the road a bit—a piece of wanton good nature that his spouse at once pounced upon as proof that he would have them all murdered in their beds by doing kindnesses to drunken rogues that ought to be taken up by the constable.

She then pulled her husband back into the house and slammed shut the window, and Victoire, giving up, turned the horse's head again towards the road.

"Sorry," she heard Tarn's voice murmur at her back. "Not much use to you there. Truth is—"

"Do not try to talk," Victoire said, making an effort to sound much more cheerful than she felt. "That woman is a great *imbécile*, I think, but there is a village not far off, her husband says. We shall go there, and then you will be safe."

He did not reply, and she could only pray that he did not fall into a swoon before they came again to some habitation. It seemed hours to her before the horse at last plodded into a cluster of alleys set round a church, which she presumed must be Fairford. By this time the first sunlight was beginning to break through the mist, and a small girl, scuttling out of a house door to clutch a calico kitten that appeared to be setting out on its own to explore the morning world, gazed up in astonishment to see stopping before her a rawboned grey horse without a saddle, its reins held by a hatless young lady with chestnut curls, seated before a tall, very pale young man half slumped against her.

"Oh, please, *petite!*" said the young lady, in a breaking voice. "Is there an inn? Will you direct me to it?"

The little girl stared, round-eyed, then set up a shrill call for "Pa!" and scampered back inside the house. A moment later she reappeared; her father, a stout, muscular man in a leather waistcoat, stepping out behind her, was just in time to catch the tall young man as he slid, unconscious, from the horse's back.

Of what happened afterwards the Marquis was to have later only the vaguest of recollections. He could remember opening his eyes in what seemed to be the taproom of a small inn or alehouse, shuttered and deserted at that time of the morning except for the several persons who appeared to be carrying on a spirited argument over his aching head; he recalled being fortified with a glass of brandy and carried up a flight of stairs to a little low bedchamber under the eaves; and his recollections ended with a euphoric dream of having his clothes stripped from him by a stout man who smelled of beer and horses and of being placed between clean sheets in a featherbed, where his head was bathed with a soothing liquid by an equally stout dame in a mob cap.

Some lingering, stubborn sense of responsibility made him ask for Victoire, but, upon her appearing beside him and assuring him that everything was well with her, he sank into a blissful slumber, from which, being a healthy young man, he awoke much refreshed in the middle of the afternoon.

It required several puzzled minutes, when he first opened his eyes on his strange surroundings, for him to piece together the events that had led to his waking in a small, dimity-hung bedchamber, with a patchwork quilt over him and a tallow candle stuck into a pewter holder on the table beside the bed; but eventually the attack in the lane behind the George, the cellar, and his escape from it with Victoire, began to fall into place in his mind. There was a large lump on his head, which was still excessively sore to the touch, and he was ravenously hungry, but the dizziness from which he had suffered during the night had disappeared, and he was conscious of no other ill effects from the strenuous events of the past day.

Looking about, he found his clothes nowhere in sight, and, as there was no bell in the room, he set up a shout for the landlord. To his surprise, it was Victoire who slipped into the room, her face brightening at the sight of him.

"Oh, you are awake!" she said. "I am so glad! You have been sleeping like the dead; in fact, I was afraid once that you *were* dead, only then you began to snore—"

"How do *you* know that?" Tarn demanded. "Where the devil are we? What time is it? Where are my clothes? And you oughtn't to be here, in the first place."

Victoire drew herself up with an air of dignity. "I cannot answer so many questions all at once, my lord," she said. "And it is quite *convenable* for me to be here, for I have told the landlord that I am your sister."

"Well, that don't make you my sister," Tarn retorted. "And he'd have to know there was something dashed smoky about that tale, my girl, for you don't look any more like me than —Well, deuce take it, I'm not going to argue with you about it, at any rate. Get out of here and send somebody to bring my clothes and shaving water and I'll talk to you when I've dressed. And tell them to lay on some breakfast, or dinner, or

84

whatever meal it is they have ready at this time of day," he called after her imperatively as she obediently departed, "because I'm devilish sharp-set!"

In a few minutes the landlord appeared, a rather wary expression upon his face, and the Marquis's clothes, which had apparently received the attention of an expert housewife, over his arm.

"We'll have your hot water in a minute, sir," he said, depositing the Marquis's coat and breeches carefully upon a chair, with the respect due such expensive items of clothing, and placing his boots upon the floor.

He lingered, obviously wishing to say more, but Tarn, who appeared to have only one thought in his mind at the moment, put him off the track of whatever enquiries he had intended to make by subjecting him instead to a searching examination on what he might find awaiting him in the way of food when he went downstairs.

Having satisfied himself that a dish of ox rumps with cabbage and a ham pie were available to satisfy his appetite, he proceeded to dress. The landlord still lingered.

"If you please, your Honour—"

"Well? What is it?"

"Why, it's—not being used to cater for the Quality, as you might say—" The man paused, in a quandary, it appeared, and finally blurted out desperately, "It's about that ring the young lady gave me, your Honour. I'm sure it's worth a deal more than the room for only one night and the expense of sending the lad with the message, but if it was convenient to you, I'd rather you paid me just what was owed me in good plain coin."

"The ring? What ring?"

The man put his hand into his pocket and, withdrawing it carefully, exhibited a diamond ring upon the broad palm of his hand. Tarn picked it up and examined it.

"Good Lord, that's Nancy's ring," he said. "How did you—?"

"The young lady did say as how she was able to hide it when you was held up and robbed, sir," the landlord said doubtfully. "But my old 'oman, not being trustful by nature—though to be sure, I says to her, if the young lady wasn't honest, why should she be so set on sending a message to Lord Eastcott, at Eastcott Park, which it stands to reason she wouldn't be wishful to do if there was anything havey-cavey about the business—"

Tarn grinned, handing the ring back to the landlord. "Well, she's a resourceful chit; I'll give her that!" he said. "And don't worry yourself over the ring; if you really have sent off a message to Lord Eastcott, you will have your shot paid in good coin of the realm before the day is out."

The arrival of his hot water interrupted the conversation at that moment, and he dismissed the landlord, who went downstairs to inform his wife that there was no doubt of it that the young gentleman was Quality, as anyone could see from his highhanded ways, but that if the young lady was his sister he himself was the King of England.

His good wife tossed her head. "As if I didn't know that, the minute ever I clapped eyes on the pair of them!" she said scornfully. "His light-o'-love is closer to the mark, for all she looks to be such an innocent. Nor I wouldn't have had them in this house—for not one word of that Canterbury tale she told of them being held up by highwaymen did I believe—if it hadn't been for the case the young gentleman was in."

"Well, he ain't in it no more," her husband retorted. "All he's thinking of now is something to line his belly, and if you don't have it set upon the table by the time he comes down, you can look to have a peal rung over you, and so I warn you!"

Meanwhile, Victoire, who had spent a most unrestful day, between her anxiety over Tarn and the landlady's obvious suspicions of her respectability, which had led her to offer her no better accommodations than a daybed in a small, closetlike room at the head of the stairs, sat in the deserted taproom waiting for Tarn. Now that she had seen his lordship apparently so fully recovered, reaction from the strain of the twenty-four hours just past had begun to set in, and Tarn, when he came downstairs, found her seated rather forlornly on the wooden settle, looking very tired and exceedingly pensive. As he was accustomed to putting first things first, he made no mention of these impressions until he had seen them both seated at table with a bountiful repast set before them; but, having directed the landlady to leave them alone, he then enquired what the matter was.

"N-nothing," Victoire said not very convincingly, looking, with a lack of interest that appeared to amount almost to revulsion, at the large portion of ham pie which his lordship had heaped upon her plate. "I—I was thinking—"

"Well, don't," Tarn recommended. "Not until you've had something to eat. What have you been doing with yourself all day? You don't look as if you'd closed your eyes."

"Well, I did not sleep *much*," Victoire acknowledged, "because first I had to argue very much with the landlord so that he would send his son to tell Lord Eastcott that he must come to help you, and then I thought perhaps you were hurt very badly and might die."

"Gammon!" said Tarn. "I was sick as a horse, but you ought to've known it was no more than that. I'm sorry to have put you into a fright—never did anything more bacon-brained in my life than going off like that this morning. I'm right as a trivet now."

"Yes. I am so glad!" Victoire said, in a voice, however, which still seemed decidedly mournful. "And I—I expect you are quite safe here now, and that Lord Eastcott must come soon, or send some conveyance for you, so I—have been thinking—that I must go—"

"Go?" Tarn looked up, frowning. "Go where?"

Victoire made a rather helpless little gesture. "Back to—that place, I suppose," she said. "I must find my cousin."

"Well, if you expect to find him there, you're fair and far off, I can tell you that," Tarn said bluntly. "If the whole lot of them aren't in Calais by now, I miss my guess. Good God, girl, you don't expect, when they found me gone, they sat there waiting peacefully to be taken up by the authorities! They must have loped off hours ago; you won't find anyone in *that* house but the rats."

Victoire nodded. "Yes, I—I have thought of that," she admitted in a rather strained voice. "But what am I to do, then? I have no money, you see—and I gave Nancy's ring to the landlord so that he would let us stay here and send the message to Lord Eastcott."

"Well, the first thing you are going to do," Tarn said decisively, "is to go back to Eastcott Park with me when we hear from my uncle. You can't stay here, and you can't go back to Ireland."

Victoire wrinkled her brow. "I could go if I had money," she said. "It is not very expensive, the journey, I think, but I have no money at all, you see. Perhaps if you would lend me what I should need—though I do *not* think," she added conscientiously, "that Fitzhugh would ever pay it back—"

"No!" said Tarn.

"Oh!" Victoire looked crestfallen. "I thought—since you are so very rich—"

"It doesn't matter how rich I am. I'm not going to see you back in that scoundrel's hands again, and I shan't give you a groat to put yourself there—even if he would have you now, which I should think highly doubtful, after the trick you served him when you let me out of that cellar." Tarn grinned, taking a deep draught from the tall tankard of home-brewed set beside his plate, and said with some meaning, "You owed me that, though, young Victoire, for writing that cozening letter to bring me into his hands in the first place."

He halted in some surprise, looking at Victoire, who had sprung up from the table and was regarding him fiercely.

"Here," he demanded, "what's the matter now?"

88

"I did not write that letter!" Victoire said vehemently. "Only a fool would believe such a thing!" Tears sprang suddenly into her eyes, in no way diminishing the anger on her face. "I did not think you would be so—so—"

"Hey-day!" said Tarn, pacifically. "Very well. You didn't write the letter. No need to fly up into the boughs over it."

Victoire looked at him suspiciously. "You do not believe any more that I wrote it? *Vraiment?*"

"No, I take you at your word. Not that I ever thought it was *your* idea, in the first place. But you *are* dependant upon Duvenay, and he might have compelled you—"

"I would not have done such a thing if he had locked me up forever with nothing to eat or drink!" Victoire said, still regarding him unforgivingly. "I knew nothing of any letter —nothing!—until he boasted to me last night of what he had done. Do you believe that?"

"If you say so." Tarn was grinning still, and a reluctant smile gradually appeared upon Victoire's face as well. "Sit down and finish your dinner," his lordship commanded. "I must think what to do with you, and I don't mind telling you it's enough of a problem without your getting up on your high ropes. But you can't go back to Ireland; that's certain. You'd only find the bailiffs in the house, and, if I know anything of your precious cousin, *he* will be prudent enough to stay out of the country as long as he thinks there is any danger that I shall set the authorities on him over last night's work."

"Will you do that?" Victoire asked, with a look of some apprehension.

A rather grim expression crossed Tarn's face. "I ought to," he said. "But it would serve no good purpose; he and the others are out of reach of the law, and *you* would certainly be dragged into the matter. And I'm not so ungrateful as to wish to do *that* to you, after what you've done for me."

Victoire looked rather relieved. "Well, I cannot help being glad that you will not do so," she said, "because Fitzhugh *is* my cousin, and a Duvenay, and, though I would like to do very bad things to him and to those other men because of what they did to *you*, it would be a great disgrace if he were put in gaol. And I cannot help thinking that, at any rate, if he *has* gone to France he will not be at all comfortable there, for he does not know anyone there and he speaks French very badly."

The Marquis said unsympathetically that he did not believe Mr. Duvenay's ignorance of the language would be a hindrance to him in the career of roguery he seemed to have taken up, as in his experience a scoundrel was a scoundrel in any country and he did not doubt that Mr. Duvenay's fertile brain would be able to invent just as many dishonest schemes in France as it had in England or Ireland.

"Yes," Victoire agreed reluctantly. "It is very mortifying, but I daresay it is quite true, what you say. But it is not at all agreeable, I can tell you, to have such a *coquin* for one's cousin. Papa," she said, lifting her chin a little, "told me when he was—before he died—that he could not leave me anything but his name, but that it was an honourable one. And that is why I told these people here that we had had our carriage and all our money taken from us by highwaymen, because I could not bear to have them know about Fitzhugh."

"Was that the message you sent to my uncle, too?" Tarn demanded.

Victoire nodded rather guiltily, but his lordship only burst out laughing, and said that if his uncle had already received a ransom note from the kidnapers, and then had to hear of highwaymen on the head of it, it would be wonderful if he did not arrive at the inn in a state fit for Bedlam.

"And speaking of my uncle," he added, cocking an ear at the sound of some sudden commotion arising outside the small latticed windows of the room in which they sat, "what odds will you give me that that doesn't mean he *has* arrived?" He got up and went over to the window, ejaculating wrathfully after a moment, "Good God! *Two* chaises—outriders—and he's even brought that curst sawbones!"

He strode from the room without ceremony, and Victoire, jumping up herself and going to the window, was in time to see him engage Lord Eastcott, who had apparently just alighted from the foremost of the two elegant travelling chaises that had halted outside, in what seemed to be somewhat acrimonious conversation. A second gentleman, in the conventional frock-coat of a doctor of medicine, stood regarding the Marquis in patent bewilderment, and the scene was further enlivened by the irruption from all quarters of the little street of a clutch of dirty-faced urchins and a number of barking dogs, all evidently irresistibly attracted to the extraordinary sight of a pair of fashionable carriages, each drawn by four blood horses, and several liveried outriders.

As Victoire stood watching, scarcely knowing whether to follow her first impulse to laugh at the animated spectacle before her or to retreat in dismay from the impressive stir the sending of her message had caused, the landlord too came hurrying from the door and added his bows and enquiries to the confusion. This was sufficient to recall Lord Eastcott and his nephew to the impropriety of engaging in a public discussion of their affairs, and in a few moments they entered the house together and were ushered into the taproom by the landlord—much to Lord Eastcott's disapproval, it seemed, for when he first appeared in Victoire's view he was vociferously demanding a private parlour.

The landlord, trembling at the magnificence of Lord Eastcott's sixteen-caped driving coat and mirror-polished top boots, was obliged to confess that there was none—a remark which caused his lordship to demand scathingly of his nephew why he found him putting up at a hedge-tavern.

"And this—this—" he added, catching sight for the first time of Victoire, who, unable to retreat, stood transfixed beside the table, "this young woman here with you!" Lord Eastcott turned fulminatingly to his nephew. "I wish you will explain yourself, Tarn!" he said. "Deuce take it, if this is your notion of a joke—! You've turned my house upside down, sent your aunt to bed with the vapours, and caused me the devil of an amount of anxiety, thinking you might be lying at death's door; yet here I find you, not even a trifle out of curl, it seems, enjoying yourself with one of your bits of muslin in a common alehouse!"

"Careful, Uncle!" said Tarn in a level voice, closing the door in the landlord's face and coming across the room to place himself beside Victoire. "You may rake me down as much as you please, but Miss Duvenay is another matter. She is here only because she helped me to escape from an excessively uncomfortable and rather dangerous situation, at considerable risk to herself."

Lord Eastcott stared. "Don't try to bamboozle me, Tarn!" he said tartly. "You are running one of your rigs, I suppose —knocking up a lark, I daresay you young fellows call it. But ransom notes, highwaymen—do you expect me to swallow *that* fling?"

"You need not swallow the highwaymen, sir," said Tarn, going to the table and pouring a glass of ale from the jug that stood upon it. "Miss Duvenay was obliged to think of something that would bring you to my aid without disclosing the whole of our adventures to the people of this house, when I was too knocked up to do anything for myself this morning, and she therefore invented the highwaymen. But the ransom note was quite genuine, I assure you." He handed the glass to his uncle with a slight smile. "Here, try some of our host's home-brewed," he said. "You'll find it excellent, in spite of the appearance of his house."

Lord Eastcott, though his jaws were still champing angrily, was not proof against this invitation, and, having drunk the ale, looked somewhat mollified and said that it was a very tolerable brew.

"But I still want an explanation from you, Lewis!" he said, returning to his original subject. "If you really have a good reason for this extraordinary behaviour—"

"I have the best of reasons, but I am not going into it here and now," said Tarn. "Since we shall be travelling back to Eastcott Park together, we shall have every opportunity of discussing the matter on the way. But, meanwhile, I have not the slightest desire to spend another hour in this place, and so I suggest that we take our departure at once. Miss Duvenay, by the way, is coming with us; I shall place her in my aunt's care for the time being."

"In your aunt's care!"

Lord Eastcott, quite dumbfounded, stared at Victoire, who coloured vividly and looked imploringly at Tarn.

But the Marquis, with his usual impetuosity, was already across the room and at the door, shouting for the landlord, and, having turned briefly in the doorway to instruct his uncle to pay the fellow what was owing him, as he had no money himself, and to collect the diamond ring from him in return, went outside to inspect the travelling arrangements offered by Lord Eastcott's entourage.

Finding that one of the carriages was his aunt's elegant travelling-chaise, which, in addition to being exceedingly well-sprung, had been fitted out with every comfort for the convenience of an invalid, pillows and rugs having been provided in profusion, he at once decided that Victoire should make the journey in this vehicle, while he, his uncle, and the doctor occupied the other chaise. Victoire, however, who had followed him outside, unwilling to remain under Lord Eastcott's censorious eye, hung back when he instructed her to mount into the carriage, looking uncomfortable and very determined.

"No! I shall not go with you," she said. "I shall—I shall sell that horse, which does not belong to me, *vraiment*, but which I cannot take back to those men if they have gone out of the country, and with the money I shall go to Ireland, where I think I shall quite easily find some work to do, for I have been taught very well to cook and sew and *faire le ménage,* and my cousin's housekeeper, who is a *femme très sympathique* and much acquainted in the neighborhood, will no doubt recommend me."

She might as well have spared her breath, for Tarn, taking no notice whatever of the latter part of her speech, merely ejaculated, "Good God! The horse! I had forgotten it. We shall make a present of the wretched beast to the landlord." He then slipped his hand under her elbow and impelled her irresistibly to the door of the chaise, remarking as he did so, "And as for you, young Victoire, let me hear no more nonsense from you about going to Ireland. I have told you, you are going to Eastcott Park."

"No—please!" Victoire said desperately. "Your uncle does not want me, and I am sure that your aunt—"

"Oh, he'll come around!" Tarn said cheerfully. "So will she. It's not as if you were going to stay there for the rest of your life, you know; we'll think of something to do for you. And now, up you go, my girl!"

She was well enough acquainted with his lordship's tactics by this time to know that if she failed to do as he bid her she was likely to find herself lifted from her feet and deposited unceremoniously inside the chaise. She therefore reluctantly entered it; the steps were let up and the door shut by one of Lord Eastcott's retainers; and in a very few minutes she was rolling off down the little street in solitary state, almost buried in a nest of velvet cushions.

The effect of all this comfort was to cause her, paradoxically, to burst into tears, a luxury that she had denied herself during the long, harrowing hours of anxiety just past. But she was too young and far too weary to continue for long in this disagreeable occupation, and soon fell asleep, lulled by the motion of the carriage. Once or twice during the journey she woke and, peering from the window, saw the long evening light dying over the peaceful Sussex landscape and, later, a thin sickle moon rising in a calm sky. It was almost dark when they arrived at Eastcott Park.

9

Tarn had evidently succeeded during the journey in convincing his uncle that Miss Duvenay merited the shelter of his roof that night, for when the party arrived at Eastcott Park a few hurried words from Lord Eastcott in his astonished lady's ear resulted in Victoire's being ushered upstairs at once to a pleasant bedchamber. Lady Eastcott herself visited her there a few minutes later, still obviously quite bewildered, to inform her that refreshment would be brought to her shortly and to offer her the nightgear with which she had come unprovided. As Victoire was too embarrassed to offer any explanations to her hostess, and Lady Eastcott was evidently under instructions to demand none, nothing passed between them but the necessary civilities, and Victoire, in one of Lady Eastcott's exquisitely embroidered nightdresses, presently slipped into the big four-poster bed and fell asleep with all the problems besetting her quite unsolved and even unbroached between her and her new protectors.

Tarn, too, who had found that the strenuous events of the past twenty-four hours had quite unfitted him for a more thorough discussion of Miss Duvenay's future plans with his aunt and uncle, was glad to be driven off at once to Tarn House, where he ate the highly unsatisfactory meal provided for him on such short notice by an indignant Mrs. Timbs and then went off straightway to bed. As soon as he had risen the next morning, however, a suitable sense of his responsibility for Miss Duvenay sent him off to Eastcott Park, where he found his aunt at breakfast with Miss Standfield and Mr. Bruce Fearon, Lord Eastcott being already gone out with his agent upon estate business.

The arrival of her nephew was the signal for an immediate volley of questions directed at him by Lady Eastcott, which made it evident at once that, whatever explanations her lord had given for the extraordinary events of the past few days, they had merely left her in a greater state of confusion than she had been in before he had offered them to her.

"I vow I can make nothing of it!" she declared. "First it appears you have been carried off and held for ransom, next waylaid by highwaymen, and then suddenly you arrive quite calmly to cast the Duvenay child upon my doorstep without so much as a nightdress to her name and tell me that I must take charge of her. *Why* must I take charge of her? Where, pray, is her brother?"

"She hasn't a brother," Tarn said.

He sat down at the table and looked with every appearance of undivided interest at the buttered eggs being offered to him by Philbrook—an action which caused her ladyship to remark with asperity that, as everyone else had quite finished breakfast, that excellent butler, together with his attendant underlings, might go and leave his lordship to fend for himself.

"And now," she said, as the door closed behind the servants, "I wish you will tell me what you mean, you provoking boy, by making such a ridiculous statement. You must be *quite* aware that I myself talked to Miss Duvenay's brother in this very house no longer than a few days ago!"

"That," said Tarn, adding a few slices from a fine York ham to his plate, "is where you are mistaken, ma'am. He isn't her brother. He's her cousin."

"Her cousin?" Lady Eastcott stared incredulously. "Her *cousin*? But he told us himself—"

"All a hum," Tarn assured her. "It's too long a story to go into, but you can take my word for it that he's her cousin. What's more, he's loped off—probably to the Continent, I should think, so that leaves Victoire on *my* hands."

Lady Eastcott put a bewildered hand to her brow. "Victoire!" she exclaimed. "But her name is Nancy!"

"No, that was t'other one," Tarn corrected her. "Duvenay's sister, the girl I knew in Ireland. I never clapped eyes on young Victoire until she turned up here the other day. She has been living in France for the past five years, you see."

Lady Eastcott said in a failing voice that she did not see in the least, and Miss Standfield, taking a hand in the proceedings at this juncture, observed placidly to his lordship that, unused as he no doubt was to giving an account of his actions to anyone, she rather believed he owed it to his aunt, since he had induced her to receive the young lady under her roof, to present her with a fuller history of Miss Duvenay than he had yet favoured them with.

"Well, but I don't want it spread all over the countryside, you know," Tarn objected, with an unfavourable glance at Mr. Fearon. "It's a curst smoky business, you see, but the girl couldn't help herself, and she was a regular Trojan in helping me to get out of those fellows' hands."

Miss Standfield shook her head in a gently disapproving fashion. "This," she said, "is *not* an explanation, Lewis. Do you not think that you would find yourself able to give us a more informative account if you set your mind firmly to the task? I do wish that you will endeavour to do so, for until you do, Miss

Duvenay's situation here must be highly anomalous. Indeed, I fear the child is too embarrassed at present even to leave her room."

This was an aspect of the situation that did not appear to have occurred to his lordship, and he said rather indignantly that he did not see why he could not bring a young lady into his aunt's home without everybody wishing to know the entire story of her life.

"Yes, but, you see," Mr. Fearon murmured, entering the conversation, "the question inevitably poses itself—*is* she a lady? Your enviable reputation with females of a certain class, Lewis—"

A slight flush crept into Tarn's cheeks. "You have a damned nasty tongue, Bruce," he said. "I don't advise you to use it on that girl, though, or I warn you that I'll take steps to stop you."

Mr. Fearon's brows rose. "Dear me!" he drawled. "How chivalrous! I confess I had not expected this of you, coz! Is it possible that I scent a romance?"

"No, you don't!" Tarn retorted. "She's only an infant, but she's a well-plucked 'un, game as a pebble, and I'm damned if you or anyone else is going to make her out to be what she's not."

He thereupon favoured the company with a brief résumé of Miss Duvenay's parentage and history, and of the events that had led up to his arrival at Eastcott Park in her company, which Miss Standfield, at least, apparently found satisfactory, for she nodded her head at its conclusion and observed that she had expected something of the sort from the start.

"It was obvious that the child was not in the least the sort of female to have drawn *your* notice, Lewis," she said, "and that she had been compelled into a situation that was highly distasteful to her. But now I ask myself," she went on, gazing thoughtfully out the window, "what you intend by your action in bringing her here. No doubt *you* have much for which to be grateful to her, but that your uncle and aunt should be equally so, to the extent of wishing to make her future well-being their concern, is rather too much to expect, I fear."

Having concluded this speech, she withdrew her gaze from distant prospects and allowed it to rest again enquiringly upon the Marquis's face. She had the satisfaction of seeing a somewhat harassed look cross it.

"Well, deuce take it, I know that!" he said. "I only brought her here because I hadn't anywhere else to take her, and I couldn't leave her there alone in that curst alehouse!" He went on, with an unwonted lack of assurance, after a few moments, "Perhaps you can tell me what is to be done for her, ma'am. Obviously it's out of the question to send her back to her cousin, even if he could be found, and she has no notion where her mother and stepfather are, or when they will be in a position to offer her a home."

Lady Eastcott, breaking into the silence that followed these words, said helpfully that perhaps the girl might go out as a governess if she were not so very young.

"But I fear that no respectable family would employ her at present in that capacity," she said. "However, I daresay there are other positions that she might fill."

"As a chambermaid, ma'am?" said Tarn, with awful politeness. "Thank you! Not while she is under *my* protection!"

Mr. Fearon complained pensively, "But the point is precisely that she is *not* under your protection, coz, or, at least, so you would have us believe. However, if you have such a burning interest in the chit, perhaps *there* is the answer to your dilemma. She might amuse you very well for a year or two."

"And it might amuse *you*," said Tarn unpleasantly, "if I were to knock your damned teeth down your throat, Bruce, which I shall certainly do if you continue in this vein!" He turned to Miss Standfield again. "But you, ma'am," he appealed to her, "have *you* no suggestions?"

Miss Standfield once more consulted the view outside the window. "Why, no," she said serenely. "You were quite correct, I believe, Lewis, when you stated on the occasion of our last conversation that there was nothing you could do to remedy Miss Duvenay's situation beyond offering her your hand in marriage—which, of course, you are *quite* unprepared to do."

She paused, and her mild, regal gaze, turning slowly to meet the Marquis's eyes, surprised a suddenly arrested look in them. Before he could speak, however, Lady Eastcott had interrupted fretfully, "Well, of course he is not going to offer for her, Cousin Amelia; it is not at all helpful of you to bring *that* up. But we must think of *some* way to rid ourselves of the girl."

Tarn's eyes narrowed; he said coolly, "Never fear, Aunt; I can assure you that you *will* soon be rid of her. As a matter of fact, it appears to me that the idea Cousin Amelia has mentioned is an excellent one."

"An—an excellent one!" Lady Eastcott's voice faltered, and a look of definite apprehension crossed her face. "Why, what in the world do you mean, Lewis? You will never *marry* the girl?"

"Why not?" said Tarn, calmly going on with his breakfast. "You have been telling me ever since I returned from the Continent last year that I ought to marry and settle down. Well, I won't engage to do the latter, but I believe I *can* oblige you in the former."

Lady Eastcott shrugged her shoulders rather pettishly. "I do *not* find this an amusing jest, Lewis," she said. "Of course you will not marry a—an adventuress!"

"An adventuress! Victoire?" The Marquis gave a crack of laughter. "Come, ma'am, you are more up to the rig than that!" he said. "You know as well as I do that she is the merest child."

"She is a very clever child if she has brought *you* into her net," Lady Eastcott retorted, with some warmth. "But I cannot believe that you are serious, Tarn! Why should you wish to marry this girl? You cannot mean to tell us that you have tumbled into love with her in the space of these few days!"

"I don't mean to tell you anything of the sort," Tarn agreed.

"I don't look for 'love' in marriage, ma'am—if there is any of that valuable commodity on the market today, which I rather doubt. But if I must marry some day—as I suppose I shall have to do, for the sake of the name—I can't think of another female less likely to make life uncomfortable for me than Miss Duvenay. And it will certainly solve the problem of what I am to do with her."

Lady Eastcott looked helplessly at Mr. Fearon, who, however, merely shrugged his shoulders and said silkily, "Oh no, Aunt, don't look to *me* to join forces with you. You had best be grateful, at any rate, that the girl is not positively common. Did you not tell me that she has at least the *appearance* of a lady? If you will lock up the spoons when she or any of her charming relations come under your roof, I am sure you will suffer no great inconvenience from the match."

He glanced blandly across the table at his cousin, whose brows had drawn together in a scowl. The presence of the two ladies, however, deterred the Marquis from giving vent to his feelings in as emphatic a manner as he would have liked, and he merely rose abruptly, saying, "That settles it. I'll marry the chit as soon as a special licence can be got. I daresay we must have one of those curst things if we are to be married at once."

Lady Eastcott gave a faint scream. "At once!" she exclaimed. "Oh, Lewis, no! You must not! You *must* consider—"

"I have considered," Tarn said. He added, with distinct menace, "And I may tell all of you that I shall expect her to be received in this family with the respect due my wife!"

Mr. Fearon gave a slight laugh. "Oh, in this family!" he said, with sneering lightness. "Really, we have very little choice —have we?—since you are its head. But in the world, my dear Lewis—! If you fancy you can assure Miss Duvenay's position in the *ton* by a huddled-up business such as this, I fear you are most sadly mistaken! It will be the most diverting *on-dit* of the season, I assure you, even surpassing the brouhaha over whether it is the Regent or Clarence that the Grandduchess of

Oldenburg has come to pursue. You are to be congratulated; it is not often that one is able to count oneself capable of amusing, not only the *ton*, but half the crowned heads of Europe as well, with one's scandals. The Regent should be particularly grateful to you, for it is said that he has anticipated some difficulty in providing suitable entertainment for all his Royal guests!"

The Marquis's face had darkened during this speech, but, unpalatable as it was to him to be obliged to admit it, he was forced to acknowledge that there was at least as much truth as malice in his cousin's words. The sudden marriage, by special licence, of any gentleman holding the rank of marquis to a young lady quite unknown in the *ton* would be certain to arouse speculation and comment; when that gentleman was the Marquis of Tarn, that comment would assuredly descend from the merely curious to the positively ribald. It would be said—he was bitterly aware, once he stopped to consider the matter—that he had been caught in parson's mousetrap at last by a bit of game too alluring, or too well provided with deter-mined male relations, for him to withstand; bets would be laid at White's as to how many months less than the proper nine would elapse between the wedding and the appearance upon the scene of a son and heir; and all but the most free-and-easy ladies of the *ton* would show the new young marchioness only that frigid civility due to her rank, excluding her with finality from their own homes.

All this flashed through his lordship's mind in a space of moments, leaving him in a state of frustration and indecision quite uncommon to him. With his usual quick impetuosity, however, he hit upon a solution to his difficulties almost at once, and turned to his aunt with an imperative air.

"Bruce is right, for once," he admitted. "I daresay it will not do to marry her out of hand; that *would* make the devil of a stir. But if you will engage to keep her for a month or two, Aunt —take her to town with you when you go up for the Season, present her to your friends—I think we may carry the business off in such a way as to keep the tattle-boxes quiet."

He got no further, for Lady Eastcott interrupted him with a little shriek of dismay.

"Take her up to town with me, present her to my friends—Lewis, you must be *quite* mad even to suggest such a thing!" she exclaimed. "A creature with *such* a background—!"

Tarn's brow darkened once more. "There is nothing amiss with her background, ma'am," he said curtly. "Her father was a gentleman, with a family a good deal older than my mother's, I daresay; and if you were to cut everyone of your acquaintance who has a rogue hanging somewhere on his family tree, you'd be obliged to lead a fairly solitary life, I think." He turned abruptly to Miss Standfield. "Will *you* do it, ma'am?" he demanded of her.

Miss Standfield, before replying, raised her eyes consideringly to his face. What she saw there appeared to satisfy her, for after a moment she nodded decisively.

"Yes," she said. "I will."

Tarn's face lightened, but Lady Eastcott ejaculated incredulously, "Amelia! My dear! You *cannot* mean it! Only think—"

"That is precisely what I *am* doing, Eleanor," said Miss Standfield, in a somewhat repressive voice, "and, if you will exert yourself to do likewise, I believe you must see that *I* have chosen the most sensible course. And now," she went on to Tarn, as she rose from the table, "I shall go up and advise Miss Duvenay that you are waiting to speak to her, Lewis. I believe you will find the Small Saloon suitable for your purpose. I shall instruct her to join you there immediately."

She walked sedately from the room, leaving Lady Eastcott staring after her in bewildered consternation. Tarn laughed.

"Well, she is a regular good 'un!" he said. "Aunt, you may expect to congratulate me in half an hour—and I hope you

105

won't be too high in the instep to drop in at Albemarle Street if Cousin Amelia should invite you there while she has Victoire with her, for she is in devilish high favour with all the best-blooded tabbies in London, you know. It might even add to *your* respectability to be seen there, my dear!"

He thereupon took himself off to the the Small Saloon, paying no heed whatsoever to the "Impertinent boy!" flung after him by his incensed aunt.

Lady Eastcott turned to her other nephew, who sat with thoughtful, almost slitted eyes and a curious smile upon his lips.

"Oh, good heavens! Was there ever such a coil!" she exclaimed, her eyes sparkling with mingled vexation and alarm. "He is in one of those freakish moods of his when he will stop at nothing; if we do not do something at once, he will offer for that girl!" She jumped up. "I shall send to fetch Eastcott."

Mr. Fearon glanced up at her without moving. "I believe that to be quite unnecessary, dear Aunt," he said calmly. She struck her hands together impatiently and he went on, a slight touch of irritation appearing in his own manner, "Pray, ma'am, do not be such a widgeon! Had you rather see him married to that chit or merely betrothed to her? Depend upon it, if you put my uncle to arguing the matter with him, it will only set his back up, and he will then be apt to carry her off and marry her as fast as he can find a parson to tie the knot. Cousin Amelia is quite right in playing for time by agreeing to take the girl."

"Playing for time!"

"Exactly. Surely you cannot believe that she is any more eager than you are to see Lewis marry the chit! She is merely wise enough to realise that opposing him will only harden his determination to do so, you know that curst obstinate temper of his! But give him a month, or even less than that, and he will have some new adventure in hand, and ten to one the idea of marriage will have gone quite out of his head."

106

Lady Eastcott sat down again, looking at him doubtfully. "Do you really think so?" she asked.

"My dear ma'am, I am sure of it! No doubt what he has in mind at present is to carry out the appearance of a conventional courtship of the girl, to end in a month or so in a public announcement of their engagement; but you may depend upon it that he has not in the least considered what that must involve. Squiring the girl to *ton* parties, taking her driving in the Park, escorting her to services at the Chapel Royal—I fancy I can see Lewis in such a role! He will be bored in a week, and if he is not casting out lures to some new bit of game before a month is out, with no further thought of marriage in his head, I shall own myself very much surprised."

"He *is* very volatile," Lady Eastcott agreed, somewhat more hopefully, "and I cannot believe, from the manner in which he speaks of her, that the girl has engaged his affections. If only we might hit upon some way of settling her respectably—"

"Exactly!" said Mr. Fearon. "Perhaps even in marriage —though not, I need hardly say, marriage to Lewis. But if the girl is as well-looking as you have described her, it is not beyond the bounds of possibility that, given a month or two, she may engage the notice of some young gentleman of less exalted circumstances, who will be glad to take her off Lewis's hands when he has begun to regret the situation he is so bent upon flinging himself into today."

"Well, yes—perhaps," Lady Eastcott said, considering the matter. "And there is the girl herself, of course. None of us appears to have thought of the possibility that *she* may reject Lewis's suit."

"For the very good reason that there is no such possibility," Mr. Fearon said, rising from the table. "What—reject the opportunity to become a marchioness! My dear Aunt, do let us confine ourselves to the realm of realities! I am not in the mood, I fear, for romance."

Meanwhile, the subject of these interesting discussions, having consumed the hot chocolate and rolls brought to her chamber by an obviously curious maid, who was quite aware that she had arrived in a most mysterious fashion under the aegis of Lord Eastcott and the Marquis, without a scrap of luggage, had dressed and sat down beside the window in nervous expectation of what was to happen to her next. She had just decided for the dozenth time to go downstairs and beg Lady Eastcott to lend her the money to return to Ireland —anything, at the moment, appearing preferable to the anomalous magnificence of her present position—when there was a tap on the door and Miss Standfield entered.

"May I come in?" Miss Standfield was already in, a somewhat austerely regal figure in a purple-bloom morning dress and a neat lace cap, surveying with mild interest the rather flushed young lady who had jumped up to face her. "I am the bearer," Miss Standfield continued, "of a message for you, my dear—but first, if you please, we shall have a few moments' conversation together."

"Yes, ma'am—*comme vous voulez*," Victoire said, looking enquiring and colouring still more deeply. "If it is that Lady Eastcott wishes me to go away—"

"Not in the least. I am not come from Lady Eastcott, but from Lord Tarn. He wishes to see you in the Small Saloon as soon as may be convenient." Miss Standfield, watching the vivid young face before her, saw puzzlement appear upon it at this announcement, and what seemed a certain apprehension as well, and went on to enquire, in a somewhat altered voice, "Are you—afraid of Lord Tarn, Miss Duvenay?"

"Afraid?" Victoire looked surprised. "But no—why should I be?"

Miss Standfield's eyes did not leave her face. "He has, you know, a somewhat ungovernable temper," she remarked. "I am a reasonably acute observer, and the expression upon your face when I mentioned that he desired an interview with you—"

"Oh!" A look of enlightenment superseded the expression that had interested Miss Standfield. "Well, I *am* afraid, you see," Victoire conceded, "that he will not *quite* like me to go back to Ireland, because he says that my cousin Fitzhugh will not be there, and that there will be bailiffs in the house; but one sees for oneself that there is nothing else for me to do. And, as I have told him, I have been taught very well to cook and sew and to be useful in the house—no, no, it is quite true," she said earnestly, as she saw an expression of slight skepticism cross Miss Standfield's face. "In France a *jeune fille bien élevée* must learn such things, Madame Rollon always said, not like the English young ladies who learn only to play upon the piano and paint in water colours. And so I am quite sure that my cousin's housekeeper, who is a very respectable person and very *bienveillante*, will be able to find work for me until my cousin returns or *Maman* sends for me to go to America." She shrugged her shoulders philosophically. "Lord Tarn will no doubt scold me, but I shall not regard it," she announced. "Men are very stupid sometimes—are they not, Mademoiselle? They do not consider enough the practicality."

Miss Standfield, looking somewhat astonished by this large-minded observation, agreed that it was indeed so, and said that she was happy to learn that the Marquis's displeasure held no terrors for Miss Duvenay.

"Oh, no!" said that young lady seriously. "You see, I quite understand how it is when he becomes enraged, because *moi*, I have a very bad temper, too."

"Indeed!" said Miss Standfield, looking fascinated by these additional disclosures. "One can only hope, in that case, that you do not murder each other"—with which cryptic remark she led the way out of the room and down the stairs, leaving Victoire to ponder its meaning as she followed her.

At the foot of the stairs Miss Standfield halted and turned again to her young companion.

"My child, there is one more thing that I wish to say to you before you see Lord Tarn," she said. "If you should feel that the future he proposes for you is in the least distasteful, do not hesitate to inform him of it and then come directly to me. Do you understand that?"

"Yes, Mademoiselle." The look of puzzlement was again on Victoire's face. "But if he has truly thought of something practical for me to do—"

"Something eminently practical," Miss Standfield said dryly. "But remember what I have told you. If it does not please you, come to me."

She then pointed out to Victoire the door of the Small Saloon and departed, leaving Victoire to enter it alone.

She found Tarn standing looking out the window with an air of impatience, as if he would have much preferred being outdoors on this fine spring morning to being obliged to conduct the interview to which he had summoned her.

111

"Oh, there you are!" he said, swinging around as she came into the room. "What took you so long? Didn't Cousin Amelia tell you I wanted to speak with you?"

"Yes, she did."

Victoire looked at him enquiringly, as if wondering whether she should seat herself or not. His lordship responded by motioning her to a chair, but he did not sit down himself. He remained standing instead before the window, looking at her with a half-rueful expression upon his face.

"Lord, I thought this would be easy, but the point is, I've never done it before!" he said. He paused and went on after a moment, "Did Cousin Amelia tell you why I wanted to see you?"

"She said you had a plan to propose for my future," Victoire said helpfully. "And I do not at all see why it should embarrass you to speak of it, for I shall be grateful for *any* position, however menial."

"It isn't menial in the least!" Tarn said, looking stung. "It's—I want you to marry me, brat!"

"To—*marry* you?" Victoire repeated the words in the politely incredulous tone of one who was quite certain that she could not have heard aright. "*Pardon*, my lord; you wished to say—?"

"I wished to say exactly what you heard me say!" Tarn said, not best pleased, it seemed, by this response to his announcement. "And don't turn missish and pretend that you don't understand me! I've made up my mind that it's the best solution to your problem."

"The best solution to my problem!" Victoire looked dazed. "The best—!" She broke off. "*Voyons*, you are quite mad," she said, with conviction. "A blow—several blows upon the head—"

The Marquis appeared to be mastering his temper with some difficulty. "Young Victoire," he said dangerously, "don't provoke me! There is nothing amiss with my head—except,

perhaps, in taking the idea into it that we should deal together!
I thought you were a sensible girl."

"I am. *Very* sensible," Victoire said firmly. "That is why I am
quite sure you are either mad or drunk, my lord. If you were
not, you would know very well that it is entirely unsuitable,
what you are proposing. *D'ailleurs,* you are not in love with
me."

The Marquis looked at her in exasperation. "What the deuce
has that to say to anything?" he demanded. "You need some
provision made for your future; I need a wife—or I shall need
one by the time you've grown up enough to want children—if
only to make sure that my cousin Bruce don't step into my
father's room some day. From what I know of you, I thought I
might deal with you better than with some simpering female
paraded by her mother at Almack's, but if you mean to be as
dashed contrary as this—"

He broke off. Victoire, seated very erect before him, her
hands clasped lightly together in her lap, looked at him, a wise
expression appearing suddenly upon her young face.

"I see," she said slowly. "We are to make a *mariage de
convenance.*" She drew a deep breath and then nodded decisively. "Very well. I will not be contrary, my lord," she said. "It
shall be as you wish. I will marry you—if you are very sure that
that *is* what you wish."

"Of course I am sure!" Tarn said impatiently. "Why should I
have asked you if I weren't?"

"Then—very well," Victoire said again, and, rising, she
went to him and held out her hand for him to take, as if it were a
grave little ritual solemnising the agreement between them.
Tarn, with a slight awkwardness that would very much have
astonished any of his intimates, well acquainted with his
lordship's easy address with females, took it and dropped a
light kiss upon the brow expectantly upturned to him.

"There!" he said. "That's settled then. My cousin
Amelia—Miss Standfield, that is—has agreed to take you up to

113

London with her, where the first thing she must do," he said, critically surveying the very plainly clad figure of his promised bride, "is to buy you some clothes, it seems. After that she will see to it that you are properly introduced into the *ton*, and then, in a month or so, we'll announce our betrothal formally and be married. The whole thing will be a devilish bore, I don't doubt, but it won't do to have you set upon by every poison-tongued prattle-box in London, so we shall have to make it appear that you are as respectable as they are."

"I *am* respectable," Victoire said indignantly. "*Very* respectable!"

"Well, I'm not," his lordship said frankly. He looked down at the little figure before him. "I'm a bad lot, you know," he said suddenly. "Anyone will tell you that. But it won't be a bad bargain for you, brat. You'll be a marchioness—I daresay you will like that—and I haven't run through my fortune yet, in spite of what the gossips will tell you."

Victoire smiled, wrinkling her brow and looking suddenly very young. "A marchioness?" she repeated experimentally. "Not a *marquise? Tiens, c'est bien drôle,* my lord!"

Tarn grinned. "Droll it is," he agreed. "And not *my lord.* Lewis."

"Lewis." She considered. "That is your name? It is very odd to become betrothed to someone whose name you do not know."

"Well, you know it now," Tarn said. He took her arm. "Come along; I must talk to Cousin Amelia," he said. "She goes up to London with my aunt and uncle in a day or two, I believe, and there'll be matters for me to settle with her before she does."

These matters, it appeared, when they presently ran Miss Standfield to earth in the morning parlour, engaged with an intricate piece of embroidery set out upon her tambour-frame, were chiefly financial, for his lordship obviously took it for granted that his previous announcement of his intentions towards Miss Duvenay precluded the necessity of his putting his cousin out of any suspense under which she had been labouring by informing her of the successful outcome of his suit. He simply told her that, since she would no doubt be put to considerable expense in the entertaining she would be obliged to do in presenting Miss Duvenay to Society, he wished she would send him a Dutch reckoning of what it came to and he would dub up the possibles, adding that, as he relied on her to see to it as well that Victoire was properly rigged out for her introduction into the *ton*, she would of course add such things as milliners' and mantua-makers' bills to the lot.

Miss Standfield, putting aside her tambour-frame to bend a mild scrutiny upon the newly engaged pair, responded to this by enquiring of Victoire if she was quite satisfied with the arrangements that had been made for her future.

"Oh, yes!" said Victoire, with such a glowing look upon her face as she turned towards the Marquis that Miss Standfield's mind was at once relieved of any lingering doubt that undue pressure had had to be exerted upon her to cause her to accede to his lordship's suit. The Marquis, however, failed to note it, and merely said that if that was settled then, all right and tight, he'd best be getting back to Tarn House.

Miss Standfield raised a commanding forefinger. "One moment, Lewis," she said. "It has possibly escaped your notice that your future bride is obviously under age, so that the consent of her parent or guardian must be obtained before she can be married to you." She turned to Victoire. "Are you aware, my dear," she enquired kindly, "whether your mama and stepfather made you the legal ward of your cousin when they placed you in his care?"

Victoire, looking a little anxious, said she was sure they had not, and she was also quite sure they would not object to her marrying a marquis—"though *Maman* would no doubt like it even better if he were a duke," she said, "for she met one once, before she met Papa, who wished very much to marry her only his family would not permit it, and she was forever telling me, after Papa died, how splendid it would have been if they had. So I think she will be very pleased if I marry Lord—Lewis," she corrected herself, smiling a little self-consciously but very warmly at her betrothed.

Miss Standfield said dryly that she too was very sure that her mama would be pleased, but that all the same it was customary for a more formal consent to be obtained.

"Yes, but that's nonsense in this case," Tarn said impatiently. "If her mother and stepfather have disappeared—"

"My dear Lewis," said Miss Standfield calmly, "do not fly into one of your pelters with me. I shall consult Dilworth"—naming her solicitor, an elderly gentleman of wide experience and long service to the Standfield family—"who will no doubt be able either to locate Madame—Rollon, is it?—or, failing that, inform us of the proper steps to be taken to ensure the legality of any marriage Victoire enters into; for not even the law," she concluded, with Royalty's superb accustomedness to going its own road, "can expect a young lady to remain a spinster until her most marriageable years are all but past simply because she has the misfortune to be separated from her parents."

The Marquis, who had implicit faith in his elderly relation's ability to come up, if necessary, with an Act of Parliament sanctioning his marriage to Victoire or some equally awe-inspiring document of an ecclesiastical nature from one of the several bishops with whom she was acquainted, said with satisfaction that he would leave the matter in her hands then, and thereupon took himself off with the most offhand of adieux to his betrothed, which caused Miss Standfield to remark rather acidly that it was obvious something would have to be done to recall him to a sense of the proper behaviour he owed his prospective bride, or no one in London would be taken in to believe that his intentions towards her were serious.

She repeated this observation some time later to Lady Eastcott, whom she found in her dressing room in conference with her housekeeper. That worthy dame having been dismissed, Miss Standfield proceeded to inform her cousin of the Marquis's betrothal, which news Lady Eastcott received with the doleful comment that she expected it was for the best, since it at least meant that he would not marry the girl at once. She added that it had been very clever of Miss Standfield to have succeeded in postponing the matter by offering to take Miss Duvenay with her to London.

"Not Miss Duvenay. Victoire," Miss Standfield reminded her imperturbably. "We must accustom ourselves to calling her so, as she is to be one of the family, Eleanor. She is a charming child, I find—a very bright, coming little thing, exactly the sort of wife one might wish for Tarn."

Lady Eastcott's mouth opened. "Exactly the sort of—!" she gasped. "Amelia, have you run mad? This—this little *intrigueuse,* of no background, no family—!"

"On the contrary, she is neither an *intrigueuse* nor a person of no background," Miss Standfield replied, as calmly as before. "I am, you are aware, reasonably well acquainted with my Debrett's, and it informs me that the Duvenays are a very ancient Norman-Irish family of excellent blood, the head of the family holding the rank of baron. No doubt this child's cousin, Mr. Fitzhugh Duvenay, may be considered in the light of a blot upon the family escutcheon, but that is in no way a reflection upon *her.*"

Lady Eastcott still appeared stunned. "Yes, yes, that is all very well!" she managed to say at last. "But it still does not alter the fact that she is in no way a suitable wife for Tarn!"

"And, pray," said Miss Standfield rather tartly, "what sort of female *would* you consider a suitable wife for him? No, no, do not trouble yourself to answer that question, for I am quite aware of the young person you would describe to me—a girl of impeccable birth and breeding, properly educated, with all the accomplishments suitable for the exalted position she will hold

117

in Society—and I will tell you to your head that there is no more likelihood that Lewis will be brought to the altar with such a paragon than that he will fly to the moon! We have a choice—of this I am *quite* sure—of seeing him continue in the way of life he has been following these past half dozen years, marrying at last, if he does so at all, some rapacious female clever enough to persuade him to legalise the improper connexion between them—or Victoire. *She* at least is virtuous, intelligent, and of respectable family. She will not disgrace him, my dear, though whether he will disgrace *her* is, I fear, another matter."

Lady Eastcott continued to look her amazement; but she had been for too long accustomed to respect her elderly cousin's perspicacity not to be swayed by her reasoning. There was no flaw, she was obliged to admit, in Miss Standfield's argument. Miss Duvenay was certainly presentable, and obviously too young and innocent to be a hardened schemer who had cunningly succeeded in entrapping the Marquis, and if Miss Standfield vouched for her antecedents—

Lady Eastcott flung up her hands. "Well, I am sure I do not know what to think!" she confessed. "My head is in a whirl! Accept the girl—welcome her into the family—good heavens, what will Eastcott say? And Bruce was so sure that it was all merely a clever ruse of yours to gain time!"

"I daresay he was," said Miss Standfield, "for that is certainly what *he* desires. Surely, Eleanor, you cannot be such a ninnyhammer as not to realise that the last thing in the world Bruce desires is to see his cousin marry, and that he will do his possible to prevent it. I have not the least doubt that he has felt these six years that the life Lewis has been leading gave him every right to expect that some violent or imprudent act of his would lead to his death before he was thirty. And in that case—*voilà* Bruce Fearon, the new Marquis of Tarn. But *not*, my dear, if Tarn has a legal heir of his own body."

Lady Eastcott, with whom Mr. Fearon was a favourite, cried

out against the idea of his being so ill-natured as to hope for his cousin's early demise, and would have gone on for some time, in her usual rather featherheaded fashion, vacillating aloud over whether it was more to be desired for Tarn to marry Victoire than to have his life develop along the disagreeable lines sketched by Miss Standfield, had not Miss Standfield put an end to the conversation.

"I shall have a great deal to do if I am to go up to London tomorrow," she said. "And if you are worrying over what Eastcott will say to the affair, Eleanor, I suggest that you send him to me."

And she thereupon proceeded to leave the room, with a final word to the effect that she expected it might be better if the dress-party held to announce the engagement were given by the Eastcotts rather than by herself, as their town house was so much more commodious than her own.

11

Miss Standfield might speak disparagingly of the slim house in Albemarle Street that was her London home, but it was a very comfortable and elegant one, in spite of its lack of size. The death of a bachelor uncle, whose favourite niece she had been, had left her in middle life in possession of an ample fortune, so that she did not suffer from the necessity of relying upon the bounty of more affluent relations that burdened so many other single females. She was able to occupy herself very agreeably with a circle of acquaintances drawn chiefly from the most austere Court circles and with frequent visits to the country houses of her many relations, where she was invariably called upon to settle domestic difficulties or to restore peace to embattled households.

Upon arriving in London with Victoire, her first action was to send out cards for the small evening-party at which she planned to introduce her young charge into Society; her second, to take into her confidence her nephew, the Honourable

Marmaduke Standfield, the same who had been mentioned by Mr. Fearon as having been instrumental in arranging Tarn's affair with the odious Captain Fryde. Mr. Standfield was a young gentleman of much the same years as the Marquis, but, unlike him, an accredited Tulip of the Ton, whose knowledge of the latest fashions and *divertissements* of the younger set was universally held to be unexcelled; and to him Miss Standfield, with a regal disregard for any reservations he himself might have felt in the matter, intended to entrust the task of acting as mentor to her young protégée's inexperience when she took her first steps in Society.

"Which I am sure, Marmaduke, you will be most happy to do," she said, when, having summoned him to Albemarle Street, she informed him of what she had planned for him.

Mr. Standfield, who was more noted for his exquisite manners than for any breadth of intellect, said obligingly that it would be his pleasure; but the news that his cousin was contemplating matrimony had drawn a frown of puzzlement to his face, and he remarked politely after a moment that he fancied he must have misunderstood his aunt somewhere along the line, as it had seemed to him that she had said it was Tarn who was to marry the young lady.

"That is exactly what I meant to imply," Miss Standfield said.

"But he can't be—he won't—dash it, not Tarn!" Mr. Standfield said incredulously. "Must be confusing him with some other fellow, ma'am! Know for a fact he don't want to get married. Told me so only the other day!"

"He has since," Miss Standfield imperturbably remarked, "changed his mind. That is *not* the exclusive privilege, I may remind you, Marmaduke, of my sex. The young lady upon whom he has fixed his choice," she went on, "has been reared in France, and, owing to the present upset conditions in that country, finds herself temporarily parted from her family and under my care. It is my wish to provide her with a wardrobe suitable for her introduction into Society, and for that purpose we shall make a tour of the shops today. By 'we,' " she concluded, fixing Mr. Standfield with a commanding eye, "I naturally mean myself, Miss Duvenay, and you."

Mr. Standfield said that he would be honoured, but it was plain, from the expression upon his face, that he still doubted either his own ears or his aunt's total possession of her faculties. The entrance of Victoire at that moment served to drive him even further into a state of helpless incredulity. She was dressed to go out, in the very plain round frock she had been obliged to wear ever since she had arrived in it at Eastcott House, and even the fashionable hat she wore—one of Lady Eastcott's demurest possessions, lent her for the journey to London, a Lavinia chip tied with broad blue ribbons under the chin —could not conceal the artless simplicity of the young face beneath it.

Introduced to her by his aunt, Mr. Standfield drew valiantly upon his reputation for *savoir faire* and made her the graceful bow for which he was noted, but when Miss Standfield rose and announced that she would just put on her bonnet and gloves and they might then go, he looked after her as she walked from the room with some alarm upon his face, which was immediately increased by his awareness that Miss Duvenay was surveying him with frank curiosity, apparently much impressed by his exquisitely fitting coat of blue superfine, his intricately arranged cravat, and his chaste buttonhole of clovepinks.

"You are a cousin of Lord Tarn—*n'est-ce pas*?" she enquired politely. "*Tiens*, he has a great many relations, it seems!"

Mr. Standfield, disclaiming, said not more than most fellows, he dared say, and then, seized with the horrid idea that Miss Duvenay's remark might be construed as implying censure towards him for adding himself to a list that she apparently felt was too long already, observed palliatingly that the cousinship was a rather distant one.

"Tarn's grandfather married a Standfield," he explained. "Our fathers were first cousins. Never could figure out what that makes him and me, but nothing for you to worry about, I assure you!"

Victoire, examining his harried face with some puzzlement, assured *him* that it did not worry her in the least.

"It is only, you understand, that Miss Standfield tells me I must meet a great many people, and that it is necessary for me to remember exactly who they are, and if they are related to Lord Tarn," she confided to him. "And you must not think," she added kindly, seeing the cloud of bewilderment still upon his face, "that I will say such things to anyone but you. Miss Standfield says that you are very discreet, and that I am to be guided by you, since Lewis is not at all to be trusted to tell me the proper way to go on."

Mr. Standfield, looking rather stunned by this new responsibility, said that he would do his best, and ventured to ask where she had made the Marquis's acquaintance, and if she had known him long.

Miss Duvenay looked at him consideringly for a moment. "I do not *think,*" she decided at last, "that I am to tell you that. He is to be presented to me, you see, for the first time at the evening party Miss Standfield is to give as soon as I have the proper clothes, and then we will fall in love very quickly and become betrothed, so that everything will be quite *comme il faut—*"

The reappearance of Miss Standfield fortunately put an end to the conversation at this moment, for her nephew's confusion was by this time so complete that he was quite incapable of bearing his part in it in a satisfactory manner. Miss Standfield's landaulet was now at the door, and she directed her coachman to drive at once to the showrooms of a famous modiste in Bruton Street, observing to Mr. Standfield that, while she did not herself patronise Mme. Fanchon's establishment, she believed a great many of the younger members of the *ton* considered that lady's creations as being superior to any others to be found in London.

This Mr. Standfield was able to assure her was indeed so, and a very knowledgeable conversation between aunt and nephew thereupon ensued on the subject of the styles and colours of the present mode that might be most becoming to Miss Duvenay. Miss Standfield, reared in a period when strong colours were in vogue, was in favour of almond greens and cerulean blues, but the Honourable Marmaduke said firmly that the lighter tones were all the crack just now, and that amber or the palest of sea greens would set off Miss Duvenay's chestnut hair and very fair skin to far greater advantage.

This led to a discussion of her deplorable lack of height, and the lines of frock and scarf and pelerine that might make this sad defect less apparent, so that Victoire, who had begun by feeling quite set up in her own conceit by so many compliments dropped into her ears during the first minutes of the conversation, felt herself, by the time Bruton Street had been reached, to be a mean bit indeed, and walked into Mme. Fanchon's elegant establishment with a very dejected air.

The dejection, however, did not long remain. One glance in the mirror at the starry-eyed young lady in the gossamer gown of delicate sea-green gauze, open down the front over a slip of white satin and ornamented with tiny shell clasps, which Mr. Standfield had unhesitatingly chosen for her, and she felt she had been transformed into a fairy princess—"or at least a *marquise*," she confided earnestly to Mr. Standfield, when Mme. Fanchon was out of hearing. "*Au vrai*, do you think Lewis will like it? Do you think he will think that I look now like a—a marchioness?"

"What Lewis thinks," said Miss Standfield, surveying her with critical eyes, "is not of the least moment, my dear; what matters is what Society *thinks* he thinks. And, really, I believe this will do very well. Would you not say so, Marmaduke? Might not this toilette strike a susceptible young man like a *coup de foudre?*"

Mr. Standfield said feelingly that he was dashed well sure it would—a compliment that drew a pretty colour to Victoire's already glowing face. She had a Frenchwoman's love of clothes, and a natural quick eye and good taste that found her and Mr. Standfield in cordial agreement upon all matters of choice; and, indeed, had it not been for the uneasy feeling that all the finery being selected for her use must cost an appalling amount of money, she would have been entirely happy.

But her scruples in this regard were not shared by Miss Standfield, who told her coolly that the Marquis was well able to afford to buy a proper wardrobe for his bride—however *im*proper the notion of his doing so in place of her own family might be.

"And at least," she added, "it is less improper than his paying the milliners' and mantua-makers' bills of the sort of female of little virtue and considerable charm with whom gossip associates his name. I can see no reason why you should be set at a disadvantage in comparison with such females, my dear —which I can assure you one is in any gentleman's eyes if one looks a dowd."

Victoire, who had been surveying the effect in the mirror of a walking dress of fawn craped muslin with Circassian sleeves, turned to look at her seriously.

"*Eh bien,* you are no doubt quite right, Mademoiselle," she said. "One must sometimes not *faire des économies, n'est-ce pas?*"

"Exactly!" said Miss Standfield, looking quite unperturbed by Victoire's calm acceptance of a statement concerning her betrothed that would have driven most young ladies into wild blushes and shocked lamentations. Mr. Standfield, less well acquainted with Miss Duvenay, choked slightly, recovered himself valiantly, and said that they had better have the walking dress then, and the flat-crowned Villager hat that suited it so well, and went on with the serious task of completing his future cousin's wardrobe.

126

A visit to the Pantheon Bazaar—this time without the company of Mr. Standfield—allowed the two ladies the opportunity of purchasing those more intimate articles of apparel and toiletry of which Victoire stood in need, and they returned to Albemarle Street late in the day with the landaulet crowded with bandboxes of all sizes.

Miss Standfield had not planned a large party for Victoire's first appearance in Society, though her standing was such in select circles that even the many festivities of this Season of the Grand Peace Celebration would not have prevented her from filling her house on short notice with the cream of the *ton*, had she so desired. Lady Jersey, the acknowledged Queen of Almack's, had been invited—and, though she had read the card of invitation with a little *moue* of annoyance, having an idea that Miss Standfield meant to ask her to provide vouchers for that most exclusive of London clubs for the unknown young lady she was rumoured to have brought up to town with her, she had sent off a note of acceptance. And there was Lady Cowper, from the Melbourne House set, and Lord Petersham, Lady Sefton, Lord Alvanley—a small but splendid selection of the most tonnish names of London Society. All this, had Victoire known it, was quite a triumph for Miss Standfield; but to Victoire it meant nothing at all, and she would have accepted with equanimity the regrets of Lord Alvanley, Lady Jersey, and all the other fashionables so carefully collected for her benefit, as long as she had been assured that Tarn would not fail, her own chief interest lying simply in an agreeable daydream of bursting upon the Marquis's view, like the *coup de foudre* Miss Standfield had predicted, in the sea-green gauze with the tiny shell clasps ornamenting the bodice.

And to say the truth, when she had been arrayed for the evening in this gown, and her bright curls dressed *à l'anglaise*, with charming simplicity, by Miss Standfield's very competent dresser, she looked so different from the plainly arrayed young lady who had arrived in London from Eastcott Park that even

Miss Standfield was moved to say that she would do very well indeed.

Miss Standfield had the satisfaction of seeing her own opinion of her protégée mirrored in the eyes of her guests when they began arriving in Albemarle Street a short time later. Mr. Bruce Fearon, who had been obliged, owing to a press of engagements, to leave Eastcott Park on the morning after Victoire's arrival there, so that he had not previously been presented to her, apparently found *his* first impression of the young lady who was destined to be his cousin's bride a favourable one, at any rate, for he murmured a very pretty compliment to her as he bowed over her fingers.

"*Bien sûr!* You are the cousin, M'sieur Fearon," Victoire said, surveying him for her own part with the utmost frankness, and puzzling to know what it was that made Tarn so cordially dislike this excessively civil, handsome young man.

Mr. Fearon's brows rose slightly. "*That* sounds suspiciously as if you have heard of me," he remarked calmly, "and if it was from Lewis, I fear it can have been no good."

"From—Lewis?"

Victoire, recollecting her rôle, tried to look at a loss, but Mr. Fearon only laughed.

"No, no—I am acquainted with your secret, *ma chère*," he said. "You need not trouble to play your part in this little comedy for *me*. But here is your Prince Charming now," he added rather sardonically, as he saw Tarn walking into the room, looking, as usual, an unconscionably wild hawk in a gathering of tamer birds, and perfectly unconscious of the flutter he was causing among them. "Now I mustn't miss this pretty little scene. May I station myself just—here?"

He took up his position, disregarding Miss Standfield's slight frown of disapproval, where he could have a full view of the proceedings as Tarn strolled up to his hostess and bowed over her hand.

"So good of you to come, Lewis," Miss Standfield said, in

such a very ordinary-sounding voice that Victoire, whose heart had given a distinct jump at his lordship's approach, was able to meet his eyes with an almost equal appearance of polite interest. "Victoire, my dear, may I present my cousin, Lord Tarn? Miss Duvenay, Lewis, who is staying with me at present—"

The Marquis bowed and took Victoire's hand, looking at her with an expression of mingled amusement and gravity that almost overset her composure. She smiled at him, mischief in her own eyes now, and said demurely, "*Je suis enchantée,* my lord."

"Not enchant*ed.* Enchant*ing,*" Tarn corrected her with great aplomb, and would have gone on, but he was interrupted at that moment by a little feminine shriek of surprise behind him.

"Lewis!" said the young lady who had uttered it—a very pretty brunette in a rather daringly diaphanous gown of pink silk, her curls arranged in the fashion known as the Sappho. "What in the world are *you* doing here? Of all places to run across you!"

"Your remark, Ernestine, is scarcely flattering to me," Miss Standfield observed, presenting to Victoire Lady Eastcott's newly married daughter, Lady Whittingham, and the latter's husband, a serious-looking gentleman of some thirty years. "Pray, why should you not find Lewis in my drawing room? If he has deigned to give up for at least one evening the frequenting of such places as Cribb's Parlour and the Daffy Club —which are, I understand, among the more respectable of his usual haunts—in favour of honouring us with his presence here, I am sure we should not be astonished, for he *has,* you must know, attained the age of reason."

Lady Whittingham giggled, and said that was no doubt true, but that it still seemed odd to see her cousin at a gathering where there was to be nothing more exciting than whist to entertain him. She then turned her attention to Victoire, saying that she had heard from her mama, Lady East-cott, that she had only recently arrived in England, and enquiring how she liked London.

"I like it very much," said Victoire, gathering thankfully, from Lady Whittingham's words, that Lady Eastcott had at least not confided her secret to *her*.

Lord Whittingham, who appeared to make up by the sobriety of his own demeanour for the obvious volatility of his wife's, then asked if she had yet seen the Elgin Marbles, or visited Somerset House to view Mr. Lawrence's latest works, both of which exhibitions, he assured her, she would find instructive and entertaining.

"No, I have not," Victoire began; but she was interrupted at once by Tarn, who said ruthlessly, "You'll want an ice, Miss Duvenay—curst hot in here!"—and dragged her off with him without ceremony.

Lady Whittingham stared after them in lively astonishment. "*Well!*" she said. "I must say I have never seen Lewis take such an instant fancy to a *nice* girl! Not that she isn't excessively pretty—but she is not at all in his style, you know! Who *is* she, Cousin Amelia?"

Miss Standfield replied that she was Colonel John Duvenay's daughter—a statement which meant nothing at all to Lady Whittingham, but which her husband undertook to expatiate upon to her at such length that she at last grew bored and said, really, it was quite unfashionable for husbands and wives to take so much notice of each other in public, and wasn't that dear Emily Cowper just coming in the door? She then rustled off in a cloud of pink silk draperies, and had soon, along with Lady Cowper, established a sort of court at the far end of the room, where they attracted all the younger gentlemen like moths to a flame.

Meanwhile, Tarn had borne Victoire off into the next room, procured an ice for her and a glass of champagne for himself, and asked her how she was getting on.

"Oh, quite splendidly!" she said, looking up at him with her face flushed with the excitement of her first party and her pleasure at being in his company. "Mademoiselle has been very kind, and we have gone shopping and bought so many things that I cannot remember them all to tell you, but there is a gown of Indian muslin—oh, *tout à fait ravissante!*—which Mademoiselle says I may wear to my first ball. Only we have spent a great deal of money—oh, a great deal!" she assured him, a worried look momentarily crossing her face. "But Mademoiselle said that it was quite all right and that you would not be cross."

Tarn laughed. "No, I'm not cross, brat," he said. "Not when my blunt is spent to such good purpose! How do you like London?"

Victoire said that she liked it very much indeed. "And I have seen the Prince Regent driving in the Park," she said, "and the Tsar's sister, and St. Paul's Cathedral, and Mr. Standfield drove us out to see the Florida Gardens—"

She went chattering happily on, made voluble by the heady excitement of her first party and the Marquis's presence, until he said at last, in some amusement, "Here, draw bridle, infant! I only asked you how you liked London, not for a catalogue of all your rakings! It seems to me that you may be going to turn into one of these rattle-tongued females one can't get in a word with."

"No—*truly*?" She turned a penitent face to him. "I am sorry. It has been so very long, you see, since I had such exciting things happen to me. But I will be very quiet now, and let you talk entirely." She folded her hands primly in her lap and looked at him hopefully. "Mademoiselle says that gentlemen like always to talk a great deal of themselves," she offered.

"Mademoiselle," he said, "knows a deal too much. But I can't find fault with her, since she has treated you so handsomely—to say nothing of rigging you out in such prime style. You look very well tonight, you know."

"Yes, I do, don't I?" Victoire said, looking down at the gossamer folds of the sea-green gown with a complacency directed so entirely at her frock instead of at herself that the gleam of amusement appeared upon Tarn's face again. "Only it was not Mademoiselle who chose this gown for me, you know," she continued. "It was Mr. Standfield."

"*Duke*? How the devil did that come about?" demanded his lordship, looking not best pleased by this piece of news.

"You do not like it?" Victoire wrinkled her brow. "Mademoiselle asked him to go with us to the shops, because she says he has very good taste, and is discreet, and will tell me how I am to go on. But if you do not like it," she offered generously, "I will not let him tell me anything. *You* may tell me, instead."

Tarn grinned rather ruefully, his good humour returning. "No," he said, "Cousin Amelia is right. If you're guided by me, young Victoire, ten to one you'll land in the basket."

"Then I shall like being in the basket, wherever that is," said Victoire firmly.

"No, you wouldn't! You'd be devilish uncomfortable, with all the tabbies in London shaking their heads and whispering in corners over you the way they do over little Caro Lamb. Duke's your man to rely on; if *he* says something is the thing for you to do, you do it, and you'll get on famously."

Victoire appeared about to contest the point for a moment, but, recollecting the compliment that had inspired this slight contretemps, said magnanimously that, since he liked her gown, she did not regret now having allowed Mr. Standfield to choose it.

"And you, too," she assured him, turning admiring eyes upon his excellently cut black coat and snowy white neckcloth, which he had allowed his valet to arrange in the intricately fashionable style known as the Mathematical, "look very nice tonight, I think. I have never seen you so—so *à la mode*, and I like it very much indeed."

He gave a shout of laughter, which drew the attention of those near him—or it might be said to have done so if it had not been for the fact that most of his fellow guests had already had their attention riveted by the extraordinary sight of the Marquis of Tarn bestowing his undivided interest upon a very young and obviously very innocent female. Lady Jersey, who was among those observing this phenomenon, presently carried her curiosity concerning it to Lady Eastcott, beside whom she seated herself on a three-backed settee of lacquered wood and cane in the front drawing room.

"Now, my dear Nell," she begged, behind the cover of her play with the delicately pierced and gilded fan she carried, "do tell me—*what* has come over Tarn? Positively, no one expected to meet him in such a totally *respectable* place as dear Miss Standfield's house, with that latest dreadful mischief of his but just hushed up—and now he caps the mystery by dancing attendance upon a chit who looks to be scarcely out of the schoolroom! Can it be that he has decided to mend his ways at last?"

Lady Eastcott, who had been torn one way and another by the conflicting opinions of the various members of her family ever since Tarn had announced his intention of marrying Miss Duvenay, could have wished that Lady Jersey, an inveterate chatterbox, known to the more satirical of her friends as Silence, had not asked her this question, for she had no idea how to answer it. She was rescued from her dilemma by Mr. Fearon, who had been standing near enough to overhear Lady Jersey's remarks, and who turned to enter the conversation at this point with the languid words, "You are speaking of Tarn, I collect, Sally dear—this latest freak of his? Surely you are well enough acquainted with him, or with his reputation, at least, for he has not, I think, spent enough time in polite circles to make himself as well known to ladies of the *ton* as he is to our—shall I say, West End comets?—to realise that he is never content unless he is causing a stir. Perhaps it suits him to be

133

.

particular in his attentions to this little nobody tonight to set the gossips' tongues wagging on a new tune—or it may even be that he is doing it on a wager: he is an incorrigible gamester, you know!"

Lady Jersey laughed. "I daresay you are right," she said. "Who is the girl? I have not seen her before, I think."

"The daughter of an Irish soldier of fortune. I cannot conceive why Cousin Amelia has chosen to take her up; but she, too, as you know, my dear, has her eccentricities."

Lady Jersey made one of her quick, restless gestures, her bracelets tinkling. "She had best keep her away from Tarn, then, if she has her interests at heart," she said. "Not, I daresay, that he means anything by this; he is far too occupied, it would seem, with one of your West End comets, Bruce. I see you know whom I mean—yes, the same he flaunted so boldly at the theatre before his hurried departure for foreign shores. I saw her driving in the Park this afternoon in an elegant new barouche lined with pale-blue satin, quite in the style of the notorious Miss Wilson's—and the *on-dit* is that she charmed it out of Tarn's pocket."

She rose and went off, to be surrounded at once by a dozen of her acquaintance, and Mr. Fearon sat down in the place she had occupied beside Lady Eastcott.

"And that," he said resignedly, "is what I daresay we shall have to look forward to until Lewis tires of this latest notion he has taken. The chit is very well, by the way, Aunt—a most attractive bud of promise; but I do not think that she will hold *his* interest."

"Do you truly believe so?" Lady Eastcott looked rather distracted. "I wish I could think so, for I can tell you that Eastcott does not like the scheme at all. He flew into one of his pelters tonight and positively refused to come here to meet the girl; I was obliged to tell Amelia a dreadful Canterbury tale about his being in the gout. But *she* is so positive that Tarn will marry the child, and that it will be all for the best—"

Mr. Fearon showed his white teeth in a faint, condescending smile. "It is a sad fact, I believe, my dear," he said, "that our esteemed relation is becoming somewhat superannuated. Oh, I am aware that she once had a reputation for astuteness—but surely this latest fancy of hers is clear proof that she is no longer, mentally, what she was. Eastcott is quite right: it is outrageous of her to foster this marriage."

"But what are we to do?" Lady Eastcott demanded in despair. "You have told me yourself that arguing with Lewis will only make him more determined to marry the girl!"

"And so it will," Mr. Fearon agreed. "But how many more evenings such as this, ma'am, do you think he will endure before he begins to wish himself well out of this affair? I am convinced that we can well leave *that* aspect of it to time, and if we can only succeed in offering him a suitable arrangement for Miss Duvenay's future that does not involve his marrying her himself—" He broke off, his eye suddenly taken by the sight of Lady Whittingham's pink draperies fluttering past as she crossed to the other side of the room. "Yes—that might do very well," he said after a moment, thoughtfully. He turned again to his aunt. "Tell me," he enquired, "are you acquainted with a young man named Swanton?"

"Swanton?" Lady Eastcott looked perplexed. "I don't believe—"

"Probably you are not," Mr. Fearon said. "But I am sure that Tina is, for I met him at one of her squeezes only a few weeks past. Not that he is at all accustomed to moving in such circles, but his father, it seems, is a man of considerable importance in the city, and was able to be of some assistance to Whittingham recently in a matter of business. I believe the elder Swanton is ambitious to establish his son in Society, and Tina's card of invitation was by way of being a *quid pro quo.*"

"Yes, but what on earth has all this to say to Tarn's marrying Miss Duvenay?" Lady Eastcott demanded, still looking much perplexed.

Mr. Fearon smiled a trifle impatiently. "Merely this, ma'am," he said, "that young Mr. Swanton, whose prospects are certainly such that he need not consider fortune when he marries, is hanging out for a wife whose antecedents lack the smell of the shop, a wife holding the entrée into the world of the *ton*. Now here, on the other hand, we have little Miss Duvenay, who is sadly in need of a wealthy husband, and who, as Miss Standfield's protégée, will appear to men as ignorant of Society as the Swantons to be exactly the sort of tonnish young female they are hopeful of snaring—"

Lady Eastcott looked at him, an expression of dawning comprehension upon her face.

"Oh!" she said. "You *are* so clever, Bruce! You mean, if we could succeed in promoting a match between Mr. Swanton and Miss Duvenay—"

"Precisely so. I have been casting about in my mind ever since Tarn broached this nonsensical scheme for a proper candidate to replace him in the girl's—er—affections, and have come up with two or three other ideas, but none, I think, so promising as this. Swanton is exactly the sort of self-conscious young puppy who can be led about by the nose by a man of address, and if Miss Duvenay is not ready enough to accept his hand and fortune when she sees Tarn cooling to the idea of offering her *his*, I shall own myself very much surprised." He looked at Lady Eastcott. "But you, ma'am," he warned her, "must do your possible, as I must, to bring this about."

"Oh, I will do anything!" Lady Eastcott assured him fervently. "You can have no notion how disagreeable Eastcott has been over this affair. I vow I have had him in the sulks the entire week!"

"Then persuade Tina to send cards to young Swanton and Miss Duvenay for the dress-party she is giving on Monday," Mr. Fearon advised. "That will do for a beginning. It is very short notice, but if we are to act to settle the matter in time we had best begin at once." He rose, a cynical look momentarily marring the smiling civility of the expression he kept for social gatherings. "And I do *not* think," he concluded, "that—short notice or no—we need concern ourselves over the possibility that either Mr. Swanton or Miss Duvenay will refuse the invitation. Shall I predict that, on the contrary, they will both be *aux anges* on receiving it? And then, ma'am, we shall begin to play out our little comedy—for the benefit, one devoutly hopes, of all concerned!"

However well Mr. Fearon's prediction concerning the reception of Lady Whittingham's card of invitation at the imposing house in Marylebone recently erected by the elder Mr. Swanton was borne out, it was certain that Victoire received hers with a sunny indifference that would have surprised Mr. Fearon if he had seen it—an indifference that persisted until she had been informed by Miss Standfield that Tarn would also be at the Whittinghams' on Monday evening. This Miss Standfield had taken care to assure, first by ascertaining from Lady Whittingham that a card of invitation had been sent to Tarn, and then by dispatching word to the Marquis that she expected him to escort her and Victoire on that evening to Berkeley Square, where the Whittinghams had their town house.

The Marquis, who had planned a very different sort of evening for himself, including a rump and dozen at Long's with a party of sporting friends whose tastes were apt to lead them to entertain themselves later with a visit to the back-slums of

Tothill Fields, where they would fraternise with the roughest elements of society in reeking gin shops, or join them in looking on at a badger-baiting or a cockfight, grimaced when he received the missive containing this command; but he did not disregard it. Instead, with exemplary obedience he excused himself to his friends and presented himself in Albemarle Street at the appointed hour; but his resignation of what he considered an evening's prime sport in favour of spending several hours of boredom in hot, overcrowded rooms at his cousin's dress-party did not improve his disposition, and he had not even a compliment for Victoire as she came running downstairs to greet him in all the splendour of her first ball gown—a ravishing creation of Indian muslin adorned with knots of fern-green ribbon.

She stopped short at the foot of the staircase, regarding him with a crestfallen look.

"*Eh bien*, you do not like it?" she asked.

"Like what?"

Miss Standfield, coming downstairs in a more leisurely manner, followed by her dresser bearing a light pelisette to be thrown over her gown of purple-bloom satin, was in time to overhear his lordship's impatient question. She said to him calmly, "The child is speaking of her gown, Lewis. It is customary, you understand, to compliment a lady upon her appearance when she is wearing a new gown and has taken particular pains to appear to advantage."

The Marquis shrugged indifferently. "Oh, if it's compliments you are after," he said, "you had better have asked Duke to escort you."

"*Moi*, I do not care for compliments," Victoire asserted stoutly. "I think they are very silly—only," she added, looking rather anxiously at Tarn, "I do not wish to embarrass you by being not—not *tout à fait à la mode* when I go into company with you."

"Embarrass him!" said Miss Standfield scornfully. "My dear

child, it is you who are embarrassed by being obliged to accept the escort of a gentleman—I use the word solely in acknowledgement of your rank, Tarn—who has made such an unenviable reputation for himself that your merely appearing in public with him must subject you to disagreeable gossip."

"Then I wonder you *didn't* ask Duke to escort you!" retorted the Marquis, now looking thunderous in good earnest.

Miss Standfield, who had Royalty's habit of complete disregard for the presence of servants, was about to give him a reply in kind when both she and the Marquis were startled out of their quarrel by the sight of Victoire rounding upon her benefactress like a small tigress.

"Now you have made him angry, Mademoiselle—and for what?" she exclaimed, her hazel eyes sparkling. "A stupid compliment that I did not wish at all! He is very *gentil* to come with us tonight, I think, when there are no doubt many other things he would rather do instead, and you must not vex him so!"

"Hoity-toity! *Must* not!" said Miss Standfield, drawing herself up and preparing to transfer her fire to Victoire; but Tarn intervened, a gleam of laughter springing into his black eyes, erasing the coldness that had been there.

"No, no!" he said. "Your quarrel is with me, ma'am, not with Victoire, even though it seems she has constituted herself my champion." He took the shawl of Norwich silk that Victoire was carrying and placed it about her shoulders. "Come along, infant," he admonished her. "And *don't* get in the way of thinking you must fight my battles for me; it's embarrassing to a man of my inches to have such a small protectress."

She chuckled, her face happy once more as she saw the lightening of his humour.

"If you do not like it, I will try not to do it; but it is very hard to be silent, you see, when people are not just to you," she confided, as they went past the bowing butler and out the front door to where Miss Standfield's landaulet was awaiting them.

When they had settled themselves inside, Victoire ventured to inform his lordship that Mr. Standfield had been so obliging as to come to Albemarle Street and give her some much-needed instruction in the dances currently popular in London.

"For there is to be dancing tonight at Lady Whittingham's party," she said, "and I was very ignorant of such things, *bien entendu.* But he says now that I go on very well, and that he will not be at all afraid to ask me to stand up with him tonight, and I thought—I thought—"

She broke off, peeping up at Tarn expectantly from under her lashes.

"You thought you might entrap a second partner in me?" Tarn asked, his voice disobliging, and the mischief in his eyes hidden by the darkness.

"Yes, please—if you would not dislike it very much," Victoire said doubtfully.

"Child, he is teasing you," Miss Standfield said. "You will have a dozen partners—never fear!—and Lewis among them, I dare swear."

"Perhaps," agreed Tarn. "If she will promise not to tread upon my toes—"

"But *naturellement* I shall not!" Victoire said indignantly. "Duke says I am very—very *adroite.*"

"Oh, so it's *Duke* now, is it? And I thought he was such a high stickler!"

"You do not wish me to call him so?" Victoire's voice was anxious again. "He said it was quite *convenable*—but not yet in public—because we are to be cousins, you see."

The Marquis was beginning to reply in a tone of virtuous disapproval, but Miss Standfield interrupted to inform him severely that it was too bad of him to take advantage of the child's inexperience, and that if he meant to do his best to shake her self-confidence before her first ball she would request him to refrain from any further conversation with her.

"But I *like* him to talk to me, Mademoiselle!" Victoire protested, thereby causing the Marquis to burst into genuine laughter, so that by the time the carriage drew up in Berkeley Square an atmosphere of entire good humour reigned within it.

The street outside Lord Whittingham's house was already crowded when they arrived, the sweating coachmen being obliged to force a laborious way for their vehicles through the crush of onlookers drawn by the expectation of seeing many of the foreign notables now in London for the Grand Peace Celebration. As the landaulet took its place in the stream of arriving carriages, each halting in turn to discharge its cargo of elegantly gowned, bejewelled ladies, and gentlemen blazoned with orders or attired in splendid dress uniforms of every conceivable style, Victoire's eyes grew large with excitement.

"*Mon Dieu,*" she breathed, "I did not know it would be so—so *magnifique!* Must I meet all these people, Mademoiselle?"

"Not all of them, child," said Miss Standfield, smiling. "Don't be frightened, my dear. You will do very well."

"Truly?" Victoire drew a long breath, preparing to step out of the carriage as it stopped before the door. "I do not know—I will try," she said. "But I am very glad, all the same," she added naively, "that I am wearing a beautiful new gown."

Miss Standfield's confidence in her young protégée was not misplaced. Victoire's eyes might be glowing with wonder as she ascended the great, crimson-carpeted staircase to where Lord and Lady Whittingham stood to receive their guests at its head, but there was not the least hint of confusion in her manner as she made her curtsey and civilly replied to their greeting. Nor was her poise shaken when, as she entered the flower-bedecked ballroom, with its long mirrors dazzlingly repeating the hundreds of candles burning in the wall sconces and in the great crystal chandelier glittering overhead, she was immediately approached by Mr. Standfield and her hand solicited for the set of country dances that was just then forming.

"Thought you'd feel more at home standing up with me first," he explained, with an apologetic glance at Tarn. "No wish to cut you out, coz, but, you see, she's used to my steps, and it's a curst rum business, one's first ball, you know."

"Of course," Tarn said agreeably, his eyes roving about the room. "I don't pretend to be in your class, Duke."

Miss Standfield said pointedly to Victoire, "You may save the *next* set for Lewis, my dear. Tarn, are you attending? I said Victoire will save the next set for you."

"Yes, I heard you," Tarn said, and strolled off in search of kindred spirits, leaving Miss Standfield to shake her head over him in exasperation.

She discovered soon enough, however, that, if the Marquis was indifferent as to whether or not he danced with Victoire, there were—as she had predicted—other gentlemen who were not. The news, spread by the guests who had been present at Miss Standfield's small evening-party, of Tarn's sudden interest in the young lady Miss Standfield had brought up to town with her had focussed attention upon Victoire, and that attention, once fixed, discovered a very unusual and attractive young miss, gowned in the first style of elegance, and possessing a certain piquancy of manner that was soon counting its victims among the ranks of the younger and more susceptible gentlemen. Tarn, bringing her back to Miss Standfield at the conclusion of the set of country dances for which he had dutifully stood up with her, found several candidates waiting to request her hand for the next set. Mr. Fearon was the first of these to urge his claim, but, just as Miss Standfield was on the point of indicating to Victoire that it would be proper for her to allow him to lead her out on the floor, he gracefully withdrew in favour of a young gentleman in a florid waistcoat and an Oriental tie of gigantic height, his hair cut and curled *à la cherubim*, whom he introduced as Mr. Alfred Swanton.

"He has been making such a curst nuisance of himself trying

to find someone to present him to you, Miss Duvenay, that it appears I had best take pity on him at once," he observed. "I am sure he would give the entire fortune to which he is heir to stand up with you, and if I were a mercenary sort of fellow I daresay I should take care to profit handsomely by this charitable deed, for he will be as rich as Golden Ball one day."

Miss Standfield, who did not fail to catch Mr. Fearon's rather obvious allusion to Mr. Swanton's wealth, looked with some disapproval at that young gentleman, mentally characterising him as precisely what he was—the son of a wealthy Cit, eager to gain a foothold in Society. But Victoire was quite as willing to stand up with Mr. Swanton as with Mr. Fearon, preferring, in fact, the former's blushing deference to the latter's satirical civilities; and, as she appeared ready to give her hand to him at once, Miss Standfield did not object.

Miss Standfield might have been less complaisant, however, if she had witnessed the prelude to this little scene, for it had not been Mr. Swanton who had approached Mr. Fearon, but the other way round, and it had been Mr. Fearon who, with careful casualness, had drawn Mr. Swanton's attention to Miss Duvenay and sketched her situation in terms that had highly exaggerated the position she held in Society. His description of the Duvenay family honours would have won the approval of Mr. Fitzhugh Duvenay himself, and Mr. Swanton, a susceptible young man, much flattered by the notice of such an obvious Tulip of Fashion as Mr. Fearon, was quite ready to be convinced by him that Miss Duvenay was the most attractive young lady at the ball, who lacked only fortune to make her one of the future leaders of the *ton*.

"Deuced good of you to stand up with me, Miss Duvenay," he blurted out to her, with a naiveté almost as pronounced as her own, as they prepared to go down the dance together. "I wouldn't have dared make a push to ask you if Mr. Fearon hadn't been so kind. Don't know anybody else here tonight, you see."

Victoire, whose attention had been chiefly given to the

145

worry that Tarn was already beginning to be intolerably bored, for she could see him standing talking to Mr. Standfield across the room in an attitude most uncivilly suggestive of that emotion, withdrew her mind from its preoccupation with the Marquis and remarked rather at random that Mr. Swanton must at least know his host and hostess.

"Oh, yes!" Mr. Swanton acknowledged, blushing hotly at the horrid thought that he might have led Miss Duvenay to believe that he had dared to present himself at Lady Whittingham's party without a card of invitation. "And—and *several* other persons, really, for I was introduced to them when I was here a few weeks ago—only I am afraid most of them don't remember me," he added dismally.

Victoire, her ready sympathy drawn by her partner's plight, assured him kindly that it was much the same with her.

"Oh, no! It couldn't be!" Mr. Swanton said, contradicting her with fervent incivility. "I mean to say—Mr. Fearon says you are just come from France, and I can see you may not be acquainted with many people in London as yet, but—but they couldn't forget *you*, Miss Duvenay! Not if they'd once met you, I mean to say!"

Victoire, her eyes dancing at the sudden realisation that she had made her first London conquest, had difficulty in returning the demure sort of answer that Miss Standfield had impressed upon her was expected of a young lady of quality when confronted with masculine admiration, and could scarcely wait to inform Tarn of her success—a piece of impropriety that would have drawn Miss Standfield's severest censure. That lady, however, in happy ignorance of the thoughts passing through her charge's head, was at the moment engaged in conversation with Lady Eastcott, who had arrived with her husband in time to see Tarn dancing with Victoire. The sight had so much displeased Lord Eastcott that he would have gone off at once to demand of his daughter what she meant by encouraging Tarn in his mad idea of marrying Miss Duvenay by inviting them both to her house, had not his wife, mindful of Mr. Fearon's advice, besought him not to do what was tantamount to informing the entire world of the story by taking Tina into his confidence, or Tarn would assuredly marry the girl out of hand.

His lordship, obliged to admit this probability, had contented himself instead with giving his nephew no more than a "Humph!" in answer to his greeting when he ran across him, and thereupon went off to one of the smaller saloons to join in a game of whist, thus preserving his sensibilities from the further exacerbation that might have been caused them if he had been obliged to see Tarn standing up again with Miss Duvenay.

As it happened, however, he might have saved himself the trouble of removing from the ballroom, for Tarn, seeing Victoire passing from one partner to another as boulanger and cotillion succeeded the country dances, had not yet felt it necessary to ask her to stand up with him a second time; and before he had made up his mind to do so something occurred that momentarily put her quite out of his head.

The "something" was the entrance into the ballroom, in an interval between dances, of a group of three persons—a small, wizened, elderly gentleman with the blue riband of the Portuguese Order of the Tower and the Sword dignifying his rather shabby and certainly not overly clean evening clothes, a lady, as large and imposing as her companion was undersized, wearing a purple turban and gown and a fabulously long rope of pearls about her neck, and a much younger lady, who immediately drew the eyes of every man, and of almost every lady, in the room. She wore a gown of dull gold satin cut along Grecian lines, and leaving one shoulder, as well as most of an exceedingly white bosom, bare; there were emeralds in her hair, which was as dusky as a crow's wing and fully as glossy; and her feet, encased in thin Grecian sandals consisting merely of thongs, were seen to be bare except for the gilt paint adorning the nails. Add to this a face distinguished by a wilful beauty

147

entirely free from any dependance upon classical lines for its appeal—a ripe mouth, oval green eyes that slanted slightly upwards, or were made to seem so by a cunning use of cosmetic art—and it will be seen why conversation momentarily halted as she came into the room, to be succeeded immediately by a buzz of question and conjecture.

"Who *is* she?" Lady Eastcott—no prude—demanded in severe disapproval of Mr. Fearon, with whom she happened to be talking at the moment. "My dear Bruce, those nails!—and if she is wearing one stitch of *anything* under that gown I shall own myself astonished. I *cannot* think that Tina is acquainted with her!"

Mr. Fearon confessed himself to be quite as much in the dark as his aunt, but obligingly went off to drop a question in Lord Whittingham's ear. He returned shortly afterwards, with an odd gleam in his eye, to inform Lady Eastcott that the lady who had excited her notice was none other than the Condessa de Vilamil, whom the Whittinghams had been obliged to include in their invitation to certain high-ranking Portuguese officials now in London to attend the Peace Celebration, as she was staying with one of their number and his wife.

"A piece of luck, ma'am," he said, "for which I believe we have reason to be profoundly grateful—"

"Grateful!" interrupted Lady Eastcott, disapproval even more manifest upon her face. "Well, I daresay *you* may be —though I should not have thought it of you, Bruce—"

"My dear Aunt," interrupted Mr. Fearon a trifle impatiently, "you quite mistake my meaning! My interest in the Condessa is not in the least personal. I think you will understand it better when I tell you that she is that same Portuguese countess with whom Lewis's name was so scandalously linked during the last year or so that he was abroad."

"What!" exclaimed Lady Eastcott, her eyes flying again to the Condessa's face. "Are you *quite* sure? But, good heavens, it must be, for he is going up to speak to her now! And is that the husband?" she enquired, gazing, fascinated, at the wizened elderly gentleman who had accompanied the Condessa into the room, and who was bowing and smiling at Tarn as he approached.

"No, he and the Amazon with the pearls are the friends with whom she is staying," Mr. Fearon replied. "The Conde, I understand, is unfortunately—or perhaps I should say, fortunately—detained in Lisbon by the gout."

"He is asking her to dance, I believe," Lady Eastcott interrupted, halfway between amusement and shock. "My dear, he *is* the most thoroughly shameless boy! The story is sure to be in everyone's ears before the two of them have taken the first turn about the room—and he is quite aware of it, of course!"

"Oh, of course," agreed Mr. Fearon, an expression of great satisfaction upon his face. His eyes searched swiftly for Victoire in the brilliant throng, and discovered her seating herself beside Miss Standfield on a small sofa against the wall. "A waltz—little Miss Duvenay will not dance," he murmured. "Dear Cousin Amelia will see to that. I daresay she still has hopes that she may prevail upon Sally Jersey or Maria Sefton to procure vouchers to Almack's for the chit, so she will not be permitted to waltz in public until she has received the approval of the august Patronesses."

"Do but see how closely he holds her!" said Lady Eastcott, not greatly interested in Miss Duvenay at the moment. "I vow, they make a handsome couple, Bruce!"

"I do hope Miss Duvenay thinks the same," drawled Mr. Fearon, his eyes never leaving that young lady's face. "Do you know, I believe I must ask her to stand up with me for the quadrille, ma'am. I am sure that she, of all persons, is quite dying of curiosity about the Condessa, and it would be too bad—would it not?—if someone were not kind enough to satisfy it!"

Victoire, as Mr. Fearon had surmised, had indeed not failed to observe the Condessa's entry into the ballroom, or the promptitude with which Tarn had approached her. It had seemed to her acute eyes that he had come in response to a signal—ever so slight, but quite unmistakable—from the lady herself, a momentary flicker of darkened lashes over those oddly shaped green eyes, the hint of a smile on those ripe lips. And the next moment there he was bowing over her hand, laughing down at her, gathering her audaciously into his embrace as the music began and they swept off together in the waltz.

If she had heard the Condessa's first words as the two reached the center of the floor, her quick jealousy, already aroused, would have been fanned into even hotter flame.

"Lewis, *mi amor!* Who would have thought to meet *you* here!"

"You would," the Marquis countered promptly. "That's why

you're here, isn't it, Eva? And *don't* try giving me that innocent look! It doesn't fool me. What are you doing in London, anyway? I thought you couldn't stand the place."

She lifted her shoulders, smiling. "I heard you were here, *caro*. Isn't that what you would like me to say?"

"I'd like you to tell me the truth," said the Marquis, quite as amicably as before, "but that's too much to expect, I suppose. By the way, love, your accent's much improved; no one would imagine you'd been born within hearing of Bow Bells. I daresay my deluded cousins have been told that affecting story of Spanish nobility fallen on hard times?"

"Don't be boring, Lewis. My father *was* Spanish, and of very good family."

"He was Spanish, right enough; I'll give you that. But nobility—! Coming it rather too thick and rare, my dear! A needy rascal, not above keeping a gaming house—I believe you did say a gaming house—?"

"Darling Lewis, you are as abominable as ever, I see," said the Condessa, smiling up at him out of her green eyes as she allowed him to turn her about the floor in great circles that swept the folds of the dull gold gown in moulded curves that clung and fell and clung again to the long, statuesque lines of her opulent form. "And if you dare breathe a *word* of that to anyone in London, I shall assuredly scratch your eyes out."

"Yes, I daresay you would," said the Marquis agreeably. "But you needn't put yourself about; I never betray confidences, especially when the confider is in his—or her—cups."

"I was *not*!"

"Yes, you were, love. It's your one weakness; I was never able to discover any other."

"I had—once—a weakness for you," the Condessa murmured. "You remember?"

"I remember. But it wasn't exactly a weakness, was it? Or if it was, I think you'd have found yourself able to resist it if there hadn't been a title and a full purse thrown into the bargain."

She looked up at him provocatively. "Turned cynic, Lewis—like Byron?" she twitted him.

"That *poseur*? He was a dead bore abroad and he's even more so in London, now he's become famous. You'd best forget about him, if you have any ideas in *that* direction," he added, with his usual brutal frankness, "for he's had Caro Lamb and half the other females in the *ton* swooning over him; he can have his pick of countesses, my dear, with more than a pinchbeck Portuguese title to go with the name."

The Condessa, who was quite used to his frankness, countered it with some of her own.

"Oh, I don't want *him*; I'd a great deal rather have *you*, *caro!*" she said, and gave him a long, full, laughing look, straight up into his eyes, that made Victoire, whose seat they passed so close by at that moment that the lady's swirling draperies actually touched her gown, stiffen visibly.

"A handsome pair, are they not?" said a voice beside her. She looked up, startled, to see Mr. Fearon smiling lazily down at her. "The lady—if you are interested, as I see you are—is the Condessa de Vilamil," he went on, in the overly civil voice that she was beginning to dislike quite as much as did Tarn.

He would have gone on, but this time it was Miss Standfield's turn to stiffen.

"Indeed!" she said, bending a penetrating gaze upon the Condessa, who, as the music came to an end, had placed her hand, as if on a sudden impulse, on Tarn's arm and stood smiling up at him in the center of the floor. "Are you quite certain of this, Bruce?"

"Quite!" said Mr. Fearon, and took Victoire's hand in his, drawing her to her feet. "I think I may claim this dance, Miss Duvenay," he said, "in place of the one I relinquished to Mr. Swanton."

She took her place in the set with him reluctantly, her mind still occupied with the Condessa. Her partner was regarding her satirically, but she did not observe this.

"Why did Mademoiselle say, 'Indeed!' in just *that* way when you spoke the lady's name?" she asked him abruptly, after a time.

"Did she?"

"You know she did." She looked straight at him now. "Is the Condessa a—a friend of Lewis's?"

"A very dear friend."

"Oh!" She digested this, a slight frown upon her face.

"Yes, my dear," said Mr. Fearon, amusement in his eyes. "It is exactly as you think. You are *not* such an innocent, after all, are you? Which is perhaps as well—for if you are to marry Lewis you had best be prepared to cope with the existence of his *chères-amies* without falling into the vapours."

"*Moi*, I never have the vapours," said Victoire austerely, making a valiant effort to show no sign of the fact that her heart suddenly seemed to have dropped into the tips of her pretty satin slippers.

"I am very happy to hear it," said Mr. Fearon. "Jealousy is such an unamiable trait—is it not?—besides being quite useless, of course, where Lewis is concerned. My poor aunt—Lewis's mother—was never able to reconcile herself to the fact that the late Marquis had, as the saying goes, a roving eye. I am delighted, for Lewis's sake, that you appear to have a far more realistic attitude towards the matter." He added casually, missing nothing of the sudden paleness that had come into Victoire's face, so happily flushed only a few minutes before, "Of course, the Condessa is a very beautiful woman. Any man might lose his head over her."

Victoire said through gritted teeth, unavoidably observing Tarn standing directly before her, still talking to the Condessa, "I do not think Lewis—*loses his head,* as you say. He amuses himself merely."

Mr. Fearon laughed. "With the Condessa?" he said. "Oh,

my poor child, it is quite otherwise, I fear. He was very much *épris*, one hears, committed the most extravagant follies for her sake; the two of them made quite the most interesting scandal in Lisbon for over a year. And now, it appears, they are prepared to begin all over again."

Victoire said nothing, allowing him to lead her through the *pas d'été* as if she had no concern other than to perform the complicated steps of the quadrille without a fault; but her partner observed with considerable satisfaction that her face was still pale and set, and that the high spirits he had previously seen in her appeared to be completely quenched.

To say the truth, the ball, which had seemed so magnificent only a short time before, had suddenly turned into a most insipid affair for her. And to make matters worse, Miss Standfield, seeing, as she thought, her charge's success so well assured, had allowed herself to be drawn off into one of the smaller saloons by some of her Court friends for a comfortable cose on the affairs of Royalty, in which the persistent rumours of the Princess Charlotte's having cried off from her engagement to the Prince of Orange were certain to be thoroughly canvassed. Lady Eastcott, she had informed Victoire before departing, would be happy to take her under her wing if she found herself partnerless—but Victoire was shy of Lady Eastcott, who she felt disapproved of her, and could not pluck up the courage to approach her when, after having refused the offers of no fewer than three gentlemen to take her in to supper, in the belief that it had been arranged that she would have supper with Tarn, she found herself left quite alone as the guests began to move downstairs into the large saloon where the collation had been laid.

She looked about for Tarn, but he was nowhere in sight. Feeling suddenly quite as friendless and out of place as Mr. Swanton had described himself, she sought refuge in a small anteroom opening from the ballroom; there was no one inside, and she sat down on a chair covered with straw-coloured satin, her head drooping childishly and a sudden rush of tears springing into her eyes. Not since the day she had first left France on the strange journey that had led her to this place had she felt so very much alone.

"Miss Duvenay?"

The sound of her name made her look up quickly. Mr. Swanton was standing in the doorway, looking at her irresolutely.

"I thought—I was watching—I saw you come in here," he stammered. "I'd have asked you before, but I never imagined—I mean to say, you've had so devilish many fellows swarming round you—"

"If it is that you would like to take me to supper," Victoire said, blinking back her tears and jumping to her feet, "you may. And it is *very* kind of you to ask me."

"Oh, I say—not at all!" said Mr. Swanton, overwhelmed.

He gave her his arm and walked with her through the now thinning throng in the ballroom down the stairs and into the saloon where tables had been set out for supper. There was a splendid array of lobster patties, creams and aspics, Chantillies, and stuffed birds, which Victoire, her appetite quite ruined by Tarn's defection, attempted to show some interest in for Mr. Swanton's sake, for he was so anxious to please her that he brought her such an extensive selection that she would have had to be famished to have eaten it all.

As it happened, however, he had no time in which to enjoy watching *her* enjoy the fruits of his labour; he had, in fact, scarcely sat down beside her when Tarn's tall figure suddenly loomed disturbingly over them. The Marquis was looking distinctly menacing, and said at once, to Mr. Swanton, "You are out of place here, sir, I believe. Miss Duvenay is engaged to me for supper."

Victoire, gazing up at him in astonishment, thought that she had never seen him look so haughty and disagreeable. As for Mr. Swanton, he wilted completely, began stammering apologies, half rose from his seat, and looked altogether so completely miserable that Victoire, still smarting from Tarn's neglect of her, found herself irresistibly impelled to fly to his aid.

"No, no—sit down again, Mr. Swanton!" she said. "His lordship has quite mistaken the matter."

"Have I, by God!" said Tarn wrathfully. "We'll see that!"

His right hand shot out and seized Mr. Swanton's elbow as that young gentleman, in the act of obeying Victoire's injunction, attempted to sink back into his seat. Mr. Swanton, thus impelled, came again, rather overabruptly, to his feet, causing several heads to turn in his direction and a number of quizzing-glasses to be levelled upon the little scene. Mr. Swanton blushed to the roots of his hair, muttered something incoherent that sounded to be in the way of an apology, and hurried off, disappearing from the supper room in a trice. Tarn sat down in the chair he had vacated.

"That's better," he said coolly, completely disregarding the quizzing-glasses, now fixed in fascination upon him. "What have we here? Lobster patties? Famous!"

And he proceeded to attack one with single-minded concentration. Victoire gazed at him indignantly.

"*Tiens!*" she said. "Do you mean to sit there and *eat*, as if nothing had happened?"

"Of course I'm going to eat," responded his lordship, quite unmoved. "And you had best do the same if you intend to have anything, for I don't mean to spend the rest of my life in this house, and we must still stand up together for a second dance if we are to do what we came here for."

Victoire pushed back her plate. "I shall not eat, my lord!" she said, looking dangerous.

"Don't, then—but you'll be missing some devilish fine things. These lobster patties, for instance—"

Victoire said, in a suffocated voice, "You are—you are altogether *abominable* tonight! You did not come to take me to

157

supper—and you have been very rude to Mr. Swanton—and now you talk about lobster patties!"

"You ought to be deuced glad I *am* talking about lobster patties," Tarn said, turning his gaze for the first time upon her, with a gleam in his black eyes that reminded her forcibly and rather uncomfortably of the first time she had met him, "instead of asking you what the devil you meant by flirting with that halfling."

"I was *not* flirting! You did not come to take me to supper, and he was kind enough to ask me. That is all."

"Yes, that's all, except that you took care to charm him half out of his senses."

"I did not! *Absolument non!* It is you who are charmed half out of your senses, so that everyone looks at you and whispers!"

Tarn glanced up at her again. "Oh, so that's it—is it?" he said. "The Condessa. Well, if you think it would have stopped them from looking and whispering if I'd never gone near her, you're wrong, my dear."

"I do not care if they look and whisper! I care that you behave foolishly before all these people!"

She stopped, seeing the thunderous look on his lordship's dark face. He did not say another word to her at the moment, however, but finished the supper Mr. Swanton had so kindly provided, quite oblivious, it appeared, to Victoire's stiff, disapproving silence and the curious glances cast at them by their neighbours. He then rose and, apparently unobservant of her untouched plate, seized her wrist and drew her up beside him.

"Come along," he said. "We'll have the next dance together."

"I do not wish to dance with you!" Victoire, still seething, said.

"Well, it don't make a ha'porth of difference whether you want to or not, because it's what you are going to do," Tarn said adamantly, his hand still upon her arm as he compelled her to mount the stairs unwillingly beside him.

As luck would have it, the orchestra was beginning a waltz as they reentered the ballroom. This gave Victoire added ammunition for the guns of her refusal; she drew back, saying triumphantly, "See, they are playing a waltz, so I cannot dance with you," and she added, quite unforgivably, "Go and dance with your Condessa; it is what you wish to do, no doubt. It is a great pity, *bien entendu,* that she has a husband, but one sees that neither of you allows that to interfere with your pleasures!"

The words had scarcely left her lips before she found her hand seized in a grip so hard that it made her wince; a muscular arm encircled her waist and she was swept off to the center of the floor, her feet automatically responding to the measure of the dance before she well knew what was happening.

"*Scélérat!*" she gasped. "Let me go—let me go at once!"

The Marquis paid her not the slightest heed. He looked down into her face, his own very grim.

"Now listen to me, you little vixen!" he said. "If ever I hear you say such a thing again—"

"I will say whatever I wish! I will! You cannot stop me! And if you do not let me go this instant, Mademoiselle will be so angry with you that she will never speak to you again! She says I am on no account to waltz in public or the Lady Patronesses of Almack's will not approve—"

"They won't approve of your entering those sacred portals anyway, as long as it's me you're marrying," Tarn said bluntly. "And if you think you'll do any better with that young nodcock of a Cit, you're fair and far out, my love!"

"He is *not* a nod—whatever the word is that you said. He is a young man *entièrement respectable,* which is a great deal more than one can say of your Condessa!"

The battle was fairly joined between them: both with flaming tempers, they were too involved in their quarrel to realise that

159

they were the focus of attention in the room. Miss Standfield, who, eschewing the indigestible lure of lobster and pastries, had been sitting all this while in the small saloon to which she had retired with her friends, returned to the ballroom at about this time to the shock of seeing her young protégée dancing the forbidden waltz and apparently engaged simultaneously in open warfare with her partner, to the intense interest of all present, and clicked her tongue in exasperation.

"Charming, is it not?" Mr. Fearon's amused voice said beside her. "My dear ma'am, you were not in the supper room, I believe, so that you did not see the outbreak of hostilities. They began, it appears, with Lewis's taking exception to Miss Duvenay's allowing young Mr. Swanton to escort her down to supper; she countered by a diversionary attack against his bestowing such extremely marked attentions upon the Condessa de Vilamil; and they have now, it seems, both brought up their heavy artillery—" He glanced down at her, the expression of malicious amusement still upon his face. "Dear cousin, tell me frankly," he said, "do you still think you can make a match of it between those two? You know Lewis's ungovernable temper; he is more likely, it appears to me, to murder the chit than to marry her."

Miss Standfield, never one to waste words, merely gave him a glance and moved away to request of Lady Whittingham that she send a footman to have her carriage brought round at once.

"Oh, are you going already?" Lady Whittingham asked, endeavouring to appear politely disappointed; but the expression of relief upon her pretty face was clear evidence that she had just been obliged to endure a pungent homily from her outraged lord on the subject of her imprudence in inviting her cousin Tarn to the house.

"Wherever he goes, there is an uproar!" he had said severely. "And, really, my dear Ernestina—this Condessa de Vilamil! It would seem that everyone in London except yourself knows that she has been his mistress!"

160

Lady Whittingham could therefore only be thankful when she saw Miss Standfield shepherding a very flushed Miss Duvenay down the stairs to the front door, with Tarn following with close-gripped lips behind them, and she was turning back to her other guests with some relief when the Condessa de Vilamil's slow alto voice spoke beside her.

"Your pardon, Madame—you are the cousin, I believe, of Lord Tarn? This child with whom he leaves now—she is his betrothed?"

"His betrothed!" Lady Whittingham looked at her in astonishment. "No—certainly not!" she said, meanwhile gazing, fascinated, at the Condessa's elegantly revealing gown, and wishing that she might buy one half so daring for herself without her husband's inexorably refusing to allow her to wear it.

"No?" The Condessa's brows rose. "But he quarrels with her so fiercely, one cannot believe he is entirely indifferent—"

Mr. Marmaduke Standfield, most urgently dispatched by Lord Whittingham, arrived on the scene at that moment to snatch his cousin from the Condessa's scandalous presence by requesting her to stand up with him for the next dance; and the Condessa, smiling her slow smile, walked thoughtfully off, to be surrounded within a space of seconds by a throng of gentlemen, each seeking the honour of leading her into the set.

Meanwhile, a very silent trio sat in Miss Standfield's carriage, being conveyed back to Albemarle Street. In Miss Standfield's presence, not even the Marquis was brave enough to continue his quarrel with Victoire, and Miss Standfield herself, aware that any reproof from her would only make matters worse at this stage, very sensibly held her tongue as well. As for Victoire, she had all she could do to keep from bursting into a storm of tears, and sat biting her lips and gazing out the window, avoiding looking at Tarn at all.

When they arrived in Albemarle Street, she accepted his

161

assistance in alighting from the carriage, still without a glance in his direction; only as she entered the house and heard him making his adieux to Miss Standfield did she suddenly turn to him, her lips quivering and the tears starting to her eyes. But he was already running down the steps without a backward glance; the butler closed the door, and she was alone with Miss Standfield.

She would much have preferred going immediately to her chamber after this exhausting and highly unsatisfactory evening, but Miss Standfield had other ideas. She led her young charge inexorably up the stairs to her own bedchamber, where, having dismissed her dresser, she instructed Victoire to sit down and then placed herself calmly opposite her.

"Now, my dear," she said, "you will tell me the whole of this ridiculous affair. Have you been foolish enough to take Lewis to task over his attentions to that scandalous young woman who calls herself a Condessa?"

Victoire gazed at her mutinously, but inside her her Frenchwoman's sensible brain, beginning to overcome her Irish temper, misgave her.

"Yes!" she said. "That is, he scolded *me* because I allowed Mr. Swanton to take me to supper when he did not come himself, and so *naturellement* I—"

"*Naturellement* you became very angry and threw the Condessa in his face." Miss Standfield sighed. "My dear child," she said, "unless you can contrive to behave a little less frankly on such occasions, I am afraid that you had best give over the idea of becoming the Marchioness of Tarn. A clever woman, you know, does not counter such an exhibition as Lewis and his Condessa favoured us with tonight by indulging in an equally public exhibition of impropriety herself."

Victoire hung her head. "I know," she said, in a small voice. "It was very stupid of me—and I have made him very, very angry, so that I have the most terrible fear that he will never forgive me. But I could not help it," she said, her eyes flashing suddenly, "when I saw him behaving so foolishly with that —that *salope!*"

Miss Standfield looked shocked. "You did *not*, I hope, use that word to Lewis!" she said.

"No—but I said something almost quite as bad," Victoire acknowledged, guilt overcoming her once more, "and that was when he said I should waltz with him whether I wished to or not—"

Miss Standfield sighed again. "Dear, dear!" she said. "You were not exaggerating, I see, when you told me your temper was quite as bad as his. And what do you intend to do now, since you have got yourself into this predicament?"

Victoire's head drooped lower, and a sob choked her voice. "You think he will never, never forgive me, Mademoiselle?" she faltered.

"Never forgive you? Nonsense!" Miss Standfield said briskly. "Ten to one he will have forgotten the whole affair by the next time he sees you, for, however undisciplined his temper may be, it is *not* a vindictive one; he has never borne a grudge in his life. And, for heaven's sake, child," she added severely, as she saw the tears welling up in Victoire's eyes, "you must on no account be so foolish as even to hint to him that you have the least notion that it is *he* who has something to forgive! You will expect him to crave *your* pardon when next he sees you—not that he will do so," she added practically, "nor that I would have you insist upon it, but you may allow him to see, by a certain reserve in your manner, that he has offended you deeply—"

Through the tears, a tiny, irrepressible gurgle of laughter escaped Victoire. "*Vous êtes bien sage,* Mademoiselle," she said, "but if he is not angry with *me*, you see, I shall not know how to be angry with *him*. And he would only laugh if I behaved to him—as you said—with reserve, and perhaps call me 'brat,' which I can tell you does not make one feel at all dignified."

163

"Yes," said Miss Standfield resignedly, "I expect he would. Neither of you, I fear, has the slightest notion of how to carry on an *affaire de coeur* in the proper manner. I daresay I should wash my hands of the two of you, but I shall not—if only to make sure that Lewis does not conclude by marrying someone like that odious Condessa!" She rose. "And now go to bed, you bad child, and don't waste your time crying over that wicked boy. I shall have to prod him, no doubt, to take the next step in this ridiculous courtship, but all is not lost yet, if you can but contrive to bridle your tongue in future!"

14

As it developed, however, it was unnecessary for Miss Standfield to do any prodding, for on the very next day a message
from Tarn arrived in Albemarle Street, requesting the pleasure
of escorting the two ladies to the theatre on an evening later in
the week. Victoire, who, now that her temper had had time to
cool, was suffering even more violent pangs of guilt over her
behaviour on the previous evening, was cast into an abyss of
self-castigation   at   this   evidence   of   her   betrothed's
magnanimity—a mood, however, which did not survive the
sight of him on horseback in the Park that afternoon, riding
beside a blonde, dashing little charmer who was queening it in
an elegant barouche lined with pale-blue satin.

Mr. Fearon, himself enjoying the fashionable promenade
hour in the Park astride a showy chestnut, was kind enough to
pause beside Miss Standfield's landaulet to satisfy Victoire's
unspoken but burning desire to learn the identity of the fair
young lady with whom Tarn was laughing and chatting so

intimately—a famous Cyprian, he told her, known familiarly as the Flyer, who it was rumoured had great reason to rejoice over the young Marquis's return to the metropolis.

But if he had expected to draw fire from Victoire with this information, he was disappointed. Her Irish temper had endured a stern curtain-lecture from her cool French wisdom during the small hours of a wakeful night, and when Tarn, catching sight of Miss Standfield's landaulet in the press of smart barouches, highperch phaetons, and tilburies, brought his raking grey through the throng to come up to it, she was able to greet him with a determined smile, quite as if she had just seen him in conversation with the most respectable of dowagers instead of with a lady who inspired in her much the same sentiments as did the Condessa de Vilamil.

As for the Marquis, he was not, as Miss Standfield had truly informed her, one to nourish a grudge over a quarrel in which he was willing, in a calmer mood, to admit that he had been quite as much at fault as his opponent, and, beyond giving her a rather quizzical glance, as if he half expected that *she* might open hostilities again, made no reference to the quarrel on which they had parted so tempestuously the night before.

It was, in fact, Miss Standfield who, surprisingly, brought the matter into the open by informing the Marquis, as he held his impatiently fidgeting grey easily beside the carriage, that if he did not intend to spend more of his time displaying an obvious interest in Victoire, he might have spared himself the trouble of bringing her up to town.

"For there is not the slightest use in your thinking you can persuade people that you have serious intentions towards the child if you dance attendance upon other females," she pointed out. "*Do* endeavour to remember that, Lewis; at your age, one's memory *should* be equal to the task."

Victoire flushed. "But I do not care if he dances attendance on other ladies, Mademoiselle!" she said quite untruthfully, but with a dogged resolution not to allow herself to be drawn again into a display of jealousy. She saw Tarn's black brows go up and went on, colouring still more deeply, "I know I behaved very badly last night, but I shall not do so again. No, I am serious! *Assurément!*" she added, as he grinned skeptically at her. "We are to make a *mariage de convenance, n'est-ce pas?* And so there will be no more scenes."

"Well, you have not made your marriage yet," said Miss Standfield tartly. "Nor is it likely that you will, if Lewis is not willing for a few weeks, at least, to behave as if he had some slight interest in bringing it about."

The Marquis seemed about to utter some intemperate retort to this speech, but Victoire said hastily, reaching out to pat the grey's gleaming neck as he pressed against the side of the carriage, "Oh, what a *beautiful* creature! How I should love to try him! What is he called, please?"

"Grey Boy," said Tarn. He glanced down at her, a smile quickly erasing the expression of displeasure that had been upon his face. "Entirely too much horse for you, infant!" he said. "But if you'd like to ride with me, I'll engage to mount you on something more suitable for a very *small* female—"

"*Not a petit cheval!*" She drew herself up. "One of those very old, *fat* ponies one sees carrying *children*—"

"No, no!" Tarn assured her. "I've seen your prowess in Kent, you'll remember! But you will, I hope, allow me to persuade you to use a saddle here."

She gave a little gurgle of amusement, looking up to meet the laughter in his eyes, and Miss Standfield, saying that they must go on now, as she saw Lady Sefton's carriage ahead and wished to have a word with her, promised the Marquis to see that Victoire was provided with a proper riding dress at once and thereupon directed her coachman to drive on.

Mr. Fearon, viewing the whole scene through smiling, narrowed eyes, was swiftly revising his opinion of little Miss Duvenay. No, not *quite* so innocent as she appeared, he thought—nor so easy to entrap again into the sort of display of

167

jealousy which, if tiresomely repeated, would be sure to drive Tarn into wishing her at the devil. Other means, obviously, would be necessary if Tarn was to be dissuaded from marrying the girl, and he would require allies—more forceful ones than young Mr. Alfred Swanton appeared likely to be. Mr. Fearon, turning his chestnut towards the Stanhope Gate, decided, as a first step, to pay a call upon the Condessa de Vilamil.

As a result, his card was taken up the following day to the suite in Ellis's Hotel where the Condessa was staying with her Portuguese friends. As he had not been presented to her at Lady Whittingham's dress-party, he was personally unknown to her, but he was aware that his name must disclose to her the fact that he was a relation of Tarn's, and he had no doubt but that she would receive him.

His assumption turned out to be correct. In a very few minutes he was ushered upstairs to find the Condessa, in a rose-pink morning robe trimmed with yards of Malines lace—a garment almost as revealing of her charms as her ball dress had been at Lady Whittingham's party—reclining upon a sofa, sipping chocolate, his card still in her hand.

"*Bruce* Fearon," she greeted him without preamble, surveying with lazy appreciation his tall figure, very well turned out, as always, in elegant town dress. "I apprehend—a relation of my Lord Tarn's?"

Mr. Fearon's white teeth gleamed in a smile as he bent over her carelessly extended hand.

"His cousin, Madame. I was at Lady Whittingham's house the other night, though I had not the pleasure of making your acquaintance upon that occasion."

"I have heard Tarn speak of you." The Condessa's green eyes measured him behind a slow, perceptive smile. "You are the heir—is it not? How disappointing it must be for you that he bears a charmed life! Most men who have run into half the dangers he has would have been long since dead—and then *you* would be my Lord Tarn, *verdad*?"

Mr. Fearon, no stranger to dealings with women of the Condessa's stamp, had entered upon this interview with few misgivings; but he found himself now suddenly uneasy. This woman, it appeared, had only to set eyes upon him to divine the ambitions of which he had succeeded in keeping his closest intimates and even his family—with the possible exception of Miss Standfield—unaware. Taken by surprise, he did not for a moment know what reply to make, and, before he could gather his wits sufficiently to speak, the Condessa, laughing, was herself speaking again.

"My dear—my very dear Mr. Fearon," she said mockingly, "shall I relieve your embarrassment and tell you why you have come to see me, as you seem quite unable to tell me yourself? You wish me to make mischief between Tarn and his betrothed—she *is* his betrothed, is she not, though it seems that no announcement has yet been made?"

Mr. Fearon had regained his composure by this time, and was able to say with a smile, "I had heard, Madame, that you were a very beautiful woman—a statement which I last night ascertained for myself to be true. What I had *not* been told is that you are also a very clever one—"

The Condessa laughed again. "Spanish coin, Mr. Fearon?" she asked. "Pray spare your breath; compliments bore me. Let us speak frankly to each other; it will save us both so much time, will it not? You, it appears, do not wish your cousin to marry this child, to whom he has become betrothed for reasons that I confess I am at a loss to understand—"

"You may well be," Mr. Fearon said, ignoring the invitation to explore the subject that the Condessa's words presented. "It is not love, Madame; so much I can tell you."

"No?" The Condessa thoughtfully set down her cup, considering for a moment. "No," she said then, decisively. "It is not love—at least, not such as I have ever seen in him before. But—not quite indifference, either, Mr. Fearon."

Mr. Fearon shrugged his shoulders. "What does it matter?"

he said. "It has not hindered him, at any rate, from renewing certain—connexions here in London that he has made since he left *your* company, Madame, as you might have seen for yourself if you had been driving yesterday in the Park. Miss Duvenay, however, by what I was able to observe of her behaviour when she met him there, seems to have made up her mind not to allow such matters to deter her from making a marriage that offers her such obvious advantages—"

"Then why do you come to me?" the Condessa enquired, lifting her brows.

Mr. Fearon smiled again. "Madame," he said, "do not let us play games with each other. You have chosen to be frank with me. Very well; I shall be equally frank with you. I have come to you because we have a mutual interest in preventing this projected marriage of my cousin's, and because we can be of mutual assistance to each other in accomplishing this end. You are, I believe, in need of money; one hears that the Conde's estates are sadly encumbered. And gowns such as you wore last night—such as you are wearing today—are ruinously expensive, are they not?—to say nothing of horses and carriages and jewels and gaming debts—you *are* addicted to play, I believe, Madame? Now Lewis, I have always heard, is a generous protector, so that, if this absurd marriage can be broken off and your connexion with him renewed with my assistance, you will really have nothing to worry about in the immediate future. And as for a more distant future, when his incurable recklessness will at last have led him into an adventure that will regrettably put a period to his existence—shall we say a post-obit bond for a handsome sum, contingent, of course, upon his deceasing unmarried—?"

He paused meaningly. The Condessa, who had been admiring a large emerald set in an antique setting upon her finger, as if she were scarcely attending to her visitor's words, startled him at this point by rising and saying in a quite colourless voice, "You may go, Mr. Fearon."

170

"What? I—" Mr. Fearon, taken completely by surprise, could only gaze at her for a moment in disbelief; then he rose quickly to his feet, advancing a step or two towards her. "Madame," he said, "if I have offended you, I can only apologise—"

"I don't want your apologies, Mr. Fearon. I want you to leave."

The Condessa was a tall woman and, Mr. Fearon realised for the first time, a formidable one. He found himself staring into a pair of green eyes full of so contemptuous an anger that, in spite of all his experience, he felt raw colour tinging his cheeks. The Condessa saw it, and shrugged slightly.

"What a pitiful creature you are, after all!" she said. "Tell me—do you really think I should need *your* assistance in getting Tarn back, if I wished to do so? Or that I should enjoy, while I shared his love, contemplating the moment when his death would put me in possession of a handsome part of his fortune?"

Mr. Fearon, still discomposed, muttered an unintelligible disclaimer, and hoped with baffled fury that the Condessa would live to regret her words. The sight of his inarticulate rage, lighting up his eyes almost in a glare, made the Condessa's own eyes suddenly narrow.

"Or perhaps," she said slowly, "we were not even to wait for that happy event to occur naturally, Mr. Fearon? There are ways—is it not so?—to lead a reckless man to his death, to contrive—oh, so carefully!—that he meets disaster without one's own hand being visible in the matter."

Mr. Fearon's eyes met hers; from red, his complexion had now turned to white.

"I think you are mad!" he said, stammering slightly over the words.

"Do you? That may be—but I shall warn Lewis of you, all the same, Mr. Fearon. I have been acquainted with your kind of man, you see. It is more common, perhaps, in my own country

171

than it is here, but I can still recognise the type, even in English dress." She turned away. "And now you will go," she said, "and I think not return—"

Mr. Fearon recovered his tongue. "No," he said, his voice shaking slightly with his rage, "I'll not return. But it will please me greatly, if you are so imprudent as to speak of this interview to Lewis, to make known to all my acquaintance the interesting secret of your origin—*Condessa!*" She turned quickly to face him again, and a smile crossed his pale countenance. "Oh, yes—I know all about that, Madame!" he said vindictively. "I make it my business to know everything that concerns my cousin. Little Evita Morales has become the Condessa de Vilamil, but there are still people in London who remember her, if one takes the trouble to find them out."

The Condessa, who had a passion for gaming, knew when she had lost. She was fond of Tarn, but she had been fond of other men before him and would be fond of others in time to come. And it did not suit her plans to be unmasked in London at this time, even if it meant coming to terms with a man who, under his languid exterior, she had perceived to be wholly unscrupulous and even dangerous. She was used to dealing with dangerous men, and generous indignation, when one's own interests were at stake, was a luxury that one could ill afford.

She moved thoughtfully to the sofa, sat down upon it again, and, arranging her rose-pink draperies in a most convenient fashion for anyone desiring to seat himself beside her, patted the cushion invitingly.

"Come and sit down, Mr. Fearon," she said. "We have made a bad beginning—have we not?—but now that we understand each other we shall get on a great deal better, I believe."

The Condessa appeared at the Opera that same evening, her gown upon this occasion an almost transparent creation of palest green gauze, beneath which not even the least censorious female beholding her was willing to hazard the opinion that she was wearing anything more than an Invisible Petticoat. She was accompanied with great propriety by her Portuguese host and hostess, but these two obliging personages soon retreated into the background to such an extent that they became as invisible as the petticoat, and in their place there appeared an astounding variety of brilliant uniforms and exquisitely cut dress-coats, none, however, able to hold its place beside the Condessa for longer than a few minutes. The Condessa, it appeared, was in a capricious mood that evening.

To anyone watching her, indeed, it might almost have seemed that she was on the lookout for someone who had not yet appeared in the Opera House. At last, however, Mr. Fearon, entering her box in the middle of the evening, dropped a word in her ear that sent her eyes to the pit, where a stir was just then being occasioned by the entrance of a group of young officers. Several were in the uniform of the Dragoon Guards, while others wore the more unfamiliar foreign regimentals that were now becoming a common sight in London in this Season of the Celebration. They were all laughing and chatting together with a complete disregard for the performance going forward on the stage, their eyes raking the boxes for a glimpse of acquaintances, or, more boldly, with great appreciation, for the feminine beauty assembled there.

The Condessa, of course, received her share of such attention. But she had a returning smile for only one of her admirers—a fair young man, resplendent in the dress uniform of a Captain of Prussian Hussars. A gesture, a slight motion of her head, sent him bolting from his companions in the direction of her box; a moment later a knock fell upon the door and he entered impetuously, with the exclamation, "Condessa! I did not know *you* would be here tonight!"

The Condessa gave him her hand to kiss. "Ah, but you *would* have known if you ever went back to your hotel to receive messages, my dear Constant," she said, "for I sent you one there this afternoon."

Her other admirers jealously regarded the young intruder,

speculating darkly on the reasons for his having been accorded the honour of a message from the Condessa. A Life Guardsman, looking down from his own six-foot magnificence upon the newcomer's more moderate inches and square, handsome, deeply bronzed face, lit by a pair of excessively bright-blue eyes, murmured to a companion that it was only young Lanner—"Austrian, I believe, though he wears a Prussian uniform now. Good family, but something of a soldier of fortune—liable to pop up anywhere. Shouldn't think he had tuppence to scratch with, unless he's had a run of luck at the tables."

And he concluded with a slighting allusion to the stiff "sugar-tongs" seat the Prince Regent's admiration for everything having to do with the Prussian Army was causing him to attempt to inflict upon the English cavalry by way of Prussian riding masters—a remark which somewhat assuaged his jealous pangs but really had very little to do with Captain Lanner, who was noted for riding in a neck-or-nothing style that would have won approval even in Ireland.

Whatever his luck at the gaming tables had been, the young Captain's luck in love was certainly in that night. She and Captain Lanner, the Condessa remarked presently, with a bland disregard for the complete lack of probability of her statement, had a great desire to attend to the performance, and what were so many gentlemen doing in her box, quite preventing one from hearing anything with their chatter? Captain Lanner's rivals were obliged to retire, and he himself, taking a chair beside the Condessa, immediately enquired, his smiling blue eyes very intent upon her face, "Well now, my angel! What do you wish me to do for you?—for I cannot flatter myself, much as I wish to, that you have sent for me for any other reason than to make use of me!"

"Constant—*dear* Constant!" said the Condessa, quite unperturbed by the bluntness of this attack. "How very perceptive you are! An understanding *quite* beyond your years—"

"Oh, we'll leave my years out of it!" Captain Lanner said cheerfully. "I shall be twenty-two next month, you know —quite old enough now to be entrapped by Circe! Isn't that the term you used three years ago when we first met in Lisbon? Believe me, I have been counting the months!"

The Condessa laughed, the full-throated, open laugh that most ladies characterised as indecorous and most gentlemen considered one of her chief charms.

"You are perfectly incorrigible, my child," she said, "and it would serve you very well if I *did* entrap you one of these days."

The provocative look she turned on him from under her eyelids as she spoke must have given Captain Lanner the hope that that day might not be far off, for the bright-blue light in his own eyes leapt a little higher; but he only said, in his deliberate, slightly accented voice, " 'One of these days' cannot come too soon for me! Shall we begin tonight?"

He laid his hand upon her arm. She said calmly, without making the least attempt to disengage herself, "Nonsense! Now do not be a tiresome boy—and before all these *very* censorious English, too! I *do* have something to ask you. Did you not tell me once that you had served under Colonel John Duvenay?"

"Under Colonel—?" Captain Lanner looked surprised at this abrupt change in the conversation, but, recovering himself quickly, withdrew his hand and relaxed again in his chair. "Why, yes!" he said. "Is that why you wished to see me —merely to ask me that? But you are blowing at a cold coal, you know; he has been dead these five years."

"I am aware. But he left a young daughter—did he not?"

"Victoire?" A sudden reminiscent smile lit Captain Lanner's face. "Lord, yes—Victoire!" he said. "I haven't seen her since Vienna. Do you mean to tell me that you know her?"

"I have seen her," said the Condessa. "The point is, my dear—how well do *you* know her?"

175

The Captain was still smiling. "Not that I see how it can possibly interest you," he said, "but I knew her very well indeed in Vienna. She was a capital little madcap and I was a very young ensign, and, as Colonel Duvenay believed he owed me some kindness for my father's sake—they were used to be comrades-in-arms, you see—I saw a good deal of the Duvenays. But that, too, has been five years ago—"

"Oh, yes. But the connexion remains." The Condessa's green eyes measured him with lazy intentness. "In short," she said, "if you were to meet her again, she would, I daresay, be delighted to see you?"

"I daresay she might be," agreed Captain Lanner. "I know I should like very much to see *her*."

"And would you also like to make love to her?"

The Captain, despite his poise, blinked, and then gave her a very blank look. "*Plaît-il?*" he said incredulously. "Make love to her? But she is a child!"

"Oh, no!" said the Condessa. "She is quite grown-up enough to receive your advances, my dear—seventeen, I should hazard, at a guess, and quite charming!"

"Yes. Very well," said the Captain, who appeared to have been making some rapid calculations of his own. "Seventeen I grant you—though it seems hardly possible to me, I must tell you. She was the veriest little hoyden when I saw her last, you see—good for any game, and the despair of her very proper mama—"

"She is now, *evidentemente,* the despair of her very proper chaperon, Miss Standfield," the Condessa said, "but that does not mean, I assure you, that you will find her still a child. On the contrary, she is my Lord Tarn's latest flirt."

"*Tarn's?*" The Captain's frank skepticism appeared again; this time, however, there was a slight frown in his blue eyes. "Oh, the devil, I can't believe *that!*" he exclaimed. "A *jeune fille*—that is not *his* kind of game."

"You know him, then?"

"I have seen him—heard of him. I cannot say I know him." A look of sudden recollection crossed his face. "The deuce!" he ejaculated. "He was in *your* train not long since, if I am not mistaken. I have heard—"

"We can very well dispense with what you have heard," the Condessa said firmly, but without the slightest *gêne*. She went on pensively, after a moment, "I will tell you that I was once excessively attached to him and that he treated me very badly indeed—and then we shall leave it at that, my dear. But now, it seems, he has begun to amuse himself with this child, and for her sake and my own I should like very much to throw a rub in his way." She gave him that long, provocative look again from under her darkened lashes. "And you, dear Constant," she said, "*you* could be that rub, if you liked—"

She waited. The Captain regarded her with an odd mixture of admiration, wariness, and frank amusement in his eyes, while on the lighted stage before them a famous soprano sang dramatically of her lost love.

"Remind me," he remarked, after this slight pause, "never to fall into your bad graces, Condessa! I think I begin to feel sympathy for my Lord Tarn."

The Condessa shrugged. "Oh, I know very well the odious habit you men have of never condemning one of your kind, no matter how badly he has behaved!" she said. "And if *that* is how you intend to take the matter, let us allow it to drop now, by all means! Tarn shall amuse himself as he pleases with your young friend, and *I* shall have the satisfaction of realising that I have been quite right in believing that all your vows of devotion were the merest fustian— Oh, no! Pray do not bore me with more of them now!" she went on, as Captain Lanner began to speak. "You do not wish to help me—very well! But do not insult my understanding, then, by more protestations of your regard!"

177

The Captain, who seemed already armoured with the pleasantly unjaded cynicism of a wide but youthful experience, only grinned at this rather dramatic speech.

"Very well. I agree not to do so," he said, "upon condition that you do not insult *mine*, my angel, by enacting for me any Cheltenham tragedies! *A la bonne heure*—you have a grudge against Tarn; you wish to lower his crest a little, in revenge, by displaying him before the world in the rôle of a man who can not only leave, but be left. But why am *I* cast as spoilsport?"

"Because you know the girl—like her—are liked by her, no doubt, in return," said the Condessa promptly, abandoning histrionics with a wisdom born of her own wide experience. "It would take time for a man unknown to her to arrive at an intimacy with her of a sufficiency to rival Tarn in her interest—and time is very much lacking, you see. In a few weeks he will of a certainty either have seduced her or—if he is in the mood for quixotry—have become betrothed to her. I should not know in which case to pity her more sincerely!"

"Ah, I can well believe that her fate would be a matter of importance to you!" the Captain said cynically, taking her up short as she allowed herself to fall into a more dramatic vein again. "Confess, my dear! Your only interest is in humbling Tarn. You care nothing for little Victoire, but it would suit you very well to see her cast him off before the eyes of all London—would it not? But what happens to *me*, then, when this interesting event occurs? I will tell you. Lord Tarn calls me out—oh, on what pretext you choose, that he does not like my cravat, or the colour of my hair—anything will suffice to a man determined to make a quarrel with a successful rival—at any rate, to such a man as Tarn has the reputation of being."

The Condessa's green eyes mocked him. "Poor Constant!" she said. "Are you afraid that he will put a bullet through you? *You*? You will not tell me so! You see, I know something of your exploits on the field of honour!"

The Captain shrugged, smiling. "At any rate, I have no wish

178

to give him the chance to try," he retorted, "not over a girl I haven't seen since she was twelve years old! If I am to die for love, *ma mie*, I'll choose my own lady to die for—thank you very much!"

The Condessa laughed. "Well, well, he will not call you out!" she said carelessly. "You may rely upon that."

"May I, indeed!" The Captain looked skeptical. "And how can you be so certain of that?"

"Because, if it becomes necessary, I shall tell him precisely what you are about," the Condessa said coolly. "Oh, yes—the whole of it," she reiterated, as she saw skepticism deepen upon the young Captain's face—"that you are paying your addresses to Miss Duvenay only to please me, and that if he quarrels with you over the matter the world shall know from me that Lord Tarn's only road to a lady's affections is to shoot his rivals. Believe me, he will not call you out to make a laughing-stock of himself before all London! He will abide by the rules of the game or face a worse humiliation than will be his if Miss Duvenay prefers you to him."

The Captain said, without rancour and with considerable admiration and amusement, that the Condessa was a devil, and that it was a pity that, since she was a female, international diplomacy could not make use of her talents.

"Or that you cannot enter a bet on the books at White's," he said. "No doubt that is what you would wish to do, to make sure that the whole world will know of it when Tarn has been bested. I should be flattered, I daresay, by your confidence in me—especially since I have failed so completely, up to this time, to make the least impression upon *your* heart!"

"My dear, I am not seventeen," the Condessa said frankly. "But you will do very well with little Miss Duvenay, I think—a companion of her childhood, a link with her dead father, to whom I am informed she was very much attached—and you can be quite charmingly attentive when you wish to be, you know! You have every advantage in your favour, while Tarn

179

—even if she is inclined to be in love with him—is certain to play his usual game of indifference, that cavalier sort of on-and-off courtship that a woman can find tantalising, but that to a very young girl is merely disagreeable and humiliating." She added, deliberately lowering her eyes and fixing them upon the ivory-brisé fan she was slowly opening and shutting, "And then there is the inspiration *you* will have, my dear—at least, if I am to believe half the protestations you have made me, I daresay I must call it so—for I should be very, very grateful to you, you know—"

She broke off, raising her eyes to meet his, an enigmatic meaning in their green depths. Captain Lanner gave a slightly unsteady little laugh.

"Oh, yes—a devil! Did I not say so?" he said, and took her hand in a strong clasp. "Very well! It is a bargain! What is my Lord Tarn to me when you look at me so? And as for Victoire —if half the stories I have heard of Tarn are true, I shall be doing her a service by leading her to break her heart over me instead of over him. If, that is, she has a heart that can easily be broken—which I very much doubt, from what I know of her! It is far more likely that she will roll *me* up, foot and guns, and march off to new triumphs! Where do I meet her?"

"In the Park—tomorrow," the Condessa said promptly. "She rides there with Tarn."

The Captain's brows lifted. "Intelligence so accurate! Who are your spies?" he asked.

The Condessa laughed, and her eyes, lifting, met those of Mr. Fearon, surveying her, without the least appearance of doing so, from the opposite box, where he was exchanging languid witticisms with Lady Cowper.

15

Tarn was as good as his word in providing Victoire with a mount for her next excursion in the Park, for on the following afternoon he appeared in Albemarle Street astride his grey, with a groom behind him leading a beautiful little bay mare. Victoire, who had been on the lookout for him from an upper window, flew down the stairs at once to the street, so much excited by the sight of the mare that she quite forgot the elegance of her new sapphire-blue riding dress, with its lace cravat, and her tall-crowned hat adorned with a curled ostrich plume. The Marquis, dismounting, tossed her up into the saddle.

"How do you like her?" he enquired. "I hope she's not too *old* and *fat* for your taste?"

"Now you are teasing me," said Victoire severely, settling herself in the saddle and expertly arranging the skirts of her habit. "You know very well that she is the most beautiful mare in the whole world! I cannot wait to try her paces! How is she called? May I gallop her in the Park?"

"Her name is Vanity, and, as far as I am concerned—yes," said the Marquis. "But Duke would tell you, positively no! You will have everyone staring at you."

She threw him a saucy glance as he mounted and they set off in the direction of the Park. "*Eh bien*, I do not care for that, if *you* do not," she said. "And Duke is not here—or Mademoiselle—so we shall do as we like and say nothing to them, and then they will not be vexed, because they will know nothing at all about it!"

Tarn, watching in entire approval the ease with which she brought the mare—who was much inclined to take exception to the bustle of London traffic—mincing sedately alongside his big grey, said with a grin that if she wished to make a spectacle of herself he was not there to stop her—a remark which apparently caused her to reconsider, for she rode on with a thoughtful air of somewhat mutinous resignation that brought a gleam of amusement to his lordship's black eyes again. If he had had someone by to whom he might have offered a wager, he would have given odds that Miss Duvenay's virtuous resolution not to make an indecorous stir in the Park would not outlive her first glimpse of a clear stretch of turf or road suitable for letting the mare have her head—and he would have won his wager. Victoire, passing inside the Park and setting longing eyes upon the stretch of tan that ran beside the carriage road, found temptation irresistible; with one guilty, determined, mirthful glance at her companion, she and the mare went flying off at the gallop.

Tarn followed, his grey easily keeping pace with the mare. When Victoire drew up and found him beside her she blushed and laughed, but reminded him that, after all, he could not scold her, as he had done exactly the same thing that she had done herself.

"Ah, but only because it was my duty!" he pointed out self-righteously. "What would Cousin Amelia have said if I had allowed you to go careering off on your own?"

"She would say you were a *grédin* to tell such a fib! You enjoyed it quite as much as I did—*Oh!*"

She broke off suddenly on a sharp exclamation. They had turned their horses' heads to proceed back along the track, and, as her gaze ranged rather shyly now over the carriage road and footway, observing with some self-consciousness that her pell-mell gallop had drawn all eyes upon her, she saw a young officer abruptly detach himself from a group of military men standing in conversation nearby and take an impetuous step towards her.

"Oh!" she ejaculated again. "It *is* Constant! Constant! *Constant!*" she called, and the next moment, flinging her reins into a surprised Tarn's keeping, she had slid off the mare's back and was running towards the young officer, holding out both her hands to him and almost tripping over the long skirts of her habit as she ran.

"Constant!" she cried, as the young officer, stepping forward to meet her, took her outstretched hands in his with an almost incredulous smile upon his bronzed, eager face. "It *is* you! It *is*! Oh, Constant, don't you know me? It's Victoire! I expect I have changed, but I knew *you* at once!"

Captain Lanner, surveying the very flushed and radiant young lady whose hands he held, said, "Good God, it *is* Victoire! But you've grown up! It's incredible!"

"Yes! Isn't it? I am a young lady now—*vraiment*! And you —you are older—and a Captain!"

She stood back, surveying him admiringly, while Captain Lanner, evidently even more struck by the alteration in his erstwhile companion than she was by the change in hers, took in all the details of the captivating little face with its clustering chestnut curls escaping from beneath the severe hat, the elegant small figure in its sapphire-blue riding dress.

"What are you doing in London?" Victoire meanwhile was demanding of him. "And why did you not let me know at once that you were here?"

"Because I didn't know *you* were here until I saw you galloping that mare *ventre à terre* through the Park, to the dismay and admiration of these English!" Captin Lanner said, with a smile. "You are the same little madcap, I see, in spite of all these grown-up airs! What does your poor *maman* have to say to such goings-on?"

"*Maman* is in America—at least, I daresay she may not be there yet, but that is where she is going—so she says nothing at all!" Victoire retorted, with a gleeful air of having scored a point over him. "Oh, but, Constant, I *am* so glad to see you! It is—it is *épatant!* And you—you are glad to see me, too, *n'est-ce pas?*"

The Captain, who was still holding her hands in his, was about to give her some highly satisfactory assurances on this head when Tarn, who had called his groom sharply to his side, dismounted and, leaving the horses, came striding up. The Marquis was not looking best pleased by the turn of events, and indeed he was not; he had been used to seeing that glowing look upon Victoire's face reserved only for himself, and, though it was of course a matter of no moment at all to him if she chose to greet a young man who was obviously an old friend with such a public display of effusiveness, his hackles had nevertheless undoubtedly risen.

Captain Lanner, observing his rather grim look, prudently released Victoire's hands, but Victoire, quite impervious to it in her excitement, merely turned to the Marquis happily and said, "Oh! It is you, Lewis! This is Constant—Captain Lanner, that is. I was used to know him—oh, so well!—in Vienna. My Lord Tarn," she said, presenting the Marquis to Captain Lanner.

The two young men shook hands with no noticeable air of enthusiasm, but this absence of cordiality was more than made up for by Victoire. She launched at once into an excited series of questions and reminiscences: What was Captain Lanner doing in Prussian uniform? Did he make a long stay in London? Had he news of Mayrhof, or Grindl, or O'Ballance? Did he remember the afternoon they had eaten so much *Gugelhupf* they were both sick, and he had had to go on parade? The Captain, laughing, good-humouredly parrying the rapid questions fired at him, appeared to be enjoying himself greatly and to be quite unaware that the gentlemen with whom he had been in company were somewhat impatiently awaiting his return to them; it was, in fact, Tarn who at length pointedly reminded Victoire that she was keeping Captain Lanner from his friends.

"Ah, bah! I am sorry! But I cannot help it; it has been so long!" she said impenitently. She went on, to the Captain, "*Eh bien*, you must come to Albemarle Street to see me, then —tomorrow! I am staying there with Miss Standfield, you know. Or, better still," she added, turning eagerly to Tarn, "Lewis must invite you to come to the theatre with us tonight. You will—will you not, Lewis? Mademoiselle says that you have taken a box."

Captain Lanner, seeing the coolness with which this suggestion was greeted by the Marquis, began to disclaim, but Victoire looked so disappointed that Tarn relented and, acceding to her request, told the Captain with rather reluctant civility that he would be happy to have him join their party. The Captain as civilly accepted the invitation and then went off to rejoin his friends, while Tarn threw Victoire up into the saddle again and remounted his own big grey.

"He was my very best friend in Vienna," Victoire, still full of the meeting, informed him as they rode off side by side. "He would do anything that I would do, which was very nice—only of course he was a soldier and so it was not at all *comme il faut* for him. I climbed up into a big tree once at a picnic when Papa and *Maman* were not looking, and he climbed up after me, only a branch broke and he fell down almost on top of the Gräfin von Heusberg, who was very fat, and she and *Maman* both had the vapours, and there were a great many important people there, *tu sais*, so that Constant said if it had not been for Papa he

185

would have been *court-martialled!* You can have no idea how exciting it was!"

"Little monkey!" said Tarn, grinning in spite of himself at this dramatic account.

"Yes, I was," Victoire agreed happily. "Very like a monkey! *I* did not fall out of any trees at all"—at which the Marquis laughed aloud, although feeling, unaccountably, not greatly disposed towards laughter at that moment.

Miss Standfield had, of course, to be informed of the meeting with Captain Lanner upon their return to Albemarle Street, and, when she saw how disinclined Tarn seemed to be to join in Victoire's pleasure over this event, said with immediate cordiality that she would be happy to make the young man's acquaintance. And, true to this promise, she was very kind to Captain Lanner when he joined them in Tarn's box at Drury Lane that evening, observing with an appearance of great satisfaction his sturdy, well-set-up figure and fair good looks, and according his easy, open manners the accolade of her approval.

What was more, she undertook to require the Marquis's entire attendance upon her conversationally, so that Captain Lanner and Victoire were left free to pursue their own agreeable reminiscences of the past. Victoire, able for the first time in many years to enjoy a conversation with someone intimately connected with the happiest period of her life, was, for once, quite oblivious of the Marquis's presence—a fact which did not escape the notice of the Condessa de Vilamil, who arrived in a box on the other side of the theatre in the middle of the first act with her Portuguese host and hostess and several very elegantly attired gentlemen in her train. The Condessa herself wore a diaphanous chemise dress of white muslin with a deep décolleté that left her dazzlingly white shoulders and bosom almost bare, and it was scarcely surprising that a good many gentlemen in the audience at the Lane that evening found her amply revealed charms of more interest than the portrayal of the melancholy Dane that Mr. Kean was offering them upon the stage.

It was not surprising, either, that Tarn, finding himself *de trop* in his own box, should have taken himself, during the first interval, to the Condessa's. Victoire was so absorbed in her conversation with Captain Lanner that she scarcely noticed his departure, but she was brought up short by the sight of him entering the opposite box. Here he was received with great cordiality by the Condessa (a fact that might have puzzled Captain Lanner if he had not already somewhat precociously learned a great deal about the deviousness of the female sex), and was soon to be seen laughing and chatting with her with a good humour that had been conspicuously lacking in his behaviour in his own box that evening.

An indignant flush arose in Victoire's cheeks, and her fingers tightened round her fan. Then her chin went up and she resumed her interrupted conversation with the Captain, chatting on with a determined gaiety that was somewhat marred by an occasional smouldering glance cast in the direction of the Condessa's box.

But Tarn did not return to his own party until the curtain was rising on the second act, so that any observations she had it in mind to make to him had necessarily to be postponed until the next interval. That she was bursting to say something was obvious from the coolly dignified air she had adopted, and Captain Lanner, with mischief in his blue eyes and a conspiratorial glance—which went quite unacknowledged—at the Condessa, was considerate enough during the next interval to leave the box himself to chat with some of his friends, thus allowing Victoire full scope to quarrel with Tarn as much as she desired.

It turned out, however, that he had underestimated her. Having spent the entire act in lecturing herself upon the undesirability of making any invidious remarks about the Condessa in such a public place as a box in the Drury Lane Theatre,

187

she had her temper well in hand by the time the curtain went down, and, though she could not quite keep the Condessa out of her thoughts or conversation, she managed, when she did speak of her, to do so with a really heroic propriety.

"Bien entendu, she is very beautiful," she acknowledged, having herself introduced the Condessa's name into the conversation by enquiring of Tarn if she intended to remain long in London—a question that he professed himself (truthfully, she could only hope) to be quite unable to answer. "Much more beautiful," she went on, twisting the knife in the wound, "than any other lady I have ever seen. And if," she added magnanimously, "she wears gowns that cause one to think she is not respectable, no doubt that is what gentlemen like." Struck by a sudden thought, she looked down at her own still childishly slender figure. "Perhaps if I—" she began inspirationally.

"No!" said the Marquis unequivocally.

She tilted up her chin. "You have not heard what I was about to say," she objected. "You cannot say *No!* until you have."

"Oh, can't I?" retorted Tarn. "Well, I've said it and, what's more, I mean it—not that it needs *my* saying," he added. "Cousin Amelia will take good care you don't rig yourself out in *that* style, my girl!"

Victoire looked rebellious. "You like it when *she* does it," she pointed out, her resolution to enter into no disputes with the Marquis on the subject of the Condessa rapidly fading, so that it was perhaps fortunate that the arrival of Mr. Fearon in the box at that moment put an end to the conversation.

Mr. Fearon had brought with him a blushing but determined Mr. Swanton—not that he placed much reliance upon that young gentleman's ability to compete with Captain Lanner for Miss Duvenay's interest, but it would not do, he felt, to put out of account entirely his obvious advantages in the way of fortune. More than one young lady, to Mr. Fearon's knowledge, had been influenced more strongly, when it came to the point of bestowing her hand in marriage, by that useful commodity than by any romantic inclinations she might have felt.

So he put on his most maliciously amusing air, and adroitly succeeded in keeping both Miss Standfield and Tarn interested in the latest crim. con. story going the rounds, so that young Mr. Swanton, finding himself free from the Marquis's terrifying scrutiny, was able to pay his modest court to Victoire without hindrance, and was going on very well until he ventured to bring out a question as to whether Miss Duvenay and Miss Standfield would give him the pleasure of their company in a drive to Richmond Park. This caused Victoire—who was quite indifferent to her young Midas of a suitor, but unwilling to wound him by an unqualified negative—to appeal to Miss Standfield.

"Drive to Richmond Park?" said that astute lady, with a speculative glance at Tarn. "Why, I believe—"

"If you and Miss Duvenay have a wish to see Richmond Park, ma'am, I shall drive you there myself," said the Marquis, looking at Mr. Swanton with such an uncompromising frown that that timid young gentleman was on the verge of withdrawing from the lists altogether when his case was improved by the return of Captain Lanner. The Captain, apprised of the matter under discussion, at once remarked that, as a newcomer to England, he himself had a great desire to see something of its famed countryside, and wished that he might make one of the party if an excursion was being planned.

"Then we shall have a picnic at Richmond one day soon! Do say yes, Mademoiselle!" Victoire said, turning to Miss Standfield with her enthusiasm rising now for an outing that would include Captain Lanner among its members.

Mr. Fearon, entering into the project, amiably remarked that he would be happy to drive his phaeton if he were permitted to join the party, and to take up in it Captain Lanner or anyone else Miss Standfield might desire to invite, for whom there would not be room in her own carriage. Upon hearing this, Mr. Swanton plucked up sufficient courage to say that he would drive *his* phaeton, too, feeling that after all, as the originator of the scheme, he could not properly be excluded from it, and an animated discussion thereupon took place as to which young ladies might be invited to join a party in which there would be such a preponderance of gentlemen.

The rising of the curtain upon the next act left the details of the excursion still unsettled, but that there would be one had been firmly decided, in spite of the Marquis's in no way committing himself to take part in it and looking as if he disapproved entirely of the whole affair. Victoire, slightly intoxicated by the feeling of having held a kind of levee in the box, exactly like the Condessa, with no fewer than four eligible gentlemen giving her almost their entire attention, did not allow this negative attitude to dampen her spirits, and presently, with what she felt was a very grown-up deviousness, suggested to Tarn that he take her for a stroll in the corridor during the next interval, thus killing two birds with one stone, for this would both keep him from making a return visit to the Condessa's box and allow her the opportunity of assuring him that she would not enjoy the Richmond Park excursion in the least if he were not to be one of the company.

Unfortunately, her plan did not work out exactly as she had proposed it. The Marquis, indeed, was amenable to leaving the box at the interval, as it gave him the opportunity of escaping from the company of Captain Lanner, which he was beginning to feel irksome, not to say positively disagreeable. But they had not been walking above three minutes, and Victoire had had no opportunity to say what was on her mind, when she saw the Condessa coming towards them with her wizened Portuguese host. What was more, she was quite certain that this meeting was by design, its being rather too much to believe that the Condessa, from her vantage point just opposite them, had not seen Tarn leaving the box with her on his arm.

She would have given a great deal to have been able to turn her back upon the Condessa and walk off, but as this was not possible she fixed what she hoped was a very composed expression upon her face and wished fervently that Tarn would not be moved to stop and talk to her. But whether he would have been or not she was not to know, for by this time the Condessa had halted directly in their path and was saying in her rich voice and with her dazzling smile that she wished his lordship would make her known to his young companion.

"For I have been admiring her all the evening," she said, with an obvious disregard for truth that made Victoire quite furiously conscious of her total inability to compete with her in any way, as far as dress and appearance were concerned.

The Marquis had on his thunderous air but was obliged to make the introduction, and the Condessa smiled again, weighing up all Victoire's points and dismissing them so kindly that Victoire longed to scratch her eyes out. But instead she merely curtsied slightly, with a look as wary and challenging as a duellist giving the salute, while the wizened Portuguese, hearing his name pronounced by the Condessa, smiled benignly on them all.

At this point, however, Victoire's luck turned. Captain Lanner, released from attendance upon Miss Standfield by the appearance in her box of an ancient beau who wished to engage in a *tête-à-tête* gossip with her on Royal affairs, came strolling by alone.

"Oh, Captain Lanner!" Victoire cried, detaining him, her voice expressing a civility quite as bland as the Condessa's. "Please—will you be so kind as to take me back to the box? I am a little *fatiguée*, I find, after all, and Lord Tarn will wish to converse with his *friends.*"

Captain Lanner looked ruefully at the Marquis, as if he rather expected he would call him out on the spot and would not have blamed him if he had, but what was there for him to do? Victoire's hand was already upon his arm, and he was obliged to lead her away. In five minutes' time, he knew, it would be all over the theatre that little Miss Duvenay had dealt the Condessa a resounding snub, being so sure of her ground, as far as Tarn was concerned—or so indifferent as to whether he preferred the Condessa's conversation to hers—that she could leave him with the charmer without a qualm.

Victoire herself did not see the matter in this light, her chief thought having been the necessity of removing herself from the Condessa's vicinity if she were to adhere to her resolution not to utter certain remarks that would be sure to be construed by these proper English as "making a scene." But Captain Lanner did, for he undertook, with the freedom of old acquaintance, to bring her to a suitable understanding of the fact that she had behaved improperly as he escorted her back to the box; and so did Tarn. He came into the box not three minutes after she had entered it herself and, finding her there alone with Miss Standfield—for the ancient beau had departed and Captain Lanner had been detained in conversation at the door by friends—demanded wrathfully what the devil she had meant by it.

"Meant by what?" Victoire said, looking at him with an innocent air.

"You know very well what I mean, you little gypsy!" Tarn said bitterly. "Walking off under my very nose with Lanner!"

"I merely thought," said Victoire, with the utmost primness, "that you wished to talk to your—I mean, to talk to the Condessa"—upon which entirely improper speech Miss Standfield saw fit to enter the fray.

"Such hints, my dear Victoire," she said disapprovingly, "are not at all suitable, as you very well know. I *hope* you have not been conducting yourself in an indecorous fashion."

"Yes, she has!" Tarn interrupted, goaded. "She's the most outrageous little baggage I've ever clapped eyes on, and if you've been trying to teach her to behave herself in a proper way, all I can say is that you've wasted your time!"

"You, of course, Lewis," Miss Standfield remarked, turning

her fire upon him, "being such an excellent judge of the proprieties!"

But Victoire, who had been reflecting on her shortcomings during this interchange, here said penitently that she was very sorry, and that she would never do it again.

"That's what you said the last time!" Tarn reminded her.

"I said I would not make a scene, and, *enfin*, I have not made a scene," she objected. "I curtsied to that—that *lady*," she hastily emended what she had been about to say, seeing the Marquis's minatory eye upon her, "and spoke to her *très doucement*—"

"You didn't speak to her at all!" Tarn said. "Not," he conceded after a moment, frowning, "that I wanted you to. The truth is that she's not a fit person for you to know, infant—and an infernal amount of brass she had, forcing herself upon you in that way! All the same, it's the outside of enough, you know, when you walk off like that with Lanner!"

"I will never do it again," Victoire assured him fervently, "never!"—rejoicing inwardly over these derogatory words about the Condessa. "And Constant did not at all *wish* to do it, you know—he scolded me all the way back to the box."

The entrance of the Captain himself, and a pointed observation from Miss Standfield that the curtain was going up, put an end here to the subject, which was not taken up again during the course of the evening. In fact, there was no opportunity to do so, for Captain Lanner did not leave Victoire's side again, and, while the party was enjoying an excellent supper at the Star Hotel in Henrietta Street, amused her so much with his recalling of several disgraceful episodes from their joint past in Vienna that she forgot all about having behaved improperly about the Condessa and laughed until she choked, which made her look as if she were twelve again instead of almost eighteen and set the Captain off on an entirely new series of reminiscences involving the unfortunate Gräfin von Heusberg and a pet goat which, owing to Miss Victoire Duvenay's negligence, had invaded a drawing room while that lady was present.

As for Mr. Fearon, he supped with the Condessa that night and they discussed the Richmond Park scheme, for which she had some excellent suggestions, so that he went back to his lodgings in Stratton Street not at all ill pleased with what he felt had been accomplished that evening.

16

Mr. Fearon had good cause to be satisfied with the results of his and the Condessa's joint endeavours during the ensuing days. If Tarn was now seen everywhere with Miss Duvenay, so too was Captain Lanner, who, thanks to Mr. Fearon and the Condessa, was well provided with knowledge as to exactly when she would appear on horseback in the Park or when Covent Garden or the Royal Italian Opera House would be graced by her presence, as well as being supplied with cards of invitation to all the dress-parties, breakfasts, and balls she attended.

This was very agreeable, not to say flattering, for Victoire, as the Captain left no doubt in anyone's mind that it was she who was the attraction for him at all these functions. But Tarn was growing heartily sick of the young Captain's face by this time, and if it had not been beneath his dignity would have told Victoire as much—not, of course, that it made the slightest difference to him if she chose to enjoy the company of a young man whom she had known long before she had ever clapped eyes upon *him*. Still he could not help feeling that life would have been much simpler if the King of Prussia had never joined the alliance against Bonaparte, so that that monarch would not now feel it necessary to visit London with a great many tiresome people in his retinue whom one could very well do without.

To make matters worse, an indiscreet remark uttered by one of a party of friends just as he was about to set off with them one evening to Cribb's Parlour, which was to be the starting point for a more or less riotous night, depending upon the mood of the company, suddenly put it into his head to entertain suspicions as to the meaning of Captain Lanner's attentions towards Victoire. The Captain, it appeared, in spite of his youth, already had an interestingly checquered past—a fact of which the Marquis had been aware in a vague and tolerant manner, befitting one whose own past also did not bear close examination. But a carelessly dropped word to the effect that Captain Lanner seemed to have ambitions towards becoming more than a Friend of Victoire's Youth came as something of a shock to him, for he had been thinking of the Captain, in his conscious mind at least, exclusively under that heading, and it at once decided him to spend the evening in Albemarle Street rather than with his friends, much to the latters' disappointment.

Upon arriving at Miss Standfield's residence, however, he was informed by Cloyden, the butler, that he would find only Mr. Standfield in the drawing room, as Miss Standfield was suffering from a slight indisposition and Miss Duvenay was abovestairs, preparing to go out. The Marquis uttered an impatient exclamation and walked into the drawing room.

Mr. Standfield, in black satin knee-breeches, striped stockings, and a waisted coat with very long tails, his snowy cravat exquisitely arranged *à la Sentimentale*, was seated in an armchair, turning over the pages of a book, and glanced up in slight surprise at the Marquis's entrance.

"Hullo!" he said. "What are *you* doing here, coz?"

The Marquis enquired with some slight acerbity if there was anything unusual in a man's coming to visit his betrothed.

"Shouldn't think so myself," Mr. Standfield judiciously granted. "The point is, though, she ain't here. I mean to say, she won't be in a brace of snaps. Going to the Pavitt masquerade, you know."

His lordship said so he had been told, and then, changing the subject abruptly, enquired if Mr. Standfield knew that fellow Lanner who seemed to be always dangling at Victoire's shoe-strings lately.

Mr. Standfield suddenly found his quizzing-glass in need of polishing, began to polish it assiduously, and said that he did.

"Why?" he added cautiously.

"Because," said the Marquis succinctly, "I've half a mind to call him out. That's why."

Mr. Standfield let the quizzing-glass fall, a look of alarm appearing upon his face.

"No, no! Can't do that, old fellow!" he objected earnestly.

"Can't I? Why can't I?" demanded Tarn, looking more enamoured of the idea by the moment.

"Well, deuce take it—for one thing, Victoire," Mr. Standfield urged. "People would be bound to say it was over her. Been very particular in his attentions to her lately, you know."

The Marquis, his face darkening, said that he did know. "And when it comes to the point of a fellow saying it wouldn't surprise him if he means to give her a slip on the shoulder," he said dangerously, "that's enough."

Mr. Standfield shook his head. "No, it ain't," he said firmly. "I don't know who said that to you, but you know as well as I do that there's always some bleater ready to talk slum the minute a fellow so much as looks twice at a girl, and you're a gudgeon if you get the wind up over it. Besides," he added, considering, "Victoire wouldn't like it. Well able to take care of herself with Lanner, you know. It's my belief she'd comb his hair with a joint-stool if he ever tried to go beyond the line."

The Marquis, who had been deriving a great deal of satisfaction during the past half hour in contemplating the idea of facing Captain Lanner across twenty yards of greensward with a Manton duelling-piece in his hand, regretfully acknowledged that this was so.

"All the same," he said, "I shall have to keep a better eye on her; I can see that. Only it's the outside of enough when a man can't spend a quiet evening once in a way with his friends—" He saw the Honourable Marmaduke's skeptical eye upon him and grinned. "Oh, very well!" he said. "*Not* such a quiet evening. At any rate, that's out the window now. Do you say she is going to the Pavitt masquerade tonight?"

Mr. Standfield said that he was to escort her there himself, adding with some caution that he hoped his cousin did not object to this.

"Well, no, I don't, because I'll take her myself," Tarn said at once.

A pained look crossed Mr. Standfield's face. "*Not* in pantaloons," he said, observing with disfavour the casual attire in which the Marquis had invested himself for his projected evening at Cribb's Parlour. "They wouldn't let you in. Fancy dress or knee-breeches, you know, dear boy."

The Marquis swore, but said that he would return home and clothe himself properly and then return to Albemarle Street to give his escort to Victoire. This, however, said Mr. Standfield, would not do either, since, owing to Miss Standfield's indisposition, as well as her aversion to masquerades, which she characterised with old-fashioned directness as nothing more than invitations to licentious behaviour, it was Lady Whittingham who was chaperoning Victoire that evening. And Arthur, he said, as Tarn very well knew, would insist upon their leaving as soon as the carriages drew up before the house so that his horses would not be left standing.

The two young men then made derisive noises indicative of their opinion of Lord Whittingham's horses and his status as a judge of horseflesh in general, after which the Marquis took himself off, stating that he would go on to the Pavitts' alone as soon as he had attired himself in the proper fashion.

Pavitt House was in Chiswick, and a solitary ten-mile drive on a rainy June evening had done little to improve the Marquis's mood when he arrived there some time later, properly attired in knee-breeches and dress coat, with a scarlet domino carelessly flung over them. Nor did it mollify him to reflect, as he paused on the threshold of the great ballroom—a breathtaking apartment hung with Spitalsfield silk of a crimson colour, where life-sized gods and goddesses of dull gold looked down in Roman splendour from atop verd-antique columns —that he had neglected to learn from Mr. Standfield in what guise Victoire had come to the ball, so that finding her out in the motley masked throng of queens and shepherdesses, knights and Turks and harlequins, might turn out to be a difficult, if not impossible, task.

He was engaged in a frowning scrutiny of the dancers when a veiled Circassian lady, whose exceedingly filmy garments revealed her form so frankly that there could be little doubt that that form belonged to the Condessa de Vilamil, gracefully disengaged herself from the group of Cossacks, satyrs, and Punchinellos surrounding her and came across the room towards him.

"Lewis—*mi amor!*" she greeted him, with mocking reproach. "So late—and in nothing more imaginative than a domino! I had thought better of you!"

"Had you?" said the Marquis, his eyes moving from the dancers to rest appreciatively for a moment upon the fair Circassian and then returning at once to their survey of the crowded floor. "I daresay you would instantly have recognised me, no matter how I had disguised myself, at any rate," he said indifferently. "A mask seems no hindrance to you. I wish I had your power!"

"But it is very simple, of course! You are the tallest man in the room," the Condessa said. She added, in a tone of decided pique, "*Mi amor*, it is not at all *galant* of you to give me one glance and then forget I exist! If you are looking for that chit, she is dancing with young Lanner, and amusing herself very well without you, I assure you!"

"Is she, by God!" said the Marquis grimly. "Where are they? I wish you will point them out to me."

The Condessa's air of pique suddenly vanished; she looked at him more closely for a moment and then shrugged, laughing.

"Well, I will not tell you while you stand there looking so ridiculously *farouche*," she said lightly. "I am very fond of Constant, you know, and I will not have you blowing a hole through him merely because he is carrying on a flirtation with a girl you appear to have taken a fancy to. Come and sit down with me for a moment and we shall talk of this calmly, and then, if you like, I shall point out your Victoire to you."

The Marquis said, in a voice of repressive civility, that he could not conceive what there was to talk about.

"Well, you shall see in a moment," the Condessa said, not at all deterred by this snub. She laid her hand upon his arm. "Now do not be tiresome, darling Lewis," she said. "You know you cannot dance with Miss Duvenay until this set has ended, nor can you call Constant out here—though I must say," she added, looking critically about her at the very free-and-easy manners being displayed by more than one of Lady Pavitt's guests, "that I doubt if anyone would notice if you did. I was told that the Pavitts were not quite the thing, and that if he were not so enormously rich I should find no one of any consequence here—"

"From *you*, love?" Tarn interrupted, grinning in spite of himself.

The Condessa tapped his arm with her fan. "Now you are being your usual abominable self," she said, "and I like you much better that way. Come along; I am sure we shall be able to find a little room in this vast house where we can be alone; it seems as full of alcoves as a rabbit warren."

She drew him away and, with a last impatient glance at the masked dancers, he accompanied her into a small anteroom, where she sat down at once upon a sofa upholstered in crimson damask and with a gesture invited him to seat himself beside her.

"Well, what is it?" Tarn demanded, when he had complied.

"My dear, how too, too brusque!" The Condessa hid behind her fan, miming distress—then laughed, threw the fan down, and said he was a beast, and she was very glad she had done what she had, after all.

"Well? What have you done?" Tarn enquired, looking at her suspiciously.

"Why, nothing—except to set young Constant on to pay his addresses to your Victoire." The Marquis, thunderstruck, said nothing at all, and she went on, picking up her fan and flirting it open again. "Isn't this a pretty thing? Vernis Martin, I was assured by the gentleman who was kind enough to present it to me—"

She looked up in well-acted surprise as the fan was snatched ungently from her hand and snapped shut.

"What the devil do you mean by that?" Tarn demanded.

"Mean by what? *Mi amor,* if you break my fan, I shall be seriously displeased with you."

"Well, I've already broken it," the Marquis admitted, diverted momentarily from his wrath and glancing down, rather appalled, at the shattered ivory sticks in his hand. "I'll buy you another. But don't think," he added, more menacingly again, "that you can fob me off—"

"Fob you off? But I shouldn't dream of it!" said the Condessa. "On the contrary, I assured Constant that I would tell

201

you the whole of it. He is *not*, you see, anxious to be called out by a man of your deadly reputation, and it is plain to me that that is exactly what you are beginning to have in mind." She shook her head, a look of mischief in her green eyes. "Confess!" she said. "You would like nothing better!"

The Marquis, whose emotions had run the gamut from incredulity to a highly dangerous wrath since she had introduced the subject, had no need to confess anything at all; his face spoke the story. However, the Condessa, who was quite used to his temper, did not allow herself to become alarmed.

"It is no use your flying into a black rage with me, darling Lewis," she said, "for you know very well that I am quite incorrigible. You had much better think what you had best do in the situation—and I can tell you frankly that that is to drop the chit while you can still do so gracefully. You can't really *wish* to marry her, you know—you, of all men, to be saddled with the responsibility for that child! And even if you do succeed in taking her away from Constant now and leading her to the altar, people will be certain to say—after the very decided preference she has been showing for him—that it was only your title and fortune that carried the day against him. As for calling him out, I have merely to spread the story to make you look exceedingly foolish, my dear—the man who could win a bride only by shooting his successful rival!—if, indeed, you *did* succeed in coming off the victor," she added thoughtfully, "which is not at all certain, for Constant is quite as cool under fire as you are yourself, I dare swear."

She broke off, looking at him with a provocative smile in her eyes, as if inviting the storm to break; for the Marquis, in her experience—once he had vented his feelings in some intemperate outburst—was invariably much easier to manage.

Somewhat to her surprise, however, this time he did not rise to the bait. Instead, he sat frowning in bleak silence for several moments, and at last said, in a heavy voice that she did not recognise, "Is it Lanner's intention to marry her?"

202

"My dear, no! I daresay the idea has never entered his head. Nor does he intend to seduce her. He will do only what I have asked him to do—which is to pay court to her and lead her to display an open preference for him. When the game has been played to an end, he will disappear and leave her to fall into the arms of young Mr. Swanton—who will be only too happy to receive her, I am sure, for he is so jealous of Constant by this time that it is obvious he would like to murder him."

She paused, observing once more, with a slight sensation of surprise and unease, the grim control that his lordship was maintaining over his temper. Only the faint, sharp sound caused by the snapping of another of the ivory sticks of the fan he still held in his hand betrayed him; his dark face by now appeared quite calm.

He looked down at her. "Perhaps," he said, after a moment, deliberately, "you will have the goodness to tell me why you have hatched this plot?"

She smiled, gazing full up into his face. "*Mi amor*, need you ask?" she said softly. "I am a shameless, jealous jade; you have told me so yourself a score of times."

He frowned again, incredulously. "And Lanner?" he said. "You'd have me believe that he'd lend you his aid in this?"

"Certainly he would not do so if he knew what I intend to gain by it," the Condessa said composedly. "It is *his* delusion, my dear, that I merely wish to be revenged upon you for your cruel and inconsiderate treatment of me. Of course I did not tell him," she added pensively, "of the exceedingly handsome presents I had of you."

"No, I daresay you did not," said the Marquis scathingly. "But what happens if *I* tell him the truth?"

"Oh, he will believe you, of course," said the Condessa, still quite unperturbed. "But it will not deter him, you know. He is a perfect young scamp and has unlimited confidence in himself, besides; he is sure to think I shall change my mind like your Victoire, and prefer *him* in the end." She looked again, with faintly smiling, cynical wisdom, into his dark, rigid face. "And do not think, either, darling Lewis, of informing Miss Duvenay that Constant's pursuit of her is a sham," she said softly, "because *she* will *not* believe you, you know. She is loyal, I think, *mi amor*—far too good for either you *or* Constant, if you will have the truth—and Constant is her friend; she will never credit that he is deceiving her."

The Marquis, who was well aware that the Condessa's reading of Victoire's character was perfectly accurate, might nevertheless, if he had been in his betrothed's company at that moment, have been hard put to it not to impart to her the secret of Captain Lanner's interest in her; but he was not in her company, nor had he, unless the Condessa disclosed to him the disguise under which Victoire had come to the ball, any immediate prospect of finding her among four hundred or so other masked revellers. The Condessa, however, was kind enough presently to do just that, having the gentlemanly quality, common to many women of her type, of keeping her word—but in the meantime other events were occurring that made it quite unlikely that either Victoire or the Marquis would be in the mood for rational discussion when they met.

These events began when Victoire—demurely attired in the green silk domino which Miss Standfield's dislike of masquerades had obliged her to wear, and dancing, as the Condessa had accurately informed Tarn, with Captain Lanner —had seen the Marquis leaving the ballroom with the Condessa. She had had no more difficulty than had the Condessa in picking him out because of his betraying height, and, having seen him enter the room, had formed the happy intention of seeking him out as soon as the set had come to an end—only to find him going into seclusion almost immediately with the fair Circassian, of whose identity neither she nor anyone else in the room could have any doubt.

The look of eager anticipation left her face at once, to be

succeeded by a hurt, angry flush. Captain Lanner, his back to the scene that had so interested her, enquired what was the matter.

"Nothing! *Rien du tout!*" she denied, and began quickly to talk with enthusiasm of her first masquerade ball, and to join him in trying to guess the identities of the other guests. The Captain himself was looking very handsome in the powdered wig of an earlier day, a coat of white brocade, and satin knee-breeches, and his successor in seeking and obtaining Victoire's hand was a turban'd Turk in rich silks, with a pair of ferocious black mustachios decorating his very youthful face—Mr. Swanton, Victoire was convinced, before he had so much as completed his stammering application for her hand.

So she danced the boulanger with Mr. Swanton, wishing all the while that duelling were not a forbidden pastime for females, thus preventing her from calling the Condessa out, and at its conclusion requested her young and—she feared—slightly tipsy partner to take her back to Lady Whittingham. Mr. Swanton had indeed been recruiting his spirits, with something of the desperation of a man staking his entire fortune upon a single throw of the dice, with a rather inordinate amount of iced champagne, for he had made up his mind to ask Victoire to marry him that evening. That is to say, he had been driven to this decision by the sight of her standing up twice with Captain Lanner, for, as he did not move in the same circles as Victoire's connexion with Miss Standfield enabled her to do, he had not been aware of her growing intimacy with the Captain, and it came as a shock to him. It had previously been his intention to take advantage of the picnic excursion, set for the following day, to press his suit upon her, but jealousy, champagne, and the licensed freedom of the masquerade were now inciting him to immediate action.

So instead of taking Victoire back to Lady Whittingham as she had requested, he pulled her quite unexpectedly into a velvet-curtained alcove behind a golden pillared Diana and, at once plumping down upon his knees before her, implored her to accept his hand and heart.

Victoire looked down at him in astonishment. "*Tiens*, you are certainly foxed!" she said. "I thought so before, and now I am sure of it. Get up at once; you look very silly, I can tell you, and someone may come in."

Mr. Swanton, looking as if cold water had been cast upon him, climbed to his feet—a process somewhat impeded by his voluminous Turkish trousers and the scimitar that swung rather awkwardly from his belt. Victoire, who had been looking severe, dissolved into a giggle, upon which Mr. Swanton, suddenly ceasing to be Mr. Alfred Swanton, the Brewer King's heir, and turning into a Cockney lad with a grievance and the manners of his class, surprised her by saying, "Don't—you—*laugh*—at me!" quite furiously. He then laid hands upon her and attempted a free and ferocious embrace, which resulted only in a painful crash of noses and foreheads and a considerable disarrangement of the green silk domino. At the same moment the velvet curtains parted and Captain Lanner came into the alcove.

"What the *devil*—!" said the Captain, in quite unintelligible German that yet instantly managed to convince Mr. Swanton that he had better stop what he was doing.

"Oh—Constant!" gasped Victoire, further confusing Mr. Swanton by speaking in French. "I *am* so glad you are come! This horrid little beast—"

She broke off with a slight shriek of dismay as Mr. Swanton, hastily backing away from the Captain, bumped against a small gilt table, causing a large Chinese vase standing upon it to topple with a crash to the parquet floor.

"*Juste ciel! Do* look what you are about!" Victoire implored, while Captain Lanner, his face relaxing at the obvious terror upon Mr. Swanton's, began to grin.

"Very well, my lad," he said. "You've had your lark, haven't you? Now get out of this before I put you out."

Mr. Swanton inadvisably began stuttering indignant self-justifications, but, on the Captain's advancing upon him, immediately desisted and attempted very rapidly to depart, only to find his way barred by a tall figure in a scarlet domino, which had suddenly appeared in the entry.

"I hope," said my Lord Tarn's voice with awful politeness, "I very much hope that I don't intrude?"

Captain Lanner looked at him cheerfully. "Not at all," he said, with equal politeness. "The Turkish gentleman is just leaving—and so, in point of fact," he added, catching Victoire's hand in his, "are we."

The Marquis, who was looking at the disarray of the green domino, did not move from his position at the alcove's entrance. "Lanner—isn't it?" he enquired, frowning at the masked figure in the white brocade coat.

The Captain bowed assentingly. "You have the advantage of me, sir," he said, "but I believe—my Lord Tarn?"

Victoire said nothing at all, but pulled her domino about her, blushing furiously with the sudden conviction that Tarn did not understand in the least how she came to be alone in this secluded place with two gentlemen, her clothing in some disarray, and a broken vase upon the floor. It seemed to her a very decadent situation, quite in keeping with the boisterous, not to say ribald, romp going on in the splendid ballroom just beyond the crimson velvet curtains, and, being far too innocent to reflect that his lordship was quite accustomed to such scenes and much worse, she looked first guilty and then defiant and wished very much that the floor would open and swallow her up.

Meanwhile, Mr. Swanton, who was always terrified of the Marquis and was even more so in his befuddled condition, which caused his lordship, in the scarlet domino, to appear at least eight feet tall, took advantage of everyone's having momentarily forgotten his existence to slip unobtrusively past Tarn and escape into the ballroom.

"You—you see, Lewis," Victoire began breathlessly, finding her voice at last, "he *would* bring me in here, though I said I wished him to take me back to Lady Whittingham, and then he asked me to marry him, and tried to kiss me, only very luckily Constant came in and stopped him, and then you came—"

The Marquis, looking at Victoire's hand still clasped in Captain Lanner's, said in the same tone of daunting politeness that he dared say Victoire was very much obliged to the Captain, which was such an unusual reaction of his to any scrape into which she had fallen that she could not help thinking the remark to be intended sarcastically and began to blush again, snatching her hand from Captain Lanner's.

"I had been looking for you myself," the Marquis went on to explain, with the painful civility that represented his repression of an intense desire to strangle Captain Lanner immediately and cast his lifeless body into the medieval moat that still surrounded Pavitt House, "and I saw you come in here with that fellow—"

"It was only Mr. Swanton," Victoire interpolated anxiously, "and he *would* bring me here! I think he is foxed."

"—but I was across the floor," Tarn continued inexorably, "and by the time I could get over here it was obvious that you were in no need of my assistance."

Captain Lanner said, again very easily, "Quite right; she was not," and then suggested that, as the set seemed to be forming for the next country dance, he and Victoire take their places in it.

Victoire looked at Tarn. If he were to ask her to dance with him instead, of course she would do so, even though he had gone off into an anteroom himself with the Condessa and had no doubt been doing far worse things with her there than Mr. Swanton had ever dreamed of doing, so that she, Victoire, had every right to be angry with him. But he did not ask her—for one thing, because the Condessa's words about his carrying the day against the Captain only by virtue of his rank and fortune had just then blightingly recurred to him, and for another, because he did not understand in the least that the light of anticipation giving the sudden glow to Victoire's face was due to her expectation that he would ask her to dance, and not to the Captain's already having done so.

So he said in his bleakest tones that he was glad to see she was enjoying the ball and walked off, leaving her quite certain that he had come to the masquerade only to be with the Condessa and that he was very angry with her for having allowed herself to be placed in a compromising situation by Mr. Swanton. If he had been angry in his usual highly direct and intemperate manner it would not have troubled her overmuch, for then she would have lost her temper herself and they would no doubt have had one of the indecorous quarrels Miss Standfield so much deplored and at once have made up. But as it was there was only a feeling of hopelessness and hurt, and she wondered if this was what people meant when they spoke of someone's heart being broken. She was sure that hers would be, even if it was not now, if there was to be only this cold politeness between her and Lewis from this time on.

She did not see him again that evening, for the simple reason that he left Pavitt House and returned to town as soon as he had parted from her, feeling quite unable to answer for his behaviour if he were obliged to stand by and watch her dancing with Captain Lanner. As for the Captain himself, he was felicitated by the Condessa, when they waltzed together later in the evening, long after Victoire had departed with Mr. Standfield and the Whittinghams, upon his success with Miss Duvenay.

"Yes, and I have enjoyed every minute of it," said the Captain unblushingly, looking at her with the little devils of mischief very bright indeed in his blue eyes.

The Condessa laughed. "Are you trying to make me jealous, my child?" she enquired indulgently.

"Could I?"

"I daresay you might. It would not be at all flattering to me, you know, if you were to find yourself *amoureux* of that chit."

The Captain agreed that it would be a very good joke on both of them, and thereupon whirled her about the floor with such expert and complicated energy that the subject could scarcely be pursued further between them. But there was a rather thoughtful expression upon his face and he found—somewhat to his own surprise—that instead of considering pressing the Condessa for some reward for his admitted success in carrying out her wishes in regard to Miss Duvenay, what he was really thinking about was the fact that he would be seeing Victoire again on the following day, when the projected picnic excursion was at last to take place.

17

The picnic scheme was one that seemed to have been doomed from the start.

In the first place, after having been put off several times owing to the weather or to the fact that some one of the participants was unable to be present, it had been decided to transfer the locale from Richmond Park to Merton, for no reason, apparently, except that Lord Whittingham did not like picnics and much preferred to eat his luncheon in a proper dining room. He and Lady Whittingham had been asked to join the party when it had become plain that Miss Standfield's indisposition would prevent her from acting as chaperon, and he had at once, with his usual inability to understand anyone's point of view but his own, made arrangements for the company to drive to Merton instead of to Richmond, and take their luncheon at the pretty Palladian villa he owned there. This, of course, gave the entire affair a revolting air of formality and made it quite plain that anything in the nature of a romp by the young people was to be severely frowned upon.

Then Mr. Swanton's reprehensible behaviour at the Pavitt masquerade obviously made it impossible for him to join any party of which Victoire was a member, and his apologies were accordingly conveyed in a very stiff little note carried to Miss Standfield in the morning. And lastly there was Tarn, who felt that if he were obliged to spend the greater part of the day watching Captain Lanner laughing and chatting with Victoire he would inevitably quarrel with him and perhaps be goaded as well into telling Victoire of her old friend's duplicity. So he took what he felt to be the coward's way out, though it was actually an example of most unusual wisdom upon his part, and declined to be present. This could scarcely be construed as rudeness, as he had never promised anyone that he would come, but Victoire had been counting upon his being one of the party, and his action in staying away seemed to her an additional indication that he was still much displeased with her.

She cheered up somewhat, however, when Mr. Fearon, arriving in Albemarle Street in his phaeton, suggested that he take her up with him and allow her to handle the ribbons for a time, for Tarn had been teaching her to drive and she was delighted to have the opportunity of improving her new skill. Captain Lanner was not best pleased, perhaps, to be deprived of her company by this scheme, but there was nothing for him to do but to make a fourth in the Whittingham barouche with the Whittinghams and the dashing young lady, whose name was Miss Domville, whom Lady Whittingham had invited to join the party.

It was an exemplary English June morning when the two carriages left Albemarle Street, with a bright sun and a pleasant breeze that tossed the horses' manes and the plumes of the huge gypsy hats affected by the ladies. Lord Whittingham, sleepy after the late hours he had kept the night before, contributed only yawns to the conversation, but Captain Lanner, with his usual good humour, exerted himself to entertain the ladies and succeeded so well that Lady Whittingham forgot her sulks over her lord's high-handed rearrangement of their plans, and the dashing young lady, who was not quite so dashing as she liked to appear, fell in love with him at once.

In the phaeton, Victoire's situation was less happy. It was true that Mr. Fearon, once they were beyond the outskirts of the town, had permitted her to take the reins, but her pleasure in driving his excellent greys was almost immediately tempered by the turn he gave to the conversation. His subject was Tarn. He said nothing openly, for that was not his way; but Victoire was treated to a series of light reminiscences of the Marquis's peccadilloes and to glancing hints of worse doings, not fit for a lady's ears, that made her feel very uncomfortable and defensive and wish that Miss Domville or Lady Whittingham was in her place and she was in the barouche. She could not very well tell Mr. Fearon that she did not wish to hear what he had to say when he was only trying to entertain her with amusing anecdotes, but it made her even more troubled than she already was that morning to be obliged to hear of all the beautiful ladies who seemed to have played such a large part in the Marquis's life, and she thought for the first time, with a little feeling of panic, that perhaps being married to him would be more, after all, than she could bear.

So she was greatly relieved when Merton was reached at last and the whole party sat down to a sumptuous luncheon of chickens à la Tarragon and fillets of turbot in an Italian sauce, with so many aspics, trifles, puptons of fruit, and creams to choose from that Lord Whittingham appeared to be almost justified in pointing out the advantages of this repast over any picnic nuncheon, however elaborate. Captain Lanner, too, was now firmly established at her side, which was very pleasant, although making her remember the previous evening and Tarn's coldness, so that she could not be quite her usual gay self with him.

"What is it?" he enquired of her after luncheon was over and he was able to get her off alone outside among the strawberry beds, where the party, except for Lord Whittingham, had decided to wander, with some vague, supererogatory idea of feasting on the ripening berries.

"What is what?" parried Victoire. She took a very rosy, perfect strawberry that the Captain had picked for her and regarded it with a frown, as though she were expected to pass judgement upon it rather than pop it into her mouth and eat it.

The Captain kindly took it from her and ate it himself. "You're in some kind of mood," he informed her. "If it's Whittingham, I understand perfectly. It would not have surprised me in the least if all those beautiful creams he offered us had curdled in their dishes when he looked at them."

Victoire chuckled, but said it was not Lord Whittingham or anyone else; she was in perfect spirits.

"No, you are not," said Captain Lanner. He fixed his blue eyes shrewdly upon her and asked, "Is it Tarn?"

A slight flush rose in Victoire's face, which was fortunately shaded by the wide brim of her hat. She said with dignity, "I don't know what you mean."

"Oh yes, you do," said the Captain. He took her arm and gave it a little shake. "Don't be a widgeon, Victoire," he said. "You couldn't marry a man like that. Even if he asked you, which I daresay he won't."

Victoire wanted very much to tell him that he already had, but the engagement was, after all, still a secret and besides the reason why the Marquis had asked her was not one she would have liked to explain to Captain Lanner. So she only said, in a very small voice, "Why couldn't I?"—which was no way to conclude a conversation that she was firmly convinced ought to be concluded.

"Because," said Captain Lanner unanswerably, "he'd make you devilish unhappy. He has Other Interests, you know"—or, at least, if the words were not spoken by him in large capitals, they appeared so in Victoire's mind.

There was so manifestly nothing that she could say to controvert this statement that she was reduced to remarking loftily that she wished the Captain would not talk nonsense and then turning the conversation into safer channels. Captain Lanner did not persist in pursuing the subject, but he did give her a shrug and a mischievous look to show that he understood her game. Then, to Victoire's relief, Lady Whittingham came up with the news that she and Mr. Fearon and Miss Domville found the notion of whiling away the rest of the afternoon at the villa insupportably insipid, and said that Mr. Fearon had thought of a very good scheme, which they were going to put into practice at once, whether Lord Whittingham liked it or not.

Lord Whittingham, as it developed, did not like it, but he was overruled by the insistence of the others, and in a very short time the horses had been put-to in the carriages again and the party was on its way to what Mr. Fearon assured them was a very ancient and interesting, not to say romantic, inn, with a history as old as the priory where King John was said to have slept before he signed the Great Charter and, what was more to the point for the gentlemen of the party, a home-brewed porter that was the equal of any to be found in England.

Victoire had a place in the barouche this time, Lady Whittingham, desirous of keeping out of the way of her lord's ill humour, having announced her intention of going with Mr. Fearon in his phaeton, and so was not at all disturbed to find that the inn was quite miles away from the Whittingham villa, by way of roads that seemed to have received little or no attention since the days of King John. But Lord Whittingham complained bitterly of the jolting he was receiving, and said he could not fancy why anyone should wish to make such an excursion in the heat of the day merely to see a country inn. Nor did his humour improve when they alighted before a low, rambling building of whitewashed stone, its ancient thatched roof laid in the diamond and scroll pattern of an earlier day, when thatching was a fine art.

"Pho!" he said, looking around disapprovingly at tangled creepers climbing the rough walls, an unkempt garden, and a tumbledown wooden bench standing under a pair of tiny latticed windows. "Nothing to see here! Nothing at all." He walked into the dim little hallway leading to the bar parlour and, his gaze fastening upon the hand-hewn oak slabs with which it was panelled, added darkly, "Mice!"

The ladies, however, pronounced the inn to be charming, and when the landlord, overwhelmed by this invasion of the Quality, hurried in with a tray bearing a blue pottery jug filled with his famed porter and a Stilton cheese wound in a napkin, even Lord Whittingham's disapproval abated slightly and he admitted the Blue Lion's tangy amber porter to be a very tolerable brew.

When he had quenched his thirst with several glasses of it, he settled himself in a Windsor chair by the window and, admonishing the landlord to see that he was not disturbed, went to sleep. The others went off to look around at the garden and grounds, where there was, as Lord Whittingham had truthfully said, nothing at all to see, although Miss Domville, who was interested in horticulture, was pleased to think she had discovered in a hideously overgrown and very thorny bush a type of rose that had been popular in Tudor times. She then complained that the sun had given her the headache and was escorted back into the house by Mr. Fearon, while Captain Lanner remained in the garden with Lady Whittingham and Victoire, regaling them with highly exaggerated tales of his exploits in several armies, which he obviously did not intend them to take seriously.

After half an hour or so of this the shadows began to fall over the little garden and Lord Whittingham suddenly appeared in the doorway, looking much refreshed and in a better humour, and said that it was high time they were starting back to town.

"Where is Bruce?" he asked, looking around and finding only three persons in the garden.

Lady Whittingham, who had forgotten about Mr. Fearon,

looked startled for a moment and then laughed, and said he had gone off with Miss Domville quite half an hour before.

"Well, he's not with her now," Lord Whittingham said positively. "She's in the parlour."

His wife stared. "Where in the world can he be, then?" she asked. "He has certainly not walked off somewhere alone without a word to any of us!"

But this, it soon appeared, was exactly what Mr. Fearon *had* done. A search rapidly instituted by Lord Whittingham and Captain Lanner discovered Mr. Fearon almost at once only a short distance down a rough little lane leading away from the inn, seated at the verge of the road with a very vexed expression upon his face. He had, he explained, thought to stroll to the top of the rise against which the inn stood for a better view of the countryside, but had unfortunately set his foot upon a loose rock in the road and wrenched his ankle so badly that he had felt quite unable to return to the inn unassisted. He had called, he added, but apparently no one had heard him, and so there had been nothing for him to do but to sit down and wait for someone to rescue him.

Lord Whittingham, always prepared to make the most of a misfortune, at once began to lament and worry. How were they to get back to town with Mr. Fearon in such a case? He had known from the start that no good would come of the expedition! Was it not possible that the ankle might be broken rather than sprained? Ought a surgeon to be sent for?

Captain Lanner, more practical-minded, suggested that he have a look at the ankle, but Mr. Fearon rather crossly vetoed this idea, saying he feared that if the boot were once removed it could never be got back on again, and he really would *not* be seen driving about the streets of London without it.

"If you and Arthur will give me your support, I am quite sure I shall be able to hobble back to the inn," he said. "But you will be obliged to drive my phaeton, Lanner. I cannot undertake to do *that*."

He stood up, wincing at the pain of the movement, and, with

Lord Whittingham and Captain Lanner supporting him, was able to limp back to the inn yard. Here questions and exclamations had to run their course again, while the shadows lengthened and the cool of evening began to fall upon the garden. Everyone, it appeared, had a different notion as to what ought to be done. Victoire and Captain Lanner, both hardy creatures themselves, were inclined to be somewhat impatient of Mr. Fearon's making so much of what was, after all, only a trifling accident, but Lord Whittingham was all solicitous concern, and even offered to return with Mr. Fearon to the villa, instead of subjecting him to the rigours of a journey back to town—although, he added worriedly, there were only a pair of elderly servants there, the others having been sent out from town merely to prepare and serve the luncheon and having by this time departed again.

But Mr. Fearon, after considering this and several other suggestions at some length, decided upon returning to town in the Whittingham barouche, remarking that, by taking a roundabout route to the post-road, he believed they might avoid much of the disagreeable jolting that must occur if they proceeded there directly. He then gave Captain Lanner directions as to what he was to do with his phaeton and horses when he reached London with them and, apparently becoming conscious at that moment of advancing time, said that the Captain had best take Victoire with him and go by the direct route, in which he would instruct him, as he had promised Miss Standfield that she would not be late back.

Victoire, who was by this time heartily sick of the whole affair, at once agreed, and though it occurred to Lord Whittingham, once the two carriages had gone their separate ways, that it might have been more proper for them to have remained together, as it would certainly be quite dark before the phaeton reached London, there was nothing that he could do about the matter then.

Meanwhile, Victoire and Captain Lanner were enjoying each other's company as they always did, although becoming presently more than a little puzzled by the fact that Mr. Fearon's directions, instead of leading them expeditiously to the post-road, appeared on the contrary to be plunging them deeper and deeper into a maze of rough lanes and byways.

"Do you think we had best stop at the next village we come to and enquire the way?" Victoire asked at last, pointing out at the same time that it was now growing dusk. "*Tiens*, you are very stupid, I think, Constant! You have certainly misunderstood Mr. Fearon's directions."

The Captain did not defend himself against this accusation. There was a rather odd expression upon his face, halfway between a sudden thoughtfulness and the kind of bright recklessness with which those of his fellow-officers who had seen him go into battle were well acquainted. He did not say anything, however, but only began to whistle in a cheerful, meditative way. And for some reason, when a few minutes later the phaeton, jolting along a particularly rough stretch of road, suddenly lurched, tilted, and then fell to one side with a crash that sent Victoire sliding down the up-ended seat on top of him, he was not quite so much surprised as he might have been. Victoire gasped, "*Mordieu!*" and Captain Lanner swore briefly and then apologised and asked Victoire if she was hurt.

"No! But what has happened?"

"We have lost a wheel, I should say."

The Captain, who with great presence of mind had kept hold of the reins, extricated himself with some difficulty from Victoire's encumbering presence and went to quiet the plunging horses. Victoire, a little dazed, climbed out as well, righted her wide-brimmed gypsy hat, and observed severely that there was a very large rent in the skirt of her gown.

"Pin it up," the Captain advised.

"But I have not got any pins!"

"Of course you have," said the Captain. "In your reticule. All females carry them. But first come and help me with this brute."

Victoire obediently came round and held one of the greys

while he extricated the other from the broken harness. The Captain, having tethered the horses, then took a look at the phaeton and observed dispassionately that it was no use their thinking they could get *that* on the road again this evening.

"But what are we to do then?" demanded Victoire, who had found her reticule and was searching, though not very hopefully, through its contents. "We *must* do something; *ça se voit.* How far are we from London?"

The Captain said that he had not the least guess. He then asked her unexpectedly if Mr. Fearon had ever expressed opposition to the marked attentions that his cousin, Lord Tarn, had been paying to her.

"Mr. Fearon?" Victoire stared. "You are joking, I think! What has he to say to anything?"

The Captain, whose quick mind was rapidly putting together a wrenched ankle, an unexplained half-hour's absence, a set of highly confusing directions concerning the road to London, and a vehicle with a wheel that obligingly parted company with it after receiving a certain amount of jolting, into what seemed a very ingenious plan to leave him and Miss Duvenay embarrassingly stranded at nightfall in a country backwater, said that he might have a great deal to say to it; but he did not pursue the subject. As for Victoire, the mention of Tarn's name had thrown her into the panic that the accident had not been able to do, for it had suddenly occurred to her that he would be certain to find out about all this and that equally certainly he would not like it. He was not disposed at any rate, she knew, to be pleased about her friendship with Captain Lanner, and perhaps this event would so anger him that he would first call the Captain out and shoot him and then inform her that their engagement was at an end.

Inspired by these horrid thoughts, she forgot all about her torn gown and Captain Lanner's inexplicable remark about Mr. Fearon, and, turning to the Captain, said rather breathlessly that they must get back to town at once.

"Yes, I have been thinking that myself," agreed the Captain

equably. "But it may not be so easy to manage, you know. And I believe that, if we don't manage it, it will be generally felt that I have compromised you, and that the only amends I can make will be to marry you as quickly as I can. I hadn't exactly considered marrying before today, but now that I think of it, it seems a very good idea. Will you marry me, *ma mie*?" he asked. And before Victoire could stop him he had slipped an arm about her and kissed her very gently and expertly.

Victoire pulled herself away. "*Parbleu*, Constant, will you be serious!" she scolded.

"But I am serious! We should really suit very well, you know!" said the Captain, laughing at her indignant face. "You've grown into an enchanting little rogue, and I rather think I have fallen in love with you!"

Victoire gazed at him in astonishment, which rapidly gave way to consternation.

"But you cannot be in love with me!" she expostulated. "I am—I am only Victoire, and you are—only Constant—"

"*Only* Constant—*only* Victoire? No, no! We are not children any longer!" said the Captain, half laughing at her still, but with a disturbing light in his eyes now that she could not remember ever having seen there before. He put his arm round her again and with his free hand tilted up her chin. The next moment, however, he released her and stepped back sharply, having received a very determined and resounding slap, delivered with the full force of his old playfellow's arm, upon his face. "*Peste!*" he ejaculated. "You little wildcat!"

"Leave me alone, then!" Victoire said, regarding him fiercely. "*Voyons*, we are in one big trouble and you are acting like a fool! If I am not back in Albemarle Street before it becomes too late, I can tell you that it is entirely likely that Lord Tarn will call you out and shoot you! So you will stop this foolishness at once and think of a way for us to return to town!"

The Captain grinned. "Oh, I don't think it will come to that," he said confidently. "I'm a pretty good shot myself, you know."

"And if you kill *him*," Victoire pursued inexorably, "*moi, I* shall get a pistol and shoot *you,* so we shall have no more of this nonsense, *hein?* Come now—there must be a village somewhere near here, and we shall see if these horses can be ridden. There is no saddle, *bien entendu,* but I shall not regard that."

Captain Lanner said she never had, but that the off horse appeared to him to have a badly strained hock, and, looking somewhat impressed, asked if she were really all that fond of Tarn.

"Yes," said Victoire baldly.

"Then I should think you were letting yourself in for a great deal of trouble," said the Captain, following her over to have a look at the near horse. "You'd much better marry me, you know. I haven't a groat now, beyond my pay, but my cousin Gerhard was killed at Leipzig last year and so when my uncle dies I shall be the Graf von Guernenberg. I daresay that is almost as good as a marquis."

Victoire, who was examining a graze on the near horse's knee, looked round at him in astonishment. "*Mon Dieu,* I think you are in earnest!" she said.

"Of course I am in earnest!" said the Captain, attempting to seize her in his arms again and adding a Teutonic term of endearment in a suddenly slightly thickened voice.

"So—am—I!" said Victoire, and thereupon proceeded to attempt determinedly to extricate herself by tactics more suitable to a small girl engaging in a tussle with an elder brother than to a young lady of quality.

How matters might have gone on from that moment was perhaps debatable, for Captain Lanner, who was well known to thrive upon opposition, did not seem inclined to lose the battle so tamely this time; but the sudden appearance of a farm horse and tumbril plodding round a turn in the road, with the farmer riding upon the shaft, put an abrupt end to the contest. The Captain released Victoire, who addressed a pair of highly uncomplimentary words to him in French and then called breathlessly to the young farmer, who was staring in astonishment at the overturned phaeton, "Oh, sir! Will you take us to the nearest village? We have had an accident, as you see!"

"Good Lord," said Captain Lanner to her under his breath, amusement conquering his natural irritation at having his love-making interrupted, "you can't ride in that thing, Victoire! He's carting dung!"

"I do not care," said Victoire obstinately. "I shall ride upon the shaft, as he is doing, for it appears to me that both Mr. Fearon's horses are lame. I daresay it will be faster than walking."

"And what about me?" demanded the Captain, crossing the road behind her to where the bemused young farmer stood regarding them in bashful silence.

"You may walk, or ride one of Mr. Fearon's lame horses," said Victoire ruthlessly. "But first," she said, "you must lend me some money, for I have only a half-crown—and *no* pins," she added darkly, "in my reticule, and I shall be obliged to hire some sort of carriage, you know, when we reach the village."

The Captain retorted that he was dashed if he would frank her to run off anywhere alone—a statement that appeared to be about to cause a resumption of hostilities between them when the young farmer diffidently observed that there was an inn just round the next bend where they could probably hire a gig, being as it wasn't Thursday, when it would be wanted to take the landlady to market. Upon hearing this, both Captain Lanner and Victoire burst out laughing, as it appeared a very good joke to them that they had been prepared to argue so vehemently over the matter of transportation to a place not a quarter mile distant, and they set off together at once in quite good humour with each other and were soon bargaining with the landlady of a very neat little inn for the use of her gig and the taking in charge of Mr. Fearon's horses and phaeton by her ostler.

Victoire then had an even more brilliant idea, for it was growing quite dark by this time and the notion of setting forth on a journey of, as they had been informed, some seven miles to London alone in a gig with Captain Lanner was one that

223

appeared to her to be fraught with some peril. She did not, however, see fit to confide this idea to Captain Lanner, and it was only as he helped her to mount into the gig that he observed that he had a second passenger waiting to enter it—a strapping young female in a print dress and a shawl, who giggled and bobbed him a curtsey before she climbed in and seated herself at Victoire's side.

"What the deuce—?" began the Captain; but he got no further.

"This is the landlady's daughter, Constant," said Victoire serenely. "She is coming with us to London—aren't you, Susan? And Mademoiselle will give her a room in Albemarle Street tonight, and tomorrow she is to have half a guinea and come back here on the coach."

The landlady, standing with arms akimbo and what Captain Lanner could only characterise as a smug smile upon her face—the smile of a respectable female who has succeeded in thrusting a spoke into the wheel of some nefarious male plot—nodded confirmation of these words. The Captain was obliged to acknowledge himself bested. He could not put Susan out of the gig, nor would it be of the slightest use to him to think any longer of the attractive schemes his fertile brain had been concocting for the purpose of causing Victoire to change her mind about him that evening. They would certainly—armed with depressingly explicit directions from the landlady as to the proper route to take—arrive most respectably in Albemarle Street in another hour, and that would be the end of that.

And so, in point of fact, it was. But that it was also the beginning of something else was apparent even before the gig, having halted before Miss Standfield's door, had been given by Captain Lanner into the hands of one of the street loungers who seemed to earn their living, with no disagreeable exertion involved, simply by being at the proper spot when someone needed a horse or horses held. For while the Captain was jumping down from his seat the front door of Miss Standfield's house opened and Tarn came out upon the doorstep.

Captain Lanner, walking round the dusty gig to assist Victoire to alight, found himself face to face with the Marquis, and noted instantly that he had on what Victoire had once described as his *formidable* look.

"Where the devil—?" began Tarn; but hostilities—if hostilities were what he had in mind—were immediately broken off by the eruption of Susan from the gig. She scrambled down unassisted, looked at Tarn, and, giggling in sheer nervous terror at the coldly wrathful expression upon his face, bobbed a curtsey to him and effaced herself against the gig.

Then Victoire, appearing behind her, held out her hands to Tarn to be helped down by him, and at once, though quite as nervous as Susan, attempted to take the situation in hand.

"Oh, I am *so* sorry, Lewis," she said hastily, anxious to get it all out before the Captain and the Marquis decided to come to blows with each other, and hoping that her torn frock and considerably dishevelled appearance were not visible in the darkness, "but Mr. Fearon sprained his ankle and Constant was obliged to drive his phaeton, and then the wheel came off and so it was necessary for us to hire this gig. And this is the landlady's daughter," she concluded, indicating Susan, "who has been with me ever since the accident, so you see that it has all been quite *convenable.*"

She halted, looking up into Tarn's face and observing with some apprehension that this rather tangled explanation did not seem to have mollified him to any appreciable extent. But his lordship said curtly that they could not stand there talking in the street and brought her inside, with Captain Lanner and Susan following behind.

In the drawing room they found Miss Standfield, who appeared considerably astonished at sight of the number of persons whom Tarn had brought into her house. The questions died upon her lips, however, as Victoire, hurrying across the room to her, plunged into renewed and voluble explanations, ending with a fervent appeal to her to assure the Marquis that everything had been perfectly *comme il faut,* so that he would at once stop looking as if he were about to murder someone.

"The someone, I expect," said Captain Lanner, stepping forward at this point in a quite unperturbed manner, "being myself." He bowed to Miss Standfield and bent over her hand, raising it to his lips with a Continental grace that did not appear to improve Tarn's temper as he observed it. "A thousand apologies, ma'am," said the Captain, "for invading your drawing room in this unseemly manner, but Miss Duvenay's tale, you must understand, is quite accurate, though a trifle incoherent, I believe."

Miss Standfield said that she did not in the least mind her drawing room's being invaded, but that as it appeared, as far as she had been able to understand Victoire's story, that the young person they had brought with them was to stay the night, she had best ring for her housekeeper so that she might arrange a room for her. She then confided Susan into the hands of that very competent female and, having instructed Cloyden to bring some sherry, said mildly to Tarn, who had been chafing visibly under these delays, that if he intended to say anything outrageous he had best say it now, while the servants were out of the room.

"Thank you, ma'am!" said the Marquis, with awesome civility. "But I do not propose to say anything outrageous, even with your kind permission. I have, it appears, merely to offer my thanks to Captain Lanner once more for his care of Victoire, and to tell him that I shall see to it in future that she will not require such services of him again."

This seemed to Victoire such a forbearing, not to say magnanimous, speech that she felt in her relief like applauding. But Captain Lanner apparently did not see it in the same light, for he said very politely and coolly that it did not quite appear to him by what right the Marquis took upon himself the exclusive concern for Miss Duvenay's future well-being.

"I'll tell you by what right," Tarn said instantly. "Miss Duvenay is betrothed to me."

Captain Lanner looked surprised—more than surprised, incredulous. "*Plaît-il?*" he said after a moment. "You said—*betrothed?*"

And he looked at Victoire, who said at once, fervently, "Yes, yes! It is true, Constant! I did not tell you because it is still a secret—"

"And why," interrupted Tarn, a look of alarming grimness

227

about his mouth, "should you have felt the necessity of telling Captain Lanner of it, more than any other of your acquaintances?"

Victoire, though feeling entirely virtuous, managed, to her consternation and fury, to look guilty, and even Captain Lanner's face took on a slight, conscious colour. But he maintained his presence of mind and said with an aplomb worthy of a soldier under fire that he and Victoire were such old friends that it would scarcely be surprising if she had felt the impulse to confide in him. Victoire, though grateful to him, could not help feeling that he had used her Christian name with provocation in mind, and when he pointedly asked the Marquis when the announcement was to be made she was sure of it and frowned at him.

"Tomorrow," said Tarn brazenly, as if the whole thing had been decided in conclave weeks before. "That is, I am sending the notice to the *Gazette* then."

The Captain offered his congratulations, looking as if he had rather not but did not see his way out of doing so under the circumstances, drank a glass of the sherry that Cloyden then brought in, and took his departure, leaving Victoire still in the rather dazed state into which Tarn's announcement had thrown her. To have been fearing having one's engagement broken off entirely by one's incensed betrothed, and then to have it publicly confirmed by him instead was something of a shock, particularly when one could not be sure that he had done it out of any more loverlike impulse than the desire to depress the pretensions of a young man towards whom he was feeling very uncordial at the moment.

"Did you—did you *really* mean that?" she asked the Marquis rather doubtfully as the door closed behind Captain Lanner.

"About the announcement? Yes!" said Tarn. "Well, I can see that that's the only thing to do to keep you from getting into scrapes like this—first that gudgeon Swanton and now Lanner! And if you intend to try to tell me," he added ominously, "that

228

he didn't act in a way that made you feel you had to have that girl with you in that gig, you can save your breath!"

"He only said he wanted to marry me," Victoire defended herself and the absent Captain. "*Voyons*, there is nothing so very wicked in that!"

The Marquis said with some satisfaction that at least the notice in the *Gazette* would put an end to that sort of thing, and then read her a trenchant homily on unprincipled young men who offered marriage to unsuspecting females with the purpose of attaining their own nefarious ends—at which point Miss Standfield said dryly that she had heard of the devil quoting Scripture and this seemed to her to be very much the same sort of situation, and would the Marquis be good enough to go away now and let Victoire go upstairs to bed after the very exciting day it seemed she had had.

It was quite evident that the Marquis had not finished what he had to say, but as he could not very well remain in the house any longer after Miss Standfield had asked him to go, he took his departure. Miss Standfield then told Victoire that he had made quite a nuisance of himself that evening, demanding why she herself had not gone to Merton and accusing her of being foolish beyond permission in allowing Victoire to go off on an excursion with Captain Lanner with no better chaperon than Lady Whittingham.

"Yes," said Victoire, feeling, though limp with relief now that the scene she had been dreading had passed off with such comparative mildness, a deep depression settling upon her for some unaccountable reason, "I could see that he was very much enraged, because he was so polite that it made one's blood freeze to hear him speak. And it was because he was so enraged, *sans doute*," she added despondently, "that he said that to Constant about sending the notice of our engagement to the *Gazette*. It was not because he really *wished* to do it—was it, Mademoiselle?"

Miss Standfield, looking at the flushed, unhappy little face before her, would have liked to tell her that she had quite misread his lordship's mind, but she was a firm believer in facing facts and was obliged to admit that Victoire's statement of the matter had probably been correct.

Victoire rose with a tiny sigh. "Well, I do not mind at all," she said rather forlornly. "Only it is very vexing, *vous voyez*, Mademoiselle, to have Constant and Mr. Swanton both saying they have fallen in love with me, when I do not care in the least to have them do so, while Lewis—"

She did not finish her sentence, which ended only with a slight catch of her breath that Miss Standfield for some reason found more eloquent than any words she might have spoken, but trailed out of the room and up the stairs to her own chamber. Here, however, she took herself very firmly to task for not being grateful that things had turned out as well as they had, and by dint of asking herself severely how she would be feeling now if the Marquis had challenged Captain Lanner to a duel instead of only reading her a lecture, managed to put herself into a tolerably cheerful state of mind before she fell asleep.

The cheerfulness, however, did not survive a morning call paid in Albemarle Street the following day by Lady Whittingham, who, it appeared, had been informed of the previous night's accident by Mr. Fearon when she had sent to enquire after his ankle that morning.

"Of course Captain Lanner was obliged to tell him what had happened to his horses and phaeton," she said, her eyes sparkling with the liveliest curiosity as she looked at Victoire, "and *of course*, too, he told him that everything had gone off with the greatest propriety, and that the pair of you had come back to London in a gig you had hired from the landlady of an inn, with the landlady's daughter sitting bodkin between you. But I am dying to hear the *true* story, and what Lewis will say when he finds out."

"Lewis," said Miss Standfield repressively, "will say nothing at all, my dear Ernestina—for the simple reason that he was here when Victoire and Captain Lanner returned last night, and so already knows all about the matter."

Lady Whittingham looked disappointed. "Well, I *did* rather expect," she said, "that he would have called Captain Lanner out, or something equally dreadful, for you *know* what he is like when he is angry, Cousin Amelia! And even though I have never believed a word of all the rumours one hears that he intends to marry Victoire himself—"

"The notice of their betrothal," Miss Standfield once more interrupted, in the same tone of resigned condescension, "will appear no later than tomorrow in the *Gazette*, you will find, to say nothing of the *Morning Post* if Lewis has not been remiss—"

Lady Whittingham stared, then began to laugh and exclaim, flying out of her chair to embrace Victoire.

"Oh, it is famous!" she said. "So Lewis has been caught at last! And I had not the least guess, you sly puss—for I told Arthur only this morning that I was sure you and Captain Lanner would make a match of it, and so it did not signify if you had had the misfortune to be caught in such a compromising situation with him! But do you mean to tell me that Lewis —Lewis, of all men!—did not fly into a pelter when you walked in last night with the Captain? Or is that when he asked you to marry him? In *my* experience, my dear, there is nothing that makes a man feel so romantic as his having been perfectly furious with you half an hour before."

Victoire said in a rather small voice that his lordship had not been furious at all, but very polite, and that the engagement had been an understood thing for some time. This made Lady Whittingham exclaim once more, but now in some vexation at her own want of perception, and in order not to be caught out again she said that, while she might not have foreseen the engagement, she *did* foresee now that there must be a duel between the Marquis and Captain Lanner.

"Because I *do* know Lewis," she said, "and he has never in his life done anything sensible and forbearing. But if you are worried about him," she added kindly, seeing the anxious expression that had appeared upon Victoire's face, "you need not be, you know, for everyone says he is the finest shot in England."

Victoire, in a tone of vivid distress, said that was all very well, but she knew Constant to be an excellent shot as well, and she did not want either him or the Marquis to be killed or hurt over what had been no more than a stupid accident—which, she added severely, no one need know anything about if Lady Whittingham and Mr. Fearon would only hold their tongues.

"Well, of course, *I* shall say nothing!" said Lady Whittingham virtuously. "And Bruce is the soul of discretion, you know, so that I am sure you need not worry, either, about *his* speaking of it to anyone."

But this latter statement was not perfectly accurate, for the "soul of discretion" was at that very moment seated in a comfortable armchair in his own parlour, with his injured foot ostentatiously propped upon a footstool before him, regaling several of his friends with a highly coloured account of the previous day's excursion. The story, he could only hope, would be all over town before the sun had set, and if *that*, he told himself with great satisfaction, did not considerably alter Tarn's intention to go through with his scheme of marrying the Duvenay chit, he would be very much surprised. Giving credit where credit was due, he acknowledged that the Condessa, whose idea the whole scheme had been, had put her finger upon the crux of the matter when she had said that, of all things, Tarn would never endure being made to appear ridiculous, and that his response to the embarrassing situation would undoubtedly be to throw himself at once into some new and scandalous adventure that would turn the attention of the town from Miss Duvenay and make it obvious that he had never been serious about her in the first place.

This pleasing conviction endured until the following day, when his valet, as usual, brought a copy of the *Gazette* in to him with his morning chocolate. To the surprise even of that imperturbable gentleman's gentleman, this event was followed within the space of three minutes by a violent execration from his master, after which Mr. Fearon instantly sprang out of bed, quite oblivious, apparently, to the pain of the ankle that he had insisted had been injured, though his valet had been unable to detect any signs of swelling upon it, and demanded his clothes. The valet, who had counted upon Mr. Fearon's remaining abed for at least half an hour longer, hastened to set them in order, incurring several scathing rebukes for his slowness, and could only breathe a sigh of relief when he saw his master out of the house at an hour when he ordinarily had not as yet sat down to his breakfast.

Mr. Fearon, remembering at the last moment to snatch up a heavy gold-headed stick to assist the limping gait he fell into once he had passed his own front door, made his way immediately to Ellis's Hotel, where he was admitted, after a short delay, to the Condessa de Vilamil's apartments. He found her looking quite as charming as usual, despite the earliness of the hour, in a morning robe of blue gauze and lace, for she was one of those voluptuously formed women who always appear to advantage *en déshabillé*.

"Have you seen this?" Mr. Fearon demanded of her without ceremony, placing the *Gazette* before her and indicating a paragraph that the newspaper had been folded back to show.

The Condessa perversely looked at him instead of at the journal.

"But you are very rude this morning, my friend!" she said.

Mr. Fearon did not trouble himself to deny the charge. He was walking up and down the room with a furious energy that rather surprised the Condessa, who, like everyone else, had become accustomed to the languid air he usually adopted. He then surprised her even further by halting before her and, thrusting the *Gazette* into her hands, saying in a voice so thick with rage that she could scarcely recognise it, "You will oblige me by reading this paragraph, ma'am!"

The Condessa, with a little shrug, let her eyes fall upon the item he had presented to her, which was a notice of the impending nuptials of Miss Victoire Duvenay and Lewis Lionel Wystan Fearon, the Most Noble the Marquis of Tarn. Mr. Fearon, standing watching her, saw a slight colour mount in her face and snatched the journal from her again.

"So much for your schemes, ma'am!" he said, casting the offending paper down contemptuously upon a table. "A pretty outcome they have had!"

The Condessa, who had, she thought, as much right to feel disappointed as Mr. Fearon, debated for a moment allowing him to see the full scope of *her* temper, which had no mean reputation in a country famed for its fiery women, but, looking at Mr. Fearon, prudently decided not to. If she had been in Spain instead of in England, she would have said that her guest had murder in his eyes, but she had a poor opinion of Englishmen on the whole and felt them, with very few exceptions, to be incapable of such interestingly violent actions.

Nevertheless, she now reserved her own emotions and merely said, with another shrug, that after all they were not married yet.

"They are as good as married," said Mr. Fearon savagely. "Even Lewis will not cry off now, after a public announcement has been made." He took another angry turn about the room. "This is what comes of letting your counsels prevail!" he said. "And if it is any satisfaction to you, I had Lanner with me yesterday to give me an account of the accident to my phaeton and greys, and if he is not fallen in love with that chit himself, you may call me a gudgeon!"

The Condessa, her eyes narrowing, said that in that event it would not surprise her if Tarn found some pretext to call him out, and was reflecting, evidently with some satisfaction, upon the possibility of the fickle Captain's living—or perhaps even more satisfactorily *not* living—to regret his fickleness when she was brought up short by Mr. Fearon's saying furiously, "If you are thinking of a duel, that can do no manner of good! Lewis is by far too cool a hand at that sort of thing; it is quite likely that he would come out of it with a whole skin!"

The Condessa stiffened slightly. Then she looked into Mr. Fearon's face, which was blotched and distorted now with his fury, and an odd, wary expression suddenly came over her own.

"*Diablos!*" she said slowly. "So I was not mistaken then, after all, the first day you came here, in saying that you wished his death!"

Mr. Fearon halted abruptly in his angry pacing. For a moment he stared at her and then, evidently composing himself with a strong effort, forced an indifferent smile to his lips.

"How melodramatic you are, my dear Condessa!" he said. "That is one of the charms of your Latin heritage, of course! But I fear we English have far too much phlegm to satisfy your notions of the proper response to situations such as this. Naturally I am vexed that our plans have gone awry, but as for desiring my cousin's death—!" The Condessa, still regarding him steadily, said nothing, and Mr. Fearon went on suddenly, an odd light leaping into his pale eyes, "If you must know, you have quite mistaken my motives in this business. *You* think that it is Lewis's title and fortune I covet—"

"And it is not so?" said the Condessa, scornfully and incredulously.

"No!" It occurred to her that Mr. Fearon's whole manner had altered now, reflecting what seemed to be some abrupt mental change. He no longer appeared angry; there was, incredibly, an air almost of triumph about him, as of a man who, in a last desperate gamble, has just picked up a winning card. "No," he repeated slowly after a moment, composing his features into the expression of sardonic languor that represented their usual appearance, "it is not. Not his title and fortune, but—his bride."

The Condessa was not easily astonished, but that this statement had accomplished that feat was plain now to be seen.

"His bride!" she ejaculated. "*Venga*, you are joking me, *evidentemente!* That little schoolgirl!"

Mr. Fearon, who knew the Condessa's powers of penetration when it came to the less admirable traits of the human character, did not protest, but instead prudently declared that he could not speak of it to her or to anyone else, and would never have done so in the first place had it not been for the shock of the announcement in the *Gazette*. He then picked up his hat and stick, apologised for having disturbed her at such an unseemly hour, and said that he would take his leave.

"One moment!" said the Condessa imperatively. Mr. Fearon paused. "What is it that you are up to now?" she demanded, rising and confronting him with a slight frown upon her face. "You have thought of some new scheme, *verdad?*"

Mr. Fearon said untruthfully that he had thought of nothing at all, and again apologised for having allowed his agitation at hearing of the approaching marriage to have led him into saying more than he ought.

"But a man in love, you know—" he concluded, with a brazen show of ruefulness which, though he knew very well it would not take her in, he appeared to be daring her to challenge.

The Condessa, however, did not trouble herself to take up the gauntlet. She merely regarded him thoughtfully, and after a moment said that if he would take a piece of advice from her he would not meddle any further in his cousin's affairs.

"I know that he is very careless, and reckless as well, but he is not stupid, my friend," she said. "You are to make a pretence now, it seems—God knows why—that you have been in love with the Duvenay girl all this while—"

Mr. Fearon looked injured, and said, "A *pretence?*"

"A pretence," repeated the Condessa inexorably. "Me you will not take in with such a story, no matter how well you may succeed in imposing on others. But for what, I ask myself, do you invent this foolishness? What have you to gain by it?"

Mr. Fearon said sententiously that he feared a man had nothing at all to gain from a broken heart, and added, in a tone that she had come to know and dislike very much, that he did not advise her to mention either his *tendre* for Miss Duvenay or her skepticism concerning it to anyone, as when people began talking of things that did not concern them other people were apt to begin talking as well. This the Condessa rightly interpreted as a threat, and so, remembering little Evita Morales who had become the Condessa de Vilamil, she swallowed the dislike she felt for Mr. Fearon and wisely determined to take his advice, allowing herself only the malicious satisfaction of reminding him as he took his leave that he was quite forgetting to limp.

19

It took Mr. Fearon very little time to establish his credentials as a secret admirer of Miss Duvenay's who had been nourishing his passion in the shadow of his cousin's more magnificent pretensions and now saw his last hope vanishing in the cold print of an announcement in the *Gazette*. Appearing that very evening at Lady Finniston's ball, after a busy day spent in some very unfashionable places, where he had held private conversation with certain individuals known more familiarly in Bow Street than in the West End, he was all punctilious politeness to the newly betrothed pair, though wearing such a melancholy countenance as to attract the attention of everyone who saw him.

His cousin, Mr. Marmaduke Standfield, was the first to comment upon this, observing solicitously that he looked a trifle out of curl and enquiring if it was the ankle that was causing him distress.

"The ankle? No!" said Mr. Fearon. "It is coming along very

well. But it is enough to curdle anyone's pleasure in life to see Lewis walk off, with his usual luck, with the most enchanting girl in England!" He added with a rather bitter air that there was, of course, no chance for poor beggars like himself when a coronet was laid in the balance.

Mr. Standfield looked his astonishment at this entirely unexpected statement. "Sounds as if you were a bit smitten there yourself, coz," he said acutely, after a moment. "Surprise to me, I must say; thought you'd no use for her. Told me so often enough yourself."

Mr. Fearon achieved a rather hollow laugh. "Oh, yes!" he said. "I believe my parade of indifference *was* quite effective. It pleases me, at any rate, to hear you say so."

And he went off to pay his court to Victoire, leaving Mr. Standfield to confide to Lady Eastcott, who was looking very well that evening in cerulean blue satin and diamonds, that he rather fancied poor old Bruce had had his nose put out of joint by Tarn's betrothal to Miss Duvenay.

"Bruce!" said Lady Eastcott, looking incredulous. "Nonsense! He can't endure the girl! Has he not been saying forever that she is *quite* an unsuitable bride for Tarn? Oh!" She broke off suddenly, a look of intelligence widening her blue eyes. "Do you mean," she said, "that he was so set against the match because he hoped that *he*—?"

Mr. Standfield nodded. "Seems so," he said wisely. "Set of gudgeons we all were, I daresay, not to have seen through it before this. Well, look at him now!" he concluded, with a glance across the room to where Mr. Fearon was standing hovering in the group surrounding Victoire, evidently waiting for his chance for a word with her.

Lady Eastcott, shaking her head, declared that she would never have believed it, and indeed it could not be; but she was so intrigued by the idea that before half an hour had passed she had communicated it to no fewer than four persons, so that there could be little doubt that in a short time Mr. Fearon's *tendre* for his cousin's affianced bride would be one of the *on-dits* of London.

The suspicion was heightened in the minds of all those who shared the secret by the fact that Mr. Fearon, evidently too smitten by despair to conceal his passion successfully any longer, now that the announcement of the engagement had actually been made, spent most of the evening observing Victoire from afar in a sombre manner that would have done credit to Lord Byron himself—a resemblance heightened by the slight limp he was still affecting. Miss Standfield, quite puzzled by his behaviour, was enlightened presently by Lady Eastcott, who had by this time decided that it was all very romantic and so could sigh sympathetically over her nephew's lovelorn plight.

"I am sure I had not the remotest guess that he felt so before this evening," she said, "for he has been very clever in hoaxing everyone to believe that he positively disliked the girl. Really, I cannot think why he did not tell Tarn before it was too late that he was willing to take her off his hands, for it is obvious that Lewis does not care for her himself. I *have* heard that he decided to announce the engagement merely in a fit of pique over her escapade with Captain Lanner the other day, which does not make the least degree of sense to me, for it would have been far more like him to have called young Lanner out, you know. But there is no understanding young people these days. There is Tina, for example, who must be forever quarrelling with Whittingham—I admit he is dreadfully dull, but, my dear, too divinely rich, so that if she will only go the right way about it there is nothing in the world she might not have from him! Yet here she is making a piece of work over his wishing to take her down to Eastcott Park when Nigel and I go there tomorrow, and setting up his back without the least need. And I hear," she went on, returning to her original subject without the slightest pause, "that Miss Duvenay has refused the Swanton boy as well; she is determined to be a marchioness, it

x

241

seems. Silly chit! She would do a great deal better to take him, or Bruce. Tarn will make a damnable husband—but I daresay she does not care for that, so long as she may be Lady Tarn."

Miss Standfield, who had long since given over trying to convince her volatile cousin that Victoire was not a predatory female, allowed her to rattle on; but there was a slight frown between her brows. She did not in the least believe in Mr. Fearon's suddenly evidenced attachment for Victoire, nor could she conceive him to be foolish enough to think that he might succeed in preventing Tarn's marriage by drawing Victoire off for himself—which was the only logical reason she could adduce for his behaviour. He was certainly far too astute for that. She was obliged to believe that there must be some other explanation for this pretence of affection, but what it could be she could not imagine.

Mr. Fearon, meanwhile, hovered in Victoire's vicinity all the evening, but remained prudently in the background during the greater part of the time. Only as the guests were beginning to depart did he approach her, where she stood with Tarn and Lady Whittingham and the Honourable Marmaduke, and ask if he would have the pleasure of seeing her at Lady Inlow's ball on the following evening.

She looked enquiringly at Tarn before replying. She, too, had had a hint dropped in her ear by Lady Eastcott concerning Mr. Fearon's newly discovered *tendre* for her, and, although she had been incredulous at the moment, she could not fail now to observe the air of suppressed devotion with which he was regarding her.

"I do not know," she said, in a civil but quite unencouraging tone. "If Lewis wishes to take me—"

"Not I," said Tarn promptly. "I go to Epsom tomorrow, you know, and I shan't promise to return in time."

Mr. Fearon raised his brows. "A prizefight, coz?" he said, looking as if, had he been in his cousin's place, he would not have permitted anything so trivial to keep him from Victoire's side. "Surely, if Miss Duvenay has expressed a wish to attend the ball—" He broke off, and after a moment said abruptly, as if coming to some resolution, "If you would care to have me escort you to the ball, Miss Duvenay, since Lewis has cried off—"

Victoire looked somewhat at a loss, for she had not the least desire to have Mr. Fearon escort her anywhere, especially as he seemed to have taken this odd idea into his head about being in love with her, and, turning her eyes hopefully upon Mr. Standfield, said she rather thought *he* was going to gallant her to the Inlows'.

But this idea was at once vetoed by Tarn, who said that Duke was coming to Epsom, too.

"Yes, but I might return in time for the ball," Mr. Standfield, always anxious to be obliging, urged.

He did not, out of a desire not to interfere in what seemed to be the already somewhat strained relations between the newly betrothed couple, add that Tarn might very well do so also; but it turned out to be unnecessary for him to say anything of the sort, for at this point Lady Whittingham entered the conversation to observe with an air of mischief that if Tarn did not care to gallant Victoire to the ball she was sure that Captain Lanner would.

Upon this the Marquis instantly snapped, "Unnecessary! I'll take her myself." And so the matter was settled.

Unfortunately, this magnanimous decision upon his lordship's part did little to heal the breach between him and his betrothed. They were both, in fact, at that moment in the disagreeably let-down state of people who had been keyed up all evening to an emotional situation that had failed to develop—that is, each had been expecting Captain Lanner to appear at the ball, and had been rehearsing in his or her mind the various possibilities for unpleasant consequences that this might entail, Tarn foreseeing his unpredictable betrothed's standing up at least three times with the dashing

243

Captain, in the teeth of her newly announced engagement and Victoire going in terror lest the incipient quarrel between Tarn and Captain Lanner that Miss Standfield had been able to interrupt in her own drawing room should break out here, unchecked, upon their meeting again.

So when the Captain did not turn up after all, this fact, far from causing them the least feeling of relief, gave them instead an aggrieved sense of disappointment, arising from the knowledge that they would now be obliged to go through the whole thing all over again, whenever Captain Lanner *did* put in an appearance at some function at which both were present.

The remainder of the company, however, found the evening most rewarding, having been offered not only the interesting spectacle of the participants in the most unusual engagement of the Season in what seemed a far from engaged mood, but also the added complication of Mr. Fearon's suddenly revealed passion for his cousin's affianced bride; and Lady Whittingham, for one, went home quite delighted that she had had the foresight not to be persuaded by her lord to leave town for Eastcott Park on the morrow, which would have caused her to miss further developments in what promised to be the most diverting romantic imbroglio in years.

As for Mr. Fearon, the resounding success of his disclosure of his pretended hopeless passion for Victoire, coupled with the chance-got knowledge that both Tarn and the Honourable Marmaduke were to go out of town on the following morning, decided him to act at once. A more favourable opportunity might never present itself, and he congratulated himself that the arrangements he had made that day had been complete in every respect, so that there was no reason, it appeared to him, why the whole plan should not succeed to admiration.

So on the following afternoon, just after Miss Standfield, having partaken of a cold nuncheon with Victoire, had retired to her bedchamber to rest according to her invariable custom, Mr. Fearon appeared in Albemarle Street, driving a pair of chestnuts in the shafts of his newly repaired phaeton. Victoire, who was alone in the small drawing room attending to some of Miss Standfield's correspondence, would much rather not have received him when Cloyden announced him, but, being unable to think of an excuse not to on the spur of the moment, told the butler to show him in and put down her pen with a disagreeable premonition that something unpleasant was about to occur.

But how unpleasant that something would be she had no notion until Mr. Fearon walked into the drawing room. One look then at his face made her realise that he had not come to embarrass her with a declaration of his feelings for her, for there was an expression of the gravest anxiety upon it and he said to her at once, as he closed the door behind him, "You are alone—good! I had thought you might be at this hour. My dear child, I have shocking news for you, and I fear I have not time to break it to you gently. This morning Lewis and Captain Lanner—"

He got no further, for Victoire's hand had gone to her mouth, half stifling the ejaculation that broke from her.

"Oh, *mon Dieu*! A duel!" she cried, all her worst fears returning in an instant at the sound of this ominous preamble. "But Lewis has not been killed? Tell me at once! Tell me!" She flew across the room, seizing him fiercely. "He has not been killed?"

"No, no!" Mr. Fearon disengaged her hands and clasped them comfortingly in his own. "My news is bad, but not so bad as that. He is alive—but, I regret to say, wounded—"

"Wounded? It is bad? But he will not die? Say he will not die!"

Mr. Fearon could feel the trembling of her hands in his own, and, apparently making an effort to reassure her, forced a slight smile to his lips.

"Pray do not be imagining the matter to be worse than it is, my dear," he said. "The wound is not at all serious, I assure you. Unfortunately"—and here his expression grew more sombre again—"most unfortunately, there are other consequences to this folly of his. Captain Lanner, you see, who was—as you no doubt have gathered—Lewis's opponent, has been killed."

"Killed? *Constant*?" Victoire stared at him uncomprehendingly. "Constant—is dead? But no—and no! Lewis would not—"

"My dear, he has. He put a bullet through him this morning at Paddington Green, and, as a consequence, must now fly the country. My mission to you is to bear his message—that he wishes you to go with him, and that, if you consent to do so, your marriage will then take place at once abroad."

She had withdrawn her hands from his, with a stunned look upon her face, and now walked away from him to the window. After a few moments she reiterated in a stifled voice, "I cannot believe it! Killed—*mon Dieu!* How could he do such a thing!—and over nothing, a trifle, a stupid accident—"

Mr. Fearon stood watching her sympathetically, but with an expression of some urgency upon his face.

"I know, of course, that this comes as a severe shock to you," he said presently. "Captain Lanner, I understand, was an old friend of yours—but, indeed, I must say in Lewis's defence that the provocation appears to have come from him, and that Lewis could scarcely have avoided the meeting." He added persuasively, as she did not speak, but remained standing at the window with the same blind look of shock and disbelief upon her face, "I must beg you to endeavour to calm yourself and look at the matter rationally, my dear. The point is that Lewis is even now on his way to Newhaven, where he will remain until he hears from me of your decision—and you will apprehend that that decision must be made quickly. Either you join him at once at Newhaven, and from there go with him to France, or Miss Standfield, he fears, may take steps, as soon as she learns of the matter, to prevent your doing so. I myself, I

246

admit, had certain scruples in undertaking this mission, and only the belief that Lewis has become sincerely attached to you—as you, I am convinced, are to him—induces me to consider that what I am doing is for your happiness, and his. Under *your* influence—"

Victoire struck her hands together suddenly, interrupting him; the colour began to return to her face. "Yes, yes!" she exclaimed. "You are quite right—*certainement* I must go to him at once! Only how?" She pressed one hand despairingly to her forehead.

"As to that," Mr. Fearon said promptly, "I have Lewis's commission to escort you to him, and I shall, of course, carry out my charge if you wish to join him. My phaeton is waiting outside; it will take us to the Bear, in Piccadilly, where I have ordered a chaise-and-four to be in readiness for us, and by this evening we may be in Newhaven. Lewis *must* leave England tonight, you know, whatever you decide; the Runners are undoubtedly already looking for him, and, with his reputation, I have the gravest apprehensions of what might occur if he were obliged to stand his trial."

Victoire nodded, her cheeks blanching once more. "Yes, yes—I understand!" she said. "But you should not have permitted him to wait for me—he should have gone at once! Now we must lose no time! I will come this very moment!"

"Good!" said Mr. Fearon. "Is it safe for you to run upstairs and fetch your hat and gloves? I fear there is no time for more; you must purchase your necessaries when you come to France."

She nodded once more and sped up the stairs, returning in a few moments to join him in the drawing room. He was standing beside the writing desk, holding a folded sheet of paper in his hand.

"I have taken the opportunity to write a few words to Miss Standfield," he explained, "telling her only that you have been unexpectedly called out of town and that I will vouch for your safety and will return tomorrow to give her a full account of the matter. Does that meet with your approval? If so, I shall give it to my groom, and instruct him to deliver it here no later than six o'clock this afternoon."

"Yes, yes!" said Victoire, only half heeding him, her mind wholly occupied now with Tarn's danger. "Only let us go at once!"

"As you wish," he said, and left the room with her.

Cloyden, the butler, showed no surprise at seeing Victoire departing from the house with Mr. Fearon, apparently for an afternoon drive, for she was carrying no more than a light pelisse over her arm, and in a few moments she had mounted into the waiting phaeton and was being driven off in the direction of Piccadilly. She was too preoccupied with the anxieties that her companion's disclosures had roused in her to wish to engage in conversation with him during the short drive to the posting-house, beyond urging him to make the greatest haste; and only when they were shut up together in a post-chaise and she saw the streets of London falling behind them did she begin to sort out her jumbled thoughts and take a more rational account of the situation.

She turned to Mr. Fearon then with an apology for her silence, and requested him to tell her what more he could of the events of the morning.

"Lewis was not badly hurt?" she asked again, for that anxiety was still preying upon her mind.

"No, no—a flesh wound merely," Mr. Fearon assured her. He added after a moment, with an air of slight constraint, "You have been wondering, no doubt, how I came to be involved in the matter, since Lewis and I are scarcely—intimates. It was Duke's doing; he—it was unforgivable, I think!—allowed himself to be persuaded to act for Lewis in this affair. I gather that afterwards he did not feel it possible to leave Lewis until a surgeon had attended him and he had been conveyed to some safe place, and so he sent off a message to me." He smiled a trifle wryly. "There is an old saying that blood is thicker than water," he said. "It is at moments such as this, I daresay, that one discovers how true it is."

Victoire nodded, biting her lip. She was remembering the conversation at Lady Finniston's ball the night before, when Tarn had said that he and Mr. Standfield were going to Epsom together to watch a prizefight, and censuring herself bitterly for not having guessed that this plan was merely a cover for the duel she had been dreading. She could never forgive herself for her stupidity, she thought, for if she had realised that the meeting was to take place, she might at least have done her possible to prevent it and Constant might be alive at this moment.

But Constant dead was what she was not going to think about now, she told herself, because no matter how positively Mr. Fearon had said it she could not really believe it yet and she had a feeling that, when she did, it would be quite too much for her to bear. Still, she did not blame Tarn for what had happened, having been brought up in a world in which masculine violence, though disturbing and sometimes frightening, was an accepted part of life, so that her chief feeling at the moment was a kind of dreary thankfulness that that violence had taken but one life and not two, and that Tarn's had been the one that had been spared.

The journey to Newhaven was a matter of something over fifty miles, and could be accomplished, as she knew from her journey up to London from Eastcott Park, in approximately five hours in a chaise-and-four. To her relief, no accident occurred to lengthen this time, and at the several posting-houses where they were obliged to change horses they alighted from the chaise only once in order to snatch hasty refreshments. Mr. Fearon appeared quite as eager as she was herself to reach the end of their journey, and, when the horses had been put-to at Cuckfield for the last stage, settled back in a corner of the chaise with such obvious relief and satisfaction that it occurred to her abruptly that his interest in seeing a happy ending to their expedition seemed somewhat excessive, especially in view of what she had been given to understand were his feelings towards her.

She puzzled over the matter for a few minutes, sitting beside him in silence as she watched the long June dusk falling more deeply outside the chaise windows and the postillions' heads bobbing rhythmically up and down before her; but her thoughts soon strayed back to Tarn and the danger in which he stood. No doubt, she told herself, dismissing Mr. Fearon's odd behaviour from her mind, the latter's *tendre* for her had been much exaggerated, and he cared for nothing except seeing that his cousin got out of the country without involving his family in a new scandal.

Some miles past Cuckfield the chaise abruptly turned off the post-road, taking a rougher side road leading to the east. Victoire, who had been immersed in her own reflections, did not immediately notice that they had left the turnpike, but, eventually becoming aware of the increased jolting of the carriage, she sat up suddenly and uttered an exclamation of dismay.

"*Voyons!* Surely they have taken the wrong turning!" she said, looking out the window at the lonely, wooded landscape, much obscured now by the thickening darkness that lay outside. "How did this happen? You must stop them at once!"

"No, no," said Mr. Fearon soothingly. "It is quite all right, I assure you. I gave the post-boys their orders at Cuckfield." He went on smoothly, seeing the puzzlement on her face, "You did not take me literally at my word, I hope, when I told you we should join Lewis at Newhaven? Naturally Duke could not risk taking him to a public inn! Fortunately, he recollected that my own house, Edmondstone, lies in the neighbourhood, and decided to bring him there."

"*Your* house?" Victoire stared at him, her brows drawing

together in a slight frown. "But I did not know that you had a house—"

"Oh dear, yes!" Mr. Fearon said with a smile. "It is a very modest one—nothing to compare with Tarn House or Eastcott Park—and even it is beyond my poor power to keep up properly, so that I spend very little time in it. But it makes a useful haven just now—don't you agree? Lewis will not be looked for there."

Victoire was obliged to admit that he was right, but the feeling of uneasiness that had gripped her a short time before now began to return. There *was* something odd, she was convinced, in her companion's manner; a suppressed excitement gleamed in his eyes, and the fingers of one hand drummed nervously upon his knee. As the chaise drew farther and farther from the post-road she began to have an unaccountable feeling that something was dreadfully wrong, and for a moment the wild thought even darted through her mind that perhaps he had lured her away from Albemarle Street in order to force her into a marriage with himself.

"But that is absurd!" she told herself severely, glancing sidelong at Mr. Fearon's quite unloverlike face. "He could not make me marry him and, *bien sûr*, it does not appear that he would even wish to!"

So she calmed her fears as best she could, and devoutly hoped that their journey might soon be at an end, with Lewis there, reassuringly, to greet her when she arrived.

And, to her relief, it was in fact not long before the chaise, which had now rattled off the road to an overgrown lane, suddenly entered a neglected carriage-sweep and an ancient country house came into view, its chimney pots vaguely outlined against a dark misty sky.

"Edmondstone," said Mr. Fearon cheerfully. "Journey's end, my dear."

He flung open the door of the chaise and, without waiting for

251

the steps to be let down, jumped quickly down and strode around to the front of the carriage, where she heard him paying off the postillions. One of them, grinning over what had apparently been a sizable *douceur*, came around to let down the steps for her; she descended and, before she had had time even to have a fair look at her new surroundings, the postillions had remounted their horses and the chaise was rattling off again down the lane.

The day had been sultry but, as she stood looking at the unlighted blackness of the house before her, it occurred to her that the air had turned damp and heavy with the fall of night and she shivered suddenly. Mr. Fearon's hand touching her elbow made her jump.

"Come along, my dear," he said, smiling down at her. "Lewis is anxious to see you, I dare swear; we must not keep him waiting."

She hung back. "It—it is so dark," she objected, a little breathlessly. "Are you *quite* sure that Lewis is here?"

Mr. Fearon laughed good-humouredly. "But of course," he said. "Naturally it would be unwise of him to have the house blazing with lights from garret to cellar. This is a secluded place, but there *is* the possibility that such signs of activity in a house that is known to be unoccupied might attract the notice of some passer-by." His hand under her elbow urged her gently towards the house. "I am sorry to be able to extend only such poor hospitality to you," he went on lightly, "but when you see Lewis inside it will make up for all my shortcomings, will it not?"

She agreed, allowing herself to be led up to the front door. As they approached it, a light flickered through a chink in the drawn blinds at a window beside it, and the next moment it had swung open to reveal a very tall, burly, masculine figure, clad in a catskin waistcoat and frieze breeches, and holding a candle aloft in one enormous fist. A broad grin split his unprepossessing face as he beheld her standing there beside Mr. Fearon.

"All's bowman, guv'nor," he said in a hoarse voice, stepping aside to allow the newcomers to walk in. "Is this the gentry-mort you're wishful to—?"

"Hold your tongue, you fool!" Mr. Fearon interrupted shortly. He turned to Victoire, who had halted on the threshold and was staring up at the stupid little eyes grinning down at her out of that coarse brown face with its broken nose and misshapen ears. "My caretaker, my dear," said Mr. Fearon, in a somewhat vexed tone of explanation. "An ignorant fellow—but it is difficult to find anyone willing to stay in this out-of-the-way spot, you see!" He drew her across the threshold, remarking to the enormous caretaker, "I daresay Lord Tarn is abovestairs, Meggs?"

Receiving an assenting growl in response, he picked up a candle from an ancient oak table and, kindling it from the flame of the one held by Meggs, guided Victoire towards the stairs. These rose, it appeared to her as she looked up, into unrelieved blackness, nor was there any sound from above. She drew back a little as Mr. Fearon urged her forward.

"*Mais non!*" she said. "Why do you not tell Lewis to come down? Should we not go at once? And how are we to travel? Are there horses here?"

"All in good time," Mr. Fearon said, his hand on her arm again irresistibly impelling her forward. "First we must see how Lewis does. I begin to fear, since he has not come down to greet us, that his wound may be more serious than I was led to believe."

He brought her up the stairs; still no welcoming light greeted them as they reached the upper hall. The doors that opened on to it all appeared to be shut.

"One moment! Are you sure—?" began Victoire, endeavouring once more to draw back; but the hand on her arm, tightening inexorably now, forced her along the passage to a door at the end.

There she was released briefly as her companion flung open

253

the door; but before she could gather her bewildered thoughts to take advantage of this moment of freedom she had been impelled through the door into a small bedchamber, empty except for a huge four-poster bed and a pair of chairs, and Mr. Fearon, closing the door behind them, had turned the key decisively in the lock.

For a moment Victoire could only stand staring at him. Then she turned quickly to the canopied bed and pulled aside the curtains. There was no Lewis lying there; a glance told her that no one had lain on that dusty bed for years. She whirled back to Mr. Fearon.

"*Allons donc*, what does this mean?" she demanded. "Why have you brought me here? And where is Lewis?"

Mr. Fearon smiled. It was not a pleasant smile, for he had dropped all pretence of civility with the locking of the door and surveyed her now with the insolent indifference with which he might have faced down the demands of an impertinent servant.

"Where is Lewis?" he repeated her words. "I have not the least idea. Certainly—as you have seen for yourself—he is not here."

"But where, then—? And why—?"

She broke off, forcing herself to control her racing thoughts, which told her that her suspicions during the journey must, after all, have been correct, that she had indeed been abducted—by deception, rather than by force, but abducted all the same. The most puzzling fact now was not the abduction itself but her abductor's abrupt change in manner—hardly the manner of a desperately earnest lover, she told herself in utter bewilderment. It was contempt, even hatred, that she saw in those pale eyes, or in her confusion she had lost all ability to read a human face.

Mr. Fearon appeared to be able to guess the questions that lay behind her sudden silence and searching gaze, for he said mockingly, "Oh no, my dear! I have not carried you off for your *beaux yeux*; you are quite out there! Did you believe that you had fascinated me as you have fascinated Lewis? Pray do not flatter yourself! It will require more than a crude little schemer to take me in her toils!"

"Then—if not for that—why? But no!" Victoire made a fierce little gesture. "I do not care for that! Where is Lewis? *That* you must tell me—"

"I have already told you that I have not the least notion," he said, going over to the single small dormer window the room possessed and drawing the faded curtains more closely across its panes. "If I were obliged to make a guess, however," he went on, turning back to her once more, "I should say that he is at this moment somewhere past Croydon, driving at his usual breakneck pace. We had, after all, a start of several hours on him."

Victoire passed a bewildered hand across her forehead. "But this—I do not understand!" she cried. "He is not wounded, then?"

"You put it quite correctly. Not even a scratch."

"And—*enfin*, there was no duel?"

"No duel, my dear. How very astute you are—but then I daresay in your line it is necessary to be astute. I scarcely dared hope, in fact, that you would be stupid enough to fall into the

256

trap I laid for you. It should be a lesson to you never to mix love with business."

She sat down abruptly upon the chair that stood beside her; for a moment she felt almost dizzy with relief, her own predicament forgotten in her joy that Tarn was unscathed and in no present danger. But the peril of her own situation was once more forced upon her as she saw Mr. Fearon preparing to leave the room. She cried out sharply, "Where are you going? And why have you brought me here? You must be mad, I think! If Lewis is not wounded, do you think he will not find out what you have done and come in search of me?"

Mr. Fearon turned from the door; a slight smile curved his lips.

"Why, yes," he said, and there was a definite note of satisfaction in his voice. "I do think he will come. In point of fact, I have made very sure that he will know without delay exactly where to find us." She looked at him, uncomprehending, wondering again if he were mad. "Why, you little fool," he went on, stung, apparently, by the suspicion he read in her eyes, "are you flattering yourself that you are dealing with a lunatic? You may disabuse yourself of that idea! I am quite sane, I assure you—only considerably more clever than you appear to give me credit for being! Did you indeed believe that I had fallen in love with a creature like you, or would dream of mingling Fearon blood with yours? I am not so unmindful as is Lewis of what I owe to my name!"

At another moment the contempt in his voice would have roused her to quick resentment; but now she only sat quietly, her hands clasped together tightly in her lap, and said in a voice that she could not manage to keep quite steady, "*Where is Lewis? And why are you so sure that he will come here?*"

Mr. Fearon held the candle high, as if the better to see her white face.

"Oh, my dear," he said mockingly, "it was *you* who made

257

sure of that! Did you not agree that you wished me to instruct my groom to deliver the note I held in my hand to Albemarle Street at six o'clock? A pity you did not take the trouble to read it first; it was really an excellent counterfeit of your hand! Fortunately I had had every opportunity to study it, you know, since you had been kind enough to write me more than once in my cousin Amelia's name." He closed his eyes for a moment. "Let me see—how exactly did I phrase that very touching missive?" he mused. "*Dear Mademoiselle, I believe it went, I am going away with Bruce. I love him, and so I cannot marry Lewis. I hope you will not be very angry with me. Lewis will not be, I think, for I know that he does not truly care for me. Pray tell him that I have gone with Bruce to his house in Sussex, where we will be married by special licence, so there is no need for him to put himself out about me any longer. In great haste, and with all my gratitude, Victoire.* A pretty effusion, don't you agree?" he concluded. "I do hope you approve of it; I laboured so diligently to give it your tone."

He halted, looking at Victoire, who was staring at him incredulously.

"But why—*why*—?" she said again.

"Why?" There was positive enjoyment in Mr. Fearon's eyes now as they met her gaze. "Why, because it was necessary, my dear—necessary for the little drama that will be played out here tonight. We might entitle it, I think, *The Jealous Lover, or Revenge Incomplete,* and you are to play the leading female rôle. It is that of a love-stricken young damsel who gives up a coronet to flee to the arms of her true love, and the plot is very simple. The wicked Marquis whom she has jilted, you see, being of a proud and ungovernable temper, pursues the lovers and attempts to put a period to their existence by shooting them both, just as he has previously shot a tiresome number of other persons who had the misfortune to cross him at an inconvenient moment. Fortunately, although one of his bullets reaches its mark, the other does not, for the young lady's true love, even outraged and horror-stricken as he is at seeing his beloved shot down by the wicked Marquis, yet contrives to kill the Marquis before the Marquis is able to kill *him*—" He paused, still holding the candle high and looking into her face with that slight, curious smile playing about his lips. "Ingenious, is it not?" he asked her suddenly. "A trifle crude, perhaps—but, believe me, I should not have resorted to violence if you and Lewis had not made it necessary. Really, it is quite unlike him, you know, to cling so pertinaciously to the idea of marrying you—and as for you, you little fool, I gave you every opportunity to make a most advantageous match with young Swanton. But now, with the engagement publicly announced, you really could scarcely expect me to wait any longer to arrange my little drama. A brat of yours to lay claim to Lewis's title and fortune when he goes to an early reward was never in my plans, my dear."

Victoire's eyes never left his face, but she spoke now at last, through stiff lips. "*Ecoutez,*" she said haltingly. "Listen —listen to me. If you will let me go now, I promise you that I will go away and never see Lewis again. There will be no marriage—no child—and no—no murders—" Slight colour came all at once into her cheeks. "Don't you believe me? *Nom de Dieu,* you *must* believe me!" she exclaimed, rising suddenly and swiftly crossing the few feet that lay between them to lay her hand imploringly upon his arm. "There is no need for this! I tell you, I will go away!"

The curiously smiling, detached expression upon his face did not change.

"And how, I wonder," he said, with a jeering note in his voice, "will you contrive to go where Lewis will not follow you? No, no, my dear; you must be got out of the way—that is true, indeed—but in a rather more final manner than that."

"But you—if you—kill me—" She brought the words out with difficulty, her eyes still fixed without moving on his face. "If you kill *me,*" she went on, "you need not also—kill *him.* Do

259

you not see that? If *I* am gone, it is not necessary that you kill Lewis as well, for there will be no marriage then, and no child—"

She halted, looking up at him with a desperate hope in her eyes; but she could read no change of expression in that pale face.

"Touching!" he commented after a moment, nodding slightly, as if in mild approval. "Very touching! So you are really prepared to offer me your life for Lewis's! I wonder what he can have done to deserve such devotion!"

She laid her hand again upon his arm, but he brushed it off with a contemptuous movement.

"Oh, I beg you—don't weary me with any more of your high flights!" he said impatiently. "Do you imagine that I am such a fool as to believe there is any way I could kill you alone and not go to the gallows for murder? No, my dear, no! Our little drama must and shall be played out here tonight; it is the only safe way for me to accomplish my purpose, besides having the splendid advantage of allowing me to come into my inheritance at once, so that I shall not be obliged to wait for Lewis to put an end to himself by his own recklessness."

He moved again towards the door; it opened briefly, and shut again with the final sound of a key turning in the lock outside. She was left alone in darkness.

For a few moments after he had gone she simply stood without moving exactly as he had left her. It was as if her brain could not yet comprehend what had already happened to her, what must soon happen both to her and to Lewis—in two hours, or three, however long it would be before Lewis walked into the trap that had been laid for him. It would all be so easy for Bruce Fearon—the pistol shot as Lewis, unsuspecting, stepped inside the front door, then herself dragged downstairs and dispatched beside him and the room disarranged at leisure to give the proper appearance of a struggle's having occurred in it. The man Meggs—well paid, of course, by his employer

260

—would give evidence that that struggle had taken place, and there would be the counterfeit note from her, so cleverly contrived to lend credence to the story of the eloping lovers and the murderous rage of the jilted Marquis, so that Bruce Fearon, the hero thenceforth of a romantic tale of love and loss, would by this single bold stroke be safe forever in possession of Tarn's title and estates.

"If I do not stop him," Victoire concluded her mental rehearsal of the situation. She drew herself together fiercely. "If I do not stop him! But I *will* stop him. I *will*!"

There were heavy footsteps mounting the stairs now —Meggs, coming up to guard the door, she thought, while Bruce Fearon remained below, waiting for Lewis. There was no hope of escape that way—but escape she must, if she were to warn Lewis before he came to the house. She flew across the bare room to where the outline of the window was just visible in the darkness and pulled aside the curtains that covered it. It was small, she saw, but not so small that, slender as she was, she might not contrive to squeeze through it.

She opened it and looked down. To her dismay, she perceived that a drop of some thirty feet lay below her. The room was at the rear of the rambling old house, and the ground, sloping down here to what looked in the darkness to be a small stream of some sort, left the upper windows at a considerably greater distance above it than would have been the case had it been level. She could not possibly hope to jump without suffering serious injury—a fact that she was bitterly certain Bruce Fearon had made quite sure of before he had allowed her the freedom of the room.

She cast about quickly for some means of lessening the fall. A rope, she thought, might be made from bed-curtains or sheets; but the bed was bare of coverings of any sort, and the curtains, when she attempted to pull them down, frayed and tore in her hands, rotted from long years of damp and neglect.

The noise she made in the attempt to wrench them free of

their rings, though it was no more than a subdued jingle, sounded ferociously loud to her in the oppressive silence of the house; and, in truth, it was enough to bring Meggs in upon her. She heard the key turn quickly in the lock and then the door opened. He stood on the threshold, holding a lantern that showed the room clearly in its steady light; and his suspicious glance at once pinned her standing there, frozen, a fragment of torn curtain still clutched in her hand.

A growl escaped him as his slow brain pieced together her purpose. The next moment, setting the lantern down upon one of the chairs, he strode across to the bed and, gripping the curtains at its foot in his enormous fists, wrested them down and flung them on the floor. Those at the sides followed; then he stooped, bundled them all into his arms, and, recrossing the room, flung them outside into the passage.

She was surprised, when he turned again to pick up the lantern, to see that there was a smile upon his face; but it was not a smile that reassured her.

"Don't you go for to try nothing like that, missy," he reproved her, standing there with that odd grin upon his misshapen face. "Break yer neck, you would—or yer back, more likely. I see a man's back broke once in the ring. Piteous sight he was—"

He turned to go, but Victoire, flinging down the fragment of curtain she held, sprang across the room towards him, detaining him.

"Wait! Wait, please!" she cried. "If you do not wish me to die, will you help me, please? It is altogether unbelievable, I know, but Mr. Fearon—your employer—it is his intention to kill me."

"Ay," said the huge man, equably. "Ay, so it is."

She stood looking up at him, dumbfounded. "You know that, then?" she stammered.

"Ay," he repeated, again with that foolish, evil grin upon his face.

262

"And—you will let it happen?"

He nodded emphatically. "Ay. And a champion good thing 'twill be for me!"

"But—you cannot! You cannot! Listen to me—I, too, will pay you money if you will let me go, and Lord Tarn also—"

But she got no farther; Meggs, advising her severely to stubble it, for he wasn't a cove as went back on his given word, retreated forthwith from the room with his lantern and locked the door behind him.

She sat down on the bed, despair overcoming her. Her worst reflection was that if Tarn had indeed been summoned to Albemarle Street by Miss Standfield as soon as Mr. Fearon's groom had delivered the note there, he would undoubtedly have set out to seek her at once, as Mr. Fearon confidently expected, and if he were driving himself in his curricle-and-four he would certainly arrive at Edmondstone in a shorter period of time than it had required for her and Mr. Fearon to make the journey in a chaise. This meant that time was growing perilously short; she *must* find some method of escape at once. She placed no reliance at all upon the possibility that Tarn would not come, or that Miss Standfield would not have summoned him, for no matter how exactly Mr. Fearon had been able to counterfeit her hand, she was positive that neither Tarn nor Miss Standfield would believe that she had left Albemarle Street with Mr. Fearon with an elopement in mind.

She rose again presently and, going to the window, pulled it open again and looked out. It was a damp, still night and a mist was rising, thickening and gathering in wisps as white as wool, which trailed and rose in wavering streamers in the heavy air. If she were once able to escape from the house, she thought, it would be a comparatively simple matter for her to elude pursuit, but—*if she were once able to escape from the house* —there was the rub. How was she to get out?

Her eyes fell upon a huge beech growing to the left of her window. The roof of the house, which was an ancient half-

263

timbered Tudor manor of very irregular form, evidently much altered and added to over the years, was some feet below her window there, and the tree had grown over it to such an extent that it seemed possible that, if she could manage to lower herself to that level, the tree itself might provide her with the means to reach the ground. To the advantage of this plan was the fact that this lower-roofed section was set at an angle to the main body of the house in which the room where she stood lay, so that an agile person might succeed without overmuch difficulty in making a somewhat perilous progress from the upper window to the lower roof.

It was a project that would have dismayed most properly brought up young females to attempt; but to Victoire, bred up in every kind of fearless sport, and only a few years removed from the period when climbing trees had been a cherished pastime, it appeared definitely feasible. Risk there undoubtedly was, for if she were to fall she must inevitably be seriously injured, but the risk seemed slight when compared with the danger both she and Tarn would face if she remained in the house.

She did not hesitate for a moment. Crossing the room in the darkness to the place where she remembered one of the chairs stood, she carried it over to the window and, mounting upon it, scrambled through the aperture to begin her precarious progress to the lower roof. Skirts and petticoats proved a bothersome impediment, but it was not, after all, more difficult than she had feared to reach it.

Once she was safely there, however—after a few very breathless moments—the tree presented a new problem: there was no way for her to be certain that the branches growing over the roof were strong enough to support her at the distance from the trunk at which she must trust herself to them. Still, she could not remain where she was; she had to make the attempt, for, even if Meggs or Bruce Fearon did not ultimately find her here, she could warn Tarn of his danger, when he arrived, no more effectually from this place than she could have done had she remained inside the house.

"*Dieu me sauve!*" she said to herself and, going to the roof's edge, grasped what appeared to be the sturdiest of the limbs overhanging it and let herself cautiously down. A moment later she was dangling perilously from a swaying, creaking branch, while her feet sought frantically for a foothold among the boughs below her. For an instant it appeared to her that the dangerously bending branch from which she hung must surely break; but then her feet found a lower branch; she was able to creep along it, still clinging to the higher bough, to the crotch where it joined the massive trunk, and finally to collapse, crouching upon her new perch in comparative safety, her arms tightly clasping the trunk against which she half sat, half lay.

For a few moments she remained as she was, her heart slamming against her ribs in such hammer-strokes of mingled fear and exertion that she felt they must be audible in the thick, still air. But there were no answering sounds from the house, and after a time she was in sufficient control of herself to proceed to a further cautious descent of the tree. There were, she saw now, no branches for the first eight to ten feet of its height, which meant that she must hang by her hands from the lowest branch and drop several feet to the ground; but this manoeuvre held no terrors for her—if only, she thought, she did not rouse Bruce Fearon by the noise she made in her fall.

She might hope, however, that he was in another part of the house, perhaps in the front hall, awaiting Tarn's arrival—but it was a hope that left her abruptly when, pulling up her hampering skirts and scrambling down through the leafy branches, a shaft of light suddenly reached her eyes. She stopped, paralysed. The light came from a window of the house. Crouching down upon the branch on which she stood, she found that she could look inside, for the curtains had been pulled back and the window itself flung open, evidently to admit fresh air into

265

the musty, stuffy room. Within, seated in an armchair beside a table on which a pistol lay, sat Bruce Fearon.

Her heart stopped, then began to thud again in slow, heavy strokes. He could not have heard her descent above him, she thought, for he sat quite immobile, at his ease, his legs stretched out comfortably before him. Obviously he did not expect Tarn's arrival as yet, nor had he any inkling of her escape. Her further descent, however, with the noise that must inevitably result from it, might well bring him to the alert. She was in a quandary, torn between the desire to escape at once and the realisation that it would be infinitely safer to remain where she was, in the hope that he might soon leave the room to go to some other part of the house.

Prudence won the day; she settled herself, with what patience she could, to wait. Minutes went by—at least ten, she believed—but Bruce Fearon, though he rose from his chair once and moved out of her sight for a few moments, returning to seat himself again with a glass in his hand, showed no inclination to leave the room. Her impatience to be gone was fast getting the better of her when the night silence was suddenly shattered by a wrathful shout from above.

"Bubbled! Dang it, if she ain't loped off! Guv'nor! Guv'nor!"

She saw Bruce Fearon spring to his feet and waited for no more. Heedless now of the noise she made, she scrambled down from her perch and dropped into an overgrown bed of ivy that broke her fall, but tangled her feet in its wiry tendrils. By the time she had succeeded in freeing herself, she could see the bobbing light of a lantern already emerging from a rear door of the house. She picked up her skirts and fled like a deer across a neglected garden, through a thick shrubbery, over a stile into fields where she soon lost her thin slippers in the mire left by a recent rain. She could hear the sounds of pursuit behind her, but she could not spare a glance for her pursuers; she was making for the wood that she could see looming blackly

266

against the sky at a little distance before her, hoping that among the thick trees she might elude them. Even as it was, she believed, moving in her light gown among the trailing wreaths of the rising mist, she must be a confusing quarry for them in the blackness.

She sped on, her heart and limbs beginning to labour now. A little more, and she would have reached the shelter of the wood; the trees, swimming before her pulsing vision, came up to receive her. Then a fallen branch blocked her path and she swerved aside, realising in sudden panic that her pursuers would be upon her within a space of moments if she could not maintain her pace. She had bought concealment, but at the price of obstacles and uncertain footing, and now to find that concealment was an imperative necessity.

She fled on through the trees, hearing curses, the blundering sounds of pursuit, behind her.

"Not that way, you fool! Stop a moment! Use your ears! We're bound to hear her now. She can't be far off."

It was Bruce Fearon's voice, coming so clearly that her heart almost stopped. She checked, fearing to move another step, trying to control her quick, uneven breathing. For the moment there was no sound but the hushed rustle of leaves above her head, the long-drawn cry of an owl, very far away. Her eyes darted through the misty darkness, anxiously seeking some safe covert.

The sounds of pursuit began again, more cautiously now, as if they realised she must be close before them, halting every few seconds as they listened, no doubt, for her movements.

She turned desperately, and a huge oak, standing at the top of a slight rise, caught her eye. It was thickly overgrown with ivy, with a scrubby tangle of bushes at its foot. If she could reach it without their hearing her—

She moved towards it, forcing herself to step slowly and carefully when every pulse in her body cried for frantic speed.

267

She gained the top of the rise. There were the bushes—a poor haven, but perhaps if, like a driven hare, she flattened herself, crouching, in among their prickly branches—

And then she saw it, like a miracle, behind the veiling ivy, the dark cavity in the huge bole of the half-dead tree, a hollow large enough to give friendly harbour to owls and foxes, a hollow tall and deep enough for one small, panting human creature—

She pressed herself inside it, pulling the trailing ivy across the betraying glimmer of gown and face. She was only just in time; in a space of moments the lantern's bobbing glow came into sight. It stopped; Meggs's hoarse voice said, between frustration and confidence, "She's bound to be about here some'eres, guv'nor! Gone to earth. We'd be sure to ha' heard her, other gait!"

"Yes," said Bruce Fearon's voice, in savagely determined tones. "Go that way, Meggs; I'll go this. Make a circle—and search any cover!"

She heard him move off. Meggs's heavy steps were coming in her direction now, up the rise, straight towards her tree. She stood rigid, her breath stopping. Lantern light shone on the tangle of bushes, paused there deliberately, swung in slow circles about them. She closed her eyes tightly; if she saw it move closer she might betray herself by a scream.

An aeon passed. Then, slowly, the heavy footsteps moved away. She opened her eyes, her fast-thudding heart beginning to steady as she drew a half-sobbing breath of relief. He had gone by without discovering her hiding place. She was safe.

It was then that she became conscious for the first time that her hands and arms were scratched and bleeding from her hasty escape from the window by way of the tree, that her dress was torn and her feet unshod and bruised after her wild flight. It did not matter; all that did matter was that she must some- how contrive to reach the lane leading to the house in time to warn Tarn of the danger that awaited him if he entered it. It would not do to rely upon Bruce Fearon's abandoning his carefully laid plan, even though she had managed to upset it by her escape. He might set Meggs to continue the search for her alone, while he returned to the house to deal with Tarn, counting on being able to track her down later if Meggs had not succeeded in finding her. At any rate, she realised that having been driven into the open now, he would be more dangerous than ever, knowing that he could not afford to allow her to live to tell her story to Tarn.

The sounds of Meggs's footsteps had died out entirely; she could hear nothing but the tranquil night noises of the wood. Uncomfortable as she was in her cramped hiding place, she would have given a great deal to be able to remain in it—but time was slipping by; at any moment now Tarn might arrive at Edmondstone, and Bruce Fearon might already have returned to the house to lie in wait for him there. She drew a long breath, said a scathing word to herself on the subject of cowardice, and, stepping out carefully from her haven, began slowly to descend the rise.

She had gone only a few feet when a sudden sound stopped her. It was merely the crack of a twig, but it sent her sharply to the rightabout; she scrambled back up the rise to the tree and again pushed her way inside. Her heart had begun to beat faster again. They were coming back, then; one of them, at least, was coming back.

She could hear the sound of footsteps now, cautious, heavy, blundering footsteps—Meggs. They paused once, and then went on again—then, stubbornly, came back, came slowly up the rise. The light of the lantern deliberately swept the tangle of shrubbery before her sanctuary. She breathed shallowly, fighting down the impulse to panic.

The light was playing on the tree now. Behind the obscuring ivy she saw it sweep past, lighting briefly a glimmer of pale gown, then go on again. Her breath escaped her in a little sobbing sigh of relief.

And then, so abruptly that she had time to do no more than shrink back against the hollow that held her, the light sank to the ground, the ivy was thrust aside, and Meggs's huge hands seized her as his pleased voice echoed hoarsely through the silence, "Found her, guv'nor! Found her! Ay, here she is, safe as a flea in a rug! Guv'nor! D'ye hear me?"

He pulled her out into the open, handling her as easily as if she had been a rag doll caught in his enormous grasp. Hurrying footsteps crashed through the wood and Bruce Fearon came into view. He paused; the lantern, which Meggs had set upon the ground before seizing her, sent its light eerily from below to illuminate his face, set in lines of savage satisfaction.

"Good work, Meggs!" he said. "There'll be an extra pony for you on the head of this!" And, to Victoire, viciously, "You little bitch! I hadn't expected you to be so clever—but you won't give me the slip so easily again! Come along now!"

He grasped her arm ungently; Meggs took the other, and together they half dragged, half carried her down the rise. She tried to struggle, to delay their return to the house, so that Tarn, arriving and finding it empty, might leave to search elsewhere for her, but between the two men she was helpless; she could not possibly break away from them, and she was soon too exhausted to do more than stumble on numbly between them.

It seemed a very long time before they arrived at last at the house.

And then, just as she was being pulled inside the front door, she heard it—the sound of horses' hooves coming fast up the lane, the rattle of wheels. She opened her mouth to cry a warning, but Meggs's hand came down hard over her face, stifling the sound before it could break from her throat.

"What's to do, guv'nor?" she heard him growl.

"Inside—quick! Bring the girl!"

She could not guess what plan Bruce Fearon had made for meeting Tarn, but certainly this confusion and hurry had no

270

part in it. Half-blinded and wholly silenced now by Meggs's enforcing hand as he dragged her inside the house, she had a glimpse of Bruce Fearon, holding the lantern, kicking open a door that led from the hall; he stepped inside, and Meggs pulled her in after and closed the door.

"No—leave it open, you fool!" Bruce Fearon's voice commanded. "I want him in here! And keep that jade quiet, whatever you do!"

There was a pistol in his hand now; she saw the glint of its barrel as Meggs pulled her back into a corner of the room. Then there was the sound of quick footsteps outside and she knew she must do something at once, or it would be too late.

She wrenched her head aside beneath the smothering hand that was clamped over her mouth and bit down on it as hard as she could. It jerked away as Meggs uttered an oath above her, and she shrieked out, just as the footsteps came up to the door, "Lewis! He has a pistol! Don't come in! Don't come—"

21

A blow struck her silent: she collapsed in a heap on the floor just as Tarn, with that split second of warning she had given him, came through the door in a silent, murderous dive for Bruce Fearon's gun hand, like a tiger for the kill. The sheer audacity of the move warranted its success: Bruce, standing facing the door, awaiting the first sight of his victim with pistol raised, pulled the trigger indeed, but only after a fraction of a second's delay, at the instant that Tarn's body hurtled into his, and the bullet flew harmlessly wide. The two men went down in a crashing welter of arms and legs. Meggs, abandoning Victoire, hurled himself into the fray. As she pulled herself up into a sitting position, half sobbing with pain and shock, she saw at a glance how the struggle must end. Against Meggs alone, with his enormous strength, Tarn must have been at a disadvantage; with Bruce as an added opponent, he could not possibly hope to come off the victor.

She glanced about her desperately for some weapon with

which to aid him. Then she realised that the room was lit only by the light of the lantern that Bruce Fearon had carried inside with him after his search for her in the wood; it stood now upon a table near the wall where he had placed it. Raising herself dizzily, she moved against the wall, keeping out of the way of the struggle going on in the centre of the room, and quickly overturned it, extinguishing the light. The room, behind the heavy draperies at its windows, was plunged into complete darkness; there could not be the slightest hope now of distinguishing friend from foe. The advantage, she knew, was Tarn's: any blow he struck must be against an enemy, while Bruce Fearon might find himself engaging Meggs as Tarn escaped from the room with her.

The struggle went on, however, apparently with no decrease in violence; not until too late, when she saw a flicker of light leap into being, did she realise that Bruce Fearon, as quick as she to see the disadvantage of his position, had immediately abandoned his part in the fray to search for the lantern—and for the pistol, which she saw glinting again in his shaking hand as the light flared up to illumine the room. She flung herself at him. There was no purpose in the movement; it was pure instinct. He struck at her with his free hand without taking his eyes from the two men locked in battle before him, and she collapsed on the floor, dazed, her senses swimming. She saw Meggs's hands at Tarn's throat, heard the sickening thud as the heavier man forced him back against a massive oak table, his hands digging cruelly into the flesh. Bruce Fearon was smiling, his lips drawn back slightly from his teeth, the pistol dropping negligently in his hand.

Il s'amuse, she thought dully. *He is enjoying this.*

She tried to drag herself to her feet, to do something, anything, to aid Tarn, but, even as she succeeded in getting to her knees, she saw him come away from the table in a lunge that sent his opponent reeling backwards. The next moment Meggs's head had snapped back before a crashing blow that

274

took him full on the jaw; he went down, but a leg hooked round Tarn's knee brought the Marquis plummeting down atop him. There was a wild melee as the two men wrestled for an advantage. Victoire, on her knees, saw Bruce Fearon's smile disappear, his pistol hand raise slowly. He could not fire now without taking the risk of hitting the wrong man, but when the struggle was over, no matter if Tarn won or lost—

Tarn's fingers were about Meggs's throat now; the huge man, his body straining awkwardly, his face suffused with blood, made a last supreme effort to break that iron grip, failed, and fell back, spread-eagled upon the floor. For a moment Tarn remained on one knee beside him, breathing harshly; then he shot a quick glance up, saw the levelled pistol, Victoire desperately trying to drag herself to her feet—

"I wouldn't," said a deliberate, slightly accented voice from the door, "fire that pistol if I were you, Mr. Fearon. It would do me a world of good, you know, to put a bullet through your head."

Mr. Fearon's eyes jerked up. In the doorway Captain Lanner, his leathers freshly splashed from hard riding, stood holding a very businesslike pistol pointed purposefully at his head.

They were seated in Tarn's curricle—Victoire and Tarn himself, with Captain Lanner riding beside them on a very tired bay—driving in the direction of Eastcott Park, where, Tarn had informed them, it was his intention to ask Lady Eastcott to put them up. Victoire, wrapped in Tarn's drab driving coat, was bruised, scratched, muddy, and aching in every limb, and she was happier than she had ever been in her life before. The look on Tarn's face when, Bruce Fearon having been disarmed, he had sprung across the room to raise her to her feet, the feel of his arms tight around her, and his anxious, furious voice in her ears—"Are you all right? Are you? By God, if you're not, I'll kill him myself"—were still with her; and afterwards, as he had lifted her into the curricle, he had kissed her, quite regardless of Captain Lanner's presence—not one of the light, careless kisses he had occasionally bestowed upon her before that night, but a hungry embrace that had left him, it seemed to her, as shaken and breathless as she was herself.

She sat in blissful silence, hugging his driving coat about her and listening to the two men matter-of-factly discussing —*pardieu,* it was like them, she thought tolerantly, to speak now as if nothing at all dangerous or exciting had occurred! —the events of the night.

"What I can't understand"—it was Tarn speaking now, in such a very ordinary voice that it was hard to believe it had been with the conviction in her mind that he had killed the man with whom he was conversing that she had left London only hours before—"what I can't understand is how the deuce you happened to turn up here at all, much less exactly in the nick of time. How did you come to—?"

Captain Lanner, also speaking in an ordinary voice, which involved a considerable effort upon his part, however, owing to the fact that that very warm embrace he had witnessed had inspired him with a strong desire to (in inelegant boxing cant) plant the Marquis a facer and then ask Victoire who she thought had saved her, said that that was quite easy to explain. He had, he said, by a piece of good luck, arrived to pay a call in Albemarle Street just as Miss Standfield had seen the Marquis go off in his attempt to extricate Victoire from what they were both convinced had been a forced elopement with Mr. Fearon.

"She had the wind up rather badly," he went on, "which, from what I've seen of her, was so unusual that I asked her what the matter was. Of course she knows how close Victoire and I have been, so she told me, and when I heard your cousin's name I began to put two and two together and decided, with her blessing, to go off after you. It appeared to me, you see, that you might be able to do with a bit of help."

The Marquis, in spite of the fact that this speech appeared to him to have been a deliberate provocation from beginning to

276

end, set his teeth and said nothing at all, upon consideration of the debt he owed Captain Lanner; but he was wishing with all his heart that he had been able in some miraculous manner to vanquish singlehanded two men, one armed and the other a professional pugilist of gigantic size, or that at least he could be sure that Victoire's gratitude towards Captain Lanner would not have caused her to respond with equal warmth to an embrace from him if she had been given the opportunity to do so.

"She gave me very good directions," Captain Lanner was continuing, meanwhile. "I hadn't the least difficulty in finding the place."

Tarn, forced by his own private code of ethics to give credit where credit was due, said that the Captain must be a bruising rider and the Captain immodestly admitted that he was. This made Victoire chuckle sleepily and confide to Tarn that he had always talked so—"which made Papa very vexed with him sometimes," she said, "for he said that a good soldier should not praise himself. But, *enfin,*" she went on, dropping the subject, "I have been thinking, and I will tell you that I do not at all understand men, at any rate. *Voyons,* I thought one of you would kill Mr. Fearon—especially you, Lewis, when you sent him spinning against the wall and took his pistol away from him after Constant appeared in such an *absolument magnifique* way in the doorway. And I think Mr. Fearon thought so too, only then, *parbleu,* in the end you let him go! *Moi,* if I had not killed him—which it is very likely I would have done if I had had a pistol, for I was very, very angry with him, you understand—I would at least have sent for a constable and had him clapped into gaol."

"Well, I won't say I wouldn't have liked to kill him for what he did to you," Tarn said, a dark gleam in his eyes indicating that he was still not beyond regretting his own magnanimity. "But, after all, he hadn't succeeded in making away with either of us, and you can't go around murdering fellows because

277

they've only planned to murder you—not when you have them at pistol-point!"

Victoire looked at him respectfully. *"Tiens,* I find that you are very clever!" she said appreciatively. "When *I* am angry, I do not think of such things!"

"Nor do I, ordinarily," Tarn had the grace to admit. "But since we're to be married"—this with a great deal of emphasis, for Captain Lanner's benefit—"it seems that one of us at least had best learn to keep his temper. And as for having him clapped into gaol," he added, "that *would* have raised the devil of a stir— and even though he and my mother will have it that I've no feeling for what's due to the family, I draw the line at dragging this affair through the courts for every gapeseed's entertainment. As it is, he won't dare show his face in England again; you may be sure of that!"

"Yes, you are right, of course," Victoire said sleepily, nestling her head down on his shoulder. "And now may I go to sleep, please, until we arrive at your uncle's house? I do not think I can stay awake any longer, for I am very, very *fatiguée*—"

Her voice trailed off. In another few moments she was fast asleep. Captain Lanner, well acquainted with the difficulties of managing a spirited team on a dark road with a sleeping female, no matter of how slight a form, reposing against one's shoulder, said unchivalrously that Tarn had better wake her, but the Marquis would not permit it.

"I shall manage," he said, allowing his eyes to move fleetingly from the road to rest upon the little figure reposing so confidingly against him.

So the Captain reflected philosophically that at least if they landed in a ditch, he would not be a participant in the disaster and said no more.

It was full dawn when the curricle rounded the carriage sweep to draw up before the famous orange-pink façade of the Earl of Eastcott's country seat, but still far too early for anyone to be stirring inside but the servants. Tarn, tossing the reins to a yawning stable boy who had appeared at the sound of wheels upon the gravelled drive, helped his equally sleepy betrothed down from the curricle and led her up the steps to the door, ignoring the stable boy's unconcealed surprise at the sight of an unshod and much dishevelled young lady, wrapped in a driving coat that swallowed up her diminutive figure entirely, arriving at Eastcott Park at this hour of the morning. Captain Lanner followed in their wake.

They had no sooner stepped inside the front door, however—which was, unexpectedly, opened for them immediately by Philbrook—when it became apparent to all three of the newcomers that they had arrived at Eastcott Park on no ordinary morning. In the front hall Lord Eastcott, wearing a drab benjamin and surrounded by several portmanteaux and cloak-bags, was drawing on a pair of York tan driving gloves and looking impatiently towards the stairs, which he appeared to be expecting someone to descend; and, in fact, even as the newcomers entered, Lady Eastcott, bonnetted and cloaked for travel, appeared above.

"Come along! Come along, my lady!" Lord Eastcott said testily; and then turned abruptly as his wife, her eyes widening at sight of the trio in the doorway, exclaimed, "Lewis! What in the world are *you* doing here?"—and came hurrying down the stairs.

"What the deuce—!" ejaculated Lord Eastcott, his own eyes expressing the liveliest astonishment as they fell upon the extraordinary company that had invaded his house.

Tarn came forward, ignoring him, and took Lady Eastcott's hands in his.

"You are not going away, Aunt?" he asked. "At this hour? What has happened?"

"Oh, it is Tina!" said Lady Eastcott, too full, apparently, of her own problems to have any thoughts to spare for the presence of either Captain Lanner or the butler. "An express from

Arthur arrived only an hour ago; they have quarrelled again and she is leaving him, she says! I vow, the girl will drive me distracted! Of course, Eastcott and I are leaving immediately for London—"

"The devil you are!" Tarn said. "You cannot leave now! That is," he added magnanimously, "my uncle may go, if he chooses—but you see I have brought Victoire to you, and I can't have her staying here with only me and Lanner. It wouldn't be proper!"

"Wouldn't be—proper!" Lady Eastcott said faintly, looking from her nephew, who had never been known to concern himself with the proprieties before this moment, to the extraordinary picture presented by Victoire, engulfed to the tips of her slipperless toes in Tarn's driving coat. "And what, pray," she enquired with considerable asperity, pointing to Victoire, "do you call this—this—?"

"Well, it's too long a story to go into now," Tarn said impatiently, "but you can take my word for it that we've all had the devil of a night, and want a bath, breakfast, and bed, in that order. You remember Lanner, Aunt, of course?" he added, belatedly recalling his social obligations to the Captain, who stepped forward and said politely that it was a pleasure to renew his acquaintance with Lord and Lady Eastcott.

Lord Eastcott, who had also been drinking in the details of Victoire's appearance, as well as of certain interesting indications upon his nephew's person that he had been engaging in some form of mayhem, here broke in to give it as his unalterable opinion that the entire younger generation had run mad, and said that he was going to London.

"An excellent idea, Uncle," Tarn said, in cordial approval. "If I know Arthur, you will find, when you arrive there, that he has exaggerated the matter out of all proportion, and that Tina has got up the whole thing only to wheedle a new court-dress out of his pocket—but do not, on any account, let us keep you. And as for you, Aunt—had you not better take off your bonnet now and speak to your housekeeper? You will need three rooms got ready, you know, as well as a very substantial breakfast for three."

"Lewis, if your entire family was expiring around you, I believe you would still call first of all for *a substantial breakfast!*" Lady Eastcott said, torn between laughter and exasperation. "But I daresay you are quite right about Tina, and Eastcott can manage very well without me—though the chief reason I shall stay behind is so that I shall be able to hear what you have been up to now!" She turned to Victoire. "Will you go into the morning parlour, my dear, and sit down until Fream has your room ready for you?" she asked. "And—oh dear, you have brought no luggage with you, I daresay, so I shall have to see to getting you something to wear."

She hurried off to seek her housekeeper, and Victoire obediently allowed herself to be shepherded by Tarn into a small room opening from the rear of the hall. Captain Lanner, with a magnanimity of which he was quite conscious, strolled outside with Lord Eastcott to examine the points of the team of match-greys that were just drawing that harassed gentleman's travelling-chaise up to the front door and wondered if the Condessa would be sufficiently grateful to him for the part he had played in removing Mr. Fearon from the London scene (for he was beginning to have a shrewd idea that that gentleman had been behind her rather excessive anxiety to prevent Tarn's marriage to Victoire) to reward him as she had almost promised to do if he had succeeded in drawing Victoire off for himself. For in spite of the depression engendered in him by the sight of the extreme cordiality with which Victoire had returned the Marquis's embrace, he was not really greatly enamoured of the idea of marriage, attractive as he found his old playfellow and ardently as he wished she might be in love with him as much and for as long as he was with her, and as a soldier he had long since learned that, while no one can win every battle, there are always compensations for defeat.

Meanwhile, in the morning parlour Tarn, entering behind Victoire, had closed the door but, contrary to her expectation, did not look at her with the eyes of a man inviting her to walk straight into his arms, as she was longing to have him do. The Marquis, in fact, was finding himself for the first time in his life suffering from a twinned attack of scruples and doubt, brought on by a sudden realisation that he could not be at all sure that he, and not Captain Lanner, was the man whom Victoire wished to marry and that if the Captain really wished to marry her, too, and was not merely pretending to be in love with her to ingratiate himself with the Condessa, he, Tarn, ought not in honour to stand in the way of their happiness. This was such a soul-wrenching thought that he walked over to the window so that he would not be obliged to look at Victoire, wondering bleakly at the same time if it might not have been better if his cousin *had* succeeded in putting a bullet through him just before the Captain's arrival, thus ensuring the happiness of everyone.

Victoire's voice came rather timidly behind him. "Lewis? *Qu'as tu?* Are you angry?"

"Angry? No!" He turned about and, feeling it was better to get it over with at once if it was to be got over at all, said abruptly and without the least preamble, "I was thinking about Lanner. You said he'd asked you to marry him the other day but you didn't tell me what answer you'd given him or rather had wanted to give him. And, after all," he finished, with a really heroic idea of giving his rival every advantage that was properly owing to him, "*he* was the one who saved us both. I wouldn't have been able to do it alone."

"But of course you would!" said Victoire, looking quite indignant. "You were *épatant!*—and I was never afraid for an instant after you had come that we would not both be perfectly safe in the end. Besides," she added anxiously, "Constant does not *really* want to marry anyone, you know."

"That isn't the point. The point is—do you want him to want

282

to?" Tarn insisted stubbornly, noting the anxiety, and feeling now that if she said she did he would at once go back to the Continent and engage in conduct of such unparalleled recklessness there that he would inevitably be dead within three months without the necessity of taking the trouble of putting an end to himself.

But luckily for him Victoire had nothing at all in common with ordinary young ladies who would have fluttered and temporised over such a bald question. She merely said quite simply, "No. I want *you* to want to marry me," which was so exactly the right thing to say that the Marquis felt the weight of the entire world fall from his shoulders and was therefore free to breathe and move again. The movement involved taking her in his arms in such an extremely close embrace that it seemed quite possible that several of her ribs would not survive the strain—a danger that did not appear to disturb her, however, especially when she heard the Marquis's voice saying huskily above her, "Oh God, infant, I've been such a fool! I didn't know until I'd read that letter, and for one wretched moment believed it was true and you really *had* gone off with someone else, how much I'd come to love you, and that life without you—well, it doesn't bear thinking of!" he said, his arms tightening even more jealously about her.

Victoire smiled up at him in tender incredulity at such foolishness, her eyes like stars in her glowing face. "But how could it have been true?" she said. "*Moi*, I knew from the first day I met you that I was yours *à tout jamais*—and that is why I said I would marry you when you asked me, because I hoped very much that one day you would feel the same. And now it has happened, which, *pour moi*, is very wonderful—"

There did not seem to be any reply adequate to this speech but a very thickened and passionate "My darling!" from his lordship, who then crushed her in his arms again and kissed her, and would no doubt have gone on kissing her indefinitely if Lady Eastcott had not come in to say that Victoire might go

283

upstairs now to the room that had been prepared for her, and what in the world was Tarn thinking of to let Captain Lanner go wandering off by himself, as if no one cared in the least if he had any breakfast or not?

"Oh, damn Lanner!" said the Marquis, but quite good-humouredly now, thinking tolerantly that the Captain was an excellent fellow, after all, and that he ought to be excessively grateful to him for turning up and rescuing him and Victoire in the nick of time.

But he did not let Victoire go until Lady Eastcott pointed out to him in some disapproval that it was really the outside of enough to be making love before breakfast to a young lady who had no shoes on, and that there would be plenty of time for all that after they were married, if that was the way he meant to go on.

"It is exactly the way I mean to go on," said the Marquis, and he looked down at Victoire with such tenderness on his dark face that it made her almost die with love.

He released her reluctantly then and she as reluctantly went upstairs, and the sun came up very dew-washed and golden upon a misty summer world still smelling of roses and night-scented stock—a world exactly like a fairy-tale one, she thought, looking from her chamber window; and thought, too, almost asleep already and dreaming of her love, that no princess in a fairy tale, reaching the point at which it is said she is to live happily ever after, had ever been half so happy or so fortunate as was she.

You're Reading in the Wrong

is meant to be read from right to left, starting in the upper-right corner.

Unlike English, which is read from left to right, Japanese is read from right to left, meaning that action, sound effects and word-balloon order are completely reversed... something which can make readers unfamiliar with Japanese feel pretty backwards themselves. For this reason, manga or Japanese comics published in the U.S. in English have sometimes been published "flopped"—that is, printed in exact reverse order, as though seen from the other side of a mirror.

By flopping pages, U.S. publishers can avoid confusing readers, but the compromise is not without its downside. For one thing, a character in a flopped manga series who once wore in the original Japanese version a T-shirt emblazoned with "M A Y" (as in "the merry month of") now wears one which reads "Y A M"! Additionally, many manga creators in Japan are themselves unhappy with the process, as some feel the mirror-imaging of their art skews their original intentions.

We are proud to bring you Yuto Tsukuda and Shun Saeki's **Food Wars!** in the original unflopped format.

For now, though, turn to the other side of the book and let the adventure begin...!

—Editor

THOSE PANTIES ARE CERTAINLY MORE... CHASTE THAN ONE WOULD EXPECT.

WOW, UH, CHECK OUT NIKUMI-CHI.

BARA BARA

*SEE INSIDE FOR DETAILS!

THE PROMISED NEVERLAND

STORY BY **KAIU SHIRAI**
ART BY **POSUKA DEMIZU**

Emma, Norman and Ray are the brightest kids at the Grace Field House orphanage. And under the care of the woman they refer to as "Mom," all the kids have enjoyed a comfortable life. Good food, clean clothes and the perfect environment to learn—what more could an orphan ask for? One day, though, Emma and Norman uncover the dark truth of the outside world they are forbidden from seeing.

DEATH NOTE
ALL-IN-ONE EDITION

Story by **Tsugumi Ohba**   Art by **Takeshi Obata**

Light Yagami is an ace student with great prospects—
and he's bored out of his mind. But all that changes
when he finds the Death Note, a notebook dropped by
a rogue Shinigami death god. Any human whose name
is written in the notebook dies, and now Light has
vowed to use the power of the Death Note to rid the
world of evil. But when criminals begin dropping dead,
the authorities send the legendary detective L to track
down the killer. With L hot on his heels, will Light lose
sight of his noble goal...or his life?

Includes a
NEW epilogue
chapter!

*All 12 volumes in ONE
monstrously large edition!*

FOR NOW, I SHALL AWAIT IT WITH PATIENCE AND JOY.

I'M CERTAIN OF IT. BUT THAT DAY IS NOT TODAY.

ERINA, ONE DAY YOU'LL FINALLY CREATE YOUR SPECIALTY.

?

OHO HO... IT'S NOTHING. PAY IT NO MIND.

END

INTERLUDE
~SENZAEMON'S MEMORIES~

THE WAY THEY DO THINGS (END)

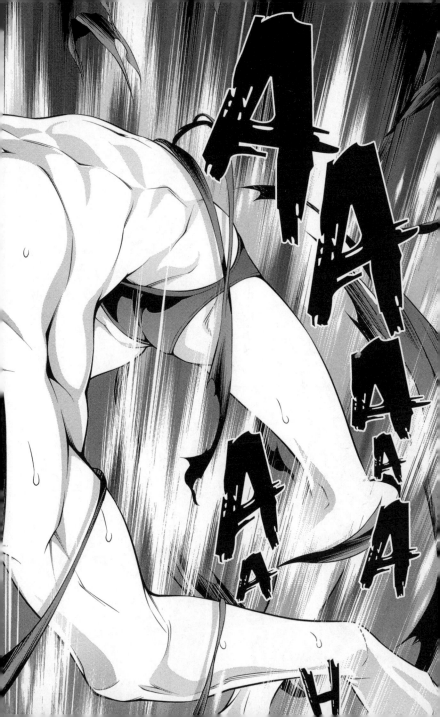

FATHER, I'M DETERMINED ...

COOKING REQUIRES FREEDOM.

AND TO PROTECT THAT FREEDOM, I WILL SPARE NO EFFORT AND SHRINK FROM NO CHALLENGE!

IT'S NO FUN IF YOU ALREADY KNOW WHAT YOU'RE GOING TO GET.

COME TO STEAL US AWAY TO A NEW LAND OF UNKNOWN DELIGHTS!

HONORED JUDGES, THAT IS THE EXTENT OF MY SPECIALTY ...

126. REBEL ANGEL

YOU SEE, MY DISH ISN'T QUITE COMPLETE.

IT HAS YET TO MORPH.

C H O K

ALL RIGHT, ALL RIGHT.

...

YEEEEAH!

IF IT'S THAT GOOD, THEN MAYBE DEAN AZAMI WILL...!

EVEN THE FIRST AND SECOND SEATS ARE SPEECHLESS!

IF YOU'RE GOING TO INSIST TO THAT DEGREE, I MAY AS WELL HAVE A BITE.

YOINK

!

NOT YET.

YOU SEE, MY DISH ISN'T QUITE COMPLETE.

146

AND THE MODERATELY SALTY BITTERNESS OF THE SQUID LEGS IS EXTREMELY EFFECTIVE IN TYING THE CROÛTE'S FLAVOR TOGETHER WITH THE MEATY JUICINESS OF THE CHICKEN!

PEANUT BUTTER'S MILD RICHNESS ADDS SUBTLE DEPTH TO THE NATURAL BODY OF THE CHICKEN, MAKING IT AN EXCELLENT SECRET SEASONING.

YES! SQUID LEGS AND PEANUT BUTTER!

APPETIZER AND MAIN DISH! THERE IS NO GREATER TIE THAT COULD BIND OUR TWO DISHES TOGETHER!

...CAN BE TRANSFORMED INTO ELEGANT GOURMET BEAUTY WHEN PUT IN MY CAPABLE HANDS.

EVEN AN ABOMINABLE MASH-UP THAT YUKIHIRA HAS TINKERED WITH FOR AGES...

...

...SO THAT AFTER YOU TASTED SOMA YUKIHIRA'S DISH...

...THE DELICIOUSNESS OF MY OWN DISH WOULD RING ACROSS YOUR TONGUES AS POWERFULLY AS POSSIBLE!

THE JIDORI CHICKEN BREASTS AND THE SQUID AND PEANUT BUTTER CROÛTE... THOSE ARE THE TWO PILLARS OF MY DISH!

TO SUPPORT THEM, I REVISED ALL THE SEASONINGS FOR THE SAUCES AND GARNISHES...

THOSE THREE THINGS DO TECHNICALLY MAKE THIS A CHICKEN-AND-EGG RICE BOWL!

CHICKEN, EGG SAUCE AND RICE CRACKERS!

THE LAYERED TEXTURES OF THE CRUNCHY YET CREAMY SAUCE PLAY AMAZINGLY OFF OF THE TENDERNESS OF THE CHICKEN!

BUT THE ONE PIECE OF THIS DISH THAT PLAYS THE BIGGEST ROLE OF ALL...

...IS THIS WRAPPING AROUND THE CHICKEN BREAST...THE CROÛTE!

CROÛTE!

IT'S A HANDY ADDITION THAT CAN BOOST THE AROMA, TEXTURES AND PRESENTATION OF A DISH WITHOUT OVERPOWERING ITS DISTINCTIVE FLAVORS!

A BASE OF BREAD OR PIE DOUGH SEASONED WITH SAVORY SPICES, CROÛTE CAN REFER EITHER TO THE DOUGH ITSELF OR A DISH WRAPPED IN IT.

...THE CROÛTE I HAD INTENDED TO USE TO WRAP THE CHICKEN BREAST REQUIRED TWO VERY SPECIFIC ADDITIONS.

THOSE TWO INGREDIENTS WERE...

GIVEN THE SUDDEN ADJUSTMENTS TO THE ORIGINAL PLAN AND MY NEED TO CREATE AN ENTIRELY DIFFERENT DISH...

YOU ARE CORRECT. THEREIN LIES THE GREATEST SECRET OF MY DISH.

VOM

THIS
FLAVOR
!

WHAT'S
GOING
ON?!

WHOA!

CHEW

S

PLSS

THE INSIDE OF THE
MEAT IS STILL TENDER,
WHILE THE OUTER
SKIN IS CRISP AND
ROBUSTLY FLAVORFUL!
IT WAS COOKED IN
A WAY PERFECT FOR
TAKING ADVANTAGE
OF THE LUXURY JIDORI
CHICKEN'S QUALITIES!

WHAT INTENSE
DELICIOUSNESS!
BOTH THE TENDER
CHICKEN MEAT
AND ITS LIGHT
JUICES ARE
SOAKED IN RICH
AND CREAMY
EGG!

FLOATING
IN IT ARE
CRUMBLES
OF SPECIALLY
MADE RICE
CRACKERS!

FRESHLY
STEAMED RICE,
SESAME OIL,
MINCED SQUID
AND A PINCH
OF SALT WERE
THOROUGHLY
COMBINED,
MOLDED INTO
THIN ROUNDS
AND THEN
TOASTED
TO CRISPY
PERFECTION.

WITH A TOUCH
OF TURMERIC
TO GIVE IT A
PLEASINGLY
VIBRANT
YELLOW COLOR,
IT'S BECOME
A THICK AND
CREAMY
SCRAMBLED-
EGG SAUCE!

THE SAUCE IS A
SIMPLE ONE OF
EGGS AND CREAM
SEASONED WITH
A BIT OF SALT
AND PEPPER AND
HEATED TO A THICK
CREAMINESS IN A
HOT WATER BATH.

SHOULD THE TWO CHEFS WHO EMBODY YOUR PERSONAL IDEAL OF *CORRECT* COOKING TASTE THIS...

...THEN WOULD YOU NOT THINK IT NECESSARY TO *REEVALUATE* YOUR DECISION?

...AND DECIDE THAT IT IS INDEED DELICIOUS...

...

I WAS CURIOUS ABOUT YUKIHIRA'S DISH ANYWAY.

I SEE NO HARM IN TASTING IT.

WHOA-HO! IS THAT A CHALLENGE? I THINK IT IS!

WHADDYA WANNA DO, TSUKASA? I THINK WE OUGHTA TAKE HER UP ON IT!

FOR MY OWN DAUGHTER TO SERVE SOMETHING LIKE THIS... I'M AT A LOSS.

IT IS SO FAR FROM THE CORRECT ANSWER THAT IT IS POSITIVELY DEPLORABLE.

PLEASE ENJOY.

WHAT AN ELEGANTLY BEAUTIFUL AND JUICY-LOOKING SLICE OF CHICKEN!

THIS IS THE MAIN DISH OF OUR TWO-COLD MEAL...

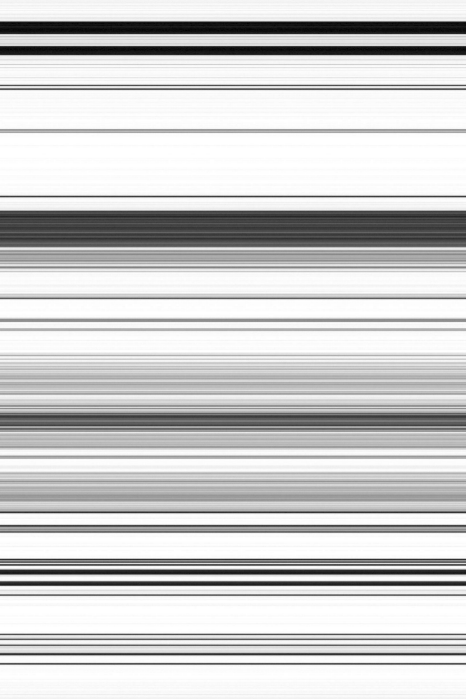

PLEASE ENJOY.

WHAT AN ELEGANTLY BEAUTIFUL AND JUICY-LOOKING SLICE OF CHICKEN!

OOOH!

#260 SPECIALTY COURSE MEAL

THIS IS THE MAIN DISH OF OUR TWO-COURSE MEAL...

WHAT SORT OF DISH IS IT?!

IS *THAT* MISS ERINA'S SPECIALTY?

IS *THAT* IT?

129

THAT IS A SPECIALTY.

A DISH THAT BRINGS TO MIND THE FACE OF THE CHEF WHO MADE IT.

THIS IS THE GREATEST POSSIBLE RECIPE...

...THAT'S CAPABLE OF BEATING YUKIHIRA!

YES. IT CAN BE THIS AND NOTHING ELSE.

BECAUSE IT'S NO FUN IF YOU ALREADY KNOW WHAT YOU'RE GOING TO GET.

BREEEEE

PHEW...

JUST IN TIME!

CROÛTE? COOLED.

GARNISHES? COMPLETE.

BUBL BUBL BUBL

SAUCE? REDUCED.

NEXT STEP! MOVE!

BROWNING UNDER THE BROILER?

COMPLETE!

THIS IS MORE... FIERCE. FORCEFUL. LIKE A RUSHING FLOOD OF PASSION!

HOW UTTERLY UNLIKE HER USUAL GRACEFUL AND RESERVED APPROACH.

121

WAAAAAA

THUS, IN A WAY...

ERINA'S DIVINE TONGUE ALLOWS HER TO TAKE ANY DISH AND ELEVATE IT TO PERFECT DELICIOUSNESS.

AND AT THE SAME TIME, NONE OF THEM ARE.

...EVERY DISH SHE CREATES IS A SPECIALTY.

...THEN...

AND WHEN SHE IS FINALLY CAPABLE OF CREATING SUCH A DISH...

A DISH THAT SURPASSES PERFECTLY DELICIOUS... ONLY IN A DISH SUCH AS THAT WILL WE SEE ERINA'S TRUE FACE.

YAMMER

YAMMER

NO MATTER WHO TRIED TO PULL THAT OFF, IT WOULD NEVER WORK!

WHAT THE HECK IS HE THINKING?!

THERE'S NO WAY IT'D COME TOGETHER AS A MEAL!

TURNING THEIR INDIVIDUAL DISHES INTO A COMPETITION?!

YAMMER

YAMMER

...AT JUST ABOUT ANY CUISINE YOU COULD NAME. HOW CAN SHE NOT?

BUT SHE'S AN ELITE PRO-LEVEL CHEF...

HOLD ON A SEC.

YAMMER

YAMMER

...BUT SIR SENZAEMON HAS YET TO AWARD THAT DISTINCTION TO ANY OF THEM.

A GOOD POINT. I'VE HEARD SHE'S MADE MULTIPLE ATTEMPTS TO CREATE ONE...

IS IT POSSIBLE ERINA-CHI DOESN'T HAVE A SPECIALTY?

WELL, GRANDFATHER? I'M SUPER-CONFIDENT IN THIS ONE.

YOU MUST ADMIT THIS HAS BECOME MY SPECIALTY!

UNFOR-TUNATELY, THAT IS NOT THE CASE. IT SEEMS YOU HAVE YET TO FIND YOUR SPECIALTY.

CHEW CHEW

HMM...

BECAUSE NONE OF THEM WERE YOUR SPECIALTY.

...NONE OF THOSE DISHES YOU MADE FOR ME LAST NIGHT CAN TOUCH IT.

WHA?! B-BUT HOW CAN YOU BE SO SURE?!

I TASTED TSUKASA'S DISH A BIT AGO, AND, MAN, IT WAS *AMAZING.* TALK ABOUT MASSIVE IMPACT!

I HATE TO SAY IT, BUT...

IF WE CAN'T PUT TOGETHER A COURSE WITH TWO DISHES OF THAT CALIBER, WE'RE GONNA LOSE.

...WE NEED NOT ONE BUT *TWO* SPECIALTIES CHOCK-FULL OF EVERY LAST OUNCE WE'VE GOT.

IF WE'RE GONNA BEAT SENPAI...

IF YOU CAN'T OUTDO ME, YOU LOSE.

IN A WAY...

YOU THINK YOU CAN MAKE A BETTER MAIN DISH THAN ME? WELL, IT'S TIME YOU PROVED IT.

...
...
...

104

YOUR APPROACH TO PREPARING THE VEGETABLES...

AZAMI NAKIRI THINKS IT'S GOOD TOO!

...

IT BRINGS TO MIND KOJIRO SHINOMIYA, LE MAGICIEN DE LÉGUME.

IT REMINDS ME OF THE RECIPE HE MADE FOR THE MOON FESTIVAL!

THERE ARE THE DIFFERENT EXCITING FLAVORS THAT POP OUT AS YOU EAT TOO.

BY BRINGING OUT THE FULL POTENTIAL OF EACH VEGETABLE, THE OVERALL FLAVOR OF THE DISH CAN BE DEEPENED WITHOUT LOSING ANY OF ITS ELEGANCE AND REFINEMENT.

...IS A CULMINATION OF THE NEW YUKIHIRA RECIPES I INVENTED, FUSED INTO ONE!

THIS DISH...

EXACTLY!

H258 SUPER SPECIALTY

...MAKING A *PÂTÉ DE CAMPAGNE* WOULD BE A WISE CHOICE.

NOW, YUKIHIRA... SHOULD YOU BE IN CHARGE OF THE APPETIZER...

1258 SUPER SPECIALTY

DURING THEIR PLANNING MEETING...

PÂTÉ DE CAMPAGNE, ALSO REFERRED TO AS A COUNTRY PÂTÉ, IS A CLASSIC FRENCH DISH.

OH YEAH! THAT SOUNDS FAMILIAR. I THINK I MADE IT ONCE DURING CLASS. HOW'D IT GO AGAIN?

A STAPLE APPETIZER CHOICE, ITS SMOOTH, MOIST TEXTURE AND ROBUST FLAVOR WHETS THE APPETITE AND RAISES ANTICIPATION FOR THE NEXT COURSE.

GROUND MEAT AND LIVER ARE MIXED WITH HERBS AND VEGETABLES, MINCED INTO A PASTE AND THEN BAKED INTO A LOAF.

PLEASE DON'T.

...IT MIGHT COME DOWN TO ROCK-PAPER-SCISSORS TO SEE WHO GETS THE MAIN DISH.

BAA——AN

SHEESH. IF I CAN'T GET HER TO GIVE IN...

OH, WAIT! HEY, ISSHIKI SENPAI?

IT IS THE ONLY POSSIBILITY.

STOP SERIOUSLY CONSIDERING THE LUDICROUS.

HM... MUCH AS I HATE TO CONSIDER IT, IT *IS* A POSSIBILITY...

AND SHOULD YOU LOSE? WOULD YOU QUIETLY ACCEPT THAT RESULT AND MAKE THE APPETIZER?

ESSENTIALLY, THE AZAMI ADMINISTRATION MEANS TO TAKE ADVANTAGE OF HER *DIVINE TONGUE.*

THAT'S CENTRAL'S MAIN GOAL IN A NUTSHELL.

WITH IT AS THE ULTIMATE GUIDE, ALL CHEFS CAN BE FREED FROM THE STRESS AND UNCERTAINTY OF HAVING TO BE CREATIVE AND ORIGINAL.

THE DIVINE TONGUE IS CAPABLE OF ACCURATELY PINPOINTING WHAT IS GOOD AND BAD ABOUT A DISH.

WHAT DOES EVERYBODY MEAN WHEN THEY SAY NAKIRI IS THE "KEY"?

MISS LINE SAID SOMETHING ABOUT IT EARLIER.

BLAH BLAH BLAH BLAH BLAH BLAH

THE SAME GOES FOR THIS DISH. ALTHOUGH IT HAS QUITE A FEW INTERESTING FEATURES TO IT, MAKING IT HIGHLY POLISHED FOR A SINGLE DISH...

HOWEVER, IT LACKS THE IMPACT AND WEIGHT OF A TRUE MAIN DISH, WHICH WOULD EXPLAIN WHY IT HAS NEVER APPEARED ON THE FORMAL MENU FOR SHINO'S TOKYO.

I CAN SEE WHY CHEF SHINOMIYA WOULD AGREE TO PLACE THIS DISH ON THE À LA CARTE MENU OF HIS FRENCH RESTAURANT.

...IT'S MUCH TOO COMPLEX TO WEAVE INTO THE TAPESTRY THAT IS A PROPER GOURMET COURSE, WHICH IS UNDERSTANDABLE, GIVEN THAT IT IS A ONE-OFF DESIGNED WITH NO THOUGHT TO WHAT COMES BEFORE OR AFTER.

GIVEN THE ADVICE AND ARRANGEMENTS *HE* OBVIOUSLY MADE, IT'S A VERY PERSUASIVE RECIPE.

*AN À LA CARTE MENU IS A LISTING OF INDIVIDUAL DISHES THAT CAN BE ORDERED AS ADDITIONS TO A SET MEAL OR COURSE.

HEY, WHOA! HOLD IT! WHO SAYS YOU'RE THE BETTER CHEF, HUH?

I'LL TELL YOU THIS NOW.

IN ORDER TO SECURE VICTORY, OUR MAIN DISH MUST BE CREATED WITH POWERFUL AND PERSUASIVE FLAVOR BY OUR MOST SKILLED CHEF.

I SAY THAT NOT OUT OF SELFISH PRIDE BUT OUT OF CONVICTION THAT IT'S OUR BEST MOVE ON A PURELY STRATEGIC LEVEL.

ON THAT MATTER, WE HAVE OBJECTIVE PROOF.

DIDN'T YOU, Y'KNOW, PLAN FOR THIS?!

WHAT HAPPENED TO THE SUPERLONG PLANNING MEETING YOU HAD LAST NIGHT, HUH?!

I'LL SAY IT ONE MORE TIME.

1257 HOW TO BUILD A SPECIALTY

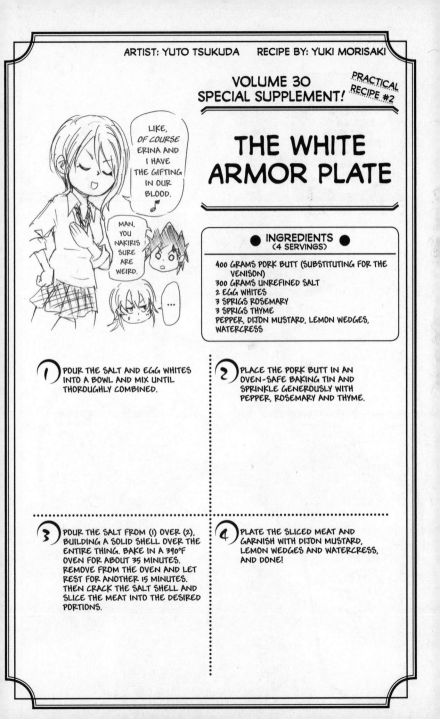

ARTIST: YUTO TSUKUDA   RECIPE BY: YUKI MORISAKI

VOLUME 30
SPECIAL SUPPLEMENT!   PRACTICAL RECIPE #2

THE WHITE ARMOR PLATE

LIKE, OF COURSE ERINA AND I HAVE THE GIFTING IN OUR BLOOD. ♪

MAN, YOU NAKIRIS SURE ARE WEIRD.

...

● **INGREDIENTS** ●
(4 SERVINGS)

400 GRAMS PORK BUTT (SUBSTITUTING FOR THE VENISON)
300 GRAMS UNREFINED SALT
2 EGG WHITES
3 SPRIGS ROSEMARY
3 SPRIGS THYME
PEPPER, DIJON MUSTARD, LEMON WEDGES, WATERCRESS

1 POUR THE SALT AND EGG WHITES INTO A BOWL AND MIX UNTIL THOROUGHLY COMBINED.

2 PLACE THE PORK BUTT IN AN OVEN-SAFE BAKING TIN AND SPRINKLE GENEROUSLY WITH PEPPER, ROSEMARY AND THYME.

3 POUR THE SALT FROM (1) OVER (2), BUILDING A SOLID SHELL OVER THE ENTIRE THING. BAKE IN A 390°F OVEN FOR ABOUT 35 MINUTES. REMOVE FROM THE OVEN AND LET REST FOR ANOTHER 15 MINUTES. THEN CRACK THE SALT SHELL AND SLICE THE MEAT INTO THE DESIRED PORTIONS.

4 PLATE THE SLICED MEAT AND GARNISH WITH DIJON MUSTARD, LEMON WEDGES AND WATERCRESS, AND DONE!

FOR ITS GREATER VARIANT— THE GIFTING— TO HAVE OCCURRED...

THE NAKIRI FAMILY IS FAMOUS FOR THE DISROBING.

IT'S PROOF THAT THIS DISH, AND INDEED THIS WHOLE COURSE, IS THE REAL DEAL!

IT'S A SIGN THAT THE DISH I TASTED WAS JUST THAT DELICIOUS.

I DIDN'T DO IT ON PURPOSE. IT SIMPLY HAPPENS.

AFTER ALL...

I CAN'T BEGIN TO IMAGINE WHAT GOURMET COURSE COULD BE GREATER THAN THIS.

WITH THAT BOOST, EISHI TSUKASA WAS ABLE TO POLISH HIS DISH TO THE GREATEST GLEAM POSSIBLE.

RINDO KOBAYASHI POURED EVERYTHING SHE HAD INTO CREATING A DISH THAT WOULD AMPLIFY THE MAIN DISH COMING AFTER IT.

THE SPECIALTY OF THE FIRST SEAT ON THE COUNCIL OF TEN, MADE WITH ALL OF HIS SKILL AND TALENT...

THE APPETIZER PRECEDING IT WAS NOTHING SHORT OF AMAZING TOO.

AND AS A RESULT, THOSE NEAR ME ARE AFFECTED WITH A SECONDHAND DISROBING.

WHEN I TASTE SOMETHING ESPECIALLY DELICIOUS, MY SPIRITUAL ESSENCE PULSES OUTWARD IN A WAVE...

THAT SOUNDS AWFULLY FAMILIAR, ACTUALLY.

ARE YOU SAYING YOU CAN FORCE OTHERS AROUND YOU TO DISROBE JUST BY EATING SOMETHING TASTY?!

UH, NONE OF THAT MAKES ANY SENSE.

UH, NIKUMI-CHI JUST LOOKS LIKE SHE'S WEARING ONE OF HER USUAL RISQUÉ OUTFITS.

SO, LIKE, SINCE UNCLE AZAMI ACCEPTED THE NAKIRI NAME, IT TOTES MAKES SENSE THAT HE'D HAVE GAINED POWERS LIKE THE GIFTING TOO.

WHEN SOMEONE OFFICIALLY MARRIES INTO THE NAKIRI FAMILY, THEY GAIN MORE THAN JUST THE NAME. THEY GAIN OUR SPECIAL ABILITIES TOO.

WELL, STUFF LIKE THAT DOES HAPPEN.

WHAT THE HECK IS UP WITH THAT FAMILY?

MY, MY. I CAN'T SAY I APPROVE OF FORCING LOVELY YOUNG LADIES TO UNDRESS IN SUCH A PUBLIC VENUE.

NO, IT DOESN'T.

EEEEK!

KYAAA!

WHAT JUST HAPPENED ?!

HUH?!

OH DEAR. I'M AFRAID IT SLIPPED OUT.

MY VERSION OF *THE GIFTING,* THAT IS.

"THE GIFTING"?!

FEH! THE MAN'S ACTING LIKE IT'S ALREADY DECIDED.

WELL, HE'S GOT ANOTHER THING COMING! YUKIHIRA AND MISS ERINA WILL SEE TO THAT!

YEAH! YOU TELL 'EM, BIG SIS NIKUMI!

HUH? WHAT'RE YOU STARING AT, YUKI? RYOKO?

HM?

A BEAUTIFUL LAND OF PEACE AND TRANQUILITY THAT WE ALL DESIRE!

IT WAS A SIGNPOST TO A GOURMET EDEN!

A PARADISE WHERE ALL CHEFS ARE FREED FROM EARTHLY TROUBLES...

NOT ONLY THAT, ITS ALREADY IMPRESSIVE FLAVOR HAS BEEN MAGNIFIED BY THE APPETIZER.

NOM

SPLSSS

...ITS DELICIOUSNESS HAS BEEN RAISED TO EVEN GREATER HEIGHTS!

BY BEING PRESENTED AFTER AN APPETIZER CENTERED ON MUSHROOMS—WHICH PAIR EXCEPTIONALLY WELL WITH VENISON—AND BEING ACCENTED WITH THE FLAVOR BOOSTER FORMIC ACID...

RINDO'S DISH POINTED THE WAY...

...BUT NOT TO A MERE FINAL DISH IN A BANQUET.

56

WHITE ARMOR'S GLEAM

Dwooop

THE WHITE ARMOR PLATE ~SAUCE CHEVREUIL~

"CHEVREUIL" IS FRENCH FOR "ROE DEER."

SIZZ SIZZ

...ITS JUICINESS AND DELICIOUSNESS SLOWLY GROWING WITHIN ITS PROTECTIVE SHELL.

BECAUSE OF THE INSULATING WALL OF SALT, THE DISH IS HEATED GENTLY AND EVENLY, WHILE IN THE OVEN...

TINK

THE DISH IS CONSIDERED COMPLETE...

KRIK

...WHEN YOU CRACK OPEN THE NOW GOLDEN-BROWN SALT CRUST.

48

LADIES AND GENTLEMEN, DID YOU HEAR THAT?!

IT APPEARS EISHI TSUKASA, THE FIRST SEAT HIMSELF, WILL BE MAKING HIS SPECIALTY!

256 WHITE ARMOR'S GLEAM

WHAT TSUKASA PUT IN THE OVEN A MOMENT AGO... IT WAS COVERED IN A SALT CRUST!

BAKING WITH A SALT CRUST!

SALT IS MIXED WITH EGG WHITES AND THEN SPREAD OVER THE TOP OF THE DISH TO FORM A THICK CRUST.

THIS ENSURES NO MOISTURE ESCAPES DURING BAKING, KEEPING THE GOODNESS OF THE INGREDIENTS CONCENTRATED INSIDE.

IT'S SAID THAT CENTURIES AGO, WHEN SHOGUN HIDEYOSHI TOYOTOMI WAS DEPLOYED ON MANEUVERS, HE'D COVER HIS FISH IN A SALT CRUST TO PREVENT IT FROM ROTTING.

ARTIST: YUTO TSUKUDA   RECIPE BY: YUKI MORISAKI

VOLUME 30
SPECIAL SUPPLEMENT!

PRACTICAL
RECIPE #1

STAAARE

MUSHROOM MILLE-FEUILLE

~WITH DUXELLES FILLING~

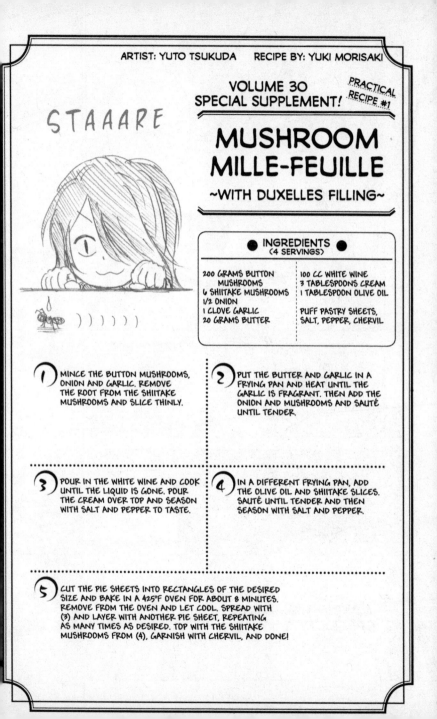

● **INGREDIENTS** ●
(4 SERVINGS)

200 GRAMS BUTTON MUSHROOMS
6 SHIITAKE MUSHROOMS
1/2 ONION
1 CLOVE GARLIC
20 GRAMS BUTTER

100 CC WHITE WINE
3 TABLESPOONS CREAM
1 TABLESPOON OLIVE OIL

PUFF PASTRY SHEETS,
SALT, PEPPER, CHERVIL

1) MINCE THE BUTTON MUSHROOMS, ONION AND GARLIC. REMOVE THE ROOT FROM THE SHIITAKE MUSHROOMS AND SLICE THINLY.

2) PUT THE BUTTER AND GARLIC IN A FRYING PAN AND HEAT UNTIL THE GARLIC IS FRAGRANT. THEN ADD THE ONION AND MUSHROOMS AND SAUTÉ UNTIL TENDER.

3) POUR IN THE WHITE WINE AND COOK UNTIL THE LIQUID IS GONE. POUR THE CREAM OVER TOP AND SEASON WITH SALT AND PEPPER TO TASTE.

4) IN A DIFFERENT FRYING PAN, ADD THE OLIVE OIL AND SHIITAKE SLICES. SAUTÉ UNTIL TENDER AND THEN SEASON WITH SALT AND PEPPER.

5) CUT THE PIE SHEETS INTO RECTANGLES OF THE DESIRED SIZE AND BAKE IN A 425°F OVEN FOR ABOUT 8 MINUTES. REMOVE FROM THE OVEN AND LET COOL. SPREAD WITH (3) AND LAYER WITH ANOTHER PIE SHEET, REPEATING AS MANY TIMES AS DESIRED. TOP WITH THE SHIITAKE MUSHROOMS FROM (4), GARNISH WITH CHERVIL, AND DONE!

TWITCH

WAIT... THIS TANG!

SHE USED OLIVE OIL TO COOK THEM INTO A CONFIT, TRAPPING AND MAGNIFYING THEIR NATURAL UMAMI FLAVOR!

THE MAIN INGREDIENT RINDO KOBAYASHI CHOSE WAS SHIITAKE MUSH-ROOMS!

*CONFIT IS A FRENCH TECHNIQUE FOR COOKING AN INGREDIENT OVER LOW HEAT IN OIL OR GREASE.

CRACKED NUTS AND HEAVY CREAM WERE BLENDED IN TO MAKE A DUXELLES, WHICH SHE THEN SANDWICHED BETWEEN THE MILLE-FEUILLE LAYERS.

AAH. CHAMPIGNON MUSHROOMS AND SHALLOTS, SAUTÉED TO A GOLDEN BROWN IN GARLIC AND BUTTER AND THEN SIMMERED TO A PASTE IN BROTH.

*DUXELLES IS A MUSHROOM PASTE OFTEN USED AS A BASE FOR FILLINGS OR SAUCES.

THOUGH I CAN'T PUT MY FINGER ON WHAT THIS SOUR FLAVOR IS FROM. WHAT IS IT?

A PERFECTLY BALANCED TART NOTE MAKES THE SALTY SAVORINESS OF THE CONFIT STAND OUT...

...WHILE ALLOWING THE MELLOW SWEETNESS OF THE SHIITAKE TO LINGER ON THE TONGUE!

BUT THE DECIDING FACTOR OF THIS DISH IS ITS SOURNESS.

SWF

EISHI, WHAT DO YOU THINK IT *TRULY* MEANS TO IMPROVE YOUR COOKING?

IT FEELS LIKE FOREVER SINCE I WAS LAST ABLE TO RELAX AND TALK WITH SOMEONE ABOUT COOKING.

AAH, HOW LONG HAS IT BEEN?

LET'S SAY PABLO PICASSO WAS STILL ALIVE.

WELL, IT NEEDN'T BE PICASSO, SPECIFICALLY. JACKSON POLLOCK WOULD DO. OR MARCEL DUCHAMP... KAZIMIR MALEVICH. ANYONE LIKE THEM, REALLY.

HUH?

I DON'T KNOW ALL THAT MUCH ABOUT ART.

UM... I DON'T THINK I COULD.

NOW, LET'S EXCHANGE PAINTINGS FOR COOKING.

EX-ACTLY.

WOULD YOU BE ABLE TO LOOK AT THAT PAINTING AND TELL IF IT WAS TRULY ART OR MERELY A CANVAS COVERED WITH RANDOM PAINT SPLOTCHES?

NOW, LET'S SAY THIS ARTIST DISPLAYS A BRAND-NEW PAINTING.

CASHMERE MAILAWHA?

IT DOESN'T MATTER IF THAT TWIST ON YOUR DISH WAS TRULY INSPIRED OR IF YOU OVERREACHED AND IT FELL FLAT...

THEIR REACTIONS WON'T CHANGE.

BUT WHAT OF THE PEOPLE WITHOUT A PROPER PALATE AND TRAINING?

SAY THAT YOU TASTED A DISH. YOU WOULD KNOW WHO MADE IT, WHAT THEY WERE AIMING FOR AND WHAT TRICKS THEY USED, YES?

11255 THOSE WHO WANDER
THE WILDERNESS

FOR THIS FINAL BOUT, BOTH TEAMS WILL PRESENT A TWO-COURSE MEAL!

THE WINNER OF THIS BOUT WILL CLAIM VICTORY IN THE RÉGIMENT DE CUISINE! THEIR PRIZE?

EACH CHEF WILL CREATE THEIR COURSE AND PRESENT THE COMPLETED DISH IN TANDEM WITH THEIR TEAMMATE.

GOOD LUCK, GUYS!

SHOULD THE RESISTANCE WIN, THEY WILL ALSO HAVE THE POWER TO RESCIND THE EXPULSION OF THEIR FRIENDS!

ALL SEATS ON THE COUNCIL OF TEN!

ALL RIIIGHT! LET'S DO THIS!

DOESN'T MATTER. WE HAVE THE TWO BEST CHEFS IN THE INSTITUTE!

EVEN WITH MISS ERINA ON THE OTHER SIDE...

YOU KNOW, I'VE BEEN TRYING HARD NOT TO THINK ABOUT IT, BUT...

...THERE'S NO WAY THE FIRST AND SECOND SEATS WILL LOSE!

HM?

NÖW!

#254 FEAST AND FAMINE

SOMA YUKIHIRA First Year High School

Helping out at his family's restaurant since he was little, Soma trained as a chef with the goal of someday surpassing his father. Out of junior high, he's suddenly sent off to culinary school. He's skilled, but sometimes invents questionable new recipes.

Shokugeki no SOMA

ERINA NAKIRI First Year High School

Granddaughter of Senzaemon Nakiri, former dean of the Totsuki Institute, she has a sense of taste so refined, famous restaurants across the nation come to her to taste test their dishes. Rebelling against her father, Azami, she has renounced her seat on the Council of Ten.

STORY

Soma grew up helping to cook at his family's restaurant, Yukihira. But one day his father enrolls him in Japan's premier culinary school, the Totsuki Institute. Having met other students as skilled as he is and with similar goals, Soma has grown a little as a chef.

In the fourth bout, Erina finally makes her battle debut. The unexpected, unorthodox dorayaki the Divine Tongue presents defeats even a confectionary master such as Akanegakubo, netting a win for the resistance. But in the final two cards, Tsukasa and Rindo of the council prevail. Now only two chefs remain on each team as the Régiment de Cuisine enters the fifth and final bout—the theme...a truly gourmet course meal!

Volume 30
Shonen Jump Advanced Manga Edition
Story by Yuto Tsukuda, Art by Shun Saeki
Contributor Yuki Morisaki

Translation: Adrienne Beck
Touch-Up Art & Lettering: James Gaubatz, Mara Coman
Design: Alice Lewis
Editor: Jennifer LeBlanc

SHOKUGEKI NO SOMA © 2012 by Yuto Tsukuda, Shun Saeki
All rights reserved.
First published in Japan in 2012 by SHUEISHA Inc., Tokyo.
English translation rights arranged by SHUEISHA Inc.

The stories, characters and incidents mentioned in this publication
are entirely fictional.

Printed in the U.S.A.

Published by VIZ Media, LLC
P.O. Box 77010
San Francisco, CA 94107

10 9 8 7 6 5 4 3 2 1
First printing, June 2019

 MEDIA

viz.com   shonenjump.com

Yuto Tsukuda

Thank you so much for all the chocolate you sent to the *Food Wars!* characters for Valentine's Day! The one who got the most chocolates was, believe it or not...Etsuya Eizan! (No, really.) Soma got more than last year, but to be outdone by Etsuya Eizan of all people! And it wasn't just chocolates. People even sent flowers and glasses wipes (*lol*). Boy, his fans truly are on another level.

Shun Saeki

Just look at my favorite little doggo. He went into his travel crate all by himself! Does he maybe want to go on a trip? I'd love to go out myself, but work has been so busy lately that I haven't even been able to set foot outside.

About the authors

Yuto Tsukuda won the 34th Jump Juniketsu Newcomers' Manga Award for his one-shot story *Kiba ni Naru*. He made his *Weekly Shonen Jump* debut in 2010 with the series *Shonen Shikku*. His follow-up series, *Food Wars!: Shokugeki no Soma*, is his first English-language release.

Shun Saeki made his *Jump NEXT!* debut in 2011 with the one-shot story *Kimi to Watashi no Renai Soudan*. *Food Wars!: Shokugeki no Soma* is his first *Shonen Jump* series.